(UN)SPOKEN

A BROTHER'S BEST FRIEND, SINGLE PARENT ROMANCE

SAINT STEPHEN'S LAKE
BOOK 3

K.C. BROOKS

To the ones who made me a mom. Life with you is the most amazing, challenging, and fulfilling gift.

And to all of the other mothers, especially the ones who fiercely love their families but feel like they've lost a piece of themselves along the way.

Find your joy, recapture your purpose, and remember that wanting to be happy isn't selfish- it's a necessity.

AUTHOR NOTE

This book contains on page, sexually explicit situations. It also contains elements of strained family relationships, alcohol abuse (past), and unplanned pregnancy. There are some chapters with on-page violence, and references to stalking and harassment. While it is the author's intention to broach these topics with sensitivity, it could still be triggering for some readers. If that is the case, please skip this book.

Protect your peace, lovelies.

PLAYLIST

1. The Other Side- Michael Marcagi
2. Hurricane- Luke Combs
3. Little Bit Better- Caleb Hearn, ROSIE
4. Spin You Around (1/24)- Morgan Wallen
5. Never Better- Wild Rivers
6. Willow- Taylor Swift
7. Sin So Sweet- Warren Zeiders
8. Hell or High Water- Bailey Zimmerman
9. Iris- Mr. FijiWiji, Matt Van
10. Bigger Houses- Dan + Shay

PROLOGUE

ELEVEN YEARS AGO

The sound of gravel crunching under the weight of the truck's tires signaled that our time was up. As I stared up at my big brother, a sea of emotions overwhelmed me—but even though sadness and fear lurked in my heart, anger was the strongest of them all. Anger that Cole was leaving before our summer even began. Anger that I didn't know the next time we'd see each other face to face. Anger that I would be here, on my own, without Cole, for the first time in my life.

Even though I was barely out of diapers when my father retired from the military, I could remember the late nights, wondering if he'd be able to call—or worse: if he'd come home at all. But that was the life of a military child, never knowing when the knock would come that would change your life. However, my father's career existed long before I was born. I'd never known anything different.

But this? Cole leaving me? That was a pain I'd never anticipated.

My brother had been my protector my entire life. With almost six years between us, he'd been more like a second father, replacing the one who was barely ever home. He was my constant, my rock in an ever-shifting river.

While Cole had always talked about joining the army, I never imagined he'd actually enlist. But here we were, only days after his high school graduation, and he was the one with the duffel slung over his shoulder, about to take off for months of grueling training. I closed my eyes, refusing to picture what would come after that.

Adam shifted at my side, bumping my hip with his. My brother's best friend had spent the last week at our house, helping Cole get ready to ship out. While they never spoke it out loud, I knew this was almost as painful for him as it was for me. Even though Adam didn't share our blood, he and Cole were brothers, and change was coming for both of them. Despite his good grades and his parent's desires, Adam was taking off for Los Angeles at the end of the summer, attempting to break into acting instead of going to college. I'd overheard enough conversations between him and Cole to know he only had a couple years to find some success before his parents would force him back home. His dad was getting up there in years, and running a dairy farm was grueling work. He was ready for his son to take over.

As much as I knew Adam didn't want that life, a small, selfish part of me wished he'd come home early. Maybe if everything else stayed the same, Cole would somehow come home sooner and be the same too.

The truck shifted into park, and my father stepped out of the cab, giving Cole a solemn nod. "Time to go, son."

My father was a man of few words, but it was clear how conflicted he felt. While he loved that his only son was following in his footsteps, he knew better than most what awaited Cole. I'd heard him confessing his fears to my mom in the middle of the night when he thought no one was listening, but come the light of day, he never wavered in his support.

Cole swallowed hard, blinking away any scrap of emotion as he looked down at me. "Try not to cause too much trouble while I'm gone, Tor."

"I'm not the one who likes to give Mom gray hair." I rolled my eyes, trying to swallow my fear. But as I looked up at him, all the humor died on my tongue. "I promise, Cole. Best behavior."

"I don't know about going that far," he laughed as he reached down to hug me. His arms encircled me, and he held me close to his chest. Cole's breath shuddered as he lowered his voice. "Me and you against the world, right, trouble?"

"You know it," I chuckled, desperately trying to hold back my tears. As much as they wanted to fall, I couldn't do that to Cole. I pulled back, pushing his hand away as he mussed up my hair. "Be safe, Cole."

"You got it, Tor."

As Cole walked up to Adam, I ducked my head, fixating on the ends of my ponytail instead of the sight in front of me. My brother whispered something to his best friend before he released him with a steady clap on the back. Cole nodded down to me, "Keep an eye on her for me, would you? Don't let her convince you she's some angel. Just ask Mr. Michaelson." He gave me a stern look. "He's still asking about what happened to his dog."

"He should have taken better care of her," I muttered, crossing my arms around my chest. I slammed my mouth shut, remembering that my official stance was the gate latch had broken and the dog must have gotten out. Whether or not she'd had a little help and found her way to a much nicer family on the other side of town, I had no idea.

Adam smirked as he glanced at me, sharing a knowing look.

He might have also had a hand with the dog's relocation plan, but that was only because he found me stranded on the side of the road, trying to tug along a dog over half my size. Without a word, he'd pulled over, lowering the gate to the back of his truck. We rode in almost complete silence, with only me pointing directions to the dog's new home. Even when he dropped me off later, we never spoke about it, Adam telling Cole he'd given me a ride home after he spotted me walking back from a friend's house.

"You got it, man," Adam said, patting Cole on the shoulder. "Just focus on what you've got to do. I'll make sure everyone is good here."

With one last nod, Cole turned, readjusting his pack as he joined my father at the truck. He glanced out the windshield, and our eyes connected, a slew of emotions and unshed words crossing the distance. I dug my nails into the palm of my hand, refusing to show any weakness. My momma said that Cole needed our strength.

"It's a tremendous honor," she'd said as she folded some of his clothes. "Cole's serving our country. He's going to need all our support."

I didn't care about any of that. I just wanted my brother to stay safe.

As we watched him pull away, the dust and gravel churned under the tires, leaving a trail of debris behind. When it settled, there was no sign of Cole, no mark to show the crater that his absence would create in my life.

"He'll be back," Adam said, almost more to himself than me. "This is the hard part, Tor. He'll be back before we even know it."

Even though we both knew it was a lie, I said nothing, knowing then that my life would never be the same.

ONE

Victoria

Present Day

"This was a mistake."

I stared at myself in the airport mirror, trying to calm my erratic nerves. My hands shook as I pushed my hair behind my shoulder, trying to fix a couple of curls that refused to cooperate. All morning, my stomach had wound itself in knots, imagining the worst-case scenarios. From the car not showing up to the plane going down in flames, it felt like my anxiety had taken control of every thought. But now that my feet were safely on the ground, all I could think about was what was waiting for me outside the airport.

When my brother's wedding invitation first arrived, I stared at it like it was a three-headed monster. For years, we'd been at odds, a result of Cole's medically induced departure from the army and the years of alcoholism that followed. He'd fallen into a deep depression, and the only solace he found was at the bottom of a bottle. I'd tried for years to get him some help, to show him he could heal without masking the pain. But that had resulted in his hostility, words that still clung to me like scars.

Five years ago, I'd had enough and entirely cut him out of my life, refusing to let him take me down with him.

I thought that was the end of our relationship, but then, almost a year ago, Cole started calling, trying to get back in contact with me. At first, I ignored his calls, waiting and listening to his voicemails, trying to ignore the cracking of the ice in my heart. When I finally took the risk and answered his call, the relief in his voice was palpable.

That was almost eight months ago, and now, Cole always attended our weekly calls. At first, I thought he'd stop, especially after we'd started to mend our rift a little. Cole was never good at facing his failures, preferring to hide behind his snark and sarcasm rather than express any vulnerabilities. But this new version of my brother not only admitted his flaws but also made up for them in spades. And I had to admit, as much as I wanted to keep my walls high, he was cracking them, little by little.

But flying across the country to attend his wedding? It felt monumental, like an unsteady step I wasn't sure I was ready to take.

I shook my head, forcing myself away from those nagging thoughts. It was just a wedding, which was pretty much a fancy party. Parties were fun, *right*? It had been a while since I attended one, but I remember having a good time. So what if I didn't know most of the guests, and the groom was my newly-reacquainted brother, and the bride was practically a stranger? I'd go, show my support, and then head back home before anyone even noticed my presence.

"This is why most people drink," my best friend, Hadley, called out from my phone screen. While mine was perched on the bathroom counter, hers was propped up on a coffee table back home, her feet wiggling as she painted her toes a shade of hot pink. She paused, thinking over her words. "But that probably wouldn't help things between you and Cole."

"You think?" I teased back, running my hands over my ratty t-shirt. I probably should have brought a change of clothes, but almost everything was meticulously folded into my carry-on, all arranged to ensure that the dress I'd brought for the wedding arrived in one piece. It was the fanciest dress I'd worn in, well, years. Hadley had convinced me to buy it, claiming to have evidence that dressing your best was the key to faking confidence. It sounded ridiculous to me, but I would take any help I could get.

I glanced at my cut-off shorts, unsure if I loved or hated how they clung to my thighs. Growing up, I'd always played sports, never having to worry about gaining weight because I was constantly rushing around to practices, scrimmages, and games. But now that that part of my life was over, it showed in my body. It had changed over the years, and although it didn't seem like much to others, I could feel the shifts. As much as I tried to love every curve, there were so many days it was more challenging than others. I ran my hands along my skin, mumbling affirmations to myself. I had enough anxiety building up. The last thing I needed was my old friend self-doubt rearing her ugly head.

"Tor?" Hadley called out from the phone, clearly noting my zone-out.

"Yeah." I swatted my hand toward the phone. "I'm sorry. I just wish I wasn't doing this alone."

"I thought your parents were there?"

"They flew up last week to spend time with Cole and his fiancée. They want to help as much as they can with the wedding." I toyed with my nail beds. "But we're kind of at odds about this trip, so I don't know if they're going to make my life any easier."

"Then maybe you should find a guy to spend the night with." She smirked through the screen. "Live a little now that you have some independence."

"Hadley Rose, you are the worst influence in the world!"

"Part of the reason why you love me, babe." She blew a kiss through the camera lens. "But I mean it, Tor. How long have you been single?"

I grimaced. "Eighteen months."

"Victoria!"

"Don't." I hide my face in my hands. "It hasn't been my priority, you know that. Plus, after everything with Cam…"

Hadley sighed, her face softening as she looked at me. "Listen, Tor, we all thought you and Cam were endgame. But you did what was best for both of you. You broke up with him because you wanted to find that soul-consuming type of love. And no offense, but you've been hiding out ever since."

"I have not!" I shook my head. "It's not like I have a lot of time for dating. And honestly, I've been with one guy my entire life. We started dating in middle school. Trying to find someone in the real world? That's freaking terrifying."

"So don't think about it that way. Think of it as a chance to try something new for a couple of days. Forget everything else in your life and focus on *you* for once," Hadley answered. "Besides, a wedding is a perfect excuse to get out there. Flirt a little. Have some fun. Ask a guy to dance. And if it's a bust, you'll never have to see them again."

"But–"

"No." She held a finger up to silence me. "I have everything handled here. Your one job this week is to have fun. And if you even think about calling twenty times every day, I will block your number."

"Don't you dare."

She arched a brow. "Don't test me, Campbell. Now, get your sexy ass out there and have some fun for both of us."

DRAGGING MY SUITCASE BEHIND ME, I stepped out of the Albany airport, scanning the crowd for Cole. The airport was significantly smaller than Dallas-Fort Worth, but being somewhere new always put me on edge. I liked to know my surroundings- I wanted to feel prepared. Just as I was about to dig out my phone and dial Cole's number, a loud honk sounded from an older Jeep parked at the end of the strip.

As my brother hopped out of the driver's side, my breath whooshed out of me. It had been so long since we saw each other in person. When I thought about our last time together, pain and regret colored all of the memories. They were filled with words I'd longed to take back, and I'm sure Cole felt the same. He'd been a shell of his usual self, his eyes dark with anger and rage.

But the man standing in front of me now looked good— healthier than I'd seen in years. His broad and genuine smile lifted some of the heaviness from my chest.

Cole walked over to me in three long strides, scooping me up into his arms. Even though we were siblings, he'd gotten all my dad's height, so my feet dangled above the ground when he tugged me up. As much as I'd been dreading this trip, having my brother here—*safe and healthy*—was more of a relief than I could put into words. He held me for a long moment before setting my feet back on the ground.

He took a step back and chuckled, "Shit, Tor. I can't believe how grown up you look."

That tends to happen when you're cut out of someone's life.

The thought rang out in my head before I could stop it, and I was glad it hadn't escaped my lips. I was trying so hard to let go of my resentment toward Cole, to escape the bitterness that overcame me when I thought of the past few years—of all the times when I needed him, only for him to ignore my calls or scold me for interrupting yet another one of his benders.

But now that his life was more settled, he was making more of an effort. Even if he had found a home in town so far from our family, I was happy for him. He was making a life for himself. It just sucked that we were strangers in each other's worlds.

Cole grabbed my bag, leading me toward the dark blue Jeep. He nodded to the missing roof. "I've got the soft top back here if the wind's too much. Alex likes to keep it off all summer. Apparently, winter comes in fast, so she tries to soak up as much warmth as she can."

Alex. His fiancée. The one who often popped up in our weekly chats, but I had yet to meet in person. I chewed on my lower lip. "Are you sure she's cool with me coming up this early?"

Cole chuckled, "Are you kidding? She was bummed you didn't fly up with Mom and Dad. She's dying to meet you."

That brought me a little relief, but I was still nervous. Besides my parents, everyone would be a stranger. What had Cole told them about me? Even though I knew I had reasons for cutting off contact with Cole, he would always be my brother. Did people hate me for placing boundaries between us? Did they judge me for being so harsh with him? Without both sides of the story, I could see me quickly becoming the villain—the bitter sister who refused to let go of past pain.

I shook my head, pushing the thoughts away as I clicked on my seat belt. Even if that was the case, I was only here for a week. I'd dealt with worse judgment than that. As I turned my mind to more positive thoughts, Cole switched on the engine, and a familiar song blasted through the speakers. I couldn't help but smile. "Your terrible taste in music hasn't changed."

He chuffed. "Not even here a minute and already giving me shit."

"You know you love it," I said absentmindedly, searching through my purse for my sunglasses.

"I do."

The somber tone in Cole's voice made my gaze snap in his direction, searching his eyes for the source of his tone. As he looked at me, I could see the regret lurking beneath the surface. All the doubts I'd had about coming to New York started to melt away. It was hard living without him for so long. As much as I knew I did it for the right reasons, it felt like a piece of me snapped back into place when he hugged me tight.

Without a second thought, I reached out, taking his hand in mine. "I missed you, big brother."

"Missed you more, trouble."

TWO

Victoria

After a couple of hours on the highway, I finally spotted the exit sign for Saint Stephen's Lake. With my eyes glued to the windows, I couldn't help but smile as we crossed into its borders. No wonder Cole was so entranced by this place. With the sun shining and the dozens of happy people on the sidewalk, it felt like I had been dropped into the middle of a Hallmark movie. The town was so quaint, with its aged brick buildings, vintage flower pots, and street lamps. People waved as we passed by, and Cole did the same. After each one, he'd stop and tell me their name, and it was clear he was a part of this community.

I could only nod, returning my gaze to the world around us. While I loved the tiny town we grew up in, it was miles and miles of grassy farmland. Seeing the mountains and water was a different but welcome sight.

We kept driving until we reached the edge of the lake. The coastline was lined with various motorboats and people coming in and out of the water. Sailboats coasted in the distance, their colorful flags painting a sharp contrast against the greenery of the surrounding mountains. Next to the beach, there were a few small food stands, pop-ups that probably only came with the summer tourists. And even though the season was practically at its end, you would never know it driving through this town. It was like a postcard come to life.

We drove down the road a little longer until we reached a sign for the Fox Creek Lodge. Although it was my first time visiting, it felt like I already knew every inch of it. During our initial conversations, Cole filled the silence by telling me all about Fox Creek, showing me their planned renovations and the options they were considering. I soon became invested in its progress, and Cole sent me constant pictures whenever they crossed another item off their list. To be honest, I'd had my doubts that it would ever open based on the sheer size of the project, but almost three months ago, it opened its doors for the first time, with a steady stream of guests ever since. Many guests had already booked stays for next year. Cole radiated with pride when he talked about Fox Creek and even more when he spoke about how Alex was running it. While my brother was the unofficial handyman, she was the one in charge, ensuring the guests had a pleasant stay.

We drove past the main lodge, a large structure at the edge of the property. The building housed Alex's office, their check-in station, and a casual restaurant for the guests to enjoy. Plans to add rooms to the second floor were made, but after renovating all the cabins, Cole and Alex decided to hold off on that for a couple more years.

Looking at the main lodge, the front looked like a typical wood cabin, complete with a wrap-around porch and swing. The side facing the lake, though, was all windows framed by black supports, giving it more of a modern edge. From the dining room, you could see almost all of Saint Stephen's Lake, a sight that drew many people in for meals, even if they weren't staying on the property.

Cole hit the blinker, passing the parking lot to follow a gravel road. Behind the main lodge was a large clearing, complete with a pavilion in the middle. On the outskirts of the property sat twelve cabins, all in a similar style to the main lodge, just on a much smaller scale. Each cabin's path was lined with bright blooms, and sunflowers grew tall around the edges.

Cole slowed down the truck as we reached the furthest one, tucked in the corner of the woods. You could barely see it from the road because trees surrounded it on one side. On the other, there was a short path to a rocky beach on the edge of the lake. As I climbed out of the cab, I stared at the water, letting out the breath I'd been holding all day.

"I thought you'd like this one," Cole admitted, running his hand over the back of his head. "It's the most private." He pointed to the edge of the forest. "And there's a break in the trees so you can see the sunrise over the lake in the morning."

"It's perfect."

As my brother grabbed my suitcase, I moved to the front door and let myself inside. There was a small kitchenette immediately when you walked in, with a vintage-looking fridge and a peninsula for seating. Behind that was an archway that led into the bedroom. As I walked toward the bed, the back window caught my eye, and I let out a small gasp. I stepped out onto the wooden porch, pressing my hands onto ledge. The lake filled my entire view. You could see the mountains, the boats, and even some of the small islands in the middle of the water. It was a hidden paradise, and it was all mine for the next seven days.

"Hey, Tor, where do you want this stuff?"

"Bedroom, please!" I called out as I walked back inside, leaving the patio door open to let in the fresh breeze. In my haste to get outside, I'd walked right past the king-sized bed in the middle of the room. My hand sunk into the white comforter, and a loud groan left my lips. Was it too early to take a nap?

Cole chuckled as he placed my suitcase next to the dresser. "It's even comfier than it looks. After Alex picked it out, we ordered one for home, too." He paused, shifting on his feet. "What do you think?"

Even though he was trying to play it cool, I could tell Cole was nervous. He constantly shuffled his feet and ran his hand through his hair when he was trying to play it cool. It had to be hard to open his world to the rest of us. My parents had already been through here, and I could only imagine what they thought.

"It's gorgeous." I smiled back at him. "I can't believe you did all this."

"All I did was put up a few walls. Everything else was all Alex." Cole beamed with pride. "She's the heart and soul of this place."

I stared at him, studying the admiration that lined his face. "You're really happy, aren't you?"

He nodded, "It took a long time to get here, but now, I can't imagine my life anywhere else." He shuffled closer to me, running his hand through his hair. "Look, Tor, I know I fucked up a lot in the past–"

"It's in the past," I said, cutting him off. His eyes studied me, as if searching for a lie in my words. "I mean it," I continued, hoping that if I said it, it would be the entire truth. "All I've ever wanted was for you to be happy, Cole."

"I am," Cole admitted quietly. "But that doesn't mean I haven't made mistakes. I know it's going to be a busy few days, but I'd like to spend some time together, get to know the grown-up version of you better. Although..." He chuckled as he pulled me into a hug. "You still fit under my arm pretty well."

I shoved him off me. "Only because you got all the tall genes and didn't leave anything for the rest of us."

As we finally started to fall into a comfortable rhythm, my phone rang out. My eyes cut to the display, hissing a sharp breath. I grabbed the device and held it to my chest, giving Cole my most innocent smile. "I have to take this."

Cole nodded, shoving his hands into his pockets. But when he reached the door, he hit the frame twice. "Dinner at the house tonight? I can pick you up in a couple of hours."

"You got it."

As I watched him exit, I hit the answer button, smiling widely at the screen. "Hey baby, how was your day?"

Emilia's toothy grin filled the whole screen, piercing a hole through my heart. It hadn't even been a day yet, and I was already missing my daughter tremendously. I was used to spending all my time with her, not having been away since before she was born four years ago. But as hard as it was to take this trip, and knowing that I wasn't ready to bring her with me, it was also nice to have some time alone. But just because I planned to take full advantage of my trip didn't mean that I didn't miss Emilia with every fiber of my being.

"Good. We played with paints!" The evidence was still all over her chubby cheeks, streaks of blue and yellow covering her sweet dimples. Her brown curls were wild, piled up on top of her head. Emilia was chaos in human form but still the most adorable thing I'd ever seen.

"You did? Are you being a good girl for Daddy?"

"Yup!" She nodded. "We're going to Target later. He said I could pick out my snacks."

I ducked my head, hiding my laughter. "Already pulling out the Target move?" I called out to my ex, Cam. "How much of the house has she destroyed?"

He chuckled as he looked over our daughter's head. "When the heck did this kid get such an appetite? I swear, last week, she wouldn't eat anything, and now, she's gone through most of the fridge."

"No idea." I knew all too well how often Emilia's tastes

changed. She might have been the light of my life, but she could also be exhausting. "You could always take her out to see the horses. Those are her favorite."

"Good plan," Cam answered. "I know Dad's working on one of the new mares today."

Cam's family lived on a vast farm on the edge of town, the same plot his great-grandfather had purchased almost one hundred years ago. After Emilia was born, we'd moved into one of the cottages on the property, wanting to be close to his family in case we needed support. Honestly, after a decade of knowing them, I was almost as close to the Sedas as I was to my own parents.

When Cam and I broke up, I expected that to change, but it was the opposite. His parents sat me down and said that no matter what happened between Cam and me, we would always be family. They even let me stay in the cottage while Cam moved back into the main house.

It was working well for us. It gave me some privacy but kept Cam close enough that he could see Emilia as much as possible. It might not have been the most traditional situation, but it suited our needs right now.

When I had a project or deadline for one of my online classes, Cam stepped up, taking care of Emilia so I could focus. And with his work as a shortstop for a minor league baseball team, I had his parents' support when he was on the road for weeks at a time. Even though our romantic relationship was over, we were a team, a family, and in many ways, he was my best friend.

Turning my attention back to my daughter, I smiled. "Where's Auntie Hadley? Did you already scare her away?"

"She was the genius who thought paints would be an amazing idea." Cam gave me a knowing look. "And then, when it came time to clean up, she had a sudden emergency and had to leave."

I chuckled; that sounded like Hadley. She was all about the bright spots in life, bringing a hefty dose of sunshine wherever she went. Ever since we were matched as roommates during my short-lived college career, she'd been my constant, my cheerleader when life tried to weigh me down, but ever since they first met, Cam and Hadley hadn't gotten along. Her free-spirited nature tended to grate against Cam's rigidity, a fact she exploited as much as possible. It was endlessly entertaining. The only thing they agreed on was Emilia, which was why I'd happily offered to let her crash at my house while I was gone. She wanted to spend more time with her goddaughter, and I knew Cam could use the help, even if he'd never admit it. Now, all I had to do was pray they wouldn't kill each other in the process.

Cam leaned down and kissed Emilia's forehead. "Why don't you go play, baby? I have to talk to Mommy for a minute."

"K, Daddy." She hopped down from the counter. "Love you, Mommy."

"Love you more, kiddo."

"Love you, foreva and eva!"

I chuckled as Cam filled the screen, his face suddenly serious. He looked behind his shoulder, watching as Emilia left the room. "How are things going there?"

"Better than I expected," I said. "Even though I was super nervous, I have to admit, it's good to see Cole. And this town is absolutely adorable; it's easy to see why he loves it so much." I exhaled slowly. "But we're taking things slowly. It's almost like we're walking on eggshells. He tried to bring up the past, but I'm not ready to get into it, at least not yet. I want to just enjoy this week without all that hanging over our heads."

"Give it time," Cam said. "This is a good step, but remember, it's just the first one. Y'all will get there, Vic." His cheek ticked, and my hackles raised. After being in each other's lives for over a decade, I knew Cam's tells almost as well as my own. And that little tick? Clear sign he was holding something back.

"What?" I asked.

"Are you sure you don't want to tell him about Emilia?"

I pushed out the remaining breath in my chest, hating how conflicted I felt. When I found out I was pregnant, it was a shock. For someone who prided herself in following a particular plan, seeing those two pink lines completely disrupted everything. Not that I'd trade my life with Emilia for anything, but the fallout still stung sometimes.

Not only did I leave school to focus on Emilia entirely, but I'd changed in my parents' eyes. I'd gone from their perfect angel to a scandal, and despite being loving grandparents, they still hadn't completely gotten over that betrayal. For weeks after I told them about my pregnancy, I called Cole, hoping he'd be the one person who wouldn't let me down. But he only answered once, and from his voice, I could tell he'd been drinking. The moment I asked about it, he became belligerent, screaming at me for fucking up his whole life. He'd said I was nothing more than a burden, and an unwanted one at that. The moment the call ended, I decided I was done, no longer willing to put him before my mental health and safety. I had to think about more than just myself, and I vowed I wouldn't let my child get involved in his mess, not until he cleaned up his act.

And while he was sober now, keeping up with our scheduled phone calls and settling down, there was still a part of me that didn't trust that his progress would last. I'd been burned too many times, gotten my hopes up, only for him to fall back into the bottle and break my heart all over again.

"I'm sure," I said quietly. "At least, not yet. Cole seems good, but..."

"Hey," Cam said, pulling my attention back to him. "You don't have to explain. I know how much it hurt when he was drinking. You're trying to make the right choice for Emilia. Don't let anyone make you question that."

"I don't want her to get used to him, only for him to disappear again." My eyes lifted to the ceiling as I tried not to cry. "I can handle him breaking my heart; it won't be the first time. But if he crushed hers, nothing in the world would get me to forgive him. I don't want her getting attached to someone if it's not a long-term thing."

"You're a good mom, Vic." Cam smiled softly at me. "And hopefully, Cole will show you how much he's changed. For what it's worth, I've got faith in the guy. Sometimes, it takes hitting rock bottom to pull yourself back up, and it seems like he's got enough to lose to make sure he never lands down there again."

THREE

Adam

The taste of bitter coffee hit my tongue as I stared out at the woods behind my cabin. No other living creature stared back at me, and for a moment, it felt like I was truly alone. Even though I was sitting on the back porch, only a handful of feet away from other people visiting Saint Stephen's Lake, it felt like I was the only person in the world.

For so long, my life was all about the hustle: making connections, taking on even the most minor role, and doing anything I could think of to break into the acting world. And while I loved it, it was also draining. How long had it been since I was able to just...be?

Since I moved here a month ago, this has been my routine. Without anything filling up my calendar, I'd make a cup of coffee and just sit on the back porch of my cabin. It was a far cry from the beach back at my house in California and the complete opposite of my penthouse in New York, but this was now my favorite view in the world. All I needed was the same Adirondack chair and the sounds of nature filling my ears.

As I relaxed in my seat, enjoying the quiet calls of birds in the nearby trees, a sudden pounding on my door shattered the illusion. It was tempting to ignore it, to pretend I'd gone out for the day, but when I heard the voice on the other side, I knew that wasn't a choice.

"Dude, open the fucking door. I know you're in there."

I rolled my eyes as I stood, tapping the screen of my phone on the side table. *Shit.* So much for wasting away the morning. It was way past morning, and I was still in my sweats, my hair all messed up from sleep. I stopped to run water over my face before heading to the door, interrupting another round of pounding knocks when I pulled it open.

"Jesus, Cole. What the hell's your issue?"

But my best friend didn't even flinch, too busy staring at my face. I could only imagine the sight he saw, from the scraggly beard I'd been rocking for far too long to the dark circles lining my eyes after another restless night of sleep. He didn't say anything as he barged inside, gripping the back of one of the chairs at the breakfast nook.

My cabin wasn't much, but it had everything I needed. It was pretty much a studio apartment with a king-sized bed and a small kitchenette, so even two people made it feel crowded. But it was all I needed.

A part of me felt guilty for squatting in one of Cole and Alex's largest cabins, but they'd insisted when I showed up at their doorstep, desperate for a place to stay. And as much as I hated relying on them, they didn't even hesitate to open their doors. I tried to pay them, to give them a date for when I'd check-out, but they wouldn't hear of it.

"It's the least I can do," Cole said at the time.

But that happy, settled man was nowhere to be found this afternoon. Even though I'd been staying here for over a month, Cole had never shown up like this, with a frantic look on his face. Shit, did something happen between him and Alex? They constantly bantered, but it was usually more playful than anything else.

Deciding to wait him out, I stood on the opposite wall of the kitchenette, crossing my arms over my chest. Cole gripped the wooden chair in his hands, his knuckles blanching. After several silent minutes, he finally relented, dragging his hand over his face. "Tori's here."

"Oh, shit, that's today?" I cursed under my breath for forgetting, knowing this had been making Cole anxious for weeks. Even though his wedding was in a handful of days, those plans never stressed him out. He never even wavered in his desire to get married, often saying it was about damn time. But seeing his little sister again after so many years apart? That was tearing him inside out.

I grabbed a bottle of water from the fridge and offered one to Cole. He shook his head. Taking a sip, I sat down across from him. "Take it the reunion didn't go well?"

"It was fine," Cole answered gruffly. "Too fine. It was like talking to a damn stranger. And she's so fucking grown up, Adam. I almost didn't recognize her at the airport."

I paused, trying to remember the last time I saw Victoria Campbell. Maybe six years ago? It had to be right after we held that disastrous intervention for Cole—the one that led him to my doorstep in California, trying to get away from his demons and triggers. As far as I knew, she cut him off right after that, refusing to deal with his self-destruction any longer. But between my career and trying to help Cole get sober, Victoria rarely crossed my mind.

Even growing up, I never paid her much attention. She was a lot younger than us, barely a toddler when Cole's family moved into my town. And while I'd always kept an eye out for her, we never really talked much. After all, what did a teenage boy have in common with a kid six years younger than them?

But seeing Cole now, a guilt gnawed in my chest. I should have tried harder and kept in contact with her. Maybe then, there wouldn't be this massive divide between her and Cole. While logically, I knew it wasn't my job to solve all my friend's problems, I'd been his guardian for so long that it was hard to let go now.

Shifting to face Cole fully, I crossed my arms over my chest. "It's the first day. Maybe she was jet-lagged."

"Maybe."

He shook his head, glancing back down at his hands. For months, he'd been trying to get Victoria to visit. After those attempts all failed, he shifted gears, trying instead to go to her, but Victoria always had some excuse, some reason they couldn't meet. Even when he'd flown down to Texas to take Alex to spend time with his parents, Victoria bailed, citing some school-related emergency.

"I know things are going to take time," Cole sighed. "But fuck, I hate this. There's so much distance between us."

"Okay, remember when you first started calling again?" He nodded. "Those first couple of calls were awkward as hell. But you pushed forward and made sure that Tori knew you weren't going anywhere. Look how far you've come already." I leaned forward on my elbows. "It'll get there, Cole. You've got her here for a week. That's already a win."

Cole nodded, finally releasing the tight breath he'd been holding. "Shit." He let out a dry laugh. "You're right, man. I think seeing her after all this time threw me off kilter. I can't stop thinking about how much I've missed being in her life. I don't want to do anything to fuck it up again."

"Then don't."

"Easy for you to say."

I tried to keep my jaw from tensing, but it was useless. I knew what Cole was implying: that everything came easily to me, that I took life in stride, never worrying about much. And while I was known for bringing my passion to my sets— outside of work, everyone else saw me as the balanced, happy-go-lucky guy.

While it was a role I'd always strived for, lately, that guy was almost non-existent. It was getting harder to project that image, to keep my emotions hidden behind a smirk. To be honest, I was over being the guy with the joke, the one who let everything slide so easily off his back. But after a lifetime of playing this part, it was harder to shake than I thought. My go-to response was to pretend everything was fine, that life was golden, and I was the same person I'd always been, no matter how much it was eating away at me.

I cleared my throat and forced a smile over my face. "Tell me what you need, Cole. I'll help however I can."

"Tori's staying in the cabin next door." Cole fidgeted with his fingers. "I know it's a lot to ask, but can you keep an eye on her? Let me know if she's okay?"

"You think something's going on with her?"

"I don't know. It's just a feeling." He glanced up at me, hurt and confusion marring his expression. "But I think Tori's holding something back. I want her to have someone she can check in with, someone she can go to if she's not comfortable talking to me. I want her to have good memories of this place."

You didn't have to know Cole well to read between the lines. He was desperate for this trip to go well. In his mind, it needed to if he wanted to be a part of Victoria's life again, and despite his best intentions, it wasn't like he had time to spare. He and Alex had been running around non-stop lately, obsessing over every detail of their property. Managing this place was a full-time job, even with a crew. Considering that they'd been working primarily alone, it was a wonder that they were still standing.

It wasn't a surprise that Cole wanted Victoria to feel comfortable staying here, knowing she might stay for longer stretches if this trip went well. As much as he loved his life here, she was the missing piece, the one thing he still beat himself up about.

Maybe, with enough time, they could get back the bond they once had.

Cole had put in the time and effort with his sobriety, digging up from rock bottom with blood, sweat, and tears. It had taken years to get to this point, but I was still so fucking proud of him. If earning Victoria's trust was the last piece he needed to move on with his life, then there was no way I'd let him do this alone.

"Of course, man. Whatever you need."

AFTER COLE LEFT to tend to some plumbing issue in Cabin Four, I ambled around the cabin for a little bit, debating what to do with my day. The only other visitor I had was my agent, Theo's, new assistant. Eloise showed up on my doorstep, like she did at the same time every week, bearing a stack of new scripts to look over. Theo was tenacious, I'd give him that, even more so since he'd broken away from his firm and started his own agency. He'd rented out office space downtown, and as far as I knew, he was keeping the firm small. Theo personally tended to every client, and the only other employee was Eloise, who he'd snaked from his old agency.

Eloise was always kind enough, but I worried about her in that office with him. Not that Theo was a bad guy, especially now that he was very happily married, but I'd seen firsthand how his temper could be, and Eloise seemed like the kind of person who would break under the slightest pressure.

She stood in the doorway, fidgeting with her fingers and

shifting on her feet, looking everywhere else but at me. As I sighed, dropping the pile on top of the ones she left last week, she spoke. "Umm, what should I tell Theo?"

"To get a different fucking hobby."

Eloise grimaced, and I knew those words would never come out of her mouth. I sighed. "Tell him the same thing as last week. I'm not ready. I need more time."

She nodded, muttering a quick goodbye before scurrying out the door.

As the screen door clattered closed behind her, I shook my head, squeezing my eyes closed. The scripts tortured me, staring at me as if they knew how much I wanted to read them. And while I might have told the world I needed a break, the truth was much more complicated.

I'd loved acting from the first time I stepped onto a stage. In the second grade, we'd performed some ridiculous winter production all about the miracle of Christmas. Even though I was just one of the reindeer, something happened when I stepped out into the bright lights. It was as if I found where I belonged, where I always wanted to be.

My parents thought it was a phase, that I would eventually settle into more realistic goals, but that wasn't me. The day before my high school graduation, my parents sat me down and offered me a deal. They'd support my dream of moving to LA, but they wanted a time frame. Two years; that was all they were willing to give me. After that, if I wasn't able to support myself, I'd come home and settle into the life they wanted for me.

Little did they know, that was never going to happen.

I'd worked my ass off from the moment I'd crossed the California state line. As I worked all day and night at dead-end jobs, every spare minute was going to auditions and casting calls. As luck would have it, I happened to get a guest spot on an up-and-coming TV show. It didn't last beyond the first season, but it was enough to get me some attention and led me to Theo. He took me under his wing and showed me what it would take to get the roles I wanted. While I may not have agreed with all his choices, I had no doubt in my mind I couldn't have gotten to this level without him.

I thumbed through the stack of scripts, waiting until the highlighter marks caught my eye. Tucked close to the bottom was one script I'd read through dozens of times, making notes as I went. Most in the pile weren't winners, but this one called to me from the moment it arrived. Scanning through the pages, I realized it was the kind of project I had dreamed of: a gritty, dark drama with a morally gray main character. It was a far departure from what I'd done so far, and I could almost imagine slipping into the role.

But just as I started to think about calling Theo, my hand tensed, moments from the past almost knocking me off my feet. Memories of white envelopes and emails with the same subject line, all filled with harrowing words and pictures, snapped of my daily life—pictures that no one should have had access to, images of me at my most vulnerable. My eyes slammed closed, sucked back into those dark months all too easily.

I sighed, trying to push that fear out of my veins. Over six months later, I still had no answers, barely beginning to pull myself out of that cycle of fear and distrust.

I erased the message to Theo and tucked my phone back in my pocket. No, I wasn't ready to jump back into that life, not yet. I was just starting to walk around town without looking over my shoulder.

Maybe one day, I'd be Adam Rice, the movie star, again. But until I could look at myself in the mirror without flinching, that was little more than a dream.

FOUR

Adam

As I left my cabin, I stretched my arms over my head, letting the lingering summer heat sink into my bones. All the locals said we were lucky; the longer the summer lasted, the more income the tourist-based businesses made. But I couldn't wait for the summer rush to end, for this town to go back to the sleepy little secret I'd fallen in love with. Until then, I'd don my usual disguise—my trustworthy sunglasses and a New York Rebels hat.

I walked over to the main lodge, a large, rustic building in the front of the Fox Creek Property. While my little cabin had most amenities, I had to venture over to the main property for food unless I wanted to cook. They always had some takeaway available, but there was also a full restaurant on the south side, with a dining room that looked out over the lake. I tended to avoid that, mostly because I could usually expect at least one person to watch me, trying to place my face. While once, being recognized gave me an indescribable thrill, now, it made my skin crawl. So, I kept to myself. Filming last year had brought enough strangers to these shores; I didn't want to be the cause of any more chaos. One picture or post could be enough to inundate the town with reports and end my respite.

Waving to the cook, Thomas, and the lone waitress, whose name I always forgot, I stepped into the buffet area. The room was between the kitchen and the dining room, and the wafting smells of fresh bread and pastries made my mouth water. But most of the lunchtime options had been picked through, and all that was left were a couple of pastries and some fruit. I glanced at my watch. Cole asked me to go over for dinner tonight, so I needed something to hold me over until then. When I was just about to say fuck it and head into the restaurant, I turned, colliding with a woman who had been trying to reach around me.

She squeaked as she started to fall. Before I could think about my actions, I reached out, pulling her into my arms. Her wide brown eyes stared up at me, shock filling her gaze.

I was equally stunned, taking in the most beautiful woman I'd ever seen. How in the hell had I missed her checking in? She must have been new, because there was no way I wouldn't have noticed her before.

As I placed her back on her feet, I took in more of her features. She had long, slightly wavy dark hair, with a few brighter pieces framing her face. Her lightly glossed lips parted in surprise, and I couldn't help but stare at the pink hue. She was adorable, almost innocent. But that thought was dashed when I scanned the rest of her, finding luscious curves that could make any man fall to his knees.

"I'm okay," her voice said as she glanced down at my arm still wrapped around her waist.

"Oh, sorry," I said quickly, gifting her an apologetic smile. "I was just..." *Staring? Distracted by your full lips?* "I need coffee."

She giggled, tucking her chin down to her chest. "Same."

She nodded behind me. "Care to pass me a cup? Don't want to risk another collision."

"You got it."

I grabbed one of the porcelain cups, but she stopped me, placing her hand on my arm. "Actually, I meant one of the to-go cups. I'm heading right back to my cabin."

"As was I," I chuckled. "But to make up for almost knocking you over, I'd love to treat you to a real meal."

Her eyes widened at my offer, her teeth sinking into her plush bottom lip. Shit. Why the hell did that move go straight to my dick? Maybe it was the lack of attention he'd received lately, and now, even the smallest gesture was conjuring dirty images in my mind.

She shook her head, barely suppressing an annoyed chuckle. "Did Cole put you up to this?"

The sound of my best friend's name on her lips doused all my thoughts. Cocking my head to the side, I stared at her a little more intensely. Why would Cole have asked— *oh, fuck*.

"Victoria?" I screeched, pulling down my sunglasses to get a good look at her. When Cole asked me to look out for his sister, I never thought about what she'd look like now. In my mind, she was still a skinny teenager with wild hair and a toothy grin.

But the woman in front of me was a goddess.

I cleared my throat, forcing away any inappropriate thoughts before I reached down and pulled her into a hug. "Holy shit, Victoria. I didn't even recognize you." I pulled back, searching her face again. Now that I knew it was her, I couldn't believe it had taken me that long. She looked almost like a clone of her mom. She had the same color eyes as Cole, but unlike his, her color danced with something I couldn't place. "You look so different."

She chuckled, taking a step out of my arms. "I hope so. The last time I saw you, I was still rocking jean overalls."

"It was a good look."

"You're sweet," she said, placing her hand on my arm again. "But we both know that's a lie."

It was hard to rectify the picture in my mind with the sight in front of me. In truth, I paid little attention to Victoria Campbell. Our age gap meant we never ran in the same circles or shared the same school. She was always just Cole's little sister, nothing more.

But the woman in front of me had ripped all other thoughts from my mind. I was consumed by her lips and smooth curves.

However, just as quickly as the thoughts overtook me, the thought of my best friend drowned them in cold water. Cole asked me to look after his baby sister—he wanted her to feel welcome and safe in his town. Something told me he didn't want my little soldier leading the welcome wagon.

Clearing my throat, I took a big step back, trying to escape the floral scent that seemed to linger around her. "You heading over to the house tonight?"

She paused and took a slow breath. "Yeah, I think so. My parents are going to expect me for dinner, and I'd like to meet Alex."

"You haven't met yet?"

I knew the answer, but I wanted to hear her version of events over the past few months. While I knew Cole was trying, Victoria had been holding back; at least, that's what Cole had said. And as much as the woman in front of me was a stranger, she was still a Campbell. They might have a tough exterior, but the inside was all warmth and love. When we tried to intervene and help Cole, she was the one leading the charge, spending all her time researching the best treatment programs and ways we could support him. She was his cheerleader, the one constant in his corner. For Victoria to cut Cole out of her life meant something must have cut her deep, and the wound wasn't likely healed.

"Nope," Victoria answered, averting her eyes from my gaze. "We've talked on the phone, and she sometimes joins our weekly calls, but I haven't met her in person." She chuckled and gave me a conspiratorial smirk. "I'm very curious about the woman who convinced my brother to settle down."

"I think it was the opposite way around," I chuckled. "Alex would have been happy to keep dating, but Cole wanted to make things official. He would have married her months ago, but they decided to wait until things were more stable here."

"That doesn't sound like the Cole I remember."

I met her gaze, taking in the pain and hurt hidden behind the dark specks of her eyes. As soon as she noticed me staring, she shook her head, rolling her eyes. "Ignore me, I'm just hangry. I promise I'll be charming tonight."

"I don't know, trouble. I think I like it when you speak your mind."

"We'll see about that," she chuckled, grabbing one more pastry and stacking it on her plate. "So, tell me what you've been up to, Adam? Besides destroying the box office and making women ages 18 to 35 lust after you."

"Are you keeping tabs on me, Campbell?" I joked, hoping she didn't notice my flinch.

"It's kind of hard not to, Rice," she chuckled, putting her plate down and adding cream to her coffee. "You're a pretty popular guy."

As she spoke, another guest joined us. Even though they paid us no mind, my defenses rose, not wanting to expose any part of myself. I cleared my throat, "I should get going, but it was..." I blanked out on words, too busy staring into Victoria Campbell's eyes. "Good. It's really good to see you again." I squeezed her shoulder as I walked past. "But you'll be there tonight?"

"Yup. I might try to squeeze in a quick nap, but Cole's coming to pick me up later."

"Good," I repeated, as if it was the only word left in my brain. "Good. Then I'll see you there."

As I walked outside, I instantly regretted it. Every fiber of my body wanted me to go back inside and keep talking to Victoria. I wanted to know more about her and find out what had happened in the years since we parted. Never did I think that Cole's little sister would knock me on my ass like she did.

When I reached my cabin, I turned, watching as she walked across the lawn. For most of my life, Victoria Campbell had been an afterthought.

But she certainly had all of my attention now.

FIVE

Victoria

As we pulled up to Cole's house, my heart started to beat a heavy rhythm. My nerves raced in my chest, and I could feel my pulse all the way down to my fingertips. Cole looked over to me as he shifted the car into park. With a soft sigh, he nodded to the house. "Ready for this?"

"Of course," I said, hoping the tone of my voice didn't betray me. As much as Cole tried to comfort me on the way over, letting me know all about the people waiting for us, I couldn't help but feel a little nauseous. These were the people closest to Cole, a good barometer to tell how others in his life would receive me. All I could hope was that this evening would go well, and I could go and hide back in my cabin until the next day.

My brother opened his door, but let me take my time exiting the vehicle. Stepping into the driveway, I took a look at Cole's new home with clearer eyes. It was something out of a storybook, this sweet little cottage in the middle of the woods. Everything from the bright flowers that lined the siding to the brightly painted teal front door screamed home. There was only one other house in view, a dark red one that looked more like a farmhouse than anything else. From our earlier conversation, I could guess that was where Marta and Curt, their close friends and neighbors, lived. They also had a son who was staying with them, but he was taking care of their restaurant so they could give Alex and Cole all their attention over the next few days.

"Hey," Cole called out. "We're back."

"Victoria?"

My shoulders tensed as my name rang out, the sound bringing flashbacks to my youth. My parents rounded the corner, greeting me with welcoming but tight smiles. I greeted them the same, hating that the last time we spoke, we were arguing about this very trip. My mom was upset that I wasn't bringing Emilia, but I was steadfast in my choice. And as much as they didn't like it, at least my parents agreed not to say anything until I was ready.

As I walked further into the foyer, my dad's eyes met mine. My father, Sam Campbell, was an imposing man to those who didn't know him. His stern, unflappable exterior was honed through years in the military, never letting anyone see his nerves. He rarely smiled, saving those primarily for my mother and us. While he was absent for most of my childhood, there was still a part of me that loved my father fiercely. On the nights he'd be out late working, I'd stay up long past my bedtime, waiting for a couple of moments with him after he got back from base, needing a least one hug before falling asleep. As an adult, as much as I tried to say I was above it, I craved his approval, wanting to see that twinkle of pride in his eyes.

While that twinkle might have died a little on the day I told him I was pregnant, my need for his approval had not. At that moment, our relationship had irreparably changed—his perception of me shifted from the little girl who always begged for bedtime stories to a flawed but adult woman who owned her choices.

However, even though we'd seen my future playing out in different ways, I knew without a doubt that he'd move worlds to keep me safe.

Standing under his arm, my mother, Julia, smiled at me, as if unsure how to proceed. If my father was our family's rock, my mother was the sun, the person who always guided me home. Growing up, our home was always filled with her laughter, making it the most welcoming place in the neighborhood, but the years had stripped some of her joy, especially when Cole felt so lost to us.

My mother's brown eyes softened as she looked at me, wanting to say more than this space would allow. I nodded, hoping they could read the unsaid apology in my expression.

I stepped forward, breaking the stalemate between us. My mother sunk into my embrace, and tears dusted my eyes when my father kissed the top of my head. Cole watched the whole exchange with a concerned frown, probably trying to understand the odd fracture between us.

No matter what happened, there was no doubt that my parents were good people. Even when they were disappointed in me, I never questioned how much they loved me. Emilia adored them, and they were the first ones to show up whenever she needed them. But they also had grown up in a different time and held onto some of those old-fashioned beliefs. My decision not to marry Cam when those two lines showed up would always be a point of contention between us, but I could put that aside for Cole's sake.

"Is that her?" a feminine voice called out. "It's so nice to —oh."

I chuckled as my parents let me go, turning to face the new arrivals. Cole chuckled, pushing me over to greet them. "Hey, Marta and Curt, this is my baby sister, Tori. She just got in from Texas this afternoon. Tor, these are our next-door neighbors."

Marta reached out first, vigorously shaking my hand. "We are so excited to meet you. Cole hasn't stopped talking about you for weeks."

"Likewise." I smiled, shaking her hand and then turning toward Curt. "Cole said you've been so helpful with getting everything up and running at the Lodge."

"Pssh," Marta said, waving her hand through the air. "Curt's picked up a couple of side projects, and I helped set up the kitchen. That's nothing compared to what these kids have been up to."

"Speaking of which," Cole said, looking around her, "where is Alex?"

Everyone visibly flinched at the same time. Marta was the one actually to speak, though. "She felt bad about not helping with dinner, so she thought she'd make a cake for dessert."

"Fuck," Cole hissed under his breath, earning a whack in the arm from our mother. "Please tell me you checked the fire extinguisher."

"Of course," Curt chuckled. "And don't worry, Marta supervised. Seemed like everything was going well, but she's refusing to leave the kitchen until it's done. Afraid she's going to burn the damn thing."

"Wouldn't be the first time," Marta chuckled.

"I'll go grab her," Cole chuckled, moving toward the kitchen. "Get settled in the dining room, and we'll bring everything in."

We walked to the other side of the house, settling into a dining room attached to the kitchen. I immediately smiled when I saw Alex perched in front of the oven, her hands on her hips, staring at the cake as if it had personally offended her. Cole came in through the other entrance, placing his hands on her shoulders and loosening some of the tension there with his thumbs. She scowled up at him for a moment but softened as soon as he bent down and kissed her forehead.

As she spotted the rest of us coming into the room, she dusted her hands on her jeans and turned out of Cole's embrace. She beelined immediately for me, her bright blue eyes crinkled with delight. "So you must be Victoria. I have to say, I was starting to have my doubts that you were real."

My face fell, and I could feel the color draining from my face. Words failed me as I stared at Alex. Even though she was a couple of inches shorter than me, my hands shook as I tried to form words. But just as I was debating darting out of the house, Alex's lips curved into a slow smile. "Sorry, that probably was a shitty thing to say. What I meant was, I'm really happy you're here. It means a lot to both me and Cole."

"Oh," I chuckled, holding my hand to my heart. "I...Yeah, I'm thrilled to be here too. This town is beautiful."

"Thanks," she beamed. "It's not as flashy as most cities, but it's home. We like it."

With that, she ushered me into my seat across from my mother. Curt and Marta sat on either side while my dad and Cole took opposing heads of the table. Alex sat on Cole's left, leaving a space between me and her. I looked down at the empty chair, hoping it was for the one person I'd been dying to see tonight. "Are you expecting anyone else?" I asked, feigning ignorance.

"Adam's supposed to be here," Cole shrugged. "But he's running late. He should be here before dessert."

Disappointment settled in my gut, and I hated that all it took was one conversation for my childhood crush to turn into full-blown lust. Truth be told, no one, and I mean no one, knew that I'd thought Adam was the most handsome man in the world when I was younger. I guarded that secret like my own field of gold, not wanting to be ridiculed for my attraction to the much older boy.

My crush had faded over time, and I'd forgotten about him outside of his work in movies. By then, he was just another handsome actor, attractive but unattainable.

But seeing him earlier made something snap inside me, a feeling I'd long buried since breaking up with Cam. Seeing him so close? Smelling the lingering cologne on his skin? Well, that made me feel more desire than I had in years.

Glancing at my brother, I knew it was a mistake even to entertain these thoughts. Adam was his best friend, more his sibling than me at the moment. To think anything different was a mistake, mainly when we lived in such very different worlds. At the end of this week, I'd go back to Texas, go back to my life of laundry, cleaning, and trying to wrangle Emilia. Adam would go back to the glistening lights of Hollywood, probably to whatever model or actress was warming his bed at the moment.

"So, Victoria," Marta said as she passed me the salad bowl. "Your mom says you're studying business?"

"Yes, ma'am," I nodded. "I'm enrolled in online classes right now, but I'm hoping to start my MBA next year."

"That's exciting," she beamed back. Something about Marta made my panic subside. She was genuine and warm, similar to my own mother in many ways, but without the disappointment that lurked underneath. "Do you know what type of business you'd like to go into?"

"My best friend and I have this dream of opening a daycare center," I answered, trying not to shift under the weight of the whole table's stares. "She's studying to be an early childhood teacher, so between our skill sets, we should be a great team. And there's a drastic need for quality childcare, especially in more rural areas. We're hoping to fill that gap."

"Good career," Curt agreed, patting his wife on the arm. "Hard work, but meaningful."

"Yes, sir."

As if a timer had gone off in her mind, my mother suddenly sat up straighter. "Marta, did you and Alex talk about those floral arrangements Calla dropped off?"

As the conversation veered back to the wedding, I exhaled slowly, using the opportunity to take a breather. Leaving the dining room, I walked across the foyer and into a quaint living room. One of the walls was lined with bookcases, hand-carved with sunflowers in the moldings. I smiled as I ran my fingers over the surface. Even after all these years, I recognized my brother's handiwork. In school, he'd taken every shop and woodworking class he could. Whittling had become a favorite hobby of his, and you could always find him chiseling some scrap of wood left over from one of Dad's projects. My room at home still had some of his carvings, from the early ones that resembled lumps more than animals to the horses he made later on that looked like they'd start galloping off the shelf.

Alongside all genres of books were pictures, mainly of Alex and Cole. In all of them, they looked so happy, it made my chest ache. There were images of others, the family Cole had created away from ours. As much as it dug a deep hole in my chest, I couldn't help but be happy for him. It was the kind of life I'd always imagined for myself, one filled with laughter and love. Knowing Cole had come so far and found it for himself gave me a new sense of hope.

As I turned out of the living room, I headed down the corridor instead of going back into the dining room. When I reached the rear kitchen entrance, my feet faltered as I took in the sight in front of me. My brother was holding Alex, brushing his lips across her forehead. They swayed together as if there was a secret melody between them, one the rest of us couldn't hear.

I started to step back, not wanting to interrupt their moment, but no matter what I told myself, I couldn't force myself to look away. Even from this distance, the love was clear between them. There was a time when I thought Cam and I had that, but time and space had taught me that I'd always love Cam as family, nothing more. We never looked at each other like Alex and Cole. What we had was young love, the kind shaped by excitement and new experiences. They had the kind of love that knocked the wind out of your lungs, that made it impossible to see anyone else in the room.

I crossed my arms around my chest and stared down at my shoes. So many nights, I ached for that kind of love, and I was almost sure it was out of my reach. I had too much going on, and there wasn't a lot of room in my life for new people. But as much as I wanted to be a strong, independent woman for my daughter to look up to, I'd be lying if I said I didn't want a partner, someone to ease some of my burdens, some of my loneliness.

But then, there were nights when Emilia would crawl into bed with me, and all those doubts and lingering loneliness crept away as her tiny body molded against mine. She was my everything; all my love was poured into my precious girl. She was my entire world, and that was enough for me. She deserved my whole heart.

I turned to shift back into the living room when I smacked into someone standing behind me. Before I could even look up, I knew who it was. My hands landed on his sculpted chest, the soft smell of cedar crowding my senses.

Adam.

I cursed myself for making a fool of myself in front of him. *Again.* Earlier, it had been his fault, almost knocking me down because I was too busy staring at him to move away. But this time, it was all me.

His blue eyes twinkled as he looked down at me, the same smirk I'd grown up with now aimed at me. As a kid, Adam was always larger than life, the person you couldn't help but gravitate toward. He was the prom king and the debate club president. He rocked the football field and the drama stage. Everyone wanted to be friends with him, yet he was fiercely loyal to my brother.

"We gotta stop running into each other like this," he chuckled as he helped me straighten.

My skin immediately prickled under his touch, coming to life with the simple gesture. It was wild how affected I was by his presence. There was no universe where I should share the same breath as Adam Rice, much less the thoughts that had plagued my mind since I saw him earlier. God, his movies did not do him justice. The years had been way too kind to him. While he still had that same old twinkle in his eye, everything else had improved with age. It made it hard to remember I'd grown up with him. He was still the same guy who would show up with lilies every Sunday for my mother, all because he knew she loved how they brightened up the room. The kid who would pass me his blueberry pie because he knew it was my favorite and my dad would never let me have more than one piece.

But staring up at him now, it was like the past and present versions of him had merged into the man of my dreams. He was chiseled, his aura radiating confidence and swagger, but he was still holding on to that boyish charm that knocked everyone off their feet.

I cleared my throat, realizing I'd been staring at Adam for far too long. "I'm so sorry," I said as I pushed back toward the wall. "I don't know what's going on with me today."

"It's been a big day," Adam said. "You don't have to explain if you're feeling a little off-kilter."

I nodded, hating that he could see how overwhelmed I felt. But being hidden in the nook with him, it was like the stress of the day melted away, swept away in the ocean of his eyes.

But just as my heart rate started to steady, Cole stepped into the room, his eyes narrowing at the two of us. "Tor, you good?"

I nodded, taking a step out of Adam's orbit. "Yeah, just needed a breather. I don't think I've ever seen Mom so excited."

"Yeah," Cole chuckled, rubbing the back of his head. "Alex and I were saying the same thing. While I love Mom and Dad's visits, I'm ready to have some time alone with my wife."

"Future wife," she corrected with a smirk.

"Close enough," Cole answered back, pressing a kiss to her forehead. "And I can't help it, sweetheart. I like the way it sounds."

I glanced at Adam with a sly smile. "Are they always like this?"

"You should have seen them when they first met." Adam shuddered. "I was pretty sure they were going to kill each other."

Alex rolled her eyes at the comment and stepped toward me. "Trust me, you make a much better first impression than your brother." She reached out like she wanted to hug me but paused before I could get any closer. I hesitated for a second then moved closer, wrapping my arms around her petite frame.

"Thank you for taking care of Cole," I whispered in her ear so my brother couldn't hear.

"That was all him," she chuckled, squeezing me a little tighter. "Thank *you* for coming. It means more than you even know."

SIX

Victoria

After dessert was served, we all sat around the table talking about Cole and Alex's impending nuptials. While the wedding planner, who turned out to be Alex's best friend, Calla, was taking care of most of the details, there were still a few things that needed to be decided. As Cole and Alex bickered over the appetizer options, I just sat back, loving how comfortable they were with each other.

When we drove up from Albany, I kept watching Cole, trying to see if this whole thing was a farce and if he was secretly hiding his darkness. After all, he'd been really good at fooling us in the past.

But here, with Alex, it was clear his happiness wasn't a façade. It beamed out of him, making him seem younger somehow. He hadn't been like this since high school, before his memories were tainted with pain and grief. For a brief moment, I could almost forget the fallout that led to our distance, could erase the years I couldn't sleep, wondering if my brother was even alive.

The cool wave of resentment washed down my spine, making me sit up a little bit straighter. I hated that it was so easy to knock me out of the moment, to take me back to the dark stages of my past. As much as I knew I needed to let it go, it wasn't that easy. One afternoon could never replace years of hurt.

As my mother excitedly talked about Alex using some of her jewelry as her something borrowed, I cleared my throat. "Excuse me. I have to make a quick phone call."

No one seemed to notice my absence—except Adam. His eyes immediately darted to me as I stood, watching as if he could read my mind. And maybe he could. I was never one with a good poker face, but I was trying like hell not to let those feelings show.

As I walked down the hall toward the powder room, I took a right turn instead, walking through the kitchen and out the side door. As I stepped outside, closing the door to the chatter inside, it was like I could take a full breath again.

Letting my feet guide me, I walked down a pebble path leading toward a fire pit at the back of the house. It was surrounded by four chairs, perfect for late-night conversations and cookouts. But that wasn't what caught my eye. No, it was the view of the lake, the sun starting to set below the tree line. Watching the still water, I let the calm, serene air wash over me, brushing away all my stress. The questions I didn't know how to answer, the future plans that were still so far up in the air, the guilt I felt every time I lied to the group of people inside, every time I didn't divulge the most significant piece of my life. Emilia was at the forefront of my mind all the time, but it was especially challenging today. To pretend she didn't exist felt like a slight against my nature, an unimaginable life where she wasn't the center of it.

But I was making the right choice, wasn't I? My job as a parent was to protect my daughter at all costs, and I needed to be sure before I brought anyone else into her life. She'd gone through four years of changes already, and if Cam's baseball career panned out as he hoped, we'd all be moving again next year. Because while he loved playing for the minor league back home, we all knew it was only a matter of time until he got the call to move up to the next level, hopefully, sooner rather than later.

"Thought I'd find you out here."

I jumped at the sound of Adam's voice behind me. My hand flew to my chest, trying to calm my now-frantic heartbeat.

He placed a hand on my shoulder as he joined me at the edge of the lake. "Sorry, thought you heard me coming up behind you. Promise I'm not doing it on purpose."

"Debatable." I smirked up at him. "They sent you to make sure I was still here?"

"I volunteered," he answered. "Cole wanted to come, but I thought it'd be better if it was someone more neutral." He glanced down at me. "How are you holding up, kid?"

"I'm fine," I answered, but the shake in my voice betrayed me.

"Bullshit," Adam chuckled. "What's going through your head, Victoria?"

I exhaled slowly, unsure if I should spill everything to Adam. He'd proven a long time ago that he was good at keeping secrets, that he'd have my back if needed. But that would ask him to betray Cole, to keep a massive secret from his best friend. And as much as it would take some of the weight from my shoulders, it wasn't fair to place it on someone else's.

Another lie sat on the tip of my tongue, but as I met Adam's understanding gaze, I couldn't do it. There was something hidden behind his kind smile, a small tell that he wasn't as perfectly happy as everyone seemed to think. I had to clench my fist to keep from reaching out to him, to take some of that pain out of his eyes. It wasn't my place to ask about his worries, not when we were practically strangers now, but I recognized his pain. Even if it wasn't the same as mine, it was the spark of a connection I wasn't expecting.

"I'm trying to take in everything," I quietly admitted. "As much as I love seeing Cole like this, it's hard to believe it. I keep waiting for the shoe to drop, to see that this is all an illusion. Because after years of not having my brother in my life, the idea of letting him back in only to be crushed again..." I glanced up at the sky, trying to keep my eyes from tearing up.

"Hey..." Adam said, wrapping his arms around me and pulling me into his chest. His warm, woodsy scent soothed me, like a comforting embrace I never knew I needed. "I know it's hard to let go of the past, and I'm not saying you automatically should. It took me a long time to stop checking on Cole—to make sure he wasn't in some ditch somewhere. But this isn't like before. He's been sober for years, Tor. He's got a sponsor, a system that has his back. And not to mention," he looked back at the house, "he's got everything to lose now. He's not going to fall back off that path. And if he ever does fumble, he has the tools and people to catch him."

And as much as his words helped, they also poked at a frayed nerve, one I'd never dare to give life. *Why weren't we enough? Why wasn't I enough?* I knew Cole had been through a lot, that he had turned to unhealthy coping mechanisms when he felt like his world was crumbling, but he still had a family. He still had people who loved him. Why weren't we enough for him to take these steps earlier? What would our relationship look like if we'd never had years of distance between us?

Adam reached down and tipped my chin up. "Don't do that."

"Do what?"

He smiled, and it sucked the air from my lungs. "Don't waste time wondering why. You'll drive yourself crazy. One thing I learned when I went to Al-Anon is that you can't spend your life resenting the person for not getting sober when they could. Just be grateful they're sober now and that you still have them in your life."

"Al-Anon?"

"Yeah..." Adam sighed as he took a step away from me. "It's a support group for family members and friends of alcoholics. I went a few times when Cole was out in LA with me."

My jaw dropped. "I...I didn't know you did that."

"I didn't tell anyone else," Adam chuckled, hiding his discomfort. "Those first few months he stayed with me after rehab, I was scared shitless, Tor. I wanted to be there for him but had no fucking idea where to start. The meetings helped." I nodded, wishing I had thought of that sooner. Adam smiled at me. "They have a support group here. I could go with you if you want."

I backed out of his hold to face him fully. "But I'm only here for a week."

Adam smiled at me like he knew something I didn't. "Offer stands."

SEVEN

Three days had passed since the dinner at Cole's house, and I still couldn't get Victoria out of my mind. It was so strange being around her, like talking to a stranger and an old friend all in one breath. There were pieces of her I immediately recognized: her shy smile and the way her eyes twinkled when she knew something no one else did.

But there was also a new side to her, one she was holding back from the rest of us. I couldn't blame her, not after everything she'd been through. Even though I was just on the periphery, it was easy to see the toll Cole's drinking took on her. She was taking a risk coming out here, at least in her mind. While I wanted to comfort her, to assure her everything would work out, that wasn't a promise I could make.

Every day, I found excuses to talk to her, to see her bright smile. I kept telling myself I was just holding up my promise to Cole, but with every conversation between us, that was moving further into the back of my mind. It had been a long time since I sought someone out, usually waiting until my friends dragged me out of my self-imposed isolation.

But Victoria was different. Maybe it was our shared history, or maybe it was because she hadn't witnessed my downfall, but I was finding it easier to confide in her than anyone else in my life.

Right now, I stared out of my cabin, watching as she hung out with Alex in the gardens. She looked so alive out there. As I got to know Victoria better, I also learned about the weight she held on her shoulders. Even if she hadn't disclosed what was causing her so much stress, she'd let me see little pieces—the way her smile faltered when people asked her about her life back home, the soft sighs she released when she thought no one was paying attention.

But out there? There was no sign of that stress, and it made her even more breath-taking.

For the first time in a long time, I could see myself wanting someone, wanting to let them into parts of my life. Not as a cover, not as something temporary, but as something real and hopefully lasting.

"Fuck," I hissed, pulling myself away from the window. Out of all people in the world, why did it have to be Victoria? I could never make a move on her. Once upon a time, I might not have given it a second thought. There were a few years, right after I started to gain some fame, when it was almost easy to find someone to share my bed. It became like a game to see how long it would take before I found someone to take home for the night. I wasn't proud of that guy, the one who treated people like they were special only for a brief moment. While I tried to treat my companions with respect, I couldn't lie and say I remembered all of them. There were images of faces and a few memories that would pop up late at night, but no one stuck. No one made me want to stick around for more than an evening.

Besides, Theo had convinced me to keep work and play separate. Fake relationships were common in my world, often helping actors build their brands and hype upcoming projects.

It seemed simple enough—keep a thick line between my personal and professional relationships. But a couple of years ago, I'd agreed to date the wrong person, one with a vindictive streak and an incredible talent for songwriting.

There's nothing like listening to twelve songs outlining all your faults to make you take a deeper look at yourself.

After that, my reputation took a nose-dive, and I wasn't able to go anywhere without my dating habits being questioned. Shame was my constant companion, and I didn't realize how deep it had buried itself inside me until it was too late.

I'd promised myself I wouldn't get involved with anyone until I worked my head out. No one else needed to be involved in my shit. But there was something about Victoria Campbell that called to me, and I fucking hated myself for it.

The timer on my phone buzzed loudly from the table. *Shit.* Rubbing my hand over my face, I pushed away all those damning thoughts. Checking my phone, I grimaced when I realized I should be ready to go. Who the fuck thought it was a good idea to throw Cole an impromptu bachelor party? Oh, that's right, me.

As I hopped into the shower, I ran through the plan for tonight. It was going to be a small crew, just Cole, Alex's friend Javi, Theo, Curt, his son, Gray, and myself. We'd invited Cole's dad, but he was going to dinner with his wife to celebrate their getaway. With limited options in town, at least alcohol-free ones, we'd settled for a poker game at the Lost Tavern. Marta and Curt graciously offered to close up for the night to give us some privacy. Tuesdays were the slow nights anyway, and while Curt would be with us, Marta was more than happy to hang with Alex and help her with any last-minute wedding emergencies.

When I finished getting ready, a knock on my door made me jump. I rushed over to push the screen open. Cole walked inside first, flanked by Tori, who was already chewing on her cuticles—nervous tick. I was glad to see that hadn't changed. We'd always laughed that you could tell report cards were coming by the length of her nails.

She'd changed since the last time I saw her, leaving behind her workout clothes for a casual dress. The soft pink fabric flowed out at her waist but cut off above her knee. The pastel color complimented her skin tone, making it appear even more golden. It was sun-kissed and supple, flawless in a way that made me want to run my tongue along every inch. Fuck, why the hell did she have to be so tempting?

"Hope you don't mind," Cole said, oblivious to my distress. "Figured she could hang with us tonight."

"Of course," I said as I wrapped my arms around him, tapping his back a few times before turning to his little sister. We both stared at each other, as if unsure if a hug was appropriate. Well, fuck that. I reached down, wrapping my arms around her waist and lifting her in the air. Damn, she fit nicely in my arms. Almost too well. It took everything in me not to take a sniff of her hair, to get another hit of that intoxicating scent that surrounded her.

Pulling back, I let out a little laugh, noticing her attire. "Didn't get the casual message?"

She scoffed. "I didn't have anything to wear, so Alex let me raid her closet." She toyed with the hem of the dress, as if not feeling entirely comfortable. The move made the fabric cling to her curves, making my throat tighten. The image of them consumed me—the flare of her hips, the softness of her skin. She was a fucking knockout.

"You look great," I said, lowering my voice so only she could hear. "We're going to have to keep guys away from you all night."

She tucked her lip between her teeth. "And what if I don't want you to?"

"Jesus, Tor," Cole said, scrubbing his hand over his face. "No hooking up while I'm around, 'kay? It's hard enough seeing you all grown up. I don't need to go to jail tonight."

Her eyes flared as she turned to her brother. "Don't even think about it, Cole. If I want to talk to someone, you're going to respect my choices and stay out of it."

He held up his hands, "Fine, fine...." But as soon as she turned her back, he mouthed to me, "Keep an eye on her."

I almost rolled my eyes as well. I had a feeling Tori could handle matters just fine, but I wasn't about to get involved in a Campbell sibling brawl, so I kept my mouth shut.

Not to mention, I'd probably stolen more looks at Victoria than any other guy would tonight.

I glanced across my kitchen, watching as Cole and Tori talked about tonight's plans. She laughed, and it struck a nerve in my chest. I loved the way it lit up her whole face. Even if she wasn't Cole's sister, she was too good for someone like me, a guy with a red mark emblazoned on his chest.

And I needed to remember that.

EIGHT

Adam

A few minutes later, we pulled into the parking lot of the Lost Tavern, finding Javi and Theo waiting by the front entrance. They were both sitting on the bench by the planters, waving as we exited the car. I almost had to laugh—you couldn't find two more different guys. While Javi had a wide smile, Theo was already scowling. It wasn't unusual for him. I only knew of Theo's soft side because I'd worked with him for so long. Most other people thought he was a power-hungry ass, but once you got to know the guy underneath, it was easy to see he was a secret sap at heart.

Javi was the complete opposite. He had a heart of gold, and everyone who met him wanted to be his best friend. But that honor went to Alex, he was almost more a brother than anything else. They had met while she was working at the Isadora, the largest hotel in the area. While Alex quit to start her own venture, Javi stayed and even got promoted. The new manager position suited him, and we were all ecstatic he was finally getting the recognition he deserved.

I walked up to them, knocking Theo on the arm. "Look alive, man. Tonight's supposed to be fun."

"I've heard that before," he grumbled. "Remember when you dragged me to Malibu for that 'can't miss' party, and I ended up with your flavor of the week, trying to keep her from puking all over their patio?" He glared at me. "I don't trust your judgment of fun."

I grimaced, sneaking a peek at Victoria over my shoulder. Luckily, she seemed to be preoccupied, talking with Javi about the hotel. "That was a long time ago." I shook my head. "And besides, we all know why you're really pissed." I glanced down at my watch. "What's it been, two hours since you left Calla's side?"

"One," he muttered. "What's your point?"

"I didn't think it was possible, but you're even more of an ass when you're missing her."

I half-expected a snarky response, but Theo just shrugged. "There's nothing wrong with being attached to my wife. She's the best part of my world. Find the right girl, and you'll know what I mean."

Those words felt so foreign coming from Theo, but they made sense. Ever since he eloped with Calla, Alex's other best friend, the guy had softened. Where relationships used to be a four-letter word to him, he was happily committed, and I was honestly envious. Between him and Cole, I quickly learned that the right partner could change your life.

I glanced again at Victoria and smiled when our eyes met. Before my thoughts could venture back into dangerous territory, I turned toward Cole, clapping him on the shoulder. "Ready, big guy?"

He shook his head, hiding his laugh. "Seriously? Big guy?"

"I don't know," I chuckled. "Man of Honor?"

He shrugged, "Better than big guy. Let's get this night started. I don't want to be away from my girl too long."

I rolled my eyes, needing to get away from all these happily coupled men. Luckily, Gray was joining us tonight, and he was even more opposed to relationships than me. While I had a bad history, at least mine was open to the world. Gray was a closed book, never talking much about the women he spent time with. The only reason I knew he went out was because some of the women at the lodge had gossiped about it over the breakfast buffet.

We pushed open the door, taking in the Lost Tavern. Even after coming here for months, it still put a smile on my face. On the other side, it looked like nothing special, just another store-front at the end of a strip mall. But inside, it was like a step back in time. From talking with Curt and Marta, I knew little had changed in the fifty years since it opened; they'd chosen to preserve the history of the restaurant. The Lost Tavern was divided into two sections, the front part being a large bar that wrapped around the entire room. On the far wall, there was an antique mirror, while the rest of the walls held pictures of patrons over the years. The back room was the dining area, with about fifteen tables of varying sizes—except for today, when they had all been cleared out, making space for the large poker table taking over the center of the room.

From the first time I visited, I loved the Lost Tavern. Marta and Curt were the most welcoming people, and they made sure I wasn't bothered when I stepped through the door.

We took a seat at the bar, and I glanced around, calling out for our last players: "Curt, Gray, you guys here?"

"In the back," Gray's gruff yell echoed out. "Get settled. I'll be out in a couple of minutes." The sound of tools clanking made me wince. "Motherf—Cole, I need you! The damn washing machine is acting up again and the old man's no help."

"Who the hell you calling an old man?"

Cole rolled his eyes and touched his sister's shoulder before heading into the back room. Victoria claimed the stool next to me, taking in the room. Her eyes widened as she searched each picture, probably looking for familiar faces. They weren't hard to find. Alex, Cole, and I had all managed to make it onto the wall a couple of times. Even Theo had been forced by his wife to take a picture or two. Calla, who Victoria hadn't met but I was sure would love, had the most after Gray, pictures over her lifetime of growing up alongside the Anders family. She happily sighed as she turned back toward me. "This place is so cool."

"Yeah, it's one of my favorite places. You have to come back when they're open. They have the best burgers I've ever had."

"Is that an invitation, Rice?" she smirked, leaning back in her seat.

Shit, I wanted to say yes, to offer to show her all my favorite places in town, ending, hopefully, in my bed. But I bit my tongue, shaking my head. "I was thinking more you and Cole. You guys should grab dinner together before you head back home. "

Her brow furrowed. "Oh, yeah. That's...that's a good idea. I'll ask Cole."

As she turned back toward Javi, I ran my hand over my face. This was getting ridiculous. I was supposed to be keeping an eye on her, helping guide Victoria and Cole back into each other's lives. But instead, I wanted to selfishly hoard her to myself, keeping everyone else away for fear of what they might say.

Gray and Cole emerged from the back, wiping their hands on a spare rag. Gray nodded to me, "Hey man, you good? Need a drink? I grabbed some ginger beers if you're interested."

"Sounds good," I said, trying to ignore Victoria's warmth next to me. Shit, I really could have used something to take the edge off, but I wouldn't do that to Cole. Even though he insisted it was okay if we drank around him, none of us felt comfortable, not wanting to put him in a bad position, especially on his night.

As Gray introduced himself to Victoria, I could see the

wheels turning in her head. It was funny—no one seemed to make the connection with Gray's name until they saw him in person. She tilted her head. "Wait, are you *the* Grayson Anders?"

He chuckled, reaching down to grab a glass under the bar. "I don't know about that, but I've played ball for a few years, so you might know me from that."

"Played ball?" she shrieked, pulling out her phone. "Umm, no. I can play ball. You're pretty much a living legend."

He reached up, took her phone, and placed it down on the bar. "Not here." He sighed, placing his hands on his hips. "I appreciate it, I really do, but I'm not that guy here. So please, let's not make it a big deal, okay?"

"Okay..." She sighed, muttering something to herself.

"What was that?" I chuckled, moving closer.

She rolled her eyes. "Between the two of you. Neither can take a compliment."

I chuckled, taking a sip of the drink Gray poured me. "In the right time and place, I think we can both handle it. But there's something different about being home and people seeing you as a person, not your achievements. It means a lot to Gray to be able to let his guard down."

She studied me, as if reading all my internal thoughts. "You seem to know a lot about how Gray feels."

"Yeah, well," I chuckled. "He might not be the only one. That's part of the reason I love this town. At first, sure, a lot of people gawked and tried to take my picture, but now, it's like they've embraced me as one of their own. Marta and Curt are incredibly protective, and once you're in their good graces, you're a resident for life. It's nice to feel like you belong." I nodded up to Gray. "They look out for us, and we look out for him. Works both ways."

She reached out, placing her hand on my arm. "I'm glad you

both found a place like that. You're pretty incredible, Adam, even without the whole movie star thing."

I burst out in a loud laugh, unable to hold it back. Maybe it was because I'd been wallowing in self-pity for so long, but it felt good to have someone say something like that to me. No, it felt good to have Victoria say that to me. My hand found hers on instinct, and I rubbed the back of it with my thumb.

God, her skin was as soft as I thought it would be. My mind went straight to inappropriate places, needing to know if she was as soft everywhere.

But when Cole beckoned all of us into the back room, reality snapped back into place. I pulled my hand back like I'd been burned, walking away without looking back. I couldn't bear to see the disappointment on her face, even though each step felt slow and painful.

I hung in the doorway as everyone else found their seat, cringing when the only empty spot was next to Victoria. I glanced at her, and she offered me a small smile. Could she tell how much I was freaking out? How was it that every time I was in the same room as this girl, all thoughts of loyalty and my best friend flew out the window? *Boundaries.* We needed *boundaries.* That was the best place to start. No more hanging out alone, no more in-depth conversations. She was only here for five more days. I could keep it together until then.

"Is it hard to learn?"

Tori's whisper broke me out of my spiral, pulling my attention back to her. Her eyes flickered over the cards and chips as she chewed on her lower lip. I couldn't help but smirk, loving the different versions of this woman. She was so confident in some regards, but the moment she was out of her comfort zone, she floundered. I tilted my chin toward the table. "You haven't played before?"

She shook her head. "Texas Hold 'Em a couple of times, but

I never got into poker. I might have lied about my experience so Cole would bring me." She turned to face me, her deep brown eyes cutting into my soul. "Teach me?"

The words did something to my cock, and I hated that he was coming to life right now. The idea of teaching Tori all sorts of things, of corrupting her innocent smile, made my thoughts turn almost feral. I cleared my throat, shifting so she wouldn't notice the effect she had on me. "Yeah, of course. You can help me for the first round, and then you can jump in."

She beamed back at me. "Really?"

"Yeah, trouble. Let's see if you live up to your name."

NINE

Victoria

As the night carried on, one thing became painfully clear: I was absolute garbage at poker. Not only did my face give me away every time, but I could barely keep track of the cards, much less the different runs and ways to win. Only three hands in, and my pile of chips was running precariously low, earning sympathetic gazes from my fellow players.

If I had known I was walking into a room full of sharks, I might have taken Alex up on her offer to stay in with her and her friends. But considering I was here to spend time with Cole, it felt like a betrayal to refuse his invitation.

And now, I felt like I was in the middle of an inside joke. You know, the one where a movie star and world-class athlete walk into a bar? I stared across the table and met the eye of Grayson Anders, also known as one of the greatest pitchers to ever grace the MLB. I couldn't believe no one thought to mention he was Curt's son. That would have probably saved me a lot of embarrassment when I first made the connection. I was tempted to snap a picture and send it to Cam. Gray's poster had been on his wall since he even decided to play baseball. He'd probably have a stroke if he knew I was sitting here now.

Adam leaned over, whispering in my ear, "You're doing it again."

I shook my head, breaking my stare down across the table. "Sorry," I said, rubbing my hand down my thighs. "I'm not used to seeing famous people just hanging out."

"I don't count?" Adam smirked. "I'm hurt, Campbell."

"I've known you almost all of my life," I chuckled. "Sorry, I don't think of you like that. You'll always just be Adam to me."

"Don't be sorry. It's one of the things I like most about you."

As Adam turned back to his cards, I had to bite the inside of my cheek to keep from blushing. It was like my insides rioted every time he looked my way, which was starting to become a habit of his. And while Cole's constant check-ins made me feel like I was still a child, Adam was a very different story. I liked having his eyes on me, especially when they studied my body when he thought I wouldn't notice. But I'd have to be dead not to feel the heat of his gaze on my skin.

"You should fold," Adam whispered, leaning in so only I could hear him. "Theo's got a good hand."

I glanced at the man, noting his ever-present frown still in place. "How can you tell?"

"He fidgets with his wedding ring when he's feeling confident."

I smiled at Theo as he sat across from me, watching him twirl the silver band three times. It was a subtle movement, but it was there. I couldn't believe Adam even noticed.

"I fold," I said as it reached my bet, tossing the cards back toward Curt.

We watched as the rest of the hand played on, leaving Gray and Theo battling it out until the end. As Theo flipped his cards, Gray cursed, dropping his own back on the pile. "This is bullshit. I swear, the man has no tells."

Adam turned and winked at me. A lightning bolt struck my

core, almost making me bite my lip. I would never admit this to her, but maybe Hadley was right. This little crush was probably just because I'd been single for so long. Blowing off some steam was definitely in order if a wink could knock me off my axis.

"As my loving wife would say, it's because I am part robot."

"Only part?" Javi chuckled.

Theo smiled. "She claims she had a new heart installed with the wedding ring. Makes me more friendly and open to people."

As the rest of the table teased Theo endlessly, I couldn't help but smile. I loved that he was a softie—a lot like my brother in that way. They were both gone for their partners, and everyone at the table had no problem calling them out on it.

"Don't be jealous, Gray," Theo chuckled. "One day, one of those girls you sneak around with will steal your heart, and you'll be just as fucked as the rest of us."

"Gray's already got one," Curt said, smiling to himself as he shuffled the cards. "The best thing that's ever happened to him."

"You do?" Cole asked. "You've been holding out on us?"

"No," Gray said, leaning back in his chair.

"Are you lying to them about that girl of yours?" Curt shook his head. "You need to tell her how you feel. It's time, kid. She's gonna go to prom with someone else if you don't own up to it soon, and we both know you don't want that."

"Enough," Gray snapped, all our eyes on the pair. He looked at the rest of us, silently daring us to ask about what the man just said. But while the rest of the guys seemed to be stuck on the girl, I was held up by Curt's mention of the prom, as if it was coming up instead of years earlier.

"Sorry, Pops," Gray whispered, placing his hand on his father's arm. "Just don't like to talk about that." He took the cards, placing them back in the assigned box. "Cole, if you don't mind, we're gonna head out. Got a busy day tomorrow."

"Yeah, of course, man." Cole stood to go with them. "I'll lock up for you."

As they moved to the front of the bar, everyone else shifted in their seats, not sure how to process what had just happened. Theo eventually excused himself to use the bathroom, and Javi stood up as well.

"I've got to check in at home," Javi said, checking his phone. "Drew's having a meltdown because our home study is coming up soon. When I left, he was convinced we needed to secure all the furniture and tape off any sharp edges."

"How's everything going with that?" Adam asked, standing to join him. "Any word about when you'll get to start fostering?"

"You're a foster parent?" I asked.

"Not yet," Javi chuckled. "But hopefully in the next month or so. We're finishing up our certification course, and Drew wants us to take a few more workshops to make sure we're prepared, but our case worker says everything looks good. Once she signs off on our home visit, we're one giant step closer."

"That's amazing," I said quietly. Even though we'd just met, I could tell any child would be lucky to be in Javi's care. The man was incredibly warm and welcoming. He made me feel like I belonged without even trying.

Adam and Javi continued their conversation as they walked toward the exit, Cole and Gray talking outside. When Theo returned, he instantly pulled his phone out of his pocket, texting a million a minute. With no one to talk to, I decided to explore the bar, starting with the line of pictures that caught my eye when we arrived.

At least fifty photographs were posted in small, black plastic frames, all with varying signs of aging. The ones in the middle were of Marta and Curt, both holding up a small boy I could only assume was Gray. They stood in front of the restaurant, beaming at the camera. The same photo was taken over the years, Gray standing on his own in the later ones.

Dozens of smiling faces were on the wall, all patrons who had found a place at the Lost Tavern. At the very end were Cole, Alex, and a bunch of other people standing around the front of Fox Creek, holding up a sold sign. While the rest of the crowd were looking at the camera, Cole was staring at Alex, only having eyes for her.

"That was a good day."

Adam's voice broke me out of my trance. I held my hand to my heart as I turned to him, trying to hide my embarrassment. "You're making that a nasty habit."

"Sorry, Tor, thought you heard me coming." He leaned in to look closer at the image. "That was the day Cole told Alex about the lodge. She'd gotten screwed over in a business deal, and he rallied all of us to help her out."

"What do you mean?"

"A bunch of us invested in the property—well, invested in Alex's dream, really. When Cole asked, it was an easy choice. Besides, they would have done the same for us."

A knot formed in the bottom of my throat, the dueling emotions making it hard to feel the world around me. The theme of this week was going to be conflicted sentiments—mostly surrounding my brother and his new home. I wanted nothing more than to be wholly happy for him. He'd clearly found his place in the world and friends who had become more like family. But he had a family, one he'd left behind as soon as he passed the Texas state line. Did he not think we'd support him? That we wouldn't want to be a part of his new world?

Or were we no longer needed?

Adam turned, his smile falling slightly as he looked at me. "What's going through that pretty head of yours?"

"Nothing," I said, shaking away the lingering doubts. "I'm fine."

"Yeah..." He sighed. "Don't believe that for one second. We've already established you have a terrible poker face, trouble." He leaned in, turning so we were standing side by side, facing where Cole and Gray were locked in conversation. "I know it's hard not to feel resentful, but remember what we talked about."

"I'm trying," I admitted. "I'm trying so hard to forget everything and start fresh. But I just..." I sighed, rubbing my hand over my eyes. "I can't help it. I hate that he's missed so much. And as horrible as it sounds, it was easier when I knew he was a mess, when I knew the reason he wasn't coming home was because he was struggling. But seeing him so happy, so put together? It rips at me a little, knowing he's rebuilt his whole life, and I barely have a part of it."

"Tor..." Adam sighed. "He's tried to get in contact with you before—"

"I know," I snapped, trying not to let my defenses rise. "I know I should have reached out sooner, that I should have let him visit. It's my fault we're not as close as we once were."

"I never said that," Adam said, taking my hand and pulling me into a corner. "What I was going to say is that there was a reason you needed time, that you waited until this moment to let Cole back into your life." He reached out, brushing a piece of hair behind my ear. "I know how easy it is to let those dark thoughts win, to believe the worst in the world. But there's a lot to be thankful for, and right now, I'm pretty damn thankful you decided to come up here."

"For Cole?" I said, slightly breathless at his proximity. From here, it was too easy to study the depth of his blue eyes, to memorize the vibrant lines and hues. What would happen if I shifted slightly? Would he kiss me, let me feel the weight of his lips against mine? I wanted nothing more than to find out, even though, logically, I knew it would be a disaster. But it seemed like every time I reminded myself of that fact, a louder voice rang out, daring me to try something new, to jump without worrying and weighing the consequences.

"For a lot of reasons."

Adam's thumb brushed my cheek, and a flush filled my skin. His gaze darted down to my lips, and for a brief moment, I let myself imagine he wanted me too. My mouth fell open, daring him to kiss me before common sense broke us apart, but it was useless. As quick as his touch had been, it left, leaving me feeling hollow and a little foolish.

TEN

"And then I touched her, and…"

My voice trailed off, and I was unsure how to even finish the thought. How could I explain that touching the one person I *shouldn't* be touching felt like the first thing I'd done right in months?

I stared up at the clock on the wall, watching as the seconds ticked by. Over these past few months, I'd spent a lot of time analyzing each of the wood-sculpted elements. The trees and animals were familiar friends, and my eyes tended to drift whenever I was stumbling through my own feelings.

"Adam?" Dr. Kedir asked, breaking me out of my stare-down.

"Sorry," I muttered, squeezing my brow between my forefingers. "Honestly, I don't know what's happening there. I keep telling myself to stay away, but every time Victoria's in the room, I feel this need to check in on her, to be close to her. It's the last thing I should be thinking about right now."

"And why is that?"

I looked up at Dr. Kedir, letting annoyance show in my

expression. This was a game we'd played for months, ever since I stumbled into her office on a lonely Monday, hoping she could fix what was broken inside me. I wanted a quick solution, instant gratification to subjugate the lingering fear. But she just chuckled, telling me therapy was a marathon, not a sprint. She was willing to help me, but I had to want to put in the work and commit to coming to her office at least once a week.

I left without any intention of returning.

But after almost suffering a panic attack at the sight of mail on the counter, I returned, knowing that if I didn't start to work through my traumas, I'd never get back to my old life.

Instead of answering her question, I sighed, crossing my arms as I leaned back on the pale green velvet couch. Dr. Kedir's office felt like it was plucked from the pages of a storybook, all her furniture antique pieces with a certain level of uniqueness. The room was covered in a pale pink wallpaper, birds and tree branches filling almost every inch. It matched the woman in front of me. Probably in her mid-fifties, Dr. Kedir always seemed like she'd be more at home in a garden or farmer's market than in the confines of her office. More than once, she suggested we meet outside to help clear our energies.

Despite our different dispositions, she was smart and insightful. She managed to cut through my bullshit pretty quickly. It only took her fifteen minutes to see I was hiding things, that I was more comfortable with things on the surface, not daring to dive in deeper.

She shifted her long, dark box braids over her shoulder, offering an understanding smile. I rolled my eyes, trying to hide my smirk. She already knew the answer, just waiting for me to voice it out loud. "Because I'm attracted to her, but it's too complicated to act on it."

"Why?"

"I'm really starting to hate that word," I groaned. "Because Cole is my best friend, and if I tried anything with his little sister, he'd kill me."

She hummed, tapping her pen on her ever-present notepad. "You've talked a lot about your relationship with Cole. You seem to be focusing more on how this would affect him, but you haven't said how this might affect you."

"What about me?"

"Are there any other reasons why you're not pursuing..."

"Victoria."

"Victoria," she said, as if reading something in how I said her name. Knowing Dr. Kedir, she probably was. "Worst-case scenario—what would happen if you decided to pursue her?"

"She could get hurt," I answered quickly, pushing the words out before I could take them back. But as soon as I spoke them out loud, I laughed at myself. "This conversation is ridiculous. She's leaving in a few days, so it's not like anything could happen even if I wanted it to. Besides, I barely know Tori anymore. I don't even know why we're talking about her."

"You brought her up, Adam," she chuckled.

"So?"

"So you know why we're talking about her. You're trying to talk yourself out of this attraction, and you're hoping I'll back you up."

"But you won't?"

"Not in the way you hope." She leaned forward, leaning her elbows on her knees. "Only you can decide how you want to proceed. There will always be reasons not to put yourself out there. Fear can—"

"I'm not afraid."

"I beg to differ," she said. "I think you're frightened this girl has already gotten under your skin. And that if you're not careful, you will be the one nursing a broken heart when she goes back home."

"Careful, Doc," I chuckled. "You know I have a fragile ego."

No smile graced her lips. Instead, she kept staring at me, waiting for me to drop the cavalier act. I groaned, dropping my head to the back of the couch. "Fine, yes, I don't want to get hurt either, but that's not what's holding me back. I meant what I said. She's Cole's little sister, and if I hurt her, he'd never forgive me. I wouldn't be able to forgive myself."

"But why is that a foregone conclusion? Why is the only option that you're going to hurt her?"

"You know my reputation, Doc."

"I know the one you hide behind, who the media portrays you to be." She shook her head. "But that is not the man who shows up here every week, the one who constantly worries if he's doing enough to support the people around him."

My face fell, and I dropped my gaze to my hands. Supporting my friends was easy. Ignoring the critics who analyzed my every move was a much more complex task. As much as I tried, their words got to me, especially when it was parts of my past I was already ashamed of.

"I'm not ready to go there yet," I answered quietly, still not looking up to face her. I knew if I saw a flicker of disappointment in her gaze, it would gut me alive.

"Okay, we can table that topic for another day." She pulled her notepad back into her lap, scribbling something on the top page. I didn't even want to know what she was thinking. "Have you received any more letters?"

My blood stilled at her words. Images of white envelopes played out in my mind, haunting my thoughts. I could still feel the crisp paper under my hands, remembering each swirl of the script. "No," I answered honestly. "I haven't received any since I moved up here."

"Good," she answered. "That has to be a tremendous weight off your shoulders."

"Yes and no," I said. "It's taking some time to let my guard down. I feel like I'm constantly looking over my shoulder, just waiting for the moment they show up again."

"That's a natural reaction to your situation, Adam. When someone invades your life like that, it puts you in a vulnerable position." She paused and breathed out through her nose. Over the past months, I'd gotten to know some of Dr. Kedir's tells as well. This one meant she was about to say something I might not like. "Have you given any more thought to going to the authorities?"

"No."

"Adam, there is no shame in your situation. Plenty of other people have dealt with stalkers—"

"I said no," I barked, standing up to face her fully. "I tried that route once, and it just made things worse. If I knew who was targeting me, then maybe the cops could help. But until then, they're useless. It's not like I can serve a restraining order on a ghost. Besides, if I make any noise up here, they'll find me. I'm enjoying my peace, and I'm not ready to give it up just yet."

She hummed, noting another damn thing on that fucking pad of hers. "What?" I snapped. "What do you have to say?"

She put her pen down on the end table, and I instantly stiffened. "If you would like my professional opinion, I think you are hiding, Adam."

"Excuse me?"

"You've stopped acting, stopped going out into the world. Before Victoria, you haven't mentioned anyone outside of your circle of trusted friends." She met my annoyed scowl. "I believe this situation rattled you more than you would like to admit, and you're afraid of what will happen if you go back to your real life."

I sunk back into the chair, hating that she could pinpoint my emotions more than I could. Because in truth, she was right. I *was* afraid of what would happen. For months, an unseen presence made my life a living hell, leaving letters and trinkets wherever I went. Being watched was part of the job, but this person invaded every private part of my life—took pictures inside of my home, stole things from my trailer. The nail in the coffin was when they broke into my apartment in the city, leaving behind one word marked in red paint on my wall.

Mine.

I tried to get help, but even with laws against stalking, they only came into effect if you knew the person trying to ruin your life. When I went to file a complaint, no one seemed to take the risk seriously. There were only half-hearted platitudes and promises they would try, but most of these cases went unsolved. The cops recommended I hire a security detail, which probably would have been a smart idea, but I hated the idea of giving up any more of my freedom.

No, instead, I cut and run up to Saint Stephen's Lake, content to hide away for the rest of my days.

But was I really content? No, not really. I missed acting, missed the way it felt to step onto a set for the first time. And even though it had only been a few months since I walked away from that world, I hated that I was watching all my hard work slip through my fingers because of someone else's actions. While I was enjoying the break from the constant hustle and pressure, this peace was wearing thin. At some point, I wanted to get back to the life I'd earned.

"We're almost out of time," Dr. Kedir said. "And I think this is a good stopping point for the week. Think about what I said, Adam. As for Victoria, only you can decide what the best steps would be."

I nodded, giving her my thanks before walking out of her

office. What Dr. Kedir failed to mention was one of my biggest hurdles was that I had no idea what the best steps would be. It felt like I was constantly making the wrong choices, and any mistakes could harm not only me but also those around me.

And that was a risk I wasn't willing to take.

ELEVEN

Victoria

The night before the wedding, everyone gathered at the Fox Creek Lodge, running through a simple but effective rehearsal. Without an official part to play in the wedding, I mostly stood on the sidelines, watching as my parents fussed over Cole and his bride.

The lawn was already decorated to perfection, with rows of seating lined up for guests to view the ceremony. I couldn't get over how Calla had managed to transform the space. It was gorgeous, filled with the region's natural beauty.

As the rehearsal wrapped up, Cole, Alex, and their guests hung around the area, looking over all the final details for the morning. While they worked, I moved to the gazebo, sitting on the bench that faced the lake. It was easy to feel at peace while staring out over the water. The mountains lined the horizon like sleeping giants protecting this town—like nothing could disturb this quiet slice of heaven.

Perhaps, in another life, I could feel at home here as well. And while I'd gained a newfound appreciation for this town, it was Cole's home, his world. I was only a bystander, watching as he got to live his dreams.

While everyone else filtered inside for dinner, I stayed out in the gazebo, enjoying the silence for a little bit longer. I fiercely missed Emilia. Cam and Hadley gave me updates every single hour, and we called each other multiple times a day. Even with the ache in my chest, though, I had to admit—it was nice to have some time to just breathe. Ever since she was born, my life had been about her, making sure all her wants and needs were tended to. In every moment, she was my first thought, my first priority. And while I didn't regret that, it had taken me coming here to realize that while worrying about her, I'd forgotten something important.

Me.

When was the last time I'd done something I wanted to, for no other reason than that? My life was carved out from Emilia's, and even in no small part, Cam's. His schedule shaped ours during baseball season, which seemed to stretch longer and longer each year. And as hard as it was when he was away, sometimes it was even more difficult during his stretches of home games. We spent a lot of our time in the stands, supporting him as he lived his dreams. Most nights, I loved it, but there were a lot of times when it was draining, especially when they went into extra innings. Dragging a tired little girl through the stands was not exactly my dream, but it was what we'd do for family. Yet over the past week, it felt like a curtain had been lifted over my eyes, and I was realizing how I'd forgotten my dreams to help Cam pursue his. Hell, even living on his parents' property was a choice we made to make his life easier; that way, he could see Emilia during his brief time off.

It had been so long since I'd been asked what I wanted that I didn't even know where to start.

Learn how to play poker. The chuckling voice in my head sounded a lot like Adam's. He'd teased me mercilessly about my terrible card skills and even offered to teach me how to play better. Maybe I should take him up on it.

A shiver crept up my spine as I thought of how he looked at me at the end of the night, how his fingers felt against the apples of my cheeks. God, how was that man able to elicit such a reaction out of me with seemingly innocent touches? It was like he was a flame and I was the moth, desperate to get closer, even if it meant getting burnt.

Without thinking, I grabbed my phone from my pocket, texting Hadley before I could freak myself out even more.

ME

So I'm starting to think you might be right

HADLEY

About what exactly? I'm right a lot of the time.

ME

Ha. Ha.

About me getting back out there.

HADLEY

HOLY LORD JESUS, IT IS A MIRACLE

Is this a purely hypothetical thought, or is there someone you have in mind?

ME

On a scale of 0-10, how stupid would it be to try and hook up with my brother's best friend?

HADLEY

100. But if we're talking about Adam Rice, then you should do it anyway

ME

You are supposed to say don't do it

HADLEY

If that's the reaction you were looking for, you
texted the wrong friend, babe

I rolled my eyes and tucked my phone back into my pocket. She was right. If I wanted a reasonable answer, Hadley was the last person I should have reached out to. The girl was the most empathetic and kind person on the planet, but Lord knew she didn't like to think things through when it came to the male sex.

I was about to join the rest of the party when someone came to my side. As if my thoughts conjured him, Adam sat down on the bench before passing me a bottle of water. "Didn't feel like joining everyone else?"

"I'm still trying to soak everything in," I sighed contentedly. "I only have a few more days, and I want to enjoy every minute of it."

He followed my gaze, smiling softly at the setting sun. "Yeah, it's something."

"You know when you see the same thing all the time, so you lose appreciation for it?" I said. "That's how I feel like my life has been lately. Like I've just been going through the motions." I turned toward him. "But here? It's like the world has forced me to stand still. Time's suddenly stopped, and I have to enjoy the world around me, notice what I took for granted before."

"I know the feeling."

My heart stuttered as he turned to look at me, letting his eyes drift across the corners of my face. Although I told myself that Adam would never see me as anything more than Cole's little sister, I let myself wonder for a moment what it would feel like to have his lips on mine.

"Poker," I blurted out, needing something to pull me out of the dangerous direction my thoughts had veered.

He chuckled. "Looking for a rematch?"

"Not yet." I chewed on my lower lip. "I was hoping you'd teach me. I'd like to learn so if I'm ever invited to another game, I can win all my money back from you fools."

"I'll always save you a seat, Tor."

My cheeks once again flushed pink. *Those traitors.* Adam stood, offering me a hand to help me do the same. But as I got to my feet, he didn't let go, instead staring past me like he was in the middle of an internal debate. Just as I was about to ask him what was on his mind, he said, "How about tonight? After everything else wraps up? We can meet out here." He cleared his throat. "Or in your cabin, if you'd like."

"Cabin would be better," I answered quickly, wondering what it would be like to have Adam in my borrowed space. Even though it wasn't my real home, the idea of having him there made me feel vulnerable and a little exposed. But I'd shied away from enough challenges in my life, and if I wanted to find myself, I had to start facing some of the things that scared me.

Adam stared at me, and for a moment, I thought he'd take it back. Then, all the pressure inside my chest evaporated when he said, "It's a date."

"THAT'S IT?" I squawked, throwing down my hand of cards. "Just all of the cards in order?"

"Yup," Adam chuckled, shuffling the deck between his hands. "That's called a straight."

I rubbed my forehead, trying to organize the rules and game-play in my mind. When Adam laid it out in basic terms, it was easy enough, but once the cards were dealt, my mind started to get frazzled, unable to keep track of what cards I needed and wanted.

"Maybe I should just stick to Go Fish."

I leaned back in the chair, studying him across the patio table. When Adam came over, my cozy little cabin suddenly felt too intimate, as if I couldn't get enough space to breathe. Luckily, on the back porch, Cole had set up a wrought iron bistro table. It was only big enough for two people, but with the fresh air filtering around us, I could break away from the brewing tension, ignore the way my pulse fluttered every time Adam took a step toward me.

"Stop stressing, Tor," Adam chuckled. "It's just me and you here. I'll take it easy on you."

My lip instinctively tucked between my teeth, hating that my mind immediately wondered what other things this man could show me. I wasn't naive when it came to sex, but if the rumors were true, Adam was a lot more experienced than me. I'd never been adventurous in the bedroom, an obnoxious parting gift from years of religious education that taught sex was a sin and only meant for procreation. Even though I'd broken away from the church years ago, the voice still nagged in the back of my mind, making me feel shameful when I wanted something that wasn't strictly vanilla.

Adam's swift hands broke me out of my spiral, forcing me to focus back on the cards in front of me. I rearranged them, trading a few duds for hopefully something better. He watched me, nodding in agreement, as if he could read my thoughts before I even had them. "So, Tor...." he said as he rearranged his own hand. "What made you want to learn how to play poker?"

"Besides a desire to keep my money in my wallet?" I chewed the inside of my cheek. "I guess it's just always something I've wanted to try. You know how my dad has those weekly games with the guys from the base?" Adam nodded. "I used to watch them, fascinated by how easily they could read each other, the way they'd make moves without flinching. It made me want to add it to my list."

"What list?"

My mouth snapped shut, hating that the words had fallen out without thought. "Nothing."

"C'mon, trouble," Adam urged. Even though it was hardly the first time he'd used my childhood nickname, now, it felt different, like there was a deeper meaning to the word. His blue eyes continued to stare into mine. "Talk to me."

"Promise you keep it between us?"

"Do you even have to ask?" He smiled. "I think I've proven I can be trusted. After all, I kept your last secret for over a decade."

"Hey!" I pointed at him across the table. "You and I both know that asshole didn't deserve to breathe the same air as his dog, much less claim ownership. She deserved a family to love and care for her."

He reached out, wrapping his hand around my finger and bringing my hand back down to the table. When I thought he'd immediately pull away, he left his hand on top of mine, his heat pulsing through my skin. "I know, Tor. That wasn't an accusation. I think it was so fucking brave."

"You do?"

"Yeah," Adam said, meeting my eyes again. "You were just a kid, and you were already fighting for the things you believed in. It was badass."

My cheeks colored for what felt like the millionth time that day. "Thank you."

"Don't have to thank me for the truth, Tor. But I do want one thing." He leaned in conspiratorially. "Tell me about this list."

I rolled my eyes, leaning away from him, "It's stupid."

"I doubt anything stupid has ever come out of your mouth."

"You'd be surprised," I chuckled. "It's something I've been thinking about for a while. I have all these things I want to do that I've been putting off for the 'future'. But now..." I stared out at the lake. "I keep asking myself what I'm waiting for. At what point am I going to be ready to do the things that scare me? If I'm waiting for some kind of sign, I'm pretty sure it's never coming, so I might as well push myself to do them now."

Adam nodded, as if he understood what I meant. "What are some of the things?"

"Oh!" I squeaked, sitting up a little more. "I haven't put them on paper or anything; it's more like these random thoughts. I haven't sat down to think them through."

He smiled. "Then don't start now."

"What do you mean?"

He placed his cards face down, leaning his elbows on the table to get closer to me. "Don't think. Right now, if you could do anything you wanted, what would you do?"

Without thinking, my eyes darted down to his lips, wishing I was bold enough to claim them for myself. Would his kiss be tender, soft, as if he thought I would break? Or would he take my mouth with just as much passion as I felt, bruising the delicate skin with his need for a deeper taste?

But I wasn't brave enough for that, especially now that we were carving a friendship for ourselves outside of Cole and their bond. So instead of doing what I really wanted, I shot him a sly wink. "Kick your ass in poker."

Adam leaned back, sighing deeply, as if that wasn't what he wanted to hear. I tried to ignore the flicker of disappointment in his gaze, wondering if he knew where my thoughts had gone. Did he want me to cross that line?

No, there was no way. He wouldn't be interested in me—not

like that, anyway. Sure, maybe his eyes lingered a little too long on my face or body sometimes, but that wasn't the same as wanting someone.

Before I could overthink anymore, Adam's careful smile returned. "You're on, Campbell."

TWELVE

Victoria

"Crap," I hissed as the strap of my heel cut into my flesh, leaving behind a nasty red line. Sitting at one of the picnic tables on the edge of the dance floor, I rubbed my sore skin. Why the hell did I think it was a good idea to dance in new heels? I glanced around; most guests had chucked their shoes off to the side and were dancing wildly in the middle of the field.

Genius.

Tossing my demonic shoes into one of the empty seats, I stood, straightening my outfit. Hadley had helped me pick out the dark violet dress, and I had to admit, the girl had fantastic taste. It was a little sleeker than I was used to, the silk fabric clinging to my body like a second skin. But instead of filling me with insecurities, it made me feel sexy and proud of my curves.

Now that my feet no longer felt like they were being tortured, I walked around the reception area, taking in all the details. I had to give Calla credit; Cole and Alex's wedding was one of the most beautiful events I'd ever seen. Fifteen round tables circled the lawn, the tops covered in different shades of lace, lanterns, and oversized sunflowers. Fairy lights had been hung from different poles, bathing the space in an enchanting glow. As the sun started to set in the distance, the soft lights illuminated the whole place. It felt like we'd been whisked away into the middle of an enchanted forest, the magical creatures celebrating at our sides.

Despite the beautiful atmosphere, the best part of the day was when Cole spotted Alex coming down the aisle. My big brother didn't show a lot of emotions. Most of the time, they were buried deep under layers of snark and sarcasm, so to see him tear up at the sight of Alex in her wedding dress knocked me in the stomach, making my own eyes well with tears. They exchanged simple vows, promises they made to only each other.

As soon as the ceremony was over, the whole place devolved into a giant party, with almost everyone in town showing up for Cole and Alex. My parents made themselves right at home in the middle of the chaos, happily sharing stories from Cole's youth.

I decided to stay more on the outskirts, feeling both at home and like an outsider at the same time. It was no secret that this town drew you in, instantly making you feel at ease. However, there was a camaraderie among its residents, one that wasn't necessarily extended to visitors right away. It was a delicate balance I wasn't quite sure how to navigate, but with every day spent at Saint Stephen's Lake, I felt like I was becoming part of it.

As I stared out at the crowd, someone tapped me on the shoulder. I turned, smiling, when I met Alex's eyes. She looked gorgeous in a tea-length lace dress. The off-white color suited her skin tone, highlighting her summer glow. I pulled her into a hug. "Congratulations! The ceremony was beautiful."

"Thanks," she chuckled, pushing her long, brown curls over her shoulder. "And thank you for being here. You know Cole's not the best at expressing his feelings, but he's beyond grateful you came."

"Me too." I was a little shocked that my words held. Even with my initial apprehensions, I knew I made the right choice. If I'd missed Cole's wedding, it would have been hard to forgive myself. "You guys seem great together."

"Eh, we're okay," Alex chuckled. "Took us a while to let down our guards, but it was so worth it when we did."

I glanced across the field, finding Adam waiting on the other side. My traitorous eyes had followed him all afternoon, all too conscious of his movements. Every time he tried to come near me, I fled, feeling too exposed after my late-night confessions. But now, watching him laugh with Theo and Calla, it made me wonder if it would be the worst thing to let him in. Sure, we were only teetering on the edge of friendship, but it felt like it could be so much more.

Alex followed my line of sight, smirking when she realized where my attention had drifted. "If you tell Cole this, I'll kill you, but..." She chuckled. "I could see it."

"See what?"

She rolled her eyes, patting my arm as she pulled away. "Just know, Adam's like a brother to me, and his heart is so big, it's almost fragile. Hurt him, and you and I are going to have a big fucking problem."

"Did you just threaten me?" I whipped my head toward her.

She smiled as she pinched her fingers together. "Just a little bit. Consider it an even trade. If I hurt Cole, you can try to kick my ass. But just so you know, I'd rather rip out my own heart, so we should be good."

I shook my head, laughing. "I'll keep that in mind."

Alex winked then flitted away into the crowd, dancing into Cole's waiting embrace. They stood in each other's arms in the middle of the dance floor, almost ignorant of the world moving around them.

My phone vibrated in my pocket, and I pulled it out,

frowning when I noticed the time. 7:30; Emilia's bedtime back home. Even with many miles between us, I refused to let my daughter start or end her day without hearing from me. I hit the green button, walking off into the field as my daughter's face filled the screen.

"Hey, baby," I cooed. "How was your day?"

"Good!" she yelled, her wide-bright smile almost making my heart burst. "Hadley took me to see the pigs." Her eyes widened. "Mommy, they're HUGE!"

"They can be," I chuckled. "What other trouble did you get into with Auntie Hadley?"

"Not much," she said, letting a yawn slip out. "Daddy came home after practice, so she left. She said Daddy didn't know how to have fun."

"That sounds about right," I grumbled, failing to hide my annoyance. Cam and Hadley had always been oil and water. I was used to navigating conflict between them, which was fine for me, but if they kept using my daughter as a buffer, we were going to have words. "Are you all ready for bed?"

"Yup!" she proudly exclaimed. "I picked Mr. Pickles as my stuffy."

"That's a great choice. Give him lots of tight hugs."

"Mommy..." Emilia's voice called out, already sounding sleepier. "When are you coming home?"

"Only two more sleeps, baby, then I'm going to give you the biggest hug and never let you go."

"Mommy..." she chuckled. "You have to! I need to help with the pigs! The farmer said I can help him feed them."

"I guess that's okay, then." I leaned in, pretending to kiss the screen. "I love you, little one."

"Love you too, Mommy. Foreva and eva."

"Forever and ever, baby."

Cam and I talked for a few minutes, going over all the

details for my trip back home. While I was getting desperate to see Emilia again, the idea of leaving didn't sit right with me. It felt like I had just scratched the surface, barely getting to spend any time with Cole.

I crossed my arms over my chest, wondering if I'd be able to return anytime soon. First things first, I needed to talk to my brother. While a week would never be enough time to erase years of hurt, it was a good start. Watching him this week made it clear that I wanted my daughter to get to know her uncle. Maybe after we talked, he could come down to Texas and get to know her in our world.

I smiled to myself as I watched a couple of ducks land on the pond, the still water rippling under their weight. Emilia would love it here. The couple of times we'd driven down to the gulf, she was obsessed with the water and all the animals. I could see her running along the shore, picking up pebbles to save for her memory jar.

With my resolve in place, I turned back to the wedding, watching my brother stare down at his new bride. In a few days, I'd sit him down and talk to him, explaining everything so he would understand my choice. He'd probably be upset, but hopefully, he'd understand where I was coming from.

At least, I hoped he would.

THIRTEEN

Adam

I watched as Victoria rejoined the party, brushing her fingers under her eyes and smudging her makeup slightly. Not that it made her any less beautiful. She'd caught my eye the moment she stepped out of her cabin, her wine-colored dress clinging to every curve. The girl was earth-shatteringly beautiful, and it was becoming a real fucking problem for me.

Last night, I couldn't sleep, wondering what her kiss would have tasted like. There was a moment when I thought we might cross that line, right after I asked her what she wanted. Her eyes darted down to my lips, and I had to clench my fists to keep from reaching for her. Being close but not claiming her was eating me up inside.

Calla and Theo talked at my side, but I paid them little mind, answering their questions with non-committal answers. How could I when my sole focus was gliding across the field, looking like a goddess plucked from a myth? Calla followed my line of sight, smirking when she realized who captured my attention. She nudged my side. "Go say hi. She's been quiet all night because she doesn't know most of these people."

I nodded and took a long sip of my ginger beer, wishing I

had something stronger to steel my nerves. That in and of itself was concerning. I wasn't used to feeling on edge around women, having gained a good amount of confidence in my youth. But there was something different about Victoria. I didn't know whether it was because she was related to Cole or because I could see myself getting lost for her.

Dr. Kedir's words flashed through my mind, making me all too aware that I was letting fear dictate my life. I'd had every intention of letting her go, not wanting to get too close, knowing nothing could ever happen between us.

But then yesterday, I saw her sitting in the gazebo, grinning at her phone, and like the Neanderthal I was, I needed to earn some of her smiles for myself. It was all too easy to fall into a comfortable routine with her, the push and pull igniting feelings I thought I'd buried. It scared the shit out of me—opening myself up, letting someone else see my fears, all of it.

But I'd encouraged her to face her fears; the least I could do was battle my own.

When I reached her on the other side of the field, she looked around, as if trying to face anything but me. "Are you avoiding me, Tori?" I asked with a smirk.

"Avoiding is a strong word," she smiled, but her cheeks maintained their red flush. It was adorable, and I loved being the one to make her blush. "More like cowering with embarrassment."

"What do you have to be embarrassed about?"

"That whole thing about my list and wanting to be braver. I know it probably sounded stupid, at least really juvenile—"

"Hey," I said, stepping closer so only she could hear me. "I already told you—nothing you've said sounds stupid. I think it's a great idea."

Her eyes lit up as she looked at me. "Really?"

"Yeah, what do you have to lose? Write some things down, and maybe it'll motivate you to try something new."

She nodded as she exhaled, taking in my words. Her eyes softened as she watched Alex and Cole sway together, ignoring the rest of the guests. I had to give them credit for even staying. Theo had bet me ten bucks they were going to stick out the whole night, and I gave them only ten minutes. Of course, the smug bastard won. Oh well. If it was my wedding, I would have snuck away hours ago.

I followed her gaze, watching as they laughed and swayed together. Even though they held Victoria's attention, my eyes kept drifting to her, my fingers itching to hold her hand in mine.

"Have you ever thought about getting married?" Victoria asked.

"No," I answered honestly. "Not because I'm against it, but I haven't met anyone who made it seem worth it. I think that's the key. Without the right person, it's just a piece of paper."

"How right you are," Victoria sighed.

"What about you, trouble?" I chuckled, bumping her with my arm. "Are any guys back home trying to tie you down?"

"Once," she said, turning to face me with a sad smile. "I almost said yes, too. But then I realized I didn't see it for us. I couldn't imagine a future with him, not beyond what we already were. And that's when I knew: I'd rather stay single than settle for someone who doesn't quite fit."

"And if you find that person?" I swallowed, hating how my throat dried up at her words. "What then?"

"Then we build a life together," she smiled. "At least, that's the dream. First, I have to find the guy, and then we'll go from there."

As the song in the background drifted to a slow country ballad, I couldn't hold back any longer. I held out my hand. "Dance with me."

Her lip instantly found its way between her teeth. "Are you sure? I don't want Cole—"

"We're just dancing, trouble. It's a wedding. You have to dance for at least a couple of songs."

With one last peek over my shoulder, she relented, placing her hand in mine. I tugged her close, letting her smaller frame nestle against my chest. Before we even started to sway, I knew this was a mistake. There was no way I'd ever forget this feeling of rightness—the smell of her perfume, her soft exhale as she laid her head against my chest; hell, even the way her hand fit in mine. Everything about Victoria Campbell felt like she was made for me.

She looked up, and her dark brown eyes consumed me. The rest of the world faded into the background and it was just us in this moment. As the singer crooned in the background, all I could see was her. Forget her being brave; I was the one who needed her strength, something to keep from falling for the woman in my arms.

The thought snapped open in my chest, letting long-buried emotions flood through my veins. For so long, I'd been coasting, letting fear of the world keep me from experiencing anything but the mundane. Dr. Kedir was right; I wasn't living, not really. I'd been hiding, too busy being afraid to take any chances.

But here, in this moment, all I wanted was a chance—a chance to show Victoria I was worth the risk, a chance to help her be brave, a chance to taste her sweet lips and make her breathless with need.

"Tor, I—"

But before I could confess anything more, Cole stepped to our side, smiling at his little sister. "Do you mind if I cut in?"

"Oh, I..." Victoria's voice trailed off as she stared at me, waiting to see if I'd finish my thought.

But my best friend's presence doused all my bravery,

reminding me she wasn't just any woman. I couldn't take any risks—not with her, not when I was still figuring out my own shit. If I brought her down with me, Cole would never forgive me, and with a limited number of people in my corner, I couldn't risk hurting two of the best ones.

I smiled back at Victoria as I backed away. "She's all yours."

STARING out at the rippling waves, I tried to sort out my thoughts and strike Victoria Campbell from my memories. I recited the usual words and pretended she meant nothing more to me than Cole's little sister. Still, the more time I spent with her, the less those sentiments rang true. She was quickly becoming my favorite sight, her smile lighting up even the darkest of moods. I wanted to spend more time with her, get another hit of having her in my arms. It was a high I never knew I needed, but now that I'd experienced it, there was nothing else I wanted.

As if she was as attuned to me as I was to her, I could feel her join me at my side, sighing softly as her gaze followed mine.

"How's Cole?" I asked, not daring to look at her.

"Ecstatic," she chuckled. "It's like my brother's been body-snatched, and they left behind this smiling, happy guy I don't recognize. It's a little jarring."

I hummed in agreement. My words were still on the dance floor when Victoria buried herself under my skin. But instead of the discomfort I usually felt when people got too close, it was a struggle to keep my distance.

She glanced up at me, her smile faltering when she saw my expression. "Adam, are you okay?"

"Of course." I gave her my best smile, the one usually

reserved for the red carpet and interviews. But unlike those people, Victoria didn't buy it, only narrowing her eyes further.

"Don't give me that look, Rice."

"I'm fine, Tor. You don't have to worry about me. You've got enough going on with Cole."

She placed her hand on my arm. "I can worry about you *and* celebrate my brother. You might not know this, but I'm a fantastic multi-tasker."

"Oh, you are?" I mused.

"Yup," she said, enunciating the pop at the end of the word. "You're avoiding talking about yourself." When I shot her a look, she smirked. "Yes, I've noticed. You change the subject as soon as anyone asks how you are doing. But whatever's going on, Adam, I'm here. And even when I'm not, I'm only a phone call away."

I turned to face her fully, needing to get another hit of her smile. Her eyes widened slightly when they met mine. Without thinking, I dragged my fingers up, playing with a tendril of her hair. "I don't want you to worry about me, trouble."

"Too bad," she said, but her breath was lighter than it was moments ago, as if my presence was impacting her as much as hers was me. "You're stuck with me, Rice. You weren't able to get rid of me years ago, and now that we're back in each other's lives, you're going to have to get used to me pushing you around."

"Gladly," I smiled. "I like it when you push me around."

"Yeah?"

"Yeah," I answered. "It's like those videos when a chihuahua tries to beat up a German Shepherd."

She rolled her eyes. "I'm not short."

"You are compared to me."

She shook her head and pointed her finger up at me. "You're changing the subject again." For a moment, Victoria looked up at me, then to her finger in the air. With slow but steady movements, she opened her hand and placed her palm on my chest. The impact of her touch burned, and I wanted so much more. "I won't push, not if you really don't want to talk, but if you do...." She sighed, darting her eyes up to meet mine. "I'm here, Adam. Always."

I reached up, capturing her hand on my chest before she could pull it away. "I'll make you a deal, Tor. I'll let you in, but only if you do one thing for me."

"What's that?"

"Make that list." My thumb brushed the back of her hand, relishing in her soft skin. "Do the things that scare you. Be brave, Tori. And if you need someone to help you face your fears, make me your first call."

"Why would you want to do that?"

"I like how your eyes light up when you're facing something new. It's quickly becoming my new favorite sight."

Her deep, chestnut eyes widened, and for a moment, I thought I'd gone too far, crossed that fragile line we'd been toeing for days.

But she surprised me when all she said was, "Deal."

Adam

"Deal."

One word, and my walls started to lower of their own volition. Staring into the depths of Victoria's eyes, I felt safe, safer than I'd felt in months. Maybe it was because of the strength she was willing to lend me. Maybe it was because of the soft understanding in her eyes. It didn't matter. All that did was that the words came out easier than they had in months, even more smoothly than when I told Dr. Kedir my darkest fears and secrets.

I sighed, settling down onto the rocky terrain. I pulled my legs up, resting my arms around them. Victoria settled next to me moments later, leaning into me, gifting me her strength. "It, uh..." I cleared my throat. "It started right after my first trip up here."

The words flowed out as if I was telling someone else's story. I told her all about my last acting job and what had brought me to Saint Stephen's Lake for the first time. The high I felt when that film was done, sure that it was a new chapter in my life. About my move to New York, wanting to try different projects and push myself to new heights.

But that all came crashing down after only a few weeks. I thought the first envelope was a joke, some obsessed fan who was desperate for my attention. In fact, I didn't take the first five to heart. It wasn't until my email inbox got bombarded with messages that I started to think this was more than a fan.

My entire body shivered as I talked about my last night in the city. While I hid some of the details about the break-in, for once, I didn't shy away from how weak and vulnerable I felt, telling her how, even now, living in an entirely different area code, I still checked the walls daily to make sure there wasn't a message waiting for me.

Victoria stayed quiet the whole time I spoke. We stayed sitting on the shore, my eyes alternating between hers and the ground below us. But Victoria never wavered, never faltered. The only reason I knew she was affected was because she would flinch, her hand moving closer to mine. Just the smallest reaction let me know she was in this with me, that she was hanging on to my every word and hating what I had gone through.

There was a part of me that expected her to turn away in disgust. To judge me because I was unable to face this invisible threat. To tell me I was foolish not to hire guards and live my life behind my gated home, keeping away from the rest of the world.

But when I met her eyes, there was no hint of pity, no other emotion than empathy. It was a welcome relief and made me continue, even when I wanted to stop and erase this painful period of my past.

"And then, I decided to come here," I sighed, thinking about the broken man who had shown up on Cole and Alex's front porch—the one so haunted by invisible demons that he left his home without packing a single item. "I needed to get away from everything that was plaguing me. As much as I miss being in front of the camera, I needed this break. For the first time in a long time, I feel like I can breathe."

Victoria's eyes darted to the side, and her lips twisted like she was holding back. "What?" I asked.

She exhaled slowly, forcing herself to meet my eyes. "I'm glad you have a place like this, somewhere you can come when you need a break. But..." She chewed on her lower lip.

"Tell me, Tor."

"I don't want you to get upset with me."

"Hey," I said, taking my fingers to tilt her chin up to meet my eyes. "If I didn't want your words, I wouldn't have opened up to you. Don't hold back on me, trouble. Tell me what you think."

She sighed. "Breaks are meant to *end*. You've already said this isn't your real life. One day, you're going to want to go back to making movies, to acting. As I think you should. You're way too talented to wallow away up here."

"You think I'm talented?"

"Of course, that's what you focused on," she groaned, turning to place both of her hands on my chest. "I'm just worried about you, Adam. You said you have no idea who's targeting you, that you don't want to go back until you know more. But what if that never happens?" She shook her head. "I hate the idea of this invisible person ruining your life and getting away with it."

"What would you do?" I asked, genuinely curious about her response.

"I don't know," Victoria answered. "I've always wanted to be this brave person, but at some point, it became easier to let my dreams stay just that—dreams. There's no risk if you don't try." Her hands bunched in my shirt. "But you're not me, Adam. You've already done the scary thing. You've worked so hard for so long. What did you tell me?" She smiled. "Be brave."

"Be brave," I repeated. "I...I'm getting there."

"You will," she said, pushing back to put some space

between us. But before she could go too far, I grabbed her wrist, bringing her back to me.

"Not so fast, trouble." I chuckled. "You owe me something."

She rolled her eyes. "I'll work on my list tonight, I promise."

I placed my hand on my chest in mock horror. "I opened up, offered you my darkest secrets, and that's all you're going to give me?" She stared at me. "I think it's time to put your guts to the test, trouble." I leaned in, inhaling another hit of her intoxicating scent. "I think you should cross something off right now."

I expected some resistance, but this girl never ceased to surprise me. Victoria glanced over my shoulder, smiling brightly at the lake. She placed her hand on mine, and I released her wrist. I almost reached for her again, but something about her smirk stopped me. She spun and walked backward toward the water, her hands going to the straps of her dress.

"You know, ever since I got here, I've wanted to swim in the lake."

I chuckled. "We gotta work on your fears, trouble. You could have gone swimming at any time. Hell, there's a great beach only a couple of miles down the road."

"You didn't let me finish," she teased. "But I didn't bring a bathing suit. Thought it would be too cold." She shrugged her shoulder. "So I guess I'm checking two things off my list today. Swimming in the lake..." She stopped long enough to let her dress pool at her feet, kicking it further into the sand. "And skinny dipping."

My mouth dried as I took in her body, my eyes tracing every line of her curves. Her sun-kissed skin glowed in the fading daylight, making her pale underwear stand out even more. She was soft and feminine, my deepest desires brought to life. As she turned, showing off the curves of her firm ass, she called out over her shoulder, "You going to stare all night, or are you going to join me?"

Without another thought, I started pulling off my shoes, fumbling to join her as she walked deeper into the lake.

Victoria Campbell was a siren, luring me into a watery grave. And like the men of legend, I was helpless to her call, needing to follow her, even at my own peril.

The water cut like glass when I stepped into it. Despite the lingering summer heat, the water was frigid, almost enough to make me doubt my choice to follow Victoria. But when she dove under the water, the cold was the least of my worries. I swam faster, almost reaching the same spot when she popped back up with a broad smile on her face. "Took you long enough," she chuckled. "God, I did not think it would be this cold."

I pulled her into my arms, sighing deeply as her legs collided with mine. "I can help you out with that."

For a moment, Cole's face flashed in my mind, sternly telling me to stay the fuck away from his baby sister. *Sorry, buddy, never going to happen.* It'd be easier to cut out my tongue than stay away from her.

She leaned in, nothing but mischief written on her face. All of Victoria had captured me, but this version? The carefree, devious one? She was quickly becoming my favorite.

As her legs wrapped around my waist, my hands found her thighs under the water. I run my thumbs along her bare skin, wanting to move closer to her core. Victoria chuckled, leaning to whisper in my ear, "Thank you for helping me out. I'm feeling warmer already."

"Trust me, trouble," I groaned as I squeezed her thighs a little harder. "This is a lot more self-serving than you realize. I've been dying to get you back in my arms. This is just a convenient excuse."

Her eyes widened as she looked at me. Her voice cracked a little as she asked, "You have?"

I pulled her harder into me, letting her feel what havoc her body was wrecking on my lower half. She gasped as she felt my length against her stomach. "You've been driving me crazy all week, Tor. I'm at the edge of my rope, and every time you wiggle in my arms, it's getting harder and harder to hold back."

"Then stop holding back." Her smile got even wider, and she shifted closer to me, her lips pressing against my ear. "But... you'll have to catch me first."

She giggled as she shoved against my chest, swimming farther out into the lake. I waited, watching her move gracefully. As she got about ten yards away, she turned back to me. "Not even going to try to keep up?"

"This fucking girl," I grumbled, unable to hold back my grin. She squealed as I pushed off, using all my swimming experience to catch up to her. When I got close enough, I reached out, grabbing her ankle. She tried to splash me back, but I had her back in my arms before she knew it. I chuckled at her pout. "Gotcha."

She shivered as I held her, and I noticed the goosebumps breaking out over her body. "Shit," I hissed. "We need to get you back to shore and into some warm clothes."

"Wait..." Victoria said, her fingernails digging into my arms. "One more moment of bravery before we go."

Tentatively, she reached up, brushing my lips lightly with hers. It was barely enough to count as a kiss, but that small gesture lit my skin on fire. She pulled back just as quickly, her eyes widened in shock or horror. "Adam, I'm so sorry—"

Her words died as I crashed my lips to hers, needing more. That one touch turned me into a man possessed, only thinking about Victoria. My hands gripped her supple curves, lifting her so I could devour her properly. Her tongue brushed mine, and all rational thoughts left my mind. I needed this woman, craved her like I did my next breath. Forget acting, forget anything else in this world—all I needed was more forbidden moments like this, with Victoria Campbell in my arms.

But just as she relaxed in my embrace, a loud cheer erupted from the party on the shores. The sound broke the dam in my mind, the one preventing me from thinking rationally. I pulled back, searching Victoria's eyes, taking in her swollen lips. "Tor, I—"

"Don't," she whispered, placing her hand on my mouth. "Don't overthink this. It's one night; that's all I'm asking for. I want one night with you before I go back to my normal life."

One night.

Her words soured on my tongue, dousing any thoughts I had of taking things further. Was that really all she wanted?

Here I was, thinking that this girl was something special, that she was the one I'd been searching for all this time. Perhaps it was a cruel twist of karma, to give me Victoria, knowing she was perfect for me, only for her to throw the words of my past in my face.

Suddenly, my throat dried up as I pictured the faces of the women I'd said similar sentiments to. How many had asked for more, begged for me to give them a chance? No wonder Victoria wasn't looking for anything real with me. I wasn't the guy you settled down with. I was the story you told your friends over drinks at the bar.

"I can't," I said, letting her out of my embrace.

"Oh..." Victoria sighed, pulling her lower lip between her teeth. "I thought—" She shook her head. "Right. That was so stupid of me to say. Of course, you don't want that. We can just pretend it never happened."

That was not even an option. Her taste was ingrained on my tongue, trapped there forever. But how did I explain to a woman I barely knew anymore that with one kiss, my world tilted on its axis? With the first tentative touch of her lips to mine, I knew those were the only ones I needed. The thought terrified me, and it was my mind that had latched onto her so suddenly. She wanted one night with me. I wanted all of hers. How could I explain that without scaring her away?

As I stared into the hurt expression in her eyes, no words came—at least, not enough to make this right.

"I don't regret that kiss, Tor," I said. "Not for a moment. But Cole—"

"Doesn't get a say in my sex life."

"Shit, Tor," I said, placing her down. "You can't just say stuff like that."

"Why?" she snapped, staring at me with a newfound fire in her glare. "Because I'm Cole's little sister? Because I'm just a kid?"

"That's not what I said." She pushed further away from me, not waiting for me to continue. "I—"

"That's fine, Adam," Victoria whispered as she backed away and moved closer to the shore. "Please, *please*; let's forget this ever happened. Blame it on a loss of self-control, and we'll go back to what we were before. You can be Cole's best friend, and I'll be his little sister. Those roles work for us, especially because I'm leaving soon."

"Tor, wait!"

She never paused, calling out one more, "It's fine," before swimming back to shore. It took me longer than I wanted to reach her, hating how much space was suddenly between us. It was more than the distance. Victoria's walls had been down. She'd completely opened herself up to me, and I shut it down without any explanation.

Fuck that. I'd baited her all night, daring her to be brave. Teased her, tempted her, then left her feeling like a fool. But when it came time for me to be honest and face my own fears, I shut down, refusing to speak the words that terrified me.

However, by the time I got to the shore, it was too late. All that remained were the remnants of her footprints along the shoreline, disappearing as she escaped into the grassy field above.

She was gone.

FIFTEEN

Victoria

As I climbed out of the lake, I thought about rejoining the party but decided my soaked attire would lead to a lot of questions I had zero desire to answer. So, while my heart pounded in my chest, replaying every moment with Adam, my feet carried me right back to my cabin. I didn't want to see anyone else, sure that they could read the embarrassment written on all my features. As soon as I pushed the door to my cabin open, I walked over to the bed and sunk into the mattress. Falling back against the plush comforter, my hands covered my face, and I let out a frustrated scream. How the hell could I have been so stupid?

Be brave. Those damn words were why. They mocked me, even now. Bravery didn't suit me, like wearing a pair of shoes that were two sizes too small. I tried and failed. Clearly, this was a sign from the universe that I wasn't meant to break out of my routine. I was better off on my own, living the quiet life I loved.

At least, I thought I loved it.

While I couldn't deny I was dying to get back to Emilia, there was another part of my heart that hated to leave Saint Stephen's Lake. While I'd only been here a week, I'd come alive in this small town, making connections and experiencing things I'd never thought possible.

Like kissing Adam Rice.

"Why would you do that?" I asked myself as I sat up to stare into the mirror. *"Be brave,"* I repeated in a mocking tone. "Bravery is so freaking overrated. Be timid and proceed with caution. That should be my new mantra."

But even as I said the words, they felt flat, like trying to force my heart back into a small cage. I couldn't deny the thrill that had overtaken me when Adam kissed me back, his fingers digging into my skin. His touch burned, leaving behind embers of our tangling desires. How was it that I felt more in his one kiss than I had for years with Cam?

The thought felt traitorous, like a betrayal of what I shared with my high school sweetheart. Even though ending it was for the best, I still held some loyalty to the man. He was the one who gave me Emilia, the one who stayed with me even after I turned down his proposal. Heck, he was still helping me, encouraging me to make amends with Cole and insisting he had everything covered at home.

But that wasn't the same as loving him.

Not that I was in love with Adam. That would be insane. However, his touch felt right, like the kind of passion people wait lifetimes to experience. And maybe it was wrong to shut him down and not let him explain, but standing there in my underwear, aching to touch him when he put a stop to the kiss, felt like the worst kind of torture, as if I'd offered him a piece of my heart and he'd felt nothing but pity for me.

Knowing the tell-tale signs of a spiral, I grabbed my phone, calling my best friend before I could shadow every moment in a darker lens. She answered on the second ring, her sleepy voice calling out, "Tor, you okay? Aren't you supposed to be at the wedding?"

"I was, but I needed to get some air," I answered with a wobbly voice. "I did something monumentally stupid, and I just...I need you to talk some sense into me."

Shuffling sounds echoed on the other side of the line, sure Hadley was sitting up in bed so we could talk. I wished she was here with me, laying at my side like we did a million times that first year of college. She was the one who knew all my fears about Cam, the one who held my hand when I took a pregnancy test, who didn't let go during the longest three minutes of my life. She let me cry on her shoulder when those two lines appeared and told me she'd support whatever choice I made.

"Tell me everything."

And I did. I explained all about reconnecting with Adam and how he was the one who had kept me steady in my moments of doubt, that what started as my brother's friend looking out for me had transitioned into a tentative friendship of our own, at least until I crossed that line. But despite telling her everything else, I couldn't bring myself to reveal any of Adam's secrets. I was still processing that he'd been dealing with a stalker for months and that no one else really knew what was going on. While I understood his reasons, it was hard not to fear for his safety. But it wasn't my place to tell. Every word would be kept between us unless Adam's safety was at risk. Even though I was upset with him right now, that was the one thing I'd never let happen. Not when he meant so much to me—*I mean, Cole.*

"And then he told me to be brave, so I just...I went for it, Hads."

She let out a little gasp. "Please tell me you fucked his brains out."

"No!" I shook my head. "We just kissed, and..." I sighed at the memory. "It was amazing. Like nothing I've ever felt before.

I could have drowned, and I would have been okay with it as long as he kept kissing me."

Hadley giggled. "Girl, you have it so bad for him! I can't believe I get to say I know someone who hooked up with Adam Rice. My best friend, ladies and gentlemen, a hero for all womankind."

"Save your accolades for after I finish," I groaned. "I would have kept going, but Adam stopped it. Just when I was really starting to throw all my caution to the wind, he just...stopped."

"Did he say why?"

I chewed on the corner of my lip. "I didn't exactly give him the chance."

"Victoria!"

"I know, I know," I squealed, hiding behind my hands. "But you weren't there, Hads. I felt so vulnerable, standing there in front of him, practically naked. So when he started to shut things down, I freaked out and needed to get as much space between us as possible. If I didn't..." I looked up at the ceiling. "I don't know what I would have done."

She sighed, putting on her therapist hat. "I get that, babe. I really do, especially because he's not a passing moment. Adam's a permanent fixture in Cole's life, so that means he'll be in yours too, especially if you've decided to forgive Cole." She paused, mulling over her next words. "But I also think you spoke too soon."

"What do you mean?"

"I love you, Tor, but you tend to cut people off before they can hurt you. I know why, and I'm not saying it isn't justified, but I've also seen you shrink yourself over the past few years. You're so focused on Emilia and making sure she has everything she needs. And while that makes you a great mom, can you honestly say it's enough?"

"I...I don't know."

Hadley sighed. "If you never open up to anyone, sure, you'll never risk rejection, but you'll also never find someone to share your life with. And that breaks my heart for you, Tori. If anyone in this world deserves that great kind of love, it's you. Your heart's too big to be kept locked away forever."

Her words hit their mark. My eyes started to water as I weighed each one. For the first time in a long time, I wondered if the way I'd been functioning wasn't enough. "Maybe," I laughed through the tears.

"I'll take a maybe," Hadley laughed. "And I'm not saying it has to be today. It doesn't have to be Adam. But maybe get a little space between the two of you and see how you want to move forward. You don't have to have all the answers tonight."

I chuckled, wiping my tears away with my thumb. "I guess you're right. God, I hate that you're right."

"That's what best friends are for, babe. Reminding you that you deserve everything, even if you refuse to believe it yourself."

THE SMASHING *of glass bottles filled my ears, but I didn't move, keeping my body flush against the door. It was probably the worst idea; who knew what was living on the surfaces of this seedy motel room? The whole place smelled like weed and rot, and most of it was coming from the man glaring at me, trying to force his way outside. My eyes threatened to close, wishing I was anywhere else, that I didn't have to watch this scene unfold in front of me. If you told me years ago that this screaming, incoherent man was my brother, I'd punch you.*

But the new reality was a bitter pill to swallow. Cole, who had left to join the armed forces, never returned. The brother who told me jokes and held my hand during thunderstorms was long gone. The man who returned was an angry, bitter shell who only showed anger as an emotion. And right now, all that anger was directed at his best friend, the same one who had answered my call on the first ring, coming to my aid without a second thought.

"Fuck you," Cole hissed, stumbling on unsteady legs. "Get the fuck out of here."

"Not going to happen," Adam hissed, shoving Cole back. With his drunken steps, he stumbled onto the bed, still hissing harsh words when his back hit the mattress. I cried out in sympathy pain, knowing that his skin was still a mottled mess from an accident overseas. What exactly happened, Cole never divulged, keeping that secret locked away in a vault inside his mind.

As Cole's head fell back, he let out a sardonic chuckle. "Fucking Saint Rice, coming to save the day. This act is getting really fucking old." He lifted his head, a shit-eating grin filling his face. But as he turned to me, it instantly fell. "Let me guess—that little bitch ratted me out?"

"Don't talk about her like that." Adam's voice was stern, harsher than I'd ever heard it. "She's the reason you're not in prison right now."

"Bullshit," Cole said. "I had it handled."

"Not even a little," I muttered, unable to hold the words back. It was true. If I'd arrived at the bar minutes later, the cops would have taken Cole away. And while that might have been better than this, some sick part of me refused to let it happen. He was my brother, my responsibility, and no matter how much damage he caused, I was there to help pick up the pieces. But it didn't mean I had to like it.

"She speaks!" Cole chuckled, sitting up to glare at me. "When you gonna get it through your head, kid? I don't need you. I don't fucking want you around. You're nothing more than a nuisance."

Adam shoved his shoulder. "Cole, stop."

"No," he said as he leaped to his feet, moving quickly to stand in front of me, his whiskey-laced breath turning my stomach. "Do you think I asked to take care of you? To have to spend my days with some brat following me around, begging for attention?" His face contorted into a sneer. "I never fucking asked for you, baby sister, and I sure as shit don't want you around now. You're pathetic, weak, begging for any scrap of attention. You disgust me."

Adam's arm came around his waist, pulling him away from me, but he couldn't stop Cole's words from piercing through my skin. "Get the fuck out of my life."

My body woke with a jolt, unable to escape that horrible look in Cole's eyes, the one that spoke of years of unearthed anger and resentment, all because I wanted to be close to him. That was the night I started to close the door on our relationship, refusing to answer his cries for help, cutting off the money for his bar tabs and benders. I'd even let the cops take him away a couple of times, forcing him to sleep it off in a cell. He said he wanted me gone, so I faded away. I was done fighting for a brother who didn't want anything to do with me. Even now, I felt like I was waiting for the moment he'd push me away, spewing those hateful words again.

A familiar ring echoed in my cabin, and I instantly reached out to grab my phone. My heart rate spiked when I saw the time and Cam's name on the screen. My hands trembled when I answered the call, terrified of what he was going to say.

"Before you even ask, Emilia is okay."

"Thank goodness," I cried out. "Are you okay? Why are you calling so late?"

"Yeah, we're all fine. But I thought you'd want to know that we're at the ER. Emilia was throwing up and spiked a high fever, so we're here now. They're going to give her some fluids and let her rest, then send us home." He paused, and I could hear a shaky rattle in his voice. "The doctors said she's going to be fine, and I knew you'd want to know."

Even with his attempt at a calming tone, guilt ripped through me. My baby was sick, likely looking for me, and here I was, pretending my life was the same as any other 23-year-old with no worries in the world.

Especially last night with Adam.

I refused to even consider that option. It had been hard enough to fall asleep last night. It was so tempting to go next door to his cabin, demanding another taste of his lips. Shame and my tattered pride were all that kept me in my bed, unwilling to face rejection twice in one day.

But now, all my focus was on my little girl, the person who held my heart outside my chest. The image of her in a hospital bed was all I could think about, hating that I was so far away when she needed me.

I climbed out of bed and grabbed my suitcase, putting the phone on speaker as I threw my clothes inside. "Okay, Cam, I'm coming home. I'll be there as soon as I can."

"Vic, you don't have to. We have everything covered, I promise."

"Don't," I snapped, taking out my frustrations on him. I stood up straighter, running my fingers across my exhausted eyes. "I'm sorry. I know you're doing everything you can, but I want to be there. I need to see her."

Cam let out a long sigh. "Text me when you have your flight times, and I'll come to pick you up from the airport."

"Thanks, Cam. Tell Em I love her and I'll be there to hug her soon."

"Will do."

SIXTEEN

Adam

A pounding on the door echoed the pounding in my head. With a groan, I reached over, grabbing the alarm clock. Okay, way too fucking early. But the urgent knocks never stopped, continuing to ruin my already limited sleep.

Last night, I stood outside Victoria's cabin for almost an hour, debating whether I should go inside. I practiced the words in my mind, trying to convey the emotions coursing through my fucked up brain. But no matter how I wanted to phrase it, they sounded like a pathetic excuse, nothing more than lip service. She deserved more than that. More than me.

It took hearing her laughter to know I would be an unwelcome visitor. Plus, some space was probably wise. I'd almost fucked my best friend's little sister in the middle of the lake, and that would have been...

I almost said mistake, but I couldn't bring myself to describe what happened last night as that. Was it smart? Not at all. But I'd never claimed to make wise decisions. And yes, developing feelings for the one woman I shouldn't be thinking about was inadvisable, but I couldn't bring myself to regret it. In fact, as my eyes opened, I was more determined to clear the air with Victoria, to get another taste of her—maybe more, if she was interested.

The knocking continued, so I threw the comforter off and stumbled to the front door. I'd barely turned the handle when Cole barged inside, his whole body radiating with anger.

"Did something happen last night with Tori?"

Oh, fuck. I racked my brain for something, anything to say to Cole. *Well, yeah, I skinny-dipped with your baby sister last night, and she thought I rejected her, so she ran off.* But those words, even the rated PG version, refused to leave my mouth, especially with so much still unsaid between Victoria and myself.

"I don't know," I forced out the words. "What's going on?"

"She left." Cole dropped down into one of the chairs in the kitchenette. "She called my dad in the middle of the night to take her to the airport, and no one will tell me why. She left me a note saying that she'll call me when she gets home. A goddamn note, Adam." I placed my hand on his shoulder, and he shook it off. He paced the kitchen, more mumbling to himself than to me. "There was a moment last night when I thought, shit, I can really fix this. We can start over, and I can make amends for all the pain I've caused her. But now..." He slammed the note down on the table. "I don't have the first fucking clue how to handle this."

"What does Alex think?"

Cole chuckled. "She wants me to follow her, to go to Texas and confront her."

My spine straightened at the idea, hating how much I wanted to do the same. How could she leave like that? As much as I hated this for Cole, he wasn't the only one who felt betrayed. I thought we were getting closer. I'd opened up to Victoria more than I had anyone in a long time. She'd seen behind my walls then went and pulled this shit? Disappearing again after we—*I meant Cole*—had just gotten her back?

"She's right." Cole's head snapped up at my words. "You should go to Texas. Shit, I'll even come with you."

"Why would you do that?"

I stopped, unsure how to respond. All my reasons were entirely selfish. I wanted nothing more than to see her face once again and finally put into words how I felt last night when she kissed me.

But instead, I went with a modified version of the truth. "Because we've become friends since she came to visit, and I think she owes you a reason as well. Plus, it'll give me a chance to see Texas again. It's been years since I went back home."

Not that I thought of Texas as home anymore. I don't know if I ever really did. It was where I'd grown up, but I'd dreamed of leaving almost the entire time. Since we'd taken a trip to the capital in the fourth grade, I'd plotted my escape, wanting to see so much more than my rural town could ever offer. Maybe it'd be different if my family still lived there, but they'd moved away after I scored my first big role, settling in their dream retirement home closer to the Gulf.

In the decade since I moved away, I'd never imagined returning to Dunville. It was a place on a map, nothing more. But knowing that Victoria was there made me anxious to head down there as soon as possible.

Cole shook his head, running his hand over his face. "This is fucking crazy, you know that, right? Am I really about to fly out the day after my wedding without my wife?"

"It was Alex's idea. I think that's a good sign she'll support this. But if you're not sure, talk to her and let me know what she thinks." I shrugged. "It's not like I have anything better to do."

But as Cole left my cabin to talk to Alex, I'd already pulled out my phone, searching for flights. I was going to Texas, with or without him.

TWO DAYS LATER, Cole and I were on a plane bound for our hometown. Traveling took longer than I expected, but it was worth it when we walked out into the hot Texas heat. Dunville was just as small as Saint Stephen's Lake, but that was one of the few similarities.

Where the lake was kept clean and pristine, like a snapshot of a time gone by, Dunville felt more rundown. We'd known the economy had hit a lot of the local businesses hard, but it was difficult seeing so many stores boarded up. The only booming business was Seda's Sporting Goods, owned by one of the most prominent families in the county. They owned a large ranch, almost 300,000 acres, on the outskirts of town.

Driving along Main Street, the only place that had stayed the same was the high school, a glowing beacon in the middle of town. The bright red banner for the Dunville Raptors covered the fence of the football field, drawing your eye into the astro-turf and towering lights. It was like I could still hear the crowds screaming my name. The years in this town had shaped me, had made me the man I was today, but I was grateful I dared to leave when I did.

I glanced down at my phone as we pulled up to a large gate, the only sign of life on an otherwise empty road. This had to be the right place; at least, it was the address Cole's parents had reluctantly given us.

"This can't be right," Cole muttered, leaning over to look at my phone. "Why the hell would she be living on the Seda Ranch?"

"No idea."

After confirming the address was correct, Cole shook his head and hit the blinker, turning onto the dirt road. The address led us to the main house, where a stern-faced man was waiting for us, leaning on the edge of the porch.

"Can I help you?" he called out as Cole parked the truck. Despite his calm exterior, I could tell this was not a guy to be fucked with. His eyes assessed us, as if trying to decide if we were a threat.

"Sorry to bother you, sir," I said, stepping around Cole. Not that I didn't trust my friend, but he wasn't known for making the best impression on people. "We might have the wrong address, but we're looking for Victoria Campbell?"

That broke the harshness in his eyes. In fact, he almost smiled when I mentioned her name. "Y'all friends with Tori?"

"I am," I said, nodding toward Cole. "This is her brother."

"No kidding," he mumbled, holding out his hand. "Marcus Seda. This is my land, and you probably know my son, Cameron."

No, but I wasn't going to contradict anything this man said— not if he was the one keeping me from seeing Tori again.

He shook both of our hands then nodded over his shoulder. "C'mon back. I'll take you over to her cabin." He glanced at Cole, studying him yet again, probably because he was silent, a dark look crossing over his eyes. I elbowed him, mouthing, 'Get it together.' Cole was pissed, but the glowering effect wasn't going to earn us any favors.

Marcus led us behind the main house, taking a small path to three small cabins in a row. Even without telling us, I knew which one was Tori's. Bold, colorful flowers lined the walkway. My guess—she'd planted them herself. She'd always complained when she was younger, wanting a little garden in the backyard, but her parents never allowed it, not wanting to attract animals into the yard.

As Cole stepped toward the door, Marcus hung back with me. Before I could take another step, he held his arm out to my chest. "This better be a friendly visit."

"It will be," I promised.

"That's good. No matter what happened with her and Cam, that girl will always be family. I don't care who you are; no one steps onto my property and hurts my family."

"Mr. Seda, sir, I promise we're here with good intentions. Cole's protective, just like you, and we want to make sure Victoria is okay. You have nothing to worry about."

"Better not," he grumbled.

Yet, as I continued walking down the path, Marcus stayed on my heels, not letting us take a breath out of his sight. Cole looked back once before knocking on the screen door. A lead weight settled in my chest as we heard Victoria call out, "One minute" from inside.

But hers wasn't the first face to come to greet us.

Instead, a little girl pushed open the screen door, scrunching her nose when she looked us over with more judgment than any child should be able to muster. "Who are you?"

"Em, what have we talked about?" Marcus chuckled. "Use your manners."

I swear, she gave him a look that would rival most teenagers. "Sorry, Pop-Pop." She smiled sweetly up at us. "How can I help you?"

Pop-pop? As in her grandfather? Wheels that had no right turning were starting to unwind in front of me. *No. It wasn't possible.* I'd spent *days* with Victoria, and she never mentioned a kid. There had to be another explanation. As I tried to connect the dots between my memories and the sight in front of me, Cole kelt down to her level.

He smiled softly at her. "Hello, my name's Cole. I'm looking for my sister, Victoria. Have you seen her?"

She stared at him like he had three heads. As she started to speak, the woman who had haunted my dreams the last few nights stepped up behind her, and the similarities almost knocked me back. The same eyes, the same hair color. Shit, they had the same fucking smile. When she saw us, her face went white, and her eyes widened in fear. "Wh—what are you doing here?"

She posed the question to Cole, but Victoria's eyes kept darting toward me, making it clear he wasn't the only unwanted one. Her hand clenched on the little girl's shoulder, pulling her closer to her legs.

Victoria's mini-me stared up at her, the same quizzical look on her face. "Mommy, who is that?"

SEVENTEEN

Mommy.

The little girl's words crashed into my mind, breaking apart every memory I had with Victoria. I prided myself on being able to read people, but I had no idea she was hiding something like this.

"Emilia, give us a minute," Victoria said, ushering the little girl behind her.

Emilia. It was a strong name. Her great-grandmother's name, if my memory served correctly. And shit, I could see so much of her mother in Emilia. *Tori is a mother.* I stepped back, running my hand over my mouth. Holy fuck. Victoria, *my Victoria*, was a mother to a beautiful, apparently strong-willed little girl who inherited her eyes and her bright smile.

I started to say something when Cole pushed past me, storming toward the car. Victoria stepped forward, but I held my hand up to stop her. "Give us a minute." When she opened her mouth to protest, I stopped her again. "Please, Tori. Just give me a minute to talk to him."

She nodded, turning to brush a couple of tears away from her eyes. As much as I wanted to stay to comfort her, I was also battling with my anger. How could she not tell me? I told her everything and showed her the darkest parts of my life, and yet, she'd hidden a significant part of hers.

As I took off after Cole, Marcus gave me a stern look, probably picturing a thousand ways to cause us bodily harm after our exchange with Victoria.

And his granddaughter.

Fuck.

Questions pelted my mind, trying to figure out how I missed this—how we all had missed it, if Cole's reaction was any indication. Besides, if he had any idea of Emilia's existence, he would have been here every chance he got. There was no way he'd choose not to be involved in his niece's life, not after the way he doted on Tori growing up.

My feet stalled, and understanding crashed through me. Of course, Tori wasn't open about her daughter. It had taken months to convince her to visit, and even then, I saw how guarded she was when she first came to town. When it came to Cole, her defenses were a mile high, and no doubt, she wanted to see him for herself before letting her child get involved.

But that didn't explain why she hadn't told me.

Was it because of Emilia's father? Marcus' words from earlier came back to me, assuming we knew his son. That must be the guy—the one Cole would probably kill if he got his hands on him. Were they together long? Were they serious? When did things end between them?

Did things end between them?

My chest ached at that thought. Maybe that was why Tori pulled away so suddenly, not wanting anything more with me. She wanted one night only. Was that because there was someone else here waiting for her? *No.* I shook my head. That couldn't be true. The girl had a golden heart and would never hurt anyone like that. If she crossed that line with me, it was because she was available, even if I was the last person she should have been with.

When I caught up with Cole, he was already seated in the truck, slamming his hand against the steering wheel. "Fuck, fuck, FUCK!" he exclaimed as I climbed into the passenger seat. He continued to grip the leather in his hand, squeezing until his knuckles turned white. I just sat there in silence, knowing there were no words that could help him through this fog.

After a long time sitting there, Cole finally exhaled. "How could she do this?" He pushed out a short breath. "How could she hide something like this from me?"

"I don't know," I answered honestly. "But I gotta assume there's a reason."

"Yeah, she fucking hates me."

It was as if the temperature dropped twenty degrees as soon as those words left Cole's mouth. I shook my head. "She doesn't hate you. We both know that. She wouldn't have come to your wedding if she did."

He stared out ahead, nodding slightly. Looking over, I could see a couple of tears gathering in his eyes, but he wiped them away before they could fall. "I hate this. I already hate I missed so much of Tori growing up, but now..." He hissed out a curse. "I don't even know her anymore."

"Then get to know her," I said, shifting to face him. "Look, I can't imagine what you're feeling right now, but we flew down here to talk to Victoria and figure out why she kept pulling away. I think we found our answer." I shook my head. "This is your chance, Cole. Prove you're not going to bail on her again. Get in there and show your sister you'll be there for her...and for your niece."

He chuckled dryly. "Shit, I have a niece."

"Yeah, looks like you do."

"I should have known," Cole chuckled. "My first thought

when she came to the door was that she looked just like Tori when she was little."

"She's got her eyes."

Cole shook his head. "Look, if you want to head back to the hotel, I can get a cab or a ride later—"

"Nah, I'll stick around. I'm invested now. I want to see how this plays out."

AN HOUR LATER, Cole and Victoria were sitting at the dining room table, continuing to talk in hushed voices. When we first went back to the cabin, Marcus was reluctant to let us inside, but Victoria insisted she was okay. Even he seemed to realize they needed this conversation, because he offered to take Emilia up to the main house with him. But for some reason, I told him I'd take her and found myself hanging out with the most stubborn four-year-old on the planet.

After we went inside, I took in the place Victoria called home. It was tiny, barely bigger than the cabin back at the lake. The living room was filled with dated furniture and a couch that looked like it had more lumps than cushions. The walls were painted a yellowing gray and covered with nonsensical drawings. Glitter and purple seemed to reign supreme in this house. Almost everywhere you looked, there was something of Emilia's. It was clear Victoria had taken a lot of time to make her daughter feel at home.

But as I looked around, I saw little traces of Victoria here. Outside of the garden out front, it was clear she'd never personalized this space, only caring that Emilia had everything she needed.

Victoria shuffled on her feet, crossing her arms over her chest. "So this is it," she said, flush filling her cheeks. "It's not exactly my dream house, but you know, you take what you can get sometimes."

Cole just nodded, walking through her home. Victoria watched each step, collapsing into herself with every passing breath. He turned back to her, and his eyes were red, lined with emotions. It was disconcerting to see Cole upset. While we all knew he felt a lot, he had a hard time showing his softer side to the world. He cleared his throat. "Can we talk?"

Victoria nodded, glancing down at Emilia, who was playing on the floor. I stepped forward. "I got her. You guys go ahead. Clear the air."

She mouthed 'thank you' as she leaned down to kiss her daughter's hair then followed Cole into the other room. I watched as they sat across from each other, looking like mirrors images. Eventually, they started to relax, speaking in hushed tones. I tried to give them privacy, but I couldn't help looking over to check that they were okay. When a sob broke free from Victoria, it took everything to keep me in my spot, wanting nothing more than to go to her. But this conversation needed to happen between them, and I wasn't about to intrude, even though it was killing me not to comfort Victoria.

"Why do you keep looking at my mom like that?"

I turned back to Emilia, giving her my biggest smile. She just stared blankly back at me, as if she could read all my thoughts. Even though we'd just met, I was already learning a lot about Emilia Campbell-Seda. Yes, that was how she introduced herself. The little thing had just turned four *and a half* and had enough sass to keep everyone in her life on her toes. She loved animals, the color purple, and all things sparkly. She'd tried to convince me to get out the glitter and help her make a picture, but before I could grab the container, Victoria called out, "Don't even think about it."

I could have sworn I heard a quiet curse escape Emilia's lips, but that might have been my imagination. *Maybe*. On top of being way too wise for her age, Emilia was funny, making little comments every time I got distracted from our game. We were in the middle of an all-out tea party filled with authentic snacks and everything. She was a great host but had strict rules for how her guests were supposed to behave. Apparently, sneaking a cookie before tea was served was a major no-no.

Movement caught my eye at the front door, and a broad man walked inside, wearing what looked like workout gear. He tossed his hat on the rack with a casual ease, as if he'd done it a million times before. When Emilia turned her head and her face burst into a broad smile, I knew who he was before she even called out, "Daddy!"

This must be Cameron.

He scooped up Emilia in a tight hug, even when her nose wriggled in disgust. She pushed on his shoulder. "Daddy, you stink."

"Sorry, darling. It was a long practice." As he placed her back down on the floor, his eyes widened when they met mine. "What the..." He closed his eyes, shaking his head a few times, as if he couldn't believe the sight in front of him. "Hey, Vic. Do you know Adam Rice is standing in your living room?"

She chuckled as she stood from the dining room table, softly placing her hand on Cole's shoulder as she did. She walked over toward him, twinning her fingers together. "Umm, yeah. Remember how I mentioned he's friends with Cole? Well," she glanced back over her shoulder at her brother, "they came for a visit."

"Really?" Cam said. My chest tightened at the look they shared, one that spoke of years together and silent understanding. She nodded, and that erased the concern from his brow. "I finally get to meet the infamous Cole, huh?" He walked over to my friend and held out his hand. "Cameron Seda, Emilia's dad."

To his credit, Cole handled it a lot better than I thought he would. I was internally bracing for a punch to ring out, for Cole to take out his frustrations on Cameron's jaw. But luckily, he kept calm, shaking the man's hand without a hint of anger. "Good to meet you. You have a beautiful little girl."

"Aww, thanks," Cameron chuckled. "But that's all Vic. Prayed every night Emilia would get all of her genes."

Victoria chuckled with nervous energy, her eyes darting between me and the other two men. She tucked her lip in between her teeth when she met my eyes.

"So, how long are y'all in town?"

"Only until tomorrow," Cole answered. "Gotta get back to my wife and our business."

Victoria turned to Cameron. "They were concerned because I took off without saying goodbye." Her amber eyes met mine. "I told Cole, but it was because Emilia was sick. She needed me."

I nodded, trying not to overthink the relief flooding over me. It wasn't because of me. I hadn't fucked up Cole's chance to get to know her again. Cameron just smiled at her side, oblivious to all the tension filling the room. "I was just coming to get the girls for dinner. Ma made some new casserole she wants you to try. But," he glanced at us, "maybe it'd be better if I brought down a few servings."

Cole shook his head. "We don't want to be a burden."

"Nonsense," Cameron said. "My mom always cooks like she's feeding the whole army. It's part of ranch life, she always says. We've got plenty for everyone." He nodded over his shoulder. "Cole, you want to help me out? I know she'd love to meet you. Em, you wanna come say hi to Gram?"

Cole glanced at me, and I motioned to the coffee table. "I'll clean up here. Least I could do after such an amazing party."

"That was me," Emilia smirked. "I was a good host, just like Mommy taught me."

"Of course, you were, baby," Cam answered, pulling her up onto his shoulders. "Let's get some food, and then we can all get to know each other a little better."

As the patio door swung closed behind them, I suddenly realized I had made a monumental mistake. Standing only a few feet from Victoria, all I could think about was how her body felt in my arms and how sweet her lips tasted.

Victoria shuffled forward, resting her hands on the back of the threadbare couch. "I owe you an explanation."

EIGHTEEN

Victoria

"I owe you an explanation."

That was probably the understatement of the century. From the moment I saw Cole and Adam standing on my doorstep, all I could think of was how to explain everything to him. It was bad enough seeing the look on my brother's face when he put the pieces together. I hadn't even dared to look at Adam.

Since I landed in Texas, I'd drafted fifteen different text messages to him and started so many calls that I ended before the phone ever rang. I told myself it wasn't worth it, that when he saw the real me, the real obligations in my life, he'd never want to talk to me again.

I hadn't counted on him showing up here.

After my heart-wrenching conversation with Cole, my emotions were wrung out, and I had little energy left. But after our time together, I owed Adam an explanation—or at least some closure so we could both move on.

I toyed with my fingers, trying to figure out how to start, but Adam beat me to it. He shook his head, tucking his hands into his pockets. "You don't owe me anything, Victoria."

Victoria. It was funny to hear my name cut through me.

Adam rarely called me by my full name. After the first day together, I was always Tori, and recently, he'd called me trouble. I never thought I'd relish hearing my childhood nickname, but with Adam, it took on another meaning. It made me feel like I was testing his control as much as he was testing mine.

"I should have told you about Emilia." I rubbed my stinging eyes on the sleeve of my cardigan. "It probably makes me sound like a selfish jerk—"

"You don't." His words were almost forceful, and I made myself meet his eyes. I was expecting some hostility and anger at the secrets I had kept from him, but instead, all I saw was understanding. He tilted his head, giving me that side smile I'd grown attached to already. "You don't owe me your secrets, Victoria. If you want to hold some things close to your chest, I get it after everything you've been through. Do I hate that Cole found out this way? Of course. But I was right there with you during the worst of his dark period. I get wanting to make sure things were good before bringing him into your daughter's life."

My jaw dropped, and I stared at him like I was seeing him for the first time. He was the only one who understood my reasoning without question. Not even my parents agreed with my choice, thinking I was being too hard on Cole. And maybe I was, but I had to see him for myself. Anyone I brought into Emilia's life had to be in it for the long haul, and Cole had proven that during my visit. It was tempting to tell him before I left, but something like this needed to be a real conversation, not something quick to squeeze in while I was packing.

To be honest, this surprise visit was a blessing in disguise. Cole got to meet Emilia, and we had the opportunity to sit down and have an honest talk about what had happened years ago. While there were still a lot of things I was holding back, it felt good to have this secret no longer hanging over my head.

But I never thought Cole would bring Adam along.

While we were talking, I couldn't help but watch him with Emilia. She was just as enchanted by his easy presence as I was. I kept expecting him to ask for space or find excuses to get out of her game. My daughter was my pride and joy, but I was under no illusion that she was a little angel. She'd developed quite a sassy attitude for her pint-sized frame, and as much as it taxed us sometimes, Cam and I didn't want to squash any of her spirit. So, as long as she was kind, we could take a little sass from time to time.

None of that seemed to phase Adam. Instead, he sat on the floor, listening to her tea party demands. My heart almost burst out of my chest when she gave him her favorite tiara. He wore it like a badge of honor, not having any idea how much that dinky piece of plastic meant to her.

I ducked my head down, not wanting Adam to see the adoration written on my face. These feelings shouldn't be there, at least not yet. After all, we'd only spent a few days together and shared one magical kiss. That shouldn't be enough to feel this pull.

But standing here, in my disorganized living room, all I wanted was to run into his arms, to let him kiss away all my anxieties from the past few days, first with Emilia being sick and then trying to figure out what I was going to do about Adam. Even though I tried to leave my feelings behind in Saint Stephen's Lake, they refused to let go, daring me to call him and tell him all my concerns.

Closure, I told myself. *This is just closure.* Adam was a movie star, with his pick of every beautiful woman on the planet. There was no way he'd ever want to stick around now that he knew I was a mom and tied down to his hometown. The best thing to do was clear the air and then forget what happened between us. I chewed on my lower lip, sparing a look at the front door before continuing, "Look, about the kiss..."

"It was amazing."

My eyes widened as I looked at Adam. He shrugged his shoulders, and an easy smile graced his lips. "Last time, I fumbled my words, and you got the wrong idea, so I didn't want to take any risks now." He stepped forward, lowering his voice. "That was the best fucking kiss of my life, Tor."

"It was?" My voice came out almost screechy, and I was sure I must be dreaming. That was it. I was still in bed, trying to catch up on two days of horrible sleep.

Adam came to my side, lacing my pinkie finger with his. "Is that so hard to believe? Pretty sure you almost killed me, trouble."

"I don't understand." I shook my head. "I wanted to keep going, so why did you stop?"

He sighed, shifting around to sit on the edge of the couch. "I'm sure you've heard about my reputation, read articles about my dating life."

"Maybe a couple," I laughed. "They called you the Heart-break Prince?"

"Such a stupid fucking nickname." He cringed. "I've been trying to work through some things. I don't want to be that guy anymore, and especially not with you." He reached out and ran his thumb along my jaw. "I want to do right by you."

I shook my head, still not fully comprehending the words coming out of his mouth. "But that was before you saw all this." I motioned around the room. "This is my life. It's not glamorous. Emilia is the center of my world, and she can be a lot to handle. It's messy and loud, and often, glitter covers every surface. But as long as she's happy and loved, that's all I can ever ask for." I reached out and placed my hand on top of his. "That moment was amazing, but that was all it was: a moment. This isn't what you want, Adam. It's too complicated."

"I don't mind complicated," he said. "Is this about Emilia's dad?"

"Cam?" I chuckled. "No, not at all. We've been over for a long time, but we're still close friends. This is about you and what you deserve. I don't want you saddled with me and all my baggage."

His blue eyes narrowed, standing so he hovered over me. His hand shifted to the nape of my neck, shifting me so our chests were touching. "Listen here, trouble. I've fought hard for everything in my life, and you are no exception. I don't know why you have it in your pretty little head that your life is too complicated for me, but that's nonsense. I want you and everything that comes with you. I'm not asking for forever, Tor, just a chance to see what this could be." He lowered his face so his lips were only a breath from mine. With the slightest shift, I'd get to taste him again, get to melt in his embrace. "Take that chance with me?"

I wanted so badly to say yes, to dive in with him despite my insecurities, but there was still too much unknown, too many factors that could change how he felt about me. Sure, he had spent an hour playing with Emilia, but would he still want to stick around when she was crawling into bed at four in the morning or vomiting all over the living room? Besides, my life was here, and it was a far cry from his world. It wouldn't even make sense to try, not when it was destined to fail.

But when I looked into his gaze, all I could see was a good man staring at me, asking me for a chance. And as much as I didn't know Adam Rice, the movie star, this Adam, the one who had been there for me all week, who had given me the best kiss of my life—he was the kind of man who was worth the risk.

"Okay," I exhaled.

Adam's face lit up. "Yeah?"

I couldn't help but grin at the excitement on his face. "Okay, let's see where this goes. I still don't know how it'll all work out in the long run," my eyes met his, "but I want to try to see what could be between us."

He smiled then softly pressed his lips to mine. It was barely a kiss, more a promise of more, but it was enough to light my entire body in flames, enough to make my thigh clench in need. "Good," he whispered as he pulled back. "Because I'm not going anywhere."

NINETEEN

Victoria

Dinner was a tense, awkward affair. Despite Emilia's lighthearted questions and Cam trying to steer all the conversations to safe topics, they inevitably turned to painful parts of our past. Emilia was very curious about her new uncle, demanding to know why he'd never been to any of her birthday parties. Every question out of her little mouth seemed to put my brother more on edge, but he answered all of them. After he promised to make up for it, she seemed satisfied, moving her chair over to sit closer to him. Once she was settled, we eventually stumbled onto a safe topic: Cam's baseball career.

"Yeah, I'm just on one of the farm teams right now," Cam said between bites of chicken casserole. "I'm hoping to make it up to the majors in the next year or two. New York or Boston would be my ideal choice, but everyone wants to play for those major brands." He shrugged, leaning back to muss up Emilia's hair. "So we'll see."

Cole's eyes darted to me. "And you're going with him?"

"Oh..." I said, almost choking on my bite of food. "We haven't really talked about that yet. I guess we were waiting to see what happens before making any major decisions." I looked down at my daughter, staring at her empty plate. "Why don't you go play, baby?"

She didn't wait another second, taking her plate to the sink before running into the living room.

Cam smiled at Cole once she was out of earshot. "Obviously, I want Emilia around all the time, but during the season, my life is chaos, and there's a lot of times I'm not home for weeks. So, if the time comes and Vic wants to settle somewhere else, I'll follow her lead. She's already given up a lot for me, and I wouldn't want her to sacrifice anything else. She'll always have a home here too."

Apparently, his answer appeased my brother, because he nodded along with Cam's words, but Adam kept staring as if he was measuring up his competition. I wanted to laugh at the thought. Cam and I were family, but I wasn't in love with him—I hadn't been for a long time. And as much as I appreciated his parents giving me this cabin so we could all be close, with Adam sitting here, it felt a little off—a little too close for comfort.

Cole leaned back in his chair. "When's your next travel stretch?"

"Actually, next week," Cam answered. "We're heading off to Arkansas for a couple weeks, and then we'll be traveling around Texas. Why?"

My brother shifted, looking at me. "I'm throwing this out there, but I'm not looking for an answer right now. Since Cam's going to be traveling and I can't really leave Alex alone during our busy season, what if you and Emilia come back with us for a while?"

"What?" I asked, almost dropping my fork.

"I want to spend more time with you, Tor. A couple of days wasn't enough." He smiled down at Emilia. "I want to get to know my niece better too."

My mouth hung open, staring at the three men watching me

expectantly. But Emilia answered first, having overheard his question from the other room. She gave my brother a scrutinizing stare. "What kind of things would we do?"

Cole looked at me as he stumbled over his words. "All kinds of things," Adam jumped in, not missing a beat. "Do you like apple picking?"

Her eyes opened wide. "I love apples!"

"Where we live, there are amazing orchards. They let you pick all the apples you want. They also have pumpkins and hayrides."

"Really?" she asked, her eyes getting bigger with each passing breath.

"Oh yeah, fall is a big deal in our town. There's even a really cool festival with apple and pumpkin-flavored treats, pony rides, and games."

"Oh my gosh," she muttered, placing her hands on her cheeks. "I can't believe it. Mommy, we *have* to go."

"We'll see," I said, narrowing my gaze at Adam. "We have some things to talk about first."

She sighed a huff but then went back to playing, talking to her dolls about everything Adam had just said. I looked at my brother. "I...I don't know. It's not like we can just take off. We have a life here." I glanced at Emilia again. "I need to think about it."

He nodded, smiling at me. "Take all the time you need. I just wanted to give you the option. You're always welcome with us."

My heart galloped in my chest, wanting nothing more than to scream yes. And maybe if it was just me, I would have, no questions asked. The idea of going back to the town that had embraced me and made me feel like myself again was more than I could ever ask for. I'd get to spend more time with Cole, Alex, and especially Adam. The idea of giving us some time to get to know each other better made my cheeks flush, wishing we were already there. But the truth was, it wasn't only me. It hadn't been for a long time.

Excuses had already formed in my mind when Cam tapped my elbow, motioning toward the front door. "Come on, Vic. Let's get some air."

I nodded, getting up to join him. But as he placed his hand on my back, I couldn't help but turn over my shoulder to meet Adam's eyes, noting how they were glued to where Cam was touching me.

That should have been a red flag, should have been a hint I might be in over my head with him. But instead, it filled me with a warmth I'd never experienced before.

"I THINK YOU SHOULD GO."

Cam's words almost knocked the wind out of me. We walked through the fields behind the house, checking each of the flower beds as we went. This was my small contribution to the lot, wanting to do something to make it feel more like ours. The cabin was designed for ranch hands, with no frills and no fuss. We'd managed to make it a little cozier, but it was small, even for just the two of us. At least out here, we had room to run and play all day. And color.

My little girl loved to color over every surface, but I never felt bold enough to paint the walls inside. As much as I appreciated that Cam's parents let me stay here, this would always be their property, their home. But out here, I was able to grow wild-flowers and other plants, letting them thrive and grow strong. Hues of pink, purple, and yellow filled my sight, making me smile. This was my way of giving her the colors she craved.

"Don't look so shocked," Cameron laughed. "Cole's right.

And as much as it'll suck not to have you guys so close, I'm barely going to be home. Hadley's already on her way back to school, and your classes are all online. Besides Emilia, what's keeping you here?"

My mouth tensed at his words. I knew he meant it to be encouraging, but it also highlighted how shallow my life had become. Was that really all I had tying me to this town?

I thought back to Saint Stephen's Lake and how full my days were. I'd spend my days with Cole and Alex, stopping by for lunch and little trips into town. Adam was also constantly by my side, pushing me and helping guide me into this new chapter of my relationship with Cole. It was strange; for so long, I'd felt like an afterthought. With Cam's family, I was usually the plus one, welcomed but more so because Emilia was by my side. I hadn't made any new friends since I left college, and the people I'd met at the playground or in town were more interested in playdates and free childcare than getting to know me. So, knowing I had people who wanted to spend time with me, as just me, made me feel special in a way I hadn't in years.

Obviously, it would be different if I decided to return with Emilia, but a small smile filled my face at the thought.

"You know I'll never tell you what to do, Vic," Cam sighed. "But next year, Emilia's going to be starting school, and who knows where we'll be. Take the chance while you have it."

Be brave.

Adam's voice sent a chill down my spine, remembering the last time he whispered those words to me. As much as I hated to admit it, they were right. Would it really be the worst thing to take Emilia to New York and let her experience life outside of this tiny town?

And not to mention, it would allow me to explore this newfound connection with Adam. The idea of spending more time with him made my skin flush, and I hated how desperate I already felt for his touch. As much as I knew I loved Cam once, I'd never craved him like I did Adam. There was this need to be close to him, as if I couldn't stand any space between us at all. It made no sense, not after only a few days back in each other's orbit. But standing near him felt like my world was spinning even faster, and I wanted to be brave enough to face it with him.

Silently, Cam and I walked back into the house, giving each other one last look before I turned back to Adam and Cole. With a shy smile, I said, "I'm in."

Adam

"Shit, do you think we should replace this couch?" Cole ran his hand over his face. "I don't know if she's going to like this. Maybe we should have gotten a sleeper?"

I chuckled as I leaned against the wall, watching my friend as he spun out for the fifth time today. For the two weeks since we'd returned from Texas, Alex and Cole had been working overtime to transform the loft above the main lodge into an apartment for Victoria and Emilia. Although Tori was cool with staying in the same cabin and sharing a bed with her daughter, Cole insisted on creating a space just for them. The loft had been sitting empty since they bought the place. It was initially designed for a groundskeeper or manager, but with Alex and Cole's house so close, they never felt the need to use it. I smiled; maybe it had been waiting for Victoria and Emilia all this time.

But because it had been empty for almost a decade, it needed a lot of work before anyone could live here. When they began, the walls were covered with warped wood panels, and everything else was a muted shade of mustard. Spiders the size of my hand had turned the bathroom into their personal paradise. But over the past two weeks, they'd made it into a home.

The living room felt light and airy, borrowing from their favorite elements of each of the cabins. The walls were painted white, with wooden and black accents. The kitchen had been updated with sleek light gray cabinets and a Beachwood island in the middle.

But the show stoppers were the bedrooms, especially the smaller one on the right-hand side. I took exceptional pride in the room we'd created for Emilia, with shades of purple covering every surface. Alex had asked some of the moms in town and gotten her replicas of some of her favorite toys back home, including a small table for her to host many tea parties. A slow smile crept over my lips at the thought, oddly hopeful I'd receive another invitation.

Alex came up behind Cole, rubbing her hands along his back. "Everything looks great, baby. She's going to love it."

"I hope so," he muttered, pulling her to his side. "I just want them to be comfortable."

"How could they not be?" I chuckled, walking around the space one more time. "You've done everything to make sure they'll love it. And knowing Victoria, the best thing you can do is let her and Emilia make it their own, even if it's just for a short time."

Alex shot me a look that made me uneasy, as if she could feel the weight of my words. Even if I tried to play it off, Cole wasn't the only nervous one. Victoria and I had talked every day since we left Texas, but my nerves were quickly fraying. I was dying to see her again without a screen in front of us. I wanted to do a whole lot more than that, if I was being honest. And while I loved getting to know her better, I was spending more time with my left hand than ever before. Shit, was she feeling this too? Was she craving my touch as much as I did hers? With every stroke of my hand, I imagined it was hers, dreaming up her mouth taking my cock. Fuck. I shifted, trying to hide my thoughts from my friends. How the fuck did this girl do this to me? She wasn't even in the same state, and I was hard as a rock just thinking about her.

However, as much as I wanted her, I also wanted so much more. She was sweet, kind, and so bright, it scared me. She'd shown me some of her school assignments, and the way her brain worked out problems amazed me. But with every step we took forward, it felt like it still wasn't enough. Even though I had spelled out my intentions to her, she was still playing things close to the chest, and I had no idea what was going through her mind.

Pulling myself out of that thought spiral, I glanced at my watch. "Shit, I gotta head out. I'm supposed to meet with Dr. Kedir in half an hour."

"How's that going?" Cole asked.

Even though I hadn't told them the reasons behind my therapy appointments, I was open about the fact that I was going, at least with them. They'd been my biggest supporters for months, encouraging me to seek help when the thoughts in my head got too loud. And maybe one day, I'd explain the whole situation, but not today.

"It's going well," I said. "Doc's helping me work through my block with acting, and she seems hopeful I'll be able to get back to it soon."

"Good." Cole nodded. "I'm glad to hear you're not giving it up for good."

"And stop gracing the world with this handsome face?" I smirked. "Not a chance."

Alex rolled her eyes and came to my side. "C'mon, egomaniac. I'll walk you out."

We walked down the steps in silence, Alex waiting until we

got outside to speak. She looked up at me with an open expression, one that had only started when Cole came into her life. While I always admired Alex's strength, it was no secret that she hid behind iron-reinforced walls. Only after letting herself fall in love did they start to fade away with everyone else as well.

"I'm worried about you, Adam."

My jaw tensed, and I hated she could see through my false smile. "There's no reason to be, I promise. I'm doing better."

She crossed her arms around her chest, leaning against the wooden support on the side of the porch. "I know you are, and for what it's worth, I'm really proud of you for taking these steps."

"But?"

"But..." She sighed. "This thing with Victoria is complicated."

I shook my head, "Nothing is going on. I'm just happy she's coming to visit Cole."

"Don't bullshit me, Rice," she laughed. "We both know you did not spend hours painting purple walls because it would make *Cole* happy. I've seen the way you two look at each other; it's clear there's something there."

I clenched my teeth, already knowing where this was going. "Look, if you're afraid I'm going to hurt her—"

"I'm worried about *you*."

My eyes snapped to her, reading the concern written in her own. Alex continued, "I like Victoria, and I think you two could be really good together, but you have to admit, this is complicated."

"And?"

"And I'm not saying don't go for it. God knows if anyone deserves to be happy, it's you. But just promise me you'll take your time. I don't want you to be hurt when she goes back home, and there are more hearts at stake than just yours and hers." She placed her hand on my arm. "Make sure this is what you really want before diving into the deep end."

As Alex went back inside, I stayed on the porch. I needed to leave if I wanted to get to the other side of town in time, but her words stilled my steps. As much as it pained me to say it, Alex was right. I was willingly free-falling into this girl, and there was so much more at stake than just me.

And I started to doubt I was worth the risk.

EVEN AFTER SETTLING in at Dr. Kedir's office, Alex's words still echoed in my mind. The entire drive over here, I'd run through every scenario, wondering if it was a mistake to bring Victoria into my world. It was unpredictable and often unstable. I was lucky I'd had some success and made enough investments to keep me going, but how long would it last? Acting was my only true career, and now, I wasn't even doing that. Even without that, my dating reputation would always be a red flag. Was that why she was holding back? I tried to explain the media's commentary, but what if it wasn't enough for her? If you looked at my track record, I wasn't a safe bet, not for a mom with a kid to think about.

Dr. Kedir shuffled in her chair. "Anything you want to talk about today, Adam?"

I leaned forward, elbows on my knees. My legs shook restlessly, unable to quiet the doubts in my mind. "I decided to take your advice. I spent more time with Victoria and talked to her about what's been going on. And we..." I scoffed. "We kissed before she left."

"And now?" Dr. Kedir asked, failing to hide her slow smile.

"I'm not sure. Things are kind of up in the air. But Victoria's coming to stay for a while, so our paths are going to cross again."

She nodded, leaning back to look at me. "And how do you feel about this development?"

"I was excited, but now, I'm not so sure," I answered honestly. "Even since Tori left, it's felt like there's a void in my life. But at the same time, I'm feeling really fucking nervous."

"Why?"

I ran my hands over my face. "She was here for a week. Six fucking days, Doc. And I'm already acting like this? What's going to happen after a month?" I shook my head. "And now there's her daughter to think about."

She nodded, jotting something on her notepad. "That definitely adds another layer of complication."

"Hell yeah, it does," I sighed. "If you had asked me before this, I would have never thought about dating someone with a kid. And a part of me still thinks it might be too much to take on. I don't want to let Victoria down, so maybe I should just walk away before anything really starts between us." I stared at my hands, clenching them. "Even though I know it's bullshit, I keep thinking about my reputation, what it would mean for her to get involved with me. Even if Cole's cool with it, which I doubt, is she going to be able to handle what it means to really be with me? The media? The fans? The articles that take minuscule crumbs and make them into the end of the fucking world?" With each word, my anger rose, hating that this was a part of my existence. And while it wasn't a part of my life here, if I went back to my real world, it could tear us apart. "I'm being fucking selfish."

"And how does that make you feel? The idea of walking away from her?"

"Like I'm going to be sick." Even saying the words made a stone drop into my stomach. "I've always followed my gut, and it's telling me that this could be something. Something real. Not just for show and not something that only lasts for a night or two. Being around her makes me feel better. I thought being around Emilia would scare me, but it's the opposite. We're still getting to know each other, but she's so damn funny. Completely filter-free. The two of them make me laugh." I watched Dr. Kedir study me. "Tell me what to do, Doc."

"I think you already know what you want to do. And I think right now, the best thing you can do is follow that feeling. But..." She smiled softly at me. "I can understand the pressure you're feeling. Dating a single parent brings its own set of challenges." She placed her notepad on her side table and leaned closer toward me. "My best advice? Take it day by day. Talk to Victoria and let her decide how to proceed with her daughter. Find out her boundaries, especially when it comes to the media. Yes, your life is different than most, but there are examples of families thriving despite outside pressure. For now, get to know each other and enjoy their time here."

"And you think that'll work?"

She smiled at me. "I'm your therapist, Adam, not a psychic. No one knows what the future holds. Only you can decide if the risk is worth it."

I nodded, leaning back on the couch, and ran my hands over the velvet material. Dr. Kedir studied me, probably waiting for a response.

But I didn't have one.

Dr. Kedir tapped her pen on the pad, bringing me back to the present. "I'm happy to hear you're taking steps to reclaim your life and that you're giving some thought to what it will be like when you return to acting. Have you thought about talking to Theo? Maybe taking on a new project?"

My skin prickled at the thought, but it wasn't unpleasant, not like it was before. It was more like an energy rushing through my veins, making me desperate to get back in front of the camera. It wasn't the same rush or roar as before, more like a house cat than a lion, but it was there for the first time in a long time.

But I still shook my head. "I'm getting there. Still not a hundred percent ready yet, but I'm feeling closer than I was before."

"And the letters?" She looked up at me, knowing I needed the push to talk about this subject. She asked every time we met, though luckily, the answer was the same.

"Nothing, not even an email." I shrugged. "Maybe they moved on to someone else."

Dr. Kedir smiled, but it didn't hold the same weight as before. "I wish I could agree, but in my professional opinion, that's not likely. I want you to remain vigilant, Adam. And if they start again, I would encourage you to file a complaint with the police or at least hire some outside security."

"No," I said. "I'm not bringing outsiders here, making people feel unsafe. If it starts again, we'll go from there, but I'm not going to look a gift horse in the mouth. It's been almost four months. Before, I was getting messages every other hour. I'm going to choose to believe it's over."

Dr. Kedir nodded, but I didn't miss the hint of doubt in her eyes. "For your sake, Adam, I truly hope you're right."

TWENTY-ONE

Victoria

As I stared up at our temporary home, my hands tensed with nerves. Coming to Saint Stephen's Lake by myself, with a firm end date, was one thing. That trip took weeks of preparation and mental Olympics, readying myself for every possible scenario. And even though I had time to prepare for this trip as well, there was something so much more daunting about it. Maybe because Emilia was by my side, making it more real. When I arrived for Cole's wedding, there was no question: my guard was up. But the people, my brother included, in this town had taken a chisel to my mental walls, leaving them little more than crumbling piles. I felt exposed.

My daughter, however, had no such qualms.

"Mommy, can we please go inside now?"

Her light voice broke me out of my daze, and my focus returned to her smaller hand clenched in mine. Although she was trying her best to be patient, Emilia radiated with excitement, unable to hold it for a moment longer. She'd also been asleep most of the plane ride and the subsequent car trip, so she had extra energy in spades. She'd fight tooth and nail at bedtime, but that was a future problem.

"Okay, let's do this," I exhaled, squeezing Emilia's hand before ascending the stairs. Walking inside, we bypassed the dining room and kitchen nook, moving toward the back end of the main cabin, near the employee offices. Cole left shortly after we arrived, dropping our luggage upstairs before taking off to deal with a guest emergency. Alex also made herself scarce, passing us the key and telling us to make ourselves at home, with a promise to return later with pizza.

I had to admit, I was already impressed by the amount of preparation Cole and Alex had gone through to get ready for our visit. They traded in their usual worn Jeep for a luxury SUV to pick us up from the airport, courtesy of Theo. There was a booster seat in the back seat, and all of Emilia's favorite snacks were tucked in the center console. My favorite upgrade? The tablet with a bunch of downloaded movies, complete with sparkling purple headphones with cat ears. Emilia let out the most excited shriek when she saw them. Not even twenty-four hours in, and my daughter was completely spoiled by her aunt and uncle.

And it was so much more than the things that had been purchased for her. Cole and Alex talked with Emilia the whole time she was awake—*granted, it wasn't much*—but my daughter enjoyed being the center of their attention. It made me realize how sheltered her life back in Texas truly was, and while she was the apple of her grandparents' eyes, I hadn't done her any favors by keeping her with them or me most days.

Maybe this was the chance to correct the course for both of us.

The door cracked open, and a smile immediately graced my face. When Cole offered up the manager's loft above the main lodge, I had no idea what to expect. But clearly, someone had spent a lot of time prepping the apartment. I couldn't help but gawk at the incredible space, in disbelief that we got to call it home, even for a limited time. The main area was an open concept, with a small but organized kitchen that flowed into a living room and play area. The vaulted ceiling led up to a large sunlight, and wooden beams stretched across the room.

"Mommy!"

Emilia's sudden gasp snapped me out of my stupor, crossing over to join her in one of the bedrooms on the left-hand side of the apartment. Her eyes almost bulged out of her head as she looked around the room. There was no question it was meant for her. It was like the room had been plucked from her imagination. Everything was covered in purple and sparkles. Buckets of toys and art supplies filled the cube storage at the base of the closet, with a purple, pink, and teal shag carpet in the center of the room. And on the far wall, there was a full-sized, white, wrought-iron sleigh bed, bigger and more beautiful than anything I could ever afford.

As Emilia started digging through all the new toys, a knock came on the door. Alex and Cole let themselves inside, carrying pizza boxes and drinks.

Tears pricked in my eyes as I turned toward Cole, who was half-hiding behind Alex with a sheepish smile on his face. With one last glance at the room, I turned, reaching out to pull him into a tight hug. "I can't believe you did all of this for us."

"Of course we did," he muttered against my hair. "Although you should probably thank Adam too. I was about to pick out pink paint, and he said purple would be a better choice."

I bit my lip, trying to hide my smile. He'd listened to me when I told him about Emilia's aversion to pink and how it was purple or nothing lately. I had no doubt that it was a phase, but right now, it made her happier than I'd ever seen. The fact that he remembered an off-hand comment and used it to bring my daughter's dream bedroom to life meant more than I could ever voice.

"It's perfect," I said, trying to keep my voice from breaking. But looking into Cole's expression, it was hard to hold back the tears. After years of not having my brother in my life, knowing he put this much effort into making me—*making us*—comfortable made my heart start to swell. "Thank you. So much. I..." My voice trailed off, not sure how to put my gratitude into words. "Thank you, Cole."

"You got it." Cole cleared his throat. "Glad you guys like it."

I turned toward Alex, embracing her as well. "Thank you too. I can feel your handiwork all over this place."

"Anytime," she voiced, squeezing me a little tighter. "But Emilia isn't the only one with a new bedroom. Did you have a chance to check out yours?"

"Not yet. I'm still taking it all in."

"Well..." She smiled. "I think you should. Save the best for last, you know?"

I let Alex guide me over to the bedroom, and my jaw fell open when she pushed forward the door. All my life, I'd had rooms that were fine, that suited my needs. But this space? It was as if someone had nestled deep into the burrows of my brain and described everything I could have ever wanted.

Light blue paint covered the walls, where pictures of the landscape and my daughter also hung. I had no idea how they got these precious photos, from the time I first held Emilia in my arms to our most recent trip to the Caldwell Zoo. They lined the antique white dresser pressed up against the far wall, and I paused, studying each one. But as much as I loved seeing the pictures of my life with my daughter, it was the furthest two that made me choke up. The first was a picture of Cole and me when we were younger, me in one of the trees that lined our backyard and him directly below me. *Just in case you fall*, he'd told me at the time. *I want to be there to catch you.*

Next to it was a more recent picture: all of us together at

Cole and Alex's wedding. The couple was in the middle, surrounded by our family. My parents were on one side while Adam and I were on the other. We all beamed at the camera. It was the first picture we'd taken together in a decade, and it was pretty perfect.

As I stared at all of us together, I couldn't help but look at Adam. We looked good together, like we belonged at each other's side. But that wasn't what caught my eye.

While the rest of us smiled brightly at the photographer, Adam's attention was on me. Was that how he looked at me? Like I was something worth memorizing?

It was one thing to hear he was interested in me. That had already taken me by surprise. But Adam was clear about his intentions and gave me no reason to doubt his words. It was my brain that made me question what was happening, unsure if I was worthy of his attention.

But to see him staring at me with that much devotion in his eyes? It made the pieces snap into place. All my doubts faded, and all my questions about timing and consequences were forced out. As much as my mind wanted me to question how I'd started to fall for him so quickly, I couldn't.

Instead, like so much about him, it gave me a sense of rightness, like it was a foregone conclusion that our paths would merge.

I placed the photo back on the dresser, clearing my throat to hide my emotions from my brother and sister-in-law. Instead, I moved over to the bed, running my hand along the linens. For the past few years, I felt like I was living someone else's life, that none of my plans would ever come to fruition. But standing in this room, it no longer felt like a shadow clung to the corners of my memories. Maybe everything was supposed to come crashing down to lead me to this moment, to a place where I could build something new with my ever-expanding family. At least, I hoped that's what it was for.

Cole ran his hand behind his hair as he stood in the doorway. "I remembered you talking about that one movie when we were kids and how much you wanted your room to look like the main character's bedroom. Hope you still have the same taste."

I nodded. "It's perfect. I..." My voice trailed off as my hand touched the metal bed frame. "Thank you, both of you. This means the world to me."

"Anything for you, trouble." Cole smiled.

And for the first time in a long time, I believed him.

As I returned to Fox Creek for the night, my eyes instantly flew to the apartment above the main lodge. The yellow lights flooding from the windows were a strange yet comforting sight. I stared at them for too long, just in case I caught sight of the woman who'd stolen my thoughts all day. I'd tried to keep busy helping Gray make sense of his dad's filing system, though even with the two of us, it was useless. At least it'd kept me away from the apartment.

Victoria and Emilia needed time with Cole; that was what this trip was really about. Cole wanted to get to know his sister and niece, and they didn't need me hanging around like an interloper. So I told myself to give them space, to not intrude on their time together. But with every ticking second, it was getting harder to convince myself to stay away.

"Fuck it," I hissed to myself, grabbing my hat before killing the engine. "You've got better willpower than this, man. You can stay away for one night."

Climbing out of the car, I started to walk toward my cabin. But as soon as I reached the back path, my feet stopped, refusing to go a step further without seeing Victoria.

"You are not going over there," I whispered to myself. "It's one fucking night."

We'd gone weeks without seeing each other, relying on texts and calls to get to know each other. There was no rush, not when I had her here for the next month. There would be plenty of time to spend together.

But even as I told myself all these truths, my body started to rush toward the main cabin, not even glancing toward my own. Chuckling to myself, I moved up the staircase, my heart beating a steady, excited rhythm in my chest. I pulled out my phone, rereading our last conversation before I knocked on the door.

VICTORIA

Thank you for Emilia's room

ADAM

Just helped pick the paint color. Everything else was Cole and Alex

VICTORIA

Really? I remember Emilia only telling one person she wanted a teapot with purple roses and a unicorn.

It took me almost a week to find it online, but it was worth it to imagine Emilia's face when she saw it.

ADAM

Okay, I might have had something to do with that. Wanted you two to be happy you came here

VICTORIA

We didn't need all of this to make us happy, but it's appreciated. Thank you, Adam.

See you soon?

Rereading her last text again, I lifted my fist, lightly tapping my knuckles on the door. One knock, and she was there, even more beautiful than I remembered. How was it that every time I thought I'd figured this woman out, she surprised me by taking more of my breath away?

"We've got another one," Victoria called out over her shoulder with a smirk.

With that, I peeked behind her, seeing the small living room filled with familiar faces. Emilia sat on Cole's lap, adding different barrettes and ribbons to Alex's hair. On the other loveseat were Calla and Theo, watching the exchange with amused grins. Normally, I loved nights like this. Throw Gray into the mix, and we'd sit around and talk for hours.

But with Victoria finally in town, all I wanted was to show her how much I'd been thinking about her during our time apart.

Victoria leaned in. "I didn't invite them here; they all just showed up."

"Everyone's happy you decided to come stay." I smiled, trying to hide my annoyance. All I wanted was to sit and talk to her, watch her easy smile in person, hear her laugh for myself. I also wanted to do a lot of other things that definitely wouldn't be appropriate in front of this crowd.

She moved to the side, letting me join the chaos in the living room. Pizza boxes covered the coffee table, and half-empty soda cans lingered on the edges. I dove into the first box, grabbing a cheese slice before settling onto the ground near Victoria's seat.

"Adam!" Emilia exclaimed, running over to jump into my lap. "Did you see my new room? It's purple everywhere!"

"That's awesome, kiddo."

She stood up, holding out her hands. "And guess what? Auntie Alex and Uncle Cole got me a new tea set!"

"Nice, Em." I lifted my hand to give her a high-five. "Does that mean I get to come to another party?"

"Only if you promise to follow the rules." She turned to face Alex, pointing her thumb at me over her shoulder. "He didn't wait for me to serve the tea last time."

"How rude." Alex smirked. "Can't take him anywhere."

"Wait a minute, how do you score an invite to these exclusive parties?" Calla asked. "Because I have a killer dress I've been dying to wear for a special occasion, and a tea party sounds like the best kind."

Emilia's eyes widened before she let out an excited giggle. "Mommy, is it okay if everyone comes for a tea party?"

"Of course," Victoria said, pressing a kiss to the top of her head.

"And can I get a new fancy dress?"

"We'll talk about it later."

Satisfied with the answer, Emilia jumped up to talk to Calla about all her clothing. I swear, the girl had more energy than most grown adults. Victoria had told us she was constantly on the go, but it had taken until now to truly believe it. But the strange thing? I didn't mind it.

As I scarfed down the rest of my pizza, my phone vibrated in my pocket. Glancing at the message, I was surprised to see Victoria's name on top.

VICTORIA

You don't have to stick around if you don't want to

ADAM

How many times do I have to tell you, trouble? I like being around you.

Three dots appeared, as if she was typing more, but before I could look, Theo caught my eye. He watched me like a hawk, smirking when, apparently, he saw something written on my expression. He leaned forward, untangling from his wife to speak with me.

"Did you look at that script I sent over?"

"The one about the murderous computer chip?" I rolled my eyes. "Yeah, I'll think about it."

Theo's eyes lit up, and I instantly realized my mistake. "But you did look at it?"

"I was curious about the title," I shrugged. "No other reason."

As Emilia slid off her lap, Calla joined our conversation. "Nothing has caught your eye? I thought that rom-com had a lot of potential."

"He's not doing a rom-com," Theo added.

"And why is that?" his wife said, arching one of her brows. "I seem to remember someone wiping away tears when he read the third act break-up."

"You weren't supposed to tell anyone that, beautiful," he said, rubbing the bridge of his nose. "I just meant that project shouldn't be his big comeback. We need something splashier, something with more box office potential."

I held my hands up to silence them. "Okay, enough. I looked at one script. I didn't say I was ready to jump back into any project."

"How much longer is this little sabbatical going to take?" Theo said. His patience was wearing thin with me, especially because I'd been evading telling him the reason behind my absence. I knew he worried about me as a friend, but the man staring back at me was all agent.

"When he's ready," Victoria snapped from behind me. All eyes turned to her, shocked and surprised to hear the fierceness in her tone. As I glanced back at her, her cheeks flushed with color. "I'm sorry," she mumbled. "But I don't think putting pressure on Adam is going to help. He'll tell you when he's ready, not the other way around."

"Thank you," I mouthed, turning back to the rest of the group. "I'm getting there, Theo. And trust me, when I decide to jump into a project, you will be the first to know."

He nodded, but I could see a look pass between him and Calla. I couldn't blame them; they had seen me at the height of my panic earlier in the year, when the emails and letters were happening multiple times a day, and I couldn't even sleep without thinking of someone busting into my apartment. They'd tried to help, but I shut them down, too scared to let anyone else in on my nightmare. After all, if the police didn't take my concerns seriously, why would anyone else?

Alex shifted the group's attention to the lodge's stand at the upcoming Fall Fest, and luckily, that took the attention off me. As they talked about signage and what they wanted to include at the booth, my phone buzzed again in my hand, alerting me to the earlier text message.

VICTORIA

Even with the chaos?

I smiled to myself as I read her message. Little did she know that there was nowhere else I'd rather be.

ADAM

Especially with the chaos

TWENTY-THREE

Victoria

Sitting this close to Adam and not being able to touch him was torture. The smell of him, all masculine and warm, made my insides tingle, like his pheromones were designed just to trap me. What I would do if I could crawl into his lap and show him all the dreams I'd had while we were apart. I was desperate to touch him, to taste him. But there was no way I could, not with my daughter and brother sitting on the opposite side of the living room, watching and happily carrying on in conversation.

As much as I appreciated everyone coming out to greet me, I kept checking my phone, wondering how much longer they'd hang out. Not because I didn't enjoy their company; Alex and Calla had welcomed me with open arms, and Cole boasted about me like a proud brother. Theo was the only one I was still feeling out, unsure if he was just tolerating me for the rest of the group's sake. But after I stood up for Adam, something shifted in his gaze, almost a little like respect.

However, every time Adam shifted behind me, his knee grazing my shoulder or back, my focus pulled entirely to him. I sucked in a sharp breath as he leaned forward to refill his cup, his fingers brushing my spine as he sat back up. Even soft, simple touches like that felt like the worst form of foreplay, all build-up, no release. If everyone didn't leave soon, I would probably explode.

Emilia's little snore came from Cole's lap, and I started to stand up. He waved me off. "Please, can I take her?" He smiled down at his niece, curled up in his lap. "I'm not ready to let her go just yet."

How could I say no to that? I nodded, smiling to myself as he lifted my daughter with ease. My throat tightened at the sight, slightly hating myself for delaying this even for a short while. As much as I still had that voice in the back of my mind, wondering how long this Cole would stick around, it was getting quieter every day. Every time he showed up when he was supposed to, every time he answered my phone calls, the doubts lessened.

"We should head out too," Calla said, lifting herself out of Theo's lap. As soon as she did, he pulled his phone out of his pocket, grimacing when he looked at the screen. She arched her brow when she saw his expression. "Everything okay?"

"Nothing we can't handle," Theo smiled, standing up to lightly kiss her lips. After watching them all night, it made a lot more sense why Theo was so head over heels for his wife. They complimented each other well and seemed to have the best kind of partnership.

While Cole tucked Emilia into her new bed, Alex walked the others to the door, Adam hanging back with me to start cleaning up. As I collected soda cans, I felt his eyes on me, watching as I worked.

"Can I help you?" I teased.

"Nope." He shook his head, dark blond hair falling across his forehead. "Just still can't believe you're actually here."

I placed the sodas in the sink, staring out across the island at him. "Thought I'd change my mind?"

"I don't know," Adam whispered, coming closer so Alex wouldn't hear us. "But I'm really fucking glad you didn't."

I tucked my head, trying to hide the color invading my cheeks. It was refreshing being around Adam, knowing he didn't really hold back his feelings, at least when it came to me. While I was back in Texas, I couldn't help but look up Adam's past, curious about the other women he'd dated. It was a horrible decision. There were models, actresses, and even a few major philanthropists dedicated to changing the world. I couldn't hold a candle to any of them. But the biggest shock of all was how they described Adam as if he was a master player who only cared about bedding beautiful women.

After reading articles about him, for a moment, I thought he'd changed and become someone who played games with women's hearts. But it only lasted for a second before my own experiences replaced those of second-hand sources. Adam had been nothing but kind to me, direct with his intentions and feelings. Maybe in the past, he wasn't the best at relationships, but I knew better than most how people could change.

As I glanced up at Adam, I caught him staring at my lips like he wanted to consume me then and there. My thighs clenched at the thought, wondering what it would be like if we'd taken a step further. Would he be gentle? Or would the rest of his body be just as demanding as his mouth? God, I hoped that was the case.

I wanted to see more of him, to let my fingers run along the cut lines of his body, to feel how much my touch affected him. The room started to get warmer, and my brain turned to mush. As much as I wanted to believe it was from all the travel, I knew it wasn't the case. It was all due to the man hovering in front of me, staring at me like he wanted to devour me.

"Okay, she's out."

My brother's voice made me jump, almost landing on the

opposite side of the kitchen. I bowed my head, hoping he didn't notice me staring at his best friend like he was a snack I was dying to unwrap.

He clapped his hand on Adam's shoulder, not seeing the flinch on Adam's face. "We're gonna head out." He looked between the two of us. "Are you sticking around?"

"Nah," Adam chuckled. "Just wanted to make sure Tori was settled before I headed down to my cabin." He looked at me, heat returning to his dark blue eyes. "You need anything, you know where to find me."

I nodded, tucking my hands behind me. "Yeah, thanks."

Closing the door behind them, I took in more of the apartment, trying to commit this moment to memory. Without the lights on, the moon shone through the skylight, casting everything in a soft glow. It was wild to think that a few weeks ago, this place had been filled with old storage and peeling wooden panels. Now, it felt like a place anyone would be honored to visit. I peeked into Emilia's room, watching her snore quietly in dreamland. In her arm was a stuffed wolf, which must have been another gift from Cole. I was going to have to cut the man off. It was like he was trying to cram five years of presents into a few days.

I pressed a kiss on her forehead, shutting her door before walking into the bathroom. My reflection stared back at me in the wide mirror, showcasing the dark circles under my eyes. Sleep should have been my priority, but I was too filled with nerves and excitement to close my eyes. Stepping back into the living area, I grabbed a bottle of water from the fridge and then settled onto the couch. Back home, our TV only had a few channels, primarily local news and a couple of kid programs. If we wanted to watch anything different, we'd have to go into the main house. And while Cam's parents always made me feel welcome, it was hard to lounge and binge-watch while everyone else was working hard around me.

Clicking through the different apps, I let out an excited squeal as I found one of my favorite old sitcoms. But before I could get comfortable, a knock sounded from the door. My traitorous heart beat heavily in my chest, hoping that only one person was waiting on the other side.

As I pulled it open and saw Adam waiting for me, a wild, almost frantic look in his eyes, I nearly fainted at the sheer need coursing through my veins. "Wh...What are you doing here?" I stumbled.

"Saying goodnight to you properly."

TWENTY-FOUR

It had taken everything in me to leave Victoria's loft when Cole did. If it wasn't suspect as fuck for me to hang around after he was gone, I would have never left, content to spend the rest of my night with the woman upstairs.

But leave I did, and then I impatiently waited for his truck lights to fade down the road before rushing back upstairs. Maybe a bigger part of me should have cared that I was crossing a line with Cole's sister, but fuck it. Being around her made me crave every touch, every slight hit of her perfume. I needed her, friendship be damned. If giving in to her made me a terrible friend, so be it.

As soon as she opened the door, Victoria's eyes widened in shock, but a sly smile played on her lips, like she wanted me here just as much as I wanted to be there.

"Wh...What are you doing here?" she asked, her voice low and almost breathless. The sound went straight to my cock, and it pressed against the confines of my jeans. Only this siren could make me hard with just a few words from her pouty lips.

"Saying goodnight to you properly."

I didn't think, didn't even breathe as I claimed her mouth,

using my hands to anchor her close to me. She clawed at my chest, wrapping her fingers in my pale gray t-shirt. It was everything I'd learned to expect from her kiss—the passion, the need, the pull to be even closer to her. The kind of high I didn't want to ever come down from.

Her tongue tangled with mine, and I let out a groan as I pressed her up against the wall behind the door. Kicking it closed with my foot, I lifted Victoria into my arms, letting her feel how much I wanted her. She fit in my embrace like it was carved just for her. With a rock of my hips against her core, she let out a small gasp, and I used the moment to move my mouth down to her neck. Pressing against her pulse point, I let her scent fill my nostrils, snapping the fraying tether of my self-control.

"Adam..." Victoria gasped as my lips traced her collarbone, shifting the neck of the sweater that had been torturing me all night. With my hips pressed against her, I lifted it and brought it over her head. She giggled as I threw it to the other side of the room.

"Hey," Victoria chuckled, pressing her back against the wall to gain some distance between us. "What if I was cold?"

"Then I'll keep you warm, trouble."

She rolled her eyes. "Do all of your girls get these cheesy lines?"

"No other girls," I said, pressing my lips to hers. "You're the only one I want. It's driving me fucking mad, Tori."

"Me?" she said, her mouth falling slightly open, as if she couldn't believe what I was saying. "I'm nothing special."

"Fuck yes, you. And don't you dare let me hear you say something like that again." I gripped the back of her neck, forcing her to meet my eyes. Red flushed the apples of her cheeks, her eyes wider than I'd ever seen them. I wasn't letting her squirm away, not when I needed her to hear my words clearly. "You have taken over all my thoughts since you showed up in town. Every night, I imagine you coming on my fingers, on my tongue, and, when I'm really lucky, on my cock. I want you, Victoria. I want every part of you. I know we should take things slow—"

My words were cut off when she kissed me, her arms tightening around the back of my neck. "I want you too, Adam." She pulled her lip in between her teeth. "I want you in my mouth."

"Fuck, Tor, you can't say stuff like that to me."

"Why?"

I motioned to my jeans. "I'm already about to bust over here like a goddamn virgin. If you put your mouth on me, I don't know how long I'll last."

She smirked, pressing her hand against my chest to get me to release her. "Then don't."

With those last words, she lowered to her knees, undoing the buttons of my fly as she went. Each pop set off something in me, my breathing labored and out of control. I brushed her hair back as she wrapped her hands around my shaft, tentatively stroking me to life. I watched her expression as she held me in her hands, almost unsure of how to proceed.

I ran my fingers through her hair, tucking it behind her ear. "You don't have to do this, Tor—"

But once again, she surprised me, licking me from base to tip, coming back along my underside to circle my opening. My chest almost imploded when the sweet heat of her mouth took me, slowly at first, but then gaining more confidence the more she was able to fit in her mouth.

"Fuck, baby," I hissed as her hands wrapped around me, taking care of what couldn't fit. "You're killing me."

"Shhh," she chuckled, popping me out of her mouth to giggle. "Be quiet, or you'll wake the monster."

That was the last thing I wanted. No offense; I really

enjoyed spending time with Emilia, but right now, the only person I wanted to spend time with was the goddess on her knees in front of me.

"If you make a sound, I'm going to have to stop," Victoria warned, even going so far as to arch one of her eyebrows in mock seriousness.

"Keep sucking me like a goddamn dream, and I'll do whatever you want."

"Good man," she said, still stroking me with her hands. "Now, stop holding back and fuck my throat like I know you're dying to."

My eyes widened, and I smiled brightly at my dream girl. She looked sweet and innocent, and no small part of me loved that only I got to see this wanton woman behind the scenes. I nodded, placing my hands in her hair. "Yes, ma'am."

Her mouth surrounded me again, and it was like all the stars blacked out in the sky. My fingers clung to her head, keeping her still as I thrust in and out of her warm lips. Watching her plush pout swallow me was the hottest thing I'd ever seen in my life, especially when her dark brown eyes locked onto mine. For a moment, I was afraid I was being too rough, especially when she gagged around me. But when I started to pull back, Victoria's nails dug into my thighs, keeping me close.

"Baby," I hissed, looking up at the ceiling. "You gotta let me go. I'm going to cum down your throat if you don't stop."

I waited for her to release me, but instead, Victoria hummed, almost in approval. As her throat constricted around the crown of my cock, my balls tightened, and my whole body felt like it was pulsing as one. Thick ropes flew out of me, and I came harder than I had in my life. I pressed my hand against the wall, leaning my forehead against it. Victoria lifted herself up, smirking at me as she brushed the corners of her mouth with her thumbnail. I almost came again as she popped it into her mouth, sucking any remnants of my release onto her tongue.

"Damn, Tori," I groaned, my voice breaking with shaky breaths. "I think you almost killed me."

"Now, where would the fun be in that?" she smiled. "I was hoping for a repeat in the future."

"Fuck that," I said, tugging her back in my arms. "You had your fun, but I'm ready for a taste of my own."

I shifted us so I could place her on the island countertop, completely overwhelmed by the beautiful woman in front of me. "Who knew you had such a filthy mouth on you?" I said, running my thumb along her lower lip.

Her cheeks flushed that deep crimson color I'd grown to love. "I don't normally," Victoria chuckled. "But with you...I guess I felt comfortable enough to let that side out." She playfully slapped my shoulder. "Not to mention, you've had me on edge since you left."

"Oh yeah?" I chuckled, moving my hands down to her thighs and massaging her soft skin. "Did you try to take the edge off?" I leaned in, licking the column of her exposed neck. Now that she was out from under me, I could take in the cotton-white bra holding back her tits. It needed to go. I needed to hold them, to have them in my mouth. I needed to find out if they were as perfect as the rest of her. "Did you touch yourself, pretending it was me?"

As I started to unhook the back, Victoria's hands drove into my hair, holding me close to her. "God, yes. I wanted you so badly."

"I'm here now," I said as I tossed away her bra, letting it join her discarded top. "And fuck, baby, if you don't make a man want to go to his knees."

"So do it," she dared, smirking up at me.

"Soon," I said, taking one of her nipples into my mouth and

swirling my tongue. I kept lavishing it until it was fully erect, then moved to the opposite side. Fuck, being with this woman felt so right, like I was born to worship at her feet. Every taste only spurred me on more, like I would never get enough. I leaned back, taking in the dark, lust-filled expression in her eyes. "But first, I want you to show me."

"Sh—show you?"

I took her lower lip with my thumb, letting it bounce back under the weight of my touch. "Don't get shy on me now, trouble. Show me how you touched yourself when you wished it was me."

TWENTY-FIVE

Victoria

I stared at Adam, unsure how he managed to turn me on with such a simple command. Nobody looked at me like he did, as if he could see into the fibers of my soul. His eyes were the darkest they'd ever been, filled with lust, longing, and so much more. It gave me a newfound confidence to unleash the more dominant parts of me, ignoring my inner voice that told me I wasn't sexy or bold enough to take the lead.

Not to mention, there'd been a mental block when it came to sex ever since I had Emilia. I'd become shy about chasing my own needs, feeling like my body didn't belong to just me anymore. Even though it had been years, I'd still let this sexual side of me remain dormant, not able to reconcile the mother I was supposed to be and the woman who wanted to own her pleasure.

But that shy, insecure woman was nowhere to be found tonight, and I had no plans of cowering back into that role anytime soon.

Not with this beautiful man promising to go to his knees just for a taste of me. I lifted my hips, sliding my yoga pants down my legs. Adam let out a sharp hiss when he saw my lace thong, the center already drenched because of him. I left it on, wanting to see how much teasing it would take to break him.

I slid my middle finger along the fabric, savoring the warmth spreading through my limbs. My gaze never left his, almost daring him to break eye contact first. He didn't—at least not until I shifted the lace to the side, baring all of me.

"Jesus Christ," Adam sighed, rubbing his hand over his face. "God, baby, you're drenched."

"Felt too good," I said, continuing to stroke small circles into my skin. "Having you in my mouth."

"Tell me more," Adam said, his voice lower and even more lethal to my self-control. As my fingers moved toward my entrance, I chewed my lower lip.

"Loved seeing you lose control," I whispered. "Feeling you at the back of my throat. It was better than I ever thought it would be."

"You liked sucking my dick, baby?"

"Yes," I breathed, increasing the pressure. "I could have come right then."

"Don't you dare," Adam snapped, moving so he could slide his hands along my thighs. "Not until I get a chance to return the favor. This pretty little pussy is begging for my tongue." His eyes jumped up to meet mine, a heady need written on his features. "Can I taste you?"

I lifted my fingers, pressing them up to his lips. Tracing my arousal along his lower one, I smiled. "Go ahead."

He didn't hesitate, licking his lip before pulling my fingers into his mouth. He groaned around them. "Fuck, you really are perfect, you know that?" I blushed, trailing my fingers along his cheek. How this man could fill all the cracks in my heart with only a few words, I'd never know. But even though it scared me to need him this much, this quickly, I was all too willing to fall if he was there to catch me.

"I need more," Adam said, reaching out to take the sides of my thong in his hands. He looked at me, waiting until I nodded before he pulled it down my legs. As soon as I was bare, I let my legs fall open, inviting him closer.

He didn't hesitate, licking me from bottom to top, lapping up my arousal like it was his favorite snack. My head fell against the counter, unable to hold back the loud moan that ripped through me.

He tsked his tongue. "Turnabout's fair play, trouble. If I couldn't make any noise, neither can you."

"Then find something to shut me up," I laughed, picking up my head to look at him. "Because I don't know if I can hold back."

For a moment, I thought he'd put his cock back in my mouth, and I couldn't lie—that idea sent thrills through my veins. But instead, Adam just smirked, taking my ruined underwear off the counter. "Open up, baby."

I didn't hesitate, which honestly shocked even me. If anyone else had tried this, I probably would have cursed them out. But with Adam, there was a level of trust I hadn't experienced before. As the lace filled my mouth, he leaned down, sucking on my clit as he teased my entrance with his fingers.

I screamed around the fabric as he continued his ministrations, alternating between sucking my clit and licking every inch of my sex. Just as my head started to swim, he pressed two fingers inside me, crooking them along my walls.

"Fuck, Tor," he groaned, placing his head on my lower stomach. "You're so fucking tight. I'm getting hard just thinking about being inside you."

My muffled cries must have told him to continue, because he went right back to work, torturing me with his twin movements. With a few more swipes of his tongue, I shattered around him, my vision going white with waves of pleasure. Adam continued working me through my orgasm, not letting a single drop go to waste.

By the time he was pulling me up off the counter, I was completely boneless, leaning on his chest to stay upright.

He smiled brightly down at me as his fingers brushed away my hair. "You're the most beautiful thing I've ever seen."

"Yeah, right," I chuckled, reaching down to hide my scar from my C-section. It was still hard to look at in the mirror, knowing my body would never be the same. But just as my arm slung across my stomach, Adam lifted it away, pressing his lips along the faded scar.

He pulled back to look at me. "Absolutely fucking perfect, baby. Every inch of you."

I placed my hand on his chest, glancing up into his eyes. There was no trace of a lie, and despite my insecurities rearing up, I believed him. I let my hands fall to the counter, pushing up so I could kiss him again. I could taste my orgasm on his tongue, and it made my thighs clench, ready for more of him. I needed this man—inside me, in my life, and so much more.

Just as he helped me back down to my feet, a soft cry came from Emilia's bedroom. "Mommy?"

"Crap," I hissed, throwing back on my sweater and leggings. "I should go check on her. I don't want her to wake up alone in a new place."

Adam nodded. "Go. I'll finish cleaning up here."

I started to argue, but he silenced me with another soft kiss. "Go take care of your girl. I'll be here when you get back."

*****

It didn't take long to soothe Emilia back to sleep, but it was just enough time to get into my mind, second-guessing my every move tonight. Was this a one-time thing? A culmination of the tension that had been simmering between Adam and me since the wedding?

Or—*and possibly even more terrifying*— was this the start of something more? As Emilia released me, slumbering back into a deep sleep, I pulled my arm slowly out from under her and crept toward the door. To my surprise, Adam sat on the couch, studying something on his phone. As soon as he heard me approach, he gave me a bright smile and tucked it back into his pocket. I stepped in front of him, and he placed his hands on the back of my thighs, pulling me into his lap.

"Did she go back down okay?"

I nodded. "Yeah, just a bad dream or something. I rubbed her back for a couple of minutes, and then she was right back out."

"Good," Adam said, tucking some of my hair behind my ear. "And what about you?"

"Me?"

"Yeah, you," he chuckled. "Freaking out on me?"

I thought about lying to him, trying to play it cool when I felt anything but. The truth was, he had tilted my axis, making me see my world through a totally different lens. And for someone who didn't handle change well, there had been a lot today—new temporary address, a new home, and a man looking at me like I was precious to him. While everything was a positive shift, there was no doubt I was starting to panic.

Looking into his ocean-blue eyes, I nodded. "Kind of. Today's been a lot. I'm still trying to wrap my mind around being here, and now, there's you." His hands clenched on my thighs, holding me close even though I was dying to squirm under his stare. "I haven't let someone get this close in a long time, and I'm nervous about what happens next."

"Next..." Adam sighed, dragging his thumbs along my skin, tracing the seam of my leggings. "Next, I think we should spend more time together. Maybe go out on a proper date?"

I smiled wide. "You want to date me, Rice?"

"I want a hell of a lot more than that, trouble."

Words lodged in my throat at his quiet admission, unwilling to voice how much they meant to me. But with the swell of excitement came its friend unease. Worry started to simmer in my stomach, wondering if this was too much too fast. As right as it felt with Adam, I'd been burned before. It was hard to fully trust words when I knew they could change so easily.

As if he knew where my mind had wandered, Adam's fingers found my chin, directing my gaze back to him. "I mean it, Tori. I haven't felt this way about anyone in a long time. But if that's too much for you to handle right now, I can wait."

"Wait?" my voice squeaked, and I hated how weak it sounded.

"Yeah," Adam chuckled. "I'm not a patient man, but I know a good thing when I see it. You're the best thing that has come into my life in a long time. I'm not going anywhere. I'll wait as long as you need."

I swallowed, forcing my fears into the back crevice of my mind. He was baring it all to me; the least I could do was tell him I was in this with him. "I don't want to wait," I whispered. "I want to date you too, Adam."

His resulting smile was the kind poets wrote sonnets about. I didn't think I'd ever had anything so breathtaking aimed at me, and I wanted to bask in its glow for the rest of my days. It was so different than his staged smile, the one I was learning to recognize. It was fine, perfect for presenting a front to the world, but after seeing Adam's true smile, the other was nothing more than a poor facsimile.

As much as I wanted to keep this moment going forever, there was something else we needed to discuss. "What are we going to do about Cole?"

Adam instantly set up straighter. "What about him?"

"I want to wait to tell him," I admitted, shifting so I could look Adam in the eyes. "Not because he should have any impact on our relationship. I'm a grown woman, and my brother does not get to dictate who I can or cannot date. But I want to see what this is before we bring other people into it." I paused, looking up at the half-closed bedroom door. "And I also want to wait to tell Emilia as well."

Adam nodded, but I could see my words struck a nerve. I placed my hand on his cheek and asked, "What's going through your mind?"

"I get it," Adam sighed. "And I agree, especially with Emilia. Once we tell people, there's no going back. And I also want this time, just us, to figure out how we work together." He exhaled slowly. "But it's going to be hard not telling Cole. The guy's my best friend. He deserves to know what's going on before it comes out. I don't want him to think I'm taking advantage of you."

"If anything, I'm taking advantage of you," I chuckled, trying to erase the frown from his face. When it didn't work, I leaned in and pressed a light kiss to his lips. "We'll tell him first. After we decide this works between us."

"Deal," Adam said. "But does that mean I have to keep my distance from you when you're with Emilia? Because I'd like to get to know her better, especially if I'm hoping to be part of her life."

"You want to spend more time with her?"

"Yeah, of course," Adam chuckled. "How else am I going to score more invites to these exclusive tea parties? I have competition now, baby."

"I'd like that," I said. "Maybe we can go apple picking next weekend? Em's been talking about it non-stop since you brought it up at the house."

"It's a date."

TWENTY-SIX

Adam

The following week moved too slowly as I counted down the days until my first date with Tori and Emilia. Our paths crossed countless times, between grabbing meals at the main lodge and hanging out with everyone else, but we hadn't spent any time together since their first night in town.

But every night before my head hit the pillow, Victoria facetimed me, recounting all the details of their day. Everyone in town was dying to get to know Cole's little sister and were even more excited to meet his niece. Emilia was already garnering a fan club led by Marta and Curt. At their insistence, Victoria brought Emilia to the Lost Tavern every afternoon. She'd spend hours being their unofficial hostess, helping out around the dining room while Victoria got to explore the town with Calla and Alex. While she was still getting to know the other women, I could tell she was enjoying her time with them, always recounting some sort of trouble they got into.

My heart warmed every time Tori told me another story, cementing her place in our little town. Without even trying, she was becoming an unofficial member of our community, integrating a little more every single day. And while I loved that she and Emilia were finding their places, I couldn't help but be a little jealous—not only because I'd barely gotten any time alone with them, but also because they had no problem going out into town. As much as I'd chosen this place because it was safe and secluded, I was still hiding. Even when I ventured away from Fox Creek, I was always in my usual disguise, with a baseball cap slung low and dark sunglasses.

Maybe it was time to try something new.

I'd discussed it at length with Dr. Kedir, who was willing to support me in any way possible. We ran through different scenarios and discussed any potential fallout from my actions, and I had to be honest—it helped. As much as I wanted to stick my head in the sand and pretend there wasn't a possibility of my monster returning to haunt me, the truth was, I had no idea what would happen in the future. But by rehearsing every possible path, I felt more at ease and was willing to try, especially if it meant more time with Tori and Emilia.

On the day of our date, I left my hat and sunglasses at home and headed into town to prepare. Gray told me about a little farm about an hour north that had some fantastic orchards and smaller crowds. But first, there was something I wanted to do to make the day a little more special.

I parallel-parked my truck on the main strip of town, taking in the view for a moment before I stepped outside.

With Fall Fest coming up quickly, the whole town was in prep mode. During the next two weeks, Main Street would be transformed into an autumn-themed paradise, complete with a carnival and petting zoo. Locals were on ladders, tying lines of artificial leaves and fairy lights between all the street lamps. On the opposite sidewalks, a couple of the local storefronts were getting their windows painted, creating a landscape of fall colors.

As I walked past the town hall, a line of vendors waited outside, ready to lobby for the best spots for their booths. Everyone wanted to be as close as possible to the town square. Alex and Javi were at the front of the pack and waved as I passed them. The two made an unusual pairing. While Javi was the manager of the Isadora, the high-end resort on one side of town, Alex had a serious grudge against the owner. She'd pulled some shady—*possibly illegal*—actions to try to keep Alex from getting the Fox Creek property. And even though it had worked out in the end, Alex was planning on holding a grudge for the rest of her days. Despite the rivalry between their workplaces, Alex and Javi still managed to stay close friends, and they supported one another at every turn.

Next up was Paddy's Wake, an old Irish bar that had been converted into a beach bar after changing owners. Waving to the owner, Aaron, I laughed as he placed hay bales all over the parking lot. From what Cole told me, everyone was excited about the artisanal beer garden he was setting up, featuring some of the local breweries' upcoming flavors. The energy was almost infectious.

But me?

I just wanted to spend more time with my girls.

Maybe it was too soon to classify them as such, especially Emilia. She already had a dad, but I still wanted some kind of role in her life. From that first scowl, she'd made me laugh with her spunky personality. She was smart and hilarious, pretty much a miniature version of her mother. And considering how much I already cared about Victoria, it was no surprise her daughter had also marked a part of my heart.

I pushed open the door to the flower shop, smiling when I saw the owner, Mags, hiding behind the counter. Her wife, Stephanie, was probably in the greenhouse, checking on all the blooms for the weekend.

Mags smiled when she spotted me. "Mr. Rice, nice to see your whole face. To what do I owe this pleasure?"

I looked over her samplings, but I wasn't quite sure what I was looking for. "I'm taking someone out today, and I wanted to make it special for her."

"Oooh," she called out. "Is this any person or someone special?"

"Someone very special. Actually, two special someones."

Mags scrunched her face, her gray hair sloshing around her shoulders as she shook her head. "I don't want to know. You crazy kids these days. One is never enough for you?"

"It's not like that," I chuckled, holding my hands up. "No offense to those who prefer that type of relationship, but I've only got one girl on my mind. But she also has a daughter, and I want to make the day special for her too."

"Oh, a daughter?" Mags smirked. "Does this have to do with the pretty brunette who's been coming in with Calla all week?"

I shook my head. "I don't kiss and tell, Mags."

"Well, if that is the girl, you're gonna need some help. She's got a good eye for flowers and will know if you cheap out on her."

I leaned forward on the counter. "Good thing I've got the owner here to help, then."

Mags muttered under her breath, something about love-sick fools, as she made her way into the backroom where her wife always tucked some special plants. I could hear bits of their conversation, so I busied myself, looking at all the blooms filling the bins around their tiny space. Under the window, there was an array of rainbow-colored roses, surrounded by bright daisies and every other color you could possibly think of.

"Hey, Mags?" I called out. "Change of plans. I'm actually going to need two bouquets."

AN HOUR after leaving the flower shop, I climbed the stairs at the back of the lodge, trying to keep my nerves under control. It had been years since I was nervous for a date, even longer since I'd gone out of my way to plan something like today. The orchard was a little over an hour away, so I'd stocked the back-seat with all of Emilia's favorite things and snacks.

As I knocked on the door to their apartment, I waited, second-guessing my decision to get flowers. Victoria's bouquet was a masterpiece, filled with flowers I couldn't even name. The pale pink and orange blooms looked great, especially against the pale green eucalyptus leaves. However, the true magnum opus was Emilia's bouquet. It looked like a painted canvas, but only with pinks, purples, and a few blues tucked in between. Hope-fully, they'd both like them.

Did it seem too desperate? Shit, the last girl I bought flowers for was my high school prom date, and that was only because my mom made me.

As my inner panic started to rise, the door swung open, Tori's bright smile waiting on the other side. "Hey, you," she said, pulling me inside. "What do you have there?"

"Oh..." I said, trying to keep my voice steady. "Stopped by the flower shop and grabbed some bouquets for you girls." I passed her the bigger one. "Hope you like them."

"They're gorgeous," Victoria cooed, pressing up on her toes to kiss my cheek. "You didn't have to do that."

"I wanted to. Wanted to make today special for all three of us." I played with the other bunch of flowers in my hand as I looked around the room. "Where's Emilia?"

"In the bathroom," Tori chuckled. "She can't decide which headband looks best with her outfit."

"Good," I muttered as I leaned down to kiss her. "Been wanting to do that for days."

"Tell me about it," she grumbled. "It's so rude that you live 100 feet away, and I've barely seen you all week."

"Agree," I said, pressing another stolen kiss to her lips. "We'll figure something out. Could pull a Rapunzel and climb into your window after Emilia's bedtime."

"She'd probably love that," Tori chuckled. "But pretty sure someone might call the cops if they see you trying to break into our apartment. Besides, the front door works just as well."

"How cliché," I chuckled, taking a sizable step back when the bathroom door pulled open.

"Adam! Adam!" Emilia's dark eyes lit up as she took me in, rushing over to join us. They were almost the size of saucers when she spotted the flowers in my arms. "Are those for Mommy?"

"Nope," I said, leaning down on my knee, "they're for you. I heard a certain little girl loves bright-colored flowers, so I thought I'd bring you some."

"Thank you," she said, smiling brightly up at me. She smelled the blooms then looked up at her mother. "Can I put them in my room?"

"You got it, baby," Victoria said, moving over to her side. "Why don't I take them and put them in a vase, and then we can put them in there later?"

As Victoria worked in the kitchen, Emilia tugged on my hand. "Mommy said you're going to take us to a real a-chad."

"Orchard, hunny," Victoria corrected.

"Orchard," Emilia said, focusing on the word as if it offended her. "And we get to pick all the apples?"

"I don't know about all of them," I chuckled. "But we'll have to work hard if we want to get a lot of apples. Know anyone good at climbing trees?"

"I can do it," she whispered. "I'm the best climber back home. Daddy said so."

"That's a big claim." I smiled at her. "Hope you're ready to prove it."

She nodded with fierce determination. From that nod alone, I had a feeling the world would never be ready for Emilia.

"You know," Victoria said, lowering down to fix her daughter's hair, "maybe if we get enough, we can show Adam that apple pie recipe Grammie taught us. The one with the good crust?"

Her eyes widened in delight. "And make that caramel sauce to go on top?" Tori nodded. Emilia looked up at me. "Let's do this."

TWENTY-SEVEN

Victoria

"Mommy, look at it!"

Emilia danced in her seat as she looked down at the apple cider donut sundae, unsure where even to begin. The plate was the size of her head, with a giant, fresh cider donut on the bottom and two giant scoops of homemade vanilla ice cream on top, drizzled with caramel and an apple pie filling. It was probably more sugar than I should have allowed, but it was a once-in-a-season kind of treat, so I couldn't bring myself to say no. It didn't help that both Emilia and Adam gave me their best pouty faces when they asked if she could have it, Adam already agreeing to help her if she had trouble finishing it.

In truth, nothing could kill the happy glow inside me right now. I'd been excited to spend more time with Adam, but I was also nervous about having him around Emilia. He was a great guy, but it was still nerve-wracking bringing my worlds together. There was no question in my mind—Emilia trumped everyone else. If she didn't like him or was uncomfortable around him, there would be no future for us. She was my whole heart, and I would never risk her happiness for my own.

Luckily, that was far from the case. I couldn't believe it

when we got into the car, finding it ready for Emilia. He'd even picked up a booster seat, the same one Cole had got for his truck.

It only got better when we got to the orchard just after lunchtime. The early fall weather was perfect—just cool enough for long sleeves, but the sun provided a little extra warmth. We'd wandered the rows of trees for hours, filling up our bags as we went. Adam never complained, not even after Emilia climbed onto his shoulders for the fifth time. They got along like two peas in a pod, chatting away excitedly all afternoon. But nothing could top when we finished picking apples and Adam took Emilia over to the petting zoo.

"Are you sure about this?" I asked him, peering down at the different animals. "I can take her through if you want a break."

"No way," he chuckled, squeezing Emilia's hand. "I've been looking forward to this all day. Go rest for a couple of minutes." He leaned in toward my ear, lowering his voice so only I could hear him. "You're going to need it later."

I chewed on my lower lip as they walked away, letting my smile fully bloom. Watching them together, feeding the different goats, soothed something inside of me. Don't get me wrong, Cam was a devoted dad. He spent every free minute with Emilia. They had the kind of relationship I could have only hoped for them to have. But the day-to-day stuff? That was almost always on my shoulders. It was a lot of pressure trying to keep my daughter alive, happy, and entertained all the time, and my heart broke every time I thought I was failing her. Having Adam lighten my load for a few minutes meant a lot to me, and I took the opportunity to breathe fully.

"Mommy!" Emilia called out with a wide smile on her face. "Look! He's tickling my hand."

I moved over to the fence, chuckling as I watched the different goats come up to Emilia. Her palms were filled with pellets as Adam held a full cup, clearly suckered into paying the overpriced fee for the animal feed. As the goats followed her around, Emilia let out a loud chuckle and climbed into Adam's lap. "Save me," she laughed, "They're trying to gobble me up!"

Adam lifted her up, tossing the rest of the food deeper into the pen. "I got you, kiddo. Just hold on tight."

His eyes met mine, and he winked, making my insides turn to mush. All I could do was mouth, "Thank you", but the simple sentiment would never be enough to convey how much I would treasure this moment forever.

My heart filled as I watched them move on to the other animals, snapping pictures on my phone as they went. Emilia giggled the entire time, loving how Adam made up voices for each of the animals.

At the end of their allotted time, when they had to say goodbye to the animals, Emilia wrapped her little arms around Adam. When she asked him to carry her and he eagerly obliged, my heart stalled in my chest. He carried her to each animal one last time, letting her whisper soft goodbyes into their fur and feathers. As she snuggled against his chest, he looked over and grinned at me, and I swear, I almost melted on the spot.

I'd seen many sides of Adam: the sexy, the confident, and the downright swoon-worthy. But this version? The one where he cradled my daughter as if she was his own? He was everything.

"So, which animal did you like the most?" Adam asked, pulling me back into the present. Emilia's spoon paused in the air, bits of ice cream sliding onto the table as she pondered his question.

"Definitely the bunny," she said. "I wanted one, but my mommy said they need room to run around."

"Is that your favorite animal?" he asked.

"Nope," she mumbled as she shoved her whole spoon into

her mouth. "I like ponies. 'Specially the ones that let you braid their hair." She peeked up at him. "What about you?"

"I think dogs are it for me," he said. "I've always wanted one, but with my schedule, I never wanted to leave it alone for too long."

"Maybe you can get it now," Emilia offered. "We can help you! I'd do such a good job walking it and loving it! Right, Mommy?"

"We'll see," I chuckled, pressing a kiss to her brow. "But that's really up for Adam to decide. Dogs are a big commitment."

The conversation died out as Emilia turned all her attention to her dessert, taking bites bigger than what should have been physically possible. I leaned back in my seat, sighing as I took in the rolling hills surrounding us. The colors of the fall were just starting to break out over the mountains, the leaves shifting to shades of red, orange, and yellow. It was beautiful, and I couldn't wait to see all the leaves change back in town. I'd taken Emilia down by the lake a couple of times, but they weren't quite there yet, still hanging on to their summer greens a little bit longer. Not that I could blame them.

"So, trouble," Adam asked. "Put any more thought into that list of yours?"

Emilia looked up at me, her cheeks stuffed with ice cream and toppings. "What list?"

"Take human-sized bites, baby," I said, wiping the excess from around her mouth. "And it's just something Mommy's been thinking about. Some things I want to do before I get too old."

She giggled, but Adam stared at me like he could read my thoughts. He could see I was hiding behind my answer, not wanting my daughter to know there were so many things that scared me. I shifted under the weight of his stare. "I haven't thought about it much."

He shook his head, pointing his spoon in my direction. "Then now is as good a time as any. C'mon, Tor, think of one thing you want to do. It can be something small to start. Maybe something we can all do before you go back home."

My stomach churned at his words. *When we go back home.* Even though we'd only been here for a week, it was already feeling more like home than Texas had in a long time. Maybe it was having our own space or because people were taking so much time to include us, but I was starting to feel like I might belong here. That Emilia and I might belong here.

That was ridiculous. My home was in Texas. *Cam* was in Texas. It wasn't even worth a second thought. *Focus on the now,* I reminded myself. *Enjoy your time while you're here.* Smiling back at Adam, I tried to shove all my negative thoughts back into their box. "I guess if I could do anything, I'd want to travel more. But with us already being here, I can check that off the list."

"Nuh-uh," Adam answered. "That's a cop-out and you know it. I want something specific, Campbell, and make it a good one."

I rolled my eyes and slid my hand over my face. "If I had to think of anything off the top of my head, I guess..." I sighed, looking up at the sky. "All of this talk about horses makes me miss riding. I've always wanted to have one of my own, but they're a lot of work. Maybe I could look into riding while I'm here."

Adam smiled. "Atta, girl. Was that so hard?"

Yes, it was. It was hard to voice my random dreams out loud, taking something so abstract and making it more concrete. If you never put your dreams into words, then you won't be disappointed if they never come true.

"I think you should do it, Mommy," Emilia said, pushing the half-eaten plate toward Adam.

"Maybe, baby. We'll have to see."

"What else?" Adam asked, diving into Emilia's leftovers.

"I'm not sure."

He paused, watching me. "I'm giving you until the end of the week to come up with two more things. No excuses, trouble."

I let out a bark of laughter. "Are you giving me homework, Rice?"

"Yup," he answered with a sly smirk. "Gotta make sure you're keeping up with this list. Don't want you slacking on me."

I rolled my eyes, but I couldn't help my smile. The fact that Adam wanted me to achieve my dreams meant a lot. For so long, I'd had these daydreams, thoughts about what I would do if I ever got free time again, but I always convinced myself that other things were more important. Something about telling Adam my dreams made them come to life, like he'd stop at nothing to make sure they came true.

Emilia hopped off the picnic table, rushing over to Adam's side. "Can I add something to Mommy's list?"

He nodded, "I think that's a great idea." She smiled, tugging the arm of his sweater until she was able to whisper in his ear. When she finished, Adam was beaming at me. "That is a great addition. You know, you're pretty awesome, kid."

She shrugged her shoulders, proudly smiling at me. "I know."

"Don't I get to know what you're adding to my list?"

"Nope," Emilia said.

I glanced at Adam, hoping for some backup, but he just smirked at me. "Trust me, trouble. It'll be worth the wait."

TWENTY-EIGHT

It was dark by the time we got back into town. The highway was quiet as we drove through the mountains, making the sights around us more serene and quiet. Emilia drifted off almost as soon as we left the orchard, her belly full after all the apples and treats she'd consumed during the afternoon.

I smiled as I spotted her slouched over in her seat, unable to keep the happiness off my face. Truth be told, today was the best day I'd had in a long time. It wasn't because of the orchards, or the animals, or even the ridiculous amount of sugar I'd consumed. Nope. It had everything to do with the two girls in my car and how I felt around them.

Every moment I spent with Tori and Emilia, I wanted a hundred more. I was becoming a greedy, selfish man when it came to them, and I couldn't bring myself to care. Where normally, I'd be itching for space after spending the entire day with someone, instead, I was already dreading when we'd separate for the night.

I stole another glance at Victoria and Emilia. How in the hell had I gotten so lucky? It wasn't the first time I'd thanked my luck, but in the past, it was usually because of my career.

Acting was a difficult way to make a living, and for every person who got their big break, hundreds were waiting for their moment. I was one of the fortunate who had met the right people, been in the right place at the right time. And as hard as I worked for my success, I'd have to be delusional not to thank my luck.

But sitting here, watching as Emilia slept in the backseat and Tori hummed along with the radio, this simple moment surpassed any role I could have earned. As much as I missed acting, if I screwed this up, I knew I'd miss moments like this more.

"What was your favorite part of the day?" Tori asked, a small smile playing on her face.

"Mrs. Campbell, is that you?" I teased, remembering the way her mother used to start every meal with the same question. "I'm having flashbacks to all those Sunday dinners at your house growing up."

"You know, I thought it was so lame when I was a kid." Tori glanced in the rearview mirror. "But once Em started getting bigger, I found myself doing the same thing." She shifted her smile to me. "Guess we really do become our parents."

"That wouldn't be the worst thing," I chuckled. "Except for the farming part. I'd be a disaster."

"Probably," she laughed. "Remember when you tried to help my mom with her garden?"

"It's not my fault I don't have a green thumb." I reached over and took her hand in mine. "But to answer your question, I can't choose one moment. The whole day was pretty damn perfect." I lifted her knuckles to my lips. "And it's not even over yet."

"Oh yeah?" Tori asked, shifting to face me fully. "And what are the plans for the rest of the night?"

"That's up to you," I said seriously. "I don't want to intrude on your space with Emilia, especially before she knows we're more than friends. But if you'd like, I could come over after bedtime..."

"And have a repeat of the other night?"

"Maybe even more, if you're into it."

"God, yes," she sighed. "I'd really like that."

"Yeah?" I questioned, releasing her hand to flicker the blinker, turning into the guest lot for Fox Creek. As I pulled into a space, I leaned in closer to her. "You're feeling a little needy, baby?"

"You have no idea," she groaned. "We fooled around once, and I'm pretty sure you've already ruined me."

I chuckled, looking down at our joined hands. She had no idea how true that was. From the moment our lips touched, Victoria was the only one I wanted. I smiled as I looked over at her, running my free fingers along her jawline. "Just returning the favor."

As I reached out to open the door, I turned to face the front of the lodge, hissing a sharp curse when I saw we weren't alone. Cole stood on the porch, his forearms resting on the wooden railing. While he wasn't looking in our direction, unease crawled down my spine. *Did he see us?* As much as I was dying to tell him about my relationship with Tori, this wasn't the way I wanted him to find out. That conversation needed to be in the light of day, and if he didn't take it well, I didn't want it attached to the memory of today.

Besides, Tori wasn't ready. As much as I wanted to tell him the truth, I'd respect her wishes and keep it between us until she was comfortable sharing our news.

I gave Tori a sympathetic smile, sure her anxiety was probably skyrocketing at the sight of him. "How do you want to do this, Tor?"

She chewed on her lower lip, looking at Emilia snoring softly in the backseat. "We're just hanging out," she said out loud, but it sounded more like she was comforting herself. "There's nothing wrong with that. We'll tell him the truth."

"The truth, huh?" I sighed, clenching my hand over the wheel. "Can I call him a cock-block, because all I've thought about all day is having you at my mercy?"

I smirked as I glanced over at Tori, loving the blush filling her cheeks. It wasn't as bright as usual, not with our only light being the overhead beacons above the parking lot. Shit, I hated the idea of calling it a night, but there was no way I'd be able to explain hanging out in Tori's apartment after dark. "C'mon," I said. "I'll walk you two inside."

Tori sighed, shifting her purse into her lap. "Maybe you should just go to your cabin, and I'll deal with him."

"Nope. Don't like the sound of that one bit." I shook my head before nodding to the backseat. "Plus, there's no way you can carry her."

"I can do it," she answered. "Who do you think usually carries her to bed?"

I cringed at the thought, not wanting to watch Tori struggle to get her daughter inside. Sure, Cole would be more than willing to help, but my pride wouldn't let him. The whole day, I'd gotten a taste of life with these two, and I wasn't ready to drop the fantasy just yet.

"Not gonna happen," I insisted. "Let me at least take her inside, and then you can hang with your brother." I leaned forward, reaching up to run my thumb along her cheekbone. "Just know I'll be thinking about you all night."

She let out a sharp hiss. "You have no idea how much I want to kiss you right now."

Oh, I knew damn well. It was taking everything in me not to claim her lips right now, audience be damned. But not until she wanted to tell Cole the truth. I brushed my thumb along her plush lower lip, lowering my voice. "Whenever you're ready, just say the word."

AFTER BRINGING EMILIA UPSTAIRS, I insisted on tucking her into bed myself. Sure, Cole had given me a strange look, probably trying to connect the dots on why I was spending so much time with his sister and niece. For a moment, I thought about handing her over to him, but then her hand curled around my shoulder, holding me a little tighter, like she also wasn't ready to let me go. There was no way I'd pass her off after that.

Tori insisted she could sleep in her day clothes and that she'd change her later when she got up to use the bathroom, so I set her on her princess bed, tucking the fluffy purple comforter up under her chin. As I stroked a couple of stray hairs away from her face, Emilia's eyes blinked open, smiling up at me. "Thanks, Adam."

"Any time, kiddo."

"Today was the bestest day ever," she yawned. "Can we go back again?"

I smiled brightly down at her. "Just say the word, and I'll be happy to pick more apples with you."

She grinned as she snuggled back into her bed, her breathing getting heavier before I even got to the door. As soon as I pulled it mostly shut, I turned back into the living room, catching the end of a conversation between Cole and Tori. Her face was scrunched, like he'd said something that upset her, and for the first time in a long time, I wanted to punch him in the jaw. I moved closer to Tori's side. "You okay?"

"Yup," she said as she smiled tightly up at me. "Cole was just talking to me about the Fall Fest. He wants me to come help at the Fox Creek booth."

Cole sighed, running his hand through his hair. "Look if you don't want to—"

"I think you should," I answered, looking at Tori. Her brow scrunched at me, trying to understand my reasoning. "Everyone's been talking about the Fall Fest and how much fun it's going to be. Maybe you should go, help Cole and Alex for a bit, and then you can enjoy the rest of it with Emilia."

"We'd really like that," Cole added. "Marta would be more than happy to watch Emilia until you're done."

"Or I could do it."

Both Campbells turned to look at me, but their looks were drastically different. Cole stared at me like he was looking at a stranger while Tori was trying to fight a grin. I focused more on her, wanting to make sure she knew my offer was genuine. "We'll spend some time here, and then I'll bring her over when you're ready. Besides, Marta and pretty much everyone else we know is going to be running a booth. I've got nothing else going on, and I'd much rather be hanging out with Em than be by myself in my cabin."

"Are you sure?" Tori asked, shifting closer to me on instinct. I loved that she needed to be near me, her feet moving with a mind of their own. "She can be a lot of work, and I don't want to ask too much of you."

"You're not asking, I'm offering."

She sighed, glancing between me and Cole, who was still watching me like he'd missed something.

And he had.

He'd missed that I was falling for his sister and, by extension, her daughter. I wanted to be the one they called, the one who helped when Tori needed someone. I wanted to be everything for her.

"You don't have to give me an answer tonight. Think about

it and let me know." I smiled down at Tori. "You know where to find me."

I walked over to the door, clapping Cole on the shoulder as I passed. If I stayed another minute longer, I'd probably do something stupid, like confess to my best friend that I wanted him to leave so I could do unspeakable things to his sister. The only choice was to head out, even though every fiber of my being was fighting every step.

"Hold up," Cole called out. "Let me walk you out."

Oh, fuck.

TWENTY-NINE

Adam

Cole said nothing as we walked outside the back door. I tried to talk to him about his booth for Fall Fest, but all I got back were grunts. Not a good sign. The angrier Cole felt, the fewer syllables he used. Now that we were down to single digits, I was royally fucked.

As I imagined which method of torture Cole was planning for me, we stepped outside into the crisp autumn air. It had dropped several degrees since the sunset, and there was a chill in the breeze that wasn't there before. Or was it my nerves playing tricks on me? It should have been soothing, but it didn't feel that way, not when my best friend was staring at me like he could read every thought I had about his sister.

He followed after me, walking over to the porch swing in the corner. He dropped down on the red cushion and looked out at all the cabins. Maybe I could make a run for it and make it back to mine before he caught up.

Just as I was about to take my chances, Cole sighed, rubbing his hand along the back of his head. "Look, man, you don't have to do this."

I stared at him, trying to comprehend what he was talking about. "What do you mean?"

"I know I asked a lot of you when Tori first came to town, wanting you to keep an eye on her. And that..." He sighed, shifting so his hands were clenched in front of him. "That was unfair of me. She's my sister, and Emilia's my niece. They're my responsibility, so don't feel like you have to look out for them just for my sake."

I could have laughed at his admission, but seeing his face, I knew that would be the wrong answer. Here I was, being the worst friend on the face of the planet, and he wanted to talk to me because he thought he'd asked too much. It would have been so easy to tell him the truth, that seeing them was the best part of my days, that I'd gladly give up everything and more if it meant spending more time with Victoria and Emilia. Spending time with her might have started off as a favor to Cole, but it was the best thing to happen to me in years.

I shook my head. "Nah, you're good. I like hanging out with them. Tori's awesome, and Emilia's funny as hell. I like helping out when I can."

Cole inhaled slowly as he leaned back in his seat, crossing his arms over his chest. "Appreciate it, man. You know there aren't many people I trust with my family, and you're at the top of that list."

Guilt ate through my chest, wanting nothing more than to stop him. Maybe his trust was misplaced, but I couldn't bring myself to believe that. My intentions were good with Tori, more than they'd ever been in the past. And maybe I was diving in too fast, head first, but I didn't know any other way to be around her. But just because I knew I wanted more than a fling with Tori didn't mean Cole would believe me.

He shifted, sighing as he looked at the closed door. "I'm glad they have you. With Tori, I feel like we're still walking on broken glass. One misstep, and all our progress is going to be for nothing. And now, I have even more to lose." He pinched his brow. "I keep trying to make things right, but I'm fucking up at every turn."

"You're not fucking up." I sighed. "Tori's here, and this time, she brought Emilia. You're getting to see them every day, getting to know your sister in a brand new way."

"What are you trying to tell me, Adam?"

"I'm telling you to get the hell out of your head," I said. "You're so worried about messing up that you're keeping your distance. Besides that first night, how many nights have you come over alone? Not with Alex, not with Marta, just you?" His frown was all the answer I needed. "Stop worrying about making a mistake and just enjoy this time with them. That's all they need. You've come so fucking far, man. How do you not see that?"

He exhaled slowly. "I do. I know I'm doing better, and I'm so damn grateful for all the support I have. But that darkness is still in there, Adam. And I'm always afraid. *Always*. I'm afraid something's gonna come along and rip this moment right out of my hands, like I don't deserve it after everything I put you all through."

I placed my hand on his shoulder, looking him directly in the eye. "You gotta stop punishing yourself for your past, Cole. None of us know what's coming tomorrow. All we can do is make the most of what's in front of us. Right here, right now. Your sister and niece are upstairs; that's what matters. *They* are what matters."

He let out a dry chuckle. "Shit, you're right."

"Why do you sound surprised?"

I expected him to join me in laughter, but instead, his stern gaze whipped to me. "And what about you?"

"What about me?" I shrugged.

"You're giving great advice, but when are you going to take it?"

I choked on my spit, hating being called out on my hypocrisy. For months, I'd been just as stuck as he was, letting something lurking in my past take the joy out of my present. And while it still stung in the back of my mind, I was trying to move forward, especially with Tori. But Cole wouldn't know that.

"I'm working on it," I mumbled, looking down at my shoes. "It's easier to give advice than to take it."

"Yeah, no shit," Cole chuckled. "But you're slowly coming back to yourself. You think we don't notice, but we do. It's been nice to see you come out and join us in the real world again."

"You missed me, buddy?"

"Don't make it fucking weird." Cole smirked. "But yeah, man, we all did. Whatever you're doing that's putting that smile back on your face, don't let it go."

I grinned to myself, knowing he'd probably hate me if he knew what exactly was making me so happy now. But instead of destroying the moment, I just nodded. "Trust me, I don't intend to."

LATER THAT NIGHT, as I lay in my bed, I stared up at the ceiling, trying to forget Cole's words. He was right—in many ways, I was pushing him to face his fears while I was still hiding from mine. I mean, shit, I acted like it was the end of the world to take off my hat and sunglasses and walk into town. After months of therapy, I thought I was making progress, but looking at it now, it seemed like I was barely treading water. Even Dr. Kedir seemed to be on Cole's side. While I was taking small steps toward reclaiming my life, I was hesitant to step out of the comfort of my routine.

At least, until Victoria stepped into my life.

Being around her, pushing her to face her fears and reclaim some of her dreams, made me want to do the same. Maybe my dreams looked different than they had last year, but they were there. I just needed to push myself to chase them.

I sat up in bed, running my hand over my face. My reflection stared out at me, watching over the dresser as I pondered my next steps. All my life, I was told I was brave, too easygoing to ever let something get me down. And maybe part of that was true, but in reality, I'd never really had to overcome anything I couldn't handle. Moving to LA was scary, but I'd done it without hesitation. Helping Cole with his sobriety was challenging and heartbreaking, but I never doubted he could do it. So why was I so quick to cower when an unseen force decided I was theirs to claim?

"Fuck it," I hissed, climbing out of my bed. I wandered into the kitchen, grabbing a glass before filling it up with water from the sink. As I sipped it, I stared out the window, instantly checking the apartment above the lodge. Most of the lights had turned off hours ago, but one was on in the living room. Knowing Victoria, she was probably reading in her favorite armchair, tired but unwilling to give up those couple of hours of silence. Fuck, it was so tempting to go over there. When I was around her, all my problems seemed to disappear. She could soothe my fears with just her presence. But as much as I wanted the escape, that was me being selfish, especially when Emilia was asleep in the next room.

Turning around, my eyes found the small table on the side of the room. The pile of scripts was tucked against the wall, gathering dust each day. Without thinking, I stepped forward, finding the project that had been lurking in my mind. Thumbing through the pages once more, I started to imagine the scenes, to picture my marks and how I would play off my co-star. It was different from most of my other roles, grittier, darker, and that called to me, especially after the past year. I wasn't the same guy who signed up for a multi-movie superhero franchise, and I didn't want to play the same characters either.

Reading through the pages, mouthing the words to myself, I could feel it: the magic that lit my fire when I found a good project. My gut reaction hadn't failed me before, and maybe it was time to trust it again. I walked back into the bedroom, dropping the script onto the bed before grabbing my phone from its charger. I pulled up my last conversation with Theo, snapping a picture of the script and sending him a message before I could back out.

ME

This dark cowboy project—is it still on the table?

THEO

Who is this?

ME

Seriously, Theo?

THEO

I'm waiting.

ME

The only person who knows you cry when reading sappy romance movie scripts.

THEO

Not anymore. Calla also finds it profusely funny.

ME

Did I pass your test?

THEO

Had to make sure. Didn't think this text would
ever come, so wanted to make sure I had the
right guy.

As for the project, it's still on the table. You
were their first choice, but with you not
interested, they're holding casting calls in a
couple of weeks.

Want me to get you on the list?

I paused, staring at my phone. Was I really doing this? There was no way it was a coincidence that the letters and messages stopped when I stepped out of the spotlight. Would they begin again if I got this role? If my face was suddenly back in the news?

I shook my head, running my hand over my face. It was just a goddamn audition. I didn't have the part; there was no telling if I'd even get it, or if I even knew what the fuck I was doing anymore. I'd taken so much time off, I might have forgotten how to step into a role and make it my own.

My fingers tapped on the screen, following through, even though my head was still playing twenty-questions.

ME

Yeah, if you could. Not saying I'd take it even if
I got it, but I'd like to at least read

THEO

You got it. I'll let you know when I have a date

I stared at my phone, clutching the device in my hand as if it had a ticking clock attached. For months, I'd been avoiding this moment, terrified of what would come if I decided to take on another role.

But I'd been hiding long enough.

Now, I just had to hope there wouldn't be any consequences.

THIRTY

Victoria

The morning after our apple-picking date, I sipped my coffee, staring out across the field at Adam's cabin. Emilia happily played with her dolls on the living room floor next to me, and I had a chance to breathe before starting my day. I usually loved mornings like this. However, today, I couldn't help the sigh that escaped my lips.

Yesterday was one of the best days of my life. I couldn't remember the last time I laughed that much or the last time I felt like there could be more to my life than just being a mom. And even though Emilia was an equal part of our day, Adam found small moments to connect with me and make sure I knew he was thinking about me just as much as I was him.

But then, it all came crashing down when Cole showed up. I hated that I resented his presence, even for a few moments, but he'd definitely put a damper on my plans for the night. I couldn't even blame Adam for leaving; it was the right call. Even after a full day of brewing tension between us, Cole would have asked questions if Adam had hung around.

I groaned, squeezing my brow between my fingers. While I was still nervous about what Cole would say if he found out I was dating Adam, this secret was beginning to get to me. I hated having to think about every action, to fear that someone would pick up on the mounting tension between us. Deciding to keep it from my daughter was one thing; she shouldn't have to worry about her parents' dating lives until it became serious. But I wanted to be able to hold Adam's hand in public and not be afraid that it would get back to my brother.

Through the window, I glanced across the field, finding Adam's cabin. At this hour, he was probably sleeping. It was tempting to cross the lawn and go to him, to throw myself into his arms, but that would have to wait until we eventually got a moment alone.

"Mommy?" Emilia's voice called out. "Can you come play with me?"

"Of course, baby." I smiled, leaving my coffee on the table next to her. She passed one of her dolls to me before resuming brushing the other's hair. "So..." I said, trying to appear more casual than I felt. "What did you think about our day with Adam yesterday?"

"It was awesome!" she squealed, smiling back up at me. It struck me then how much her face had changed in the last few months. She'd lost the roundness in her cheeks, and there were two gaps where her little bottom baby teeth used to reside. She was growing up in front of my eyes, and soon enough, she'd be too cool for moments like this with her mother. I pulled her into a side hug, dropping a kiss to the top of her head. She squirmed under my hold. "Mommy! You're squeezing me."

"I'm sorry," I chuckled. "I'm just happy you had fun yesterday. I think Adam really liked hanging out with us."

"Do you think he'll come over again?"

"Adam?" She nodded. "I'm sure he will. Would you like that?"

"Yup," she said, standing up to survey all her toys. "He's funny, and you smile a lot when he's here."

My brow furrowed as I looked at her. "What do you mean?"

She let out a dramatic sigh, placing her hands on her hips. "Like this," she grumbled, giving me the biggest smile she could form.

I couldn't help but laugh. God, this girl might be the death of me in her teenage years, but hopefully, she'd use her powers for good later in life. "You think he makes me happy?"

She shrugged. "I think so. And he looks at you a lot. Like you're the prettiest girl in the whole world."

My face flustered at her words, both hating and loving that she'd picked up on his looks. As much as I tried to keep this burgeoning thing between us, it was hard to contain my joy when I was in Adam's presence. And the fact that he looked at me like I was someone important to him? That meant more than I could even put into words.

A knock came on the door, and I called out for them to come in without worrying who it was. We'd had a pretty steady stream of visitors since our arrival. Secretly, I was hoping it'd be Adam, but he was always good about texting me first thing in the morning to see how I slept. Since I hadn't received a text yet, I had to assume he was still sleeping.

"Hey," Cole called out, holding up bags from the bakery in town. The smell of cinnamon and sugar made my mouth instantly water. "Stopped by Poppy's to grab a couple of things, and she said these were your favorites. Hope you don't mind the early morning visit."

"Only if you don't have an almond bear claw in there."

He tugged out one of the pastries, holding it out for me. "C'mon, Tor, you think I have a death wish?"

I hurried over to the kitchen, grabbing a couple of plates before sneaking a peek into his bag. Emilia tugged on the hem of my sweater, hoping for a special treat of her own. Cole must have done something to get on Poppy's good side, because there were almost a dozen sugar cookies in the shape of a cat, dusted with purple edible sand on the bottom.

Her eyes widened into the size of saucers. "Are those for me?"

"You bet, Ems," Cole chuckled, pulling her into a hug. "You think I'd stop by here without something special for my favorite girl?"

She looped her little arms around his neck, hugging him so tightly, his face turned a little red. But he didn't let go until she dropped her hands, squirming for him to put her down.

"Only one!" I called out, sure the parenting police were going to come for me if I gave her too many cookies for breakfast. "We can save the rest for later."

"Okay, Mommy," she huffed, rushing back to play with her dolls.

As she played on the floor of the living room, Cole leaned forward onto the counter. "She seems to be doing really well here."

"She's a trooper," I sighed. "She misses Cam, but she's also used to these long stretches. He facetimes her from the locker room every night, telling her she's his good luck charm."

"I like that," Cole said. "He seems like a good guy." He sipped his coffee, looking down at the lid as he asked his next question. "No chance of that becoming something again?"

I almost choked on my coffee. Even if there were lingering feelings between Cam and me, they would have been squashed the first moment I kissed Adam. He had bulldozed his way into my heart, not leaving room for any other man to lay claim to it. But since I'd stupidly decided to keep that from my brother, I couldn't tell him.

"Nope," I answered. "We're good as friends and co-parents.

It wasn't some drawn-out or dramatic break-up. We both knew it wasn't working and decided to end it before things got worse. Sure, it hurt like hell at first, but it's what was right for us." I stared out at my daughter. "And it was right for her. I'll always love him for giving me the greatest gift, but I haven't been in love with him for a long time."

He smirked as he stared at me. I scrunched my nose, feeling awkward under his watchful eye. "What? Do I have crumbs on my face?"

"Nah, nothing like that," Cole answered. "I was just thinking how fucking proud I am of you, Tori. I haven't told you that enough, but I am."

I cleared my throat, trying to hide the way my eyes started to well. "Thanks, Cole."

Tense silence brewed between us for a moment, both of us staring at the little girl on the floor like she was a buffer. Finally, Cole leaned in. "What do you have planned today?"

"Not too much. I have a test coming up this week for Econ. I'm taking a light course load this semester because I only have a few classes left, but I don't want my grades to slip this close to the end. Probably just studying and hanging out with Em." I arched my brow. "Why?"

"I was thinking we could do something, just the two of us. Alex is downstairs with Calla and Marta, and they offered to spend the day with Emilia, maybe get some of the baking done for breakfast tomorrow."

"Oh!" I said, chewing on my lower lip. I was torn about what to do. Since I'd stepped foot into town, Cole and I had spent little time alone, always having someone else join us, whether it was Emilia, Alex, or Adam. In truth, I was nervous, not sure if this weird tension between us would just continue to rise or if we'd finally be able to move past it.

Adam's words played out in my mind, reminding me to be

brave. I came here to spend time with Cole, and so far, I'd made every excuse in the book not to. My days had been filled with familiar faces in town, and my nights were consumed by the handsome face of the actor next door. But if I ever wanted to make amends with Cole, I had to start somewhere, and he was here, begging for a piece of my time.

I nodded. "I'd like that. What were you thinking?"

His smile was wide as he looked back at me, "How do you feel about an old-fashioned fishing competition like when we were kids?"

I rolled my eyes as I took a giant bite of my treat. Fishing competitions were how my dad solved most disagreements between us, from who got to pick dinner to the one who had to help do the dishes after Thanksgiving. He'd take us out to a little pond in the back of their property, hand us a Styrofoam cup full of worms, and leave us to it. Whoever caught the most by night-fall was declared the winner.

It had been years since I'd been out, no longer able to visit that spot once I'd kicked Cole out of my life. But the idea of capturing that youthful magic made me smile.

"You're on."

THIRTY-ONE

Victoria

"You've been practicing."

Cole huffed at my side, watching as I reeled in another small bass on my line. I smirked as I pulled the hook from its mouth, posing for a picture with Cole's phone. It was my fifth today, trumping his measly two.

"Don't be jealous, big brother," I teased. "Not everyone can have natural talent like me."

He cursed under his breath, but I could see the corners of his mouth tick up. In fact, I'd seen him smile more today than I had in years, and it soothed my damaged heart that I was the cause of it.

Our first hour together was awkward, and the air was stifled with tension. Although neither of us was willing to talk about the past, it was still a barrier between us, our last conversation little more than a band-aid on a gaping wound. But as the sun rose in the sky and our reels caught tension, it started to lessen. When I caught my first fish in almost a decade, I let out a care-free laugh and wrapped my arms around his waist. He stilled at first, as if he wasn't sure he should hug me back. But with a relieved sigh, he held me close, tucking me into the crook of his shoulder like he did when we were young.

From that moment, we laughed freer and talked about our lives without the pain of the past clouding our memories. It was strange; every time I thought I'd let go of my resentment toward Cole, it seemed like another layer was hiding, lying dormant until something snapped one of my triggers. Then, memories of abandonment and pain would overtake me, making it almost hard to look at the man responsible.

But I was tired of letting my fears control me, letting them define my relationship with Cole. He was my family, and despite our rocky history, he was still here, standing next to me without a sign of wavering. Even after all this time, he'd started to be my river again, a constant strength I could pull from, even after our time apart. While I might not need him now like I did back then, I had to admit, it was good to know he'd be there.

"Whatcha thinking over there, trouble?" he asked, smirking over at me as I picked up my rod.

I cleared my throat, looking out over the lake instead of at Cole. "I missed this," I whispered. "Hanging out, just you and me."

"Me too," he sighed. He held his hand out, taking my reel from me and motioning for me to follow him out of the water. As our feet hit the rocky shores, he turned toward me, his face now carved out of granite. "Look, Tor, about what happened—"

"We don't need to go back there," I said quickly, not wanting to let those memories taint this day.

"That's the thing—we do," Cole said firmly. "We keep dancing around this issue, and it's making things harder between us. I keep thinking, if we don't talk about what happened, then we can just move on." He looked up at me, his similar dark eyes piercing into mine. "But that's not how it works. We can't keep pretending, not if we want to move on to better things. So please, Tori. Please, let me apologize to you."

I let out a dry chuckle. "Pulling the please card on me? You must be serious."

"Just wait; my next move was pulling out the recovery card. You do know that making amends is step number eight, right?" I laughed, but there was only seriousness looking back at me. I nodded, letting him continue. Cole led me over to a picnic table on the edge of the beach, sitting on top while I settled on the bench.

"I don't even know where to start," he said quietly, wringing his hands together. "When I came home from the hospital, I was so lost. I wanted nothing more than to hide myself away and lose all the memories that plagued me. And then, there was you, always trying to make me smile and reminding me of who I used to be. As much as I wanted to be that guy, I wasn't anymore. I'd seen too much."

He sighed, staring out at the sky as if it held all the answers. "There was one night when I went out with some of my friends from high school."

I nodded, remembering that night all too well. It was the first time Cole had stumbled home wasted, crashing into almost every piece of furniture as he tried to navigate back to his room. Hearing the noise, I got nervous and went to help, but he pushed me away, snarling about not needing my help. Cole had never talked to me like that before, and it cut deep, leaving behind a scar that lingered to this day.

"I should never have gone," Cole continued. "I knew those guys were bad news, but they didn't care about me. They didn't want me to work through things or make myself better. They were just looking for someone else to join their ring of misery. And I was, Tori. I was so fucking miserable, and it was almost comforting to be around them. To not have to think, to not have to remember what a fuck up I was."

"You're not a fuck-up," I said, lifting to my feet.

"Yes, I was," Cole insisted. "And the worst part was, I didn't care about that. I just wanted to feel numb. And then, when a couple of drinks turned into a whole bottle, I still couldn't muster enough energy to care. I was chasing oblivion. And when all you want is the darkness, you start to resent the light."

He reached out and took my hand. "You've always been that, trouble. The light to my dark. The good, strong daughter with an even stronger heart. I resented you because I knew if you were in my position, you wouldn't have failed. You would have fought and would never have stopped until you felt whole again. And I failed. Failed you, failed everyone who cared about me."

"Don't say that."

"It's the truth." Cole blinked up at me, tears filling his dark eyes. "In my mind, you were better off without me. So I kept pushing until you snapped, and all I could think was good; now, she can live in the sunshine without me pulling her down anymore."

I shook my head. "That wasn't what I wanted. Never did. You know how much it hurt to cut you off? How much it killed me to know I wouldn't have you in my life?" Anger I'd tried to bury now broke free, letting loose years of hurt feelings. "You had everything, Cole! And you were too damn stubborn to see it." I turned around, wrapping my hands around my waist. "You were my hero, Cole, even after you came home. I could see how much you were hurting, and all I wanted was to help. Then you kept pushing me away, and still, I kept coming back, hoping I would see a glimpse of my brother again."

I sniffled, turning to face him, hating the look of defeat on his face. But he was right—there was no going back, not after we'd already started exposing our wounds. If we didn't say everything, then they would just continue to fester, causing an even bigger divide between us. "When I found out I was pregnant, you were one of my first calls. Mom and Dad were so disappointed in me, and all I wanted was for you to say I'd be okay. That I could do this." I shook my head. "Do you even remember my call?"

He sucked in a sharp breath before shaking his head. I scoffed. "That's what I thought. That was the moment I decided I was done. Not for me. I would have kept fighting for you, kept pushing you to get help, no matter the cost." I held my hand to my heart. "Except for her. Emilia was the reason I had the strength to walk away. Because I knew if you ever hurt her, I'd never be able to look at you again."

"I'm glad you did," Cole said. "You were just a kid, Tor. You never should have had to deal with any of that. And I wish I was a stronger man and had gotten help the first time you offered it."

"Why didn't you?" I cried. "Why wasn't it enough to make you stop?"

Cole cursed under his breath. "I wish I knew, Tor. I wish more than anything that I had a perfect answer for you, but I don't." He exhaled and stepped forward. "But know this: there has not been a minute when I haven't wanted to make amends with you, to apologize for being a shitty excuse of a brother. To be a part of your life again."

"You didn't say anything."

"I couldn't," he answered. "At first, it was the shame, not wanting to face the horrible things I'd done. And then, I didn't want to push you, not until you were ready."

"I want to be," I admitted. "I see how much you've changed, how great you're doing here. All I want is to be able to forgive you." I blinked, trying to push my tears away. "But there's a small part of me that can't let go, and I'm afraid it's going to ruin things between us."

Cole stepped forward, pulling me into a hug. "It won't. As much as I wish we could snap our fingers to go back to before, it doesn't work like that. Forgiveness takes time, and I'm going to put in the work to earn your trust back. Don't worry about how long it takes. I'm not going anywhere."

I sniffled, burying my face further into his shirt. "When did you get so smart?"

"I've had a lot of sins to atone for, Tori, and there's a strong chance I'll make more mistakes along the way. But all I'm asking is for you to talk to me. Give me a chance to be there for you again."

"I can do that."

He smiled against the crown of my head. After a long hug, he pulled back, searching my face for any sign of distress. "Love you, little sister."

"Love you too, big brother."

I pushed away, wiping my tears on the back of my hand. As much as it hurt to dig through our painful history, there was a part of me that felt lighter than I had in years. I'd been putting so much pressure on myself to completely forgive Cole and ignore any negative emotions for fear of making things worse between us. But Cole was right—there was no way we could heal if we didn't face the things that haunted us.

For a moment, I was tempted to tell him about Adam, to expose the final secret lingering between us. But as much as I appreciated my brother, he didn't have a place in my relationship. If we were going to take this step, Adam needed to have input to decide if he was ready to talk to his best friend.

As I thought about Adam, all I wanted was to be near him, to feel his skin on mine. I turned to Cole, trying to hide my excitement. "So, can we agree I won?"

"Obviously," Cole snorted. "What's your price?"

I chewed on my lower lip, playing with an idea in my head. "I want to ask a favor, but you can't ask any questions."

"Which immediately makes me want to ask questions."

I rolled my eyes. "I'm serious."

"Fine," Cole huffed. "What are you thinking?"

"Can you take Emilia for the night? She's been begging for a sleep-over at your house all week, and I think tonight's a good time for one."

"And you'll be..."

"Somewhere that is none of your business."

Sitting on the back porch of my cabin, I watched as the sun set over the hills. The entire day, I'd been on edge, wondering what had happened between Victoria and Cole. When she first sent me a text saying he was taking her fishing, I was elated; it later turned to anxiety as the time kept on ticking.

What if they argued? Would Victoria want to leave? As much as I told myself I was worth sticking around for, it still nagged in the back of my mind.

Because there was no question in my mind—I was falling for Victoria. Every moment I spent with her only added to my desire to be close to her. She'd roped me in with her sweet smile, but there was so much more to her than that. She understood me in a way other people hadn't before. Being around her, and being around Emilia, made me want to be the man they saw, the one they looked at with light in their eyes.

After half-living in the shadows, being around Victoria and Emilia was like a light in the darkness, twin beacons leading me back to where I belonged.

That became even clearer after my phone call with Dr. Kedir earlier in the day. Even though my next appointment wasn't scheduled until the middle of the week, she always insisted I call her if I was struggling. And while I'd never taken her up on it before, I needed her quiet confidence to talk me through all the major changes in my life.

As we talked about my decision to step back into acting, Dr. Kedir started asking about my plans for the future. As I pondered returning to New York, every inch of my body tensed, unwilling to even entertain the thought.

Due to the nomadic nature of my job, I'd never given too much thought to the idea of settling down. For the past few years, I'd bounced around to different sets, and during the promotional period, I'd spend weeks on the road for premieres and press circuits. But now that I'd started to plant some roots, the idea of a true home was incredibly appealing. I wanted somewhere I could grow into, a place to call my own, away from the rest of the world.

I'd always assumed it would be a city or town that called to me, begging me to make it my home. However, now, home didn't make me think of a place I could point to on a map. No, it made me think of Victoria and Emilia. There was nothing that compared to the way I felt when I was around them.

Everything else was just window dressing.

Now, I just had to make sure Victoria was on the same page.

Even though she'd opened up to me, there was still something she was holding back. As I spoke with my therapist about our relationship, I realized how much of it was me leading the charge. I didn't mind, not when she had so much more on her plate, but it also made room for doubts to grow. So as much as it killed me, I was determined to wait for her to make the next move. Even though I'd cursed his appearance at the time, maybe it was a good thing that Cole interrupted us last night. After spending the day at her side, I was unable to hold back, needing to be as close to her as possible. Now that I had time to clear my head, I was willing to let her take charge and set our pace.

I wasn't going anywhere.

I grabbed my now-cold coffee, bringing it to the sink in the kitchen. As I rinsed it out, a knock sounded at my door. I frowned, trying to figure out who was waiting on the other side. God, hopefully, it wasn't Cole coming to yell about the disaster of his day.

But as I pulled the door open, my breath caught in my chest. Victoria stood on my porch, her dark eyes devouring me as soon as our gazes met. She smiled brightly at me. "Are you going to invite me in?"

"Depends," I chuckled. "What do you need, Tori?"

"You," she said breathlessly. "I need you. Now."

I pulled Victoria inside, not giving a single fuck if someone saw us together. Normally, we'd never be this bold, never risk flaunting our connection where Cole could catch us. But when the woman of your dreams shows up at your house and says she needs you?

Yeah, you don't bother worrying about the consequences.

Taking her hand in mine, I led her into my room then turned to face her as we crossed the threshold. My fingers ghosted her cheeks, pushing back into her hair so I could take her expression in fully. "You sure about this, Tori?"

She nodded. "More than anything in my life, Adam. I need you."

I inhaled slowly, as if I could taste her words written in the space between us. They went straight to my cock, already starting to harden in my jeans. But as much as I wanted to dive straight into her, I couldn't, not until she knew what this meant for me.

"If we do this, that means you're mine. I don't care what Cole or anyone else has to say about it." I reached down, thumbing her plush lower lips. "This mouth, this body, your mind, and your heart—they all belong to me." I leaned forward so she could see I meant every word. "You okay with that?"

Her wide, brown eyes searched mine, looking for any sign of hesitation. She wouldn't find any. Slowly, she nodded, placing her hand on my chest. "I'm yours as long as you're mine."

"Oh, trouble," I chuckled, bringing her closer to me. Before our lips could touch, I whispered, "You already have all of me. I was just waiting for you to realize it."

Victoria let out a let gasp as my lips collided with hers, consuming her just as I promised. Our kisses had been amazing before, full of fire and desire, but this one was different. It wasn't a stolen moment, wasn't a taste of what we couldn't have. No, this kiss was a sacred oath. It was us giving in to each other, knowing it would change everything. It was coming home.

My hands traced Victoria's curves until I leaned down, cupping her thighs. Without breaking our kiss, I lifted her, bringing her into the bathroom with me. As I placed her on the counter, she pulled back and looked at me with an adorable pout. "What are we doing in here?"

"No offense, baby, but you've been in the lake all day," I chuckled, shifting to raise her sweater over her head. "So I thought the shower might be the best place to start." I pressed a kiss to her sternum as I toyed with the top of her leggings. "How much time do we have?"

"All night," she said breathlessly as I pulled the fabric down her legs. "Emilia is spending the night with Cole and Alex."

I pulled back, searching her eyes. "And did you tell him you were coming over here?"

"No," she whispered, reaching up to force me to face her. "I wanted to. It almost slipped out, but I needed you there with me. I would never tell him about us without talking to you first." Her shoulder sank. "I think we should, though. Tell Cole, I mean. This secret is eating away at me, and I don't want to hide us from anyone."

"Then we'll tell him tomorrow." I lifted her hand, kissing her palm before placing it on the spot above my heart. "No matter what happens with Cole, remember—I'm yours."

"I'm yours," Victoria repeated as she lifted herself off the counter. She reached out and unbuckled my jeans so fast, it almost knocked me on my ass when she palmed my length through my briefs. "Now, get these off and join me in the shower. You have some proving to do, mister."

I cursed as she slipped behind the white, gauzy curtain and turned on the shower. I watched for a moment, studying her outline through the fog and fabric. As her hands soaped up her body, I was done waiting. Those needed to be my hands caressing her supple skin.

My shirt came flying off as I dropped my jeans and boxers into the same pile as her clothes, scurrying in like a man on fire. She chuckled as I filled the space behind her. "Damn, Rice. In a hurry?"

"To get another taste of you?" I chuckled, guiding her against the far wall. "You're damn right I am."

I pressed her front into the tiles, the water spray hitting her back. I watched for a moment as the rivulets of water curved against her perfect ass, making my cock even harder. I needed to be inside this woman, needed to feel when she came to life around me. However, I'd promised her I'd take my taste, and there was no way I was missing that now.

I lifted her right leg onto the edge of the tub as I sank to my knees, angling her hips so I could trace her core with my tongue. She shuddered at that first light brush. My girl liked those soft moments, but she got off so much harder when she took control.

With that thought, I reached up and shifted her hips so she was facing me, placing her legs on my shoulders. The water made everything a little more slippery, but I didn't care. Not when my girl's pussy was in front of my face and her hands were gripping my hair to death.

"Something you want, baby?" I chuckled as I teased her thighs.

Victoria glared down at me, increasing her grip on my hair. "You wanted a taste, so do it, Adam. Do not make me ask you again."

"Yes, ma'am," I chuckled as I dove into her, letting my tongue feverishly lick every inch of her pussy. There was nothing more I wanted than to take my time, but the way Victoria was squirming right above me made it difficult. For every moan, I wanted another. I wanted her to rip my damn hair out of my head.

"I need more," she cried, staring down at me like I was bringing her to life. I lifted my fingers, not giving her any warning before spearing her with two. As they dragged along her walls, I continued to lick and suck her clit, bringing her closer and closer to the edge.

When she came, it was a work of art, watching her try to find purchase on the slippery shower tiles. She had nothing to grasp at but me, and I loved every mark she left on my skin. I continued to work her through her high, only letting her feet back on the ground once I knew she was stable. As I climbed back to my feet, she lifted onto her toes, kissing me with reckless abandon.

God, this girl was my everything, the pure reason for the breath in my lungs. There was nothing I wouldn't do to make sure she was always this content, always this satisfied.

But as she lowered to her knees for me, I stopped her, pulling her back into my arms. "Not yet, baby." Her face furrowed in surprise, but before she could protest, I explained. "You said we have all night, right?"

"Yeah..." she answered. "I don't have to pick up Emilia until eight tomorrow."

"Good," I sighed. "Because as much as I love your mouth, there's something else I need even more." I passed her the body wash and motioned for her to turn around so I could scrub her back. I leaned in to whisper in her ear. "You ready for me to fuck you, baby?"

"Yes," she shuddered. "So ready."

"Then finish up. I've got plans for you, and we're going to need more room than this shower for what I have in mind."

THIRTY-THREE

Victoria

Anticipation filled me as I walked into Adam's bedroom, the towel he placed around me still warm from the dryer. This was the reason I came over. I wanted him to have every part of me. Still, I couldn't hide that tiny shred of nerves that came over me as I looked down at his bed.

As if he could feel my rising apprehension, Adam stepped out from behind me and sat down on the mattress. His chest was bare, and all that covered his body was a similar white terry cloth towel wrapped around his hips. He reached out and took my hand, intertwining our fingers. "If you want to stop–"

"I don't," I insisted, even though my body was starting to tremble. "I guess I'm just nervous."

"Nervous?" Adam said, pulling back to search my face.

I nodded, heat and embarrassment flushing my cheeks. "I've only been with one other person. And you've been with–"

"More than that," Adam answered for me.

"What if I'm not good at this?" I said, forcing the words out of my mouth. Even though I hated how vulnerable they made me feel, something about Adam made me want to give them to him anyway. Instinctively, I knew he'd never judge me, never make me feel like less because I wasn't as experienced as him.

"Hey," Adam whispered as he toyed with the edge of my towel. "You don't have anything to worry about, Tor. It's going to be amazing because it's us."

I chuckled, sliding my hand over my face. "How can you be so confident?"

"Well, for one," Adam said, smirking up at me, "you've already given me the best head of my life, so I'm definitely in awe of your skills." He lifted my hand away from my face, placing it on his heart. "And because I've never felt like this before. You've claimed every piece of me without even trying, Tor. I have doubt that something that feels so right could ever be anything less than fantastic."

I stared at him, memorizing his dark blue irises. I knew exactly what he meant. Even though I'd never dated anyone else besides Cam, I knew there was more than just a passing connection between Adam and me. He made me come alive, and that was just with the way he looked at me.

"But if you want to stop, " Adam continued, "you say the word. No matter what's happening, you say stop, and we will." He brought our hands up to his mouth and kissed the back of mine. "I'm just happy you're here right now, Tori."

"You are?"

"Of course I am," he chuckled. "Trouble, haven't you realized you're the best thing in my life?"

I tucked my head, unable to accept that level of praise. He was the same for me, but that felt different, like I wasn't worthy of his affection. "I'm not–"

He pulled me forward, depositing me into his lap. Even though I could feel his erection behind his towel, this hold didn't feel as sexual as it did intimate, as if he needed me close to make sure I heard his words clearly. "Don't you dare try to argue with me, baby. You and that little girl pulled me out of the shadows and made me whole again."

I shook my head, but at least my hands had stopped shaking. "We didn't do anything, Adam. That's all you."

He leaned forward and gripped my neck, bringing my forehead to his. "When are you going to hear me, Tori? You are mine. My everything, my purpose. My goddamn sun."

My fingers curled around his shoulders, gripping him close, as if he'd slip away if I loosened my grip. "I feel the same way, Adam."

The quiet promise between us made something cement in my chest, and all my doubts died away. All that was left was an aching need, and based on the way Adam's eyes darkened, he felt the same. Our lips met in a tentative kiss at first, as if sealing the words we'd given each other. But as I wrapped my arms around his neck, it all faded into something more primal, the kind of need that erased the rest of the world.

I shifted my hips, sliding my drenched pussy along the length of his cock. Shit, I had him in my mouth before, but now, it seemed like he'd grown even more since the last time we were together.

"I've been hiding for so long, letting my life pass me by so I could give Emilia everything," I said, savoring the soft curse that came out of his mouth when I ground down a little harder. "You made me remember what it feels like to want something, to need someone. And I've never wanted anyone more than I want you right now."

His hands shifted to my hips, helping guide me up and down his length. "Fuck, baby. You can't say stuff like that when you're soaking my lap." His fingers dug harder into my flesh. "I need you, Tori."

"You have me," I answered, my voice barely above a whisper. He shifted, tossing me onto the bed behind us. I propped up on my elbows as he walked over to his nightstand, grabbing a few condoms and tossing them next to me.

He pressed his hand to my chest, lowering me against the pillows. "I'm going to start slow, baby. Make sure you're ready to take me."

"I'm ready," I huffed, continuing to search him out. Adam's fingers coasted along my sensitive skin before he entered me, stretching my core until I was squirming for more. I almost cried when he removed them, sucking his digits dry before settling into the crevice of my hips. I sucked in a deep breath as he notched his cock at my entrance, pushing inside inch by inch.

God, what was the word for pain mixed with pleasure? Because it was everything I wanted and needed in that moment. As his cock continued to fill me, I could feel my walls stretching to accommodate his size to the brink of my limits. But as soon as he was seated to the hilt, a warmth coasted through my veins, urging me to shift against him.

"Slow down, trouble," Adam laughed as he kissed me. "I don't want to hurt you."

"I want you to," I said, staring down at where we were joined. "Please, Adam. Fuck me hard. I need to feel you everywhere."

"Shit, Tori," he said, lowering his lips to my throat. "Hold on to me, baby."

My nails dug into his back as he started to move, pulling almost all the way out before slamming back into me. That slight bite of pain was still there, but it was quickly overshadowed by the pleasure each shift brought me. Adam's eyes never left mine, watching as I opened for him. "Damn, Tori, I knew you were made for me, but I never thought you'd feel this good." He leaned back on his haunches, gripping my hips so he could fuck me properly. Adam's eyes turned almost black as he looked at me, a desperate edge filling his voice. "You're taking me so well, baby. Just like that."

"Adam," I cried, tensing around his cock. "God, don't stop."

"Never." His fingers tightened on my skin—hard enough that I knew there would be marks tomorrow, but I wanted every single one, to know this night hadn't been a dream. I wanted to feel him in every step, to know I completely and wholly belonged to him, just as he did to me.

His hand shifted so his thumb could rub circles along my clit. That was enough to force me over the edge, to force me to completely shatter around his cock. My eyes went white as he continued to fuck me through my pleasure, not stopping until he found his release right after me. Even when we both came down, we stayed in the same position, staring at each other like we could see our hearts pulsing as one.

As I stared into his dark blue eyes, one thought overcame the rest: I loved him. How hard and real that thought felt was enough to make me jolt. It was probably too soon, too early, to feel this way, but I knew with absolute certainty that I was in love with Adam Rice and that I never wanted to be without him again.

After we relaxed, Adam pulled out of me, walking into the bathroom to dispose of the condom. He came back with a warm washcloth, tenderly washing away the remnants of my orgasm. I chuckled, holding my hand up to my face. "You really don't have to do that."

"I want to," he responded. "If I didn't think you were too sensitive right now, I'd be doing it with my tongue."

"There's always later," I laughed.

"You're damn right about that." He winked as he stood, depositing the washcloth in the laundry basket. He crawled into the bed, lifting the comforter so it covered us both. "C'mere."

His strong arms surrounded me, pulling me into his chest.

His lips pressed into my forehead and hair, as if he couldn't get enough of me. I chuckled as I traced the planes of his chest, nuzzling into the crook of his shoulder. "Sleep," Adam said, pressing one last kiss against my lips. "I've got you, Tori."

I squeezed him a little tighter before I shut my eyes. "I have you too."

THIRTY-FOUR

Victoria

The following day, I woke up slowly, letting my eyes drift open to take in the light. As much as I loved our apartment, there was something about staring at the lake when you first opened your eyes. I let out a content sigh as I shifted, feeling someone else's weight on my back. I reached down, running my fingers along Adam's forearm.

Adam nuzzled into me, leaving a soft kiss on the back of my neck. "I could get used to this."

I chuckled as I turned to face him, running my fingers through the soft stubble that had formed on his cheeks and chin. "It's been a long time since I woke up to someone besides Emilia in my bed."

"Been even longer for me," Adam sighed as he kissed my forehead. "You're my first."

I stared at him for a moment as his words clicked in my sleep-addled mind. When they did, I sat up, turning to face him fully. "You've never had someone stay the night before?"

Adam chuckled, reaching up to take my elbow so I settled into the crook of his arm again. "Nope," he admitted, kissing the top of my head. "For a while, that felt like a serious step, one I wasn't willing to take. Even if I did fall asleep, I'd always be gone before the morning. And then, it became about protecting myself. I wasn't willing to let someone come into my world and ruin what I'd built for myself."

I shifted to face him. "And that's different with me?"

"Baby, *everything* is different with you."

We were silent as his words filled the air, giving life to this new yet profound connection. Because as scary as it was, I knew what he meant. Even though I'd been in a relationship before, everything felt different with Adam. Being around him made me feel confident, secure, and, most of all, safe. For so long, I'd been on my own, doing everything possible to ensure Emilia was happy. But now, I realized my happiness mattered too. Growing up, I learned a lot from my parents, but more than anything, they gave me an example of unconditional love. It wasn't perfect, wasn't glamorous. There were days that they fought like hell. But no matter what happened, they were a team and weathered life's storms together. I never felt that with Cam, not even during our good days.

But with Adam, it was innate, as natural as breathing.

And if I could give my daughter an example like that, I'd consider my job well done.

"Same here," I chuckled as he pulled me closer, his erection digging into my hip. It was hard not to shift against it, wanting to feel him inside me again. But as I moved closer to him, I winced, the ache between my legs evidence of the many rounds we went last night.

Adam frowned at the sight. "Did I hurt you?"

"No," I chuckled, pressing a kiss to his chest. "Just a little spent after last night."

He shook his head, hiding his face in my neck. "I would say I'm sorry, but last night was everything and more, so I can't bring myself to apologize."

"I don't want you to," I laughed. "It was amazing for me too."

He smiled so brightly back at me, my heart almost burst out of my chest. This moment, this man—this was that life-affirming joy people always talked about. It felt like the start of something big, like the kind of love people always aspired to find.

I gently pushed back on his chest to climb out of bed, grabbing his spare shirt from the end of the mattress. He leaned on his elbow, smirking as I walked with a little limp. "Where are you going?" he called as I walked into the bathroom.

"To pick up Emilia," I responded. "It's almost eight. Cole has to head out to get some stuff for Fall Fest, so I promised I'd grab her early."

I heard some shuffling in the bedroom as I finished cleaning up. Looking into the mirror, I found Adam standing at the bathroom door in a clean shirt and a pair of jeans. He looked too good, too presentable after our all-night marathon. Meanwhile, I looked like I had just crawled out of a hole, my eyes circled in dark rings, my hair a tangled mess.

"What are you doing?" I asked, crossing my arms over my chest.

"Going with you." Adam shrugged, stepping around me to grab his toothbrush.

I shook my head, leaning against the doorframe. "You don't have to. It's really early, and you should get more sleep."

Adam chuckled as he rinsed his mouth, stepping forward to press a kiss to my lips. "I already told you, trouble. Last night meant something to me. I'm yours, and I don't want to wait any longer." He frowned, taking a step back to look at me. "Unless you've changed your mind about wanting to tell Cole."

"No," I insisted, placing my hands on his broad chest. "I do. Today. But I just thought you'd want to wait until later."

"Not a chance." Adam winked as he walked past me. "I want to get this over with so I can kiss you anytime, anywhere."

I chewed on my lower lip. "About that..." I sighed as I stepped out of the bathroom into his bedroom. Sitting on his bed, all I wanted was to crawl back inside and ignore the rest of the world for a little longer. Adam stepped forward, watching me with an uneasy frown on his face. I exhaled slowly. "With Emilia, I want to wait a little bit longer, let her get to know you a little bit more as my friend before I explain that you're my boyfriend."

"Boyfriend?" Adam smirked. "Is that what I am?"

"Oh!" I said, dropping my gaze down to my hands and twisting my fingers together. Insecurity filled my lungs as I stared at them, hoping I didn't shatter our newfound bond by speaking out of turn. "I just thought... Well, you said I was yours—"

"Hey, hey," Adam said as he dropped to his knees in front of me. He pulled my hands apart, holding them tightly in his. "I was just kidding. I'd love to be your boyfriend, at least for now."

"For now?"

Adam leaned forward and kissed me, consuming me with one touch of his lips. "I want a lot more than that, trouble. But a boyfriend is a good start."

My cheeks reddened as he gave me one last kiss before heading into the bathroom. I grabbed my phone from his nightstand, cursing that I'd forgotten my charger in my haste to come over last night. I looked around his home, finally finding a charger in the kitchen. As I plugged in my phone, I started to pick up my clothes, frowning as I looked at them. There was no way I could show up at Cole's house wearing the same outfit as yesterday. I wanted to talk to Cole, not give him a heart attack.

"Hey," I called to Adam as he walked into the room. "Do

you mind if I borrow some clothes to head over to my place? I've got to change before we pick up Emilia."

"Course," Adam said as he grabbed something from his drawers and passed it to me. I pulled his shirt over my head, and he watched me with a reverent look.

"What?" I asked, toying with the hem.

"Nothing," he chuckled. "Just really enjoying the look of you in my clothes. It might be my second favorite, after nothing at all. In fact, you should just wear them all the time..." He ducked as I chucked a pair of socks at his head. "No? Not feeling it?"

"Not going to happen," I chuckled as I walked over to him, lifting onto my toes to kiss him deeply. "But the naked part, I could definitely agree to." I toyed with his hem. "Maybe tonight?"

"You inviting me over, trouble?"

"Maybe." I shrugged. "Probably should see how today goes first, make sure Cole doesn't try to drive me out of town when he finds out what we've done."

I tried to keep my tone light, but my real insecurities came barreling through. As much as I tried to say my brother's opinion wouldn't matter, it was everything to me. We were just getting back onto solid ground, and I didn't want to destroy our tentative foundation.

As if he could pick up on my growing anxieties, Adam pulled me into his arms. "You don't have anything to worry about, trouble. I'll be with you every step of the way. He's not going to be mad at you. Me, that might be a different story." He kissed the top of my head. "But he's not going to try and tear us apart. Even if he does, anywhere you go, I'm going with you."

I shook my head. "Don't say that, Adam."

As I tried to pull away, he held my arms, keeping me close. "I mean it, Tori."

I studied his expression, not wanting to believe the swell of hope in my chest. This moment, this man, was everything I wanted and more. But I couldn't focus on it, not when we still had a huge hurdle to overcome.

"Thank you," I whispered, placing my hand over his heart. "For last night, for the past month, just for..." I looked up into his adoring eyes. "For being you."

"Anything for you, trouble." He kissed me one last time before taking my hand and leading me toward the front door. After he pulled me outside, he took my hand and kissed my knuckles. "We'll get through this. Together."

And as much as I believed him, my stomach dropped at the sound of a grumble coming from the bottom of the steps. When I pulled away from Adam, I met my brother's stormy expression, his eyes narrowing at where our hands were intertwined.

Cole's face turned downright lethal as he looked between Adam and me. "Why the fuck are you holding my sister's hand?"

THIRTY-FIVE

Cole's eyes blazed with promises of bloodshed as he stared at his little sister's hand clenched in mine, but no matter how hard he stared, I wasn't letting go. After last night, when we promised each other we belonged together, there was no way I'd walk away from her right now. He'd have to pry my cold, dead hand from Victoria if he wanted to separate us.

"Cole..." Victoria stumbled. "I, uh..." Her dark eyes glanced up at me, unsure how to even start. I just smiled back at her, trying to give her the confidence I wanted to feel. Because even though I knew we'd get through this okay, I couldn't say the same about my relationship with Cole. From the look he was shooting in my direction, I was lucky to be still breathing. It was hard not to feel like I'd been punched in the chest, with my best friend looking at me with such vitriol in his eyes.

I hadn't seen that look since he was drinking, hating when we tried to get him to kick the habit. In the past few years, I forgot how fucking terrifying it was to have Cole look at you like that. Even though I was a big dude, Cole still had a couple of inches on me, and I knew the power his punch could pack. I'd have no chance if his fist decided to destroy my face.

"This is where you were?" he snapped at Victoria. "I've been fucking worried sick!"

"Don't talk to her like that," I practically growled, pushing her behind me.

Cole's eyes turned dark. "You think you need to stand between us? She's *my* sister." He stared at Victoria over my shoulder. "I've been calling you for the last hour, and this is where you were?"

"I'm sorry, my phone died. We were just about to come to your house," she said, her voice raising with nerves. "Is everything okay? Is Emilia okay?"

"She's fine," Cole said, his voice lowering. "She's inside with Alex right now. We came here to save you the drive. But when I couldn't find you..." His voice trailed off, his anger now reverting to fear. "I didn't know where you went, and I was so fucking afraid something happened to you. So, I was coming here to ask Adam if he saw you last night. *Clearly*, he had." His eyes narrowed at me again. "Tori, go inside. This asshole owes me a fucking explanation."

"*Excuse* me?" Victoria barked, taking a step closer to him.

"Please, Tori," he said, his voice softening as he looked at her. "I'm sorry, I'm just..." His voice trailed off as he glared at me. "Could you please go inside? You can check on Emilia while Adam and I talk."

Victoria's shoulders stiffened, facing off with her brother without an ounce of fear. Now that she knew Emilia was well, a force came out of her, ready to defend us at any cost.

She stepped around me, her finger pointed directly at him. "Get that look off your face, Cole. If you want to talk about our relationship, you can talk to *both* Adam *and* me. This isn't some boys' club where I don't get a say in my own love life." She turned and motioned for me to join her. I didn't hesitate, too shocked by what I just witnessed to argue. She wrapped her hand in mine and pulled me next to her. "Because yes, Adam and I are together. If you have anything to say about it, you will talk to *both* of us."

Cole placed his hands on his hips, inhaling slowly before staring back at us. "How long?"

Victoria said, "None of your business," while I smirked and said, "Since your wedding."

She elbowed me, but I just shrugged, not willing to lie to Cole a moment longer. Plus, I had nothing to hide, not when it came to this girl. I was all in, and Cole and everyone else needed to know it.

He groaned, turning to face away from us. My heart cracked at the sight. My feelings were all twisted up, and I felt an odd sense of loyalty to Cole while also hating that he was putting us in this position. But while Cole might have won out before, now, my loyalty was to Victoria—a fact he would hopefully get over quickly.

I squeezed Victoria's hand once before releasing it and stepping closer to my best friend. "Look, man, I'm sure you're pissed—"

"I'm not pissed," Cole answered as he stood up a little straighter. "Okay, I'm not *only* pissed. I'm also fucking confused. Why her, Adam? Out of all the women in town who are dying to sleep with you, why did it have to be my little sister?"

"Because it's Tori," I said. "Listen, I tried like hell to fight this, tried to push her out of my mind, but from the moment she stepped into town, I was drawn to her. She's not only beautiful, but she's smart, confident, and makes me see the bright side of things. Every time she looks at me, I feel like the luckiest damn guy in the entire world. So no, it couldn't be anyone else. Because there is no one else like Tori." I risked stepping another foot closer to him. "You told me not to give up what was making me happy again." I turned over my shoulder and met Victoria's eye. "It's her. Her and Emilia." I shifted back toward my best friend. "And I get it if you need time to accept this. But I'm not going anywhere, not even if you disagree with it."

Cole placed his hands on his hips and cursed under his breath. He directed his attention to Victoria. "And you feel the same way?"

She nodded. "I do. I didn't want to get involved with Adam either. I was content with just Emilia. But being with him..." She exhaled slowly. "It's made me happier than I've been in years. So no, we're not ending, no matter what you say."

Cole shook his hand, squeezing his brows together with his forefingers. "I get that, Tor, I really do." He smiled softly at his sister. "Look, if I promise not to hit him, can I talk to Adam alone for a couple of minutes?"

She narrowed her glare at him. "Best behavior?"

"Don't push your luck, trouble."

Victoria slid her gaze over to me, silently asking if I was alright talking to Cole. I nodded. I wasn't not going to lie—his promise not to hit me made me feel a little better. "Fine," she scoffed. "I'm going to head inside. Call me if anyone starts bleeding."

We waited until she crossed the yard before Cole turned toward me. While his glare wasn't as angry, it still wasn't the usual expression he wore when we hung out. I'd known the guy for most of my life, and there was no question—he was pissed. But I could take it, all his anger. None of that was going to change anything.

I crossed my arms over my chest as I leaned against the pole. "Let's get this over with. Say what you have to say."

"Do you love her?"

Cole's question shocked the hell out of me. Maybe it shouldn't have, but between the lack of sleep and the unex-pected interruption, my mind wasn't working at peak performance. I ran my hand over my face, trying to buy myself some time while I put my feelings into words. *Did I love her?* I sure as fuck did. I felt it every time she glanced my way, every time she took my hand. I'd never loved someone more than I did last night, when we destroyed any remaining walls between us.

But there was something so wrong about admitting it to Cole before I had a chance to tell Victoria.

"I care a lot about her, Cole, but I can't say anything more than that until I tell Tori how I feel. She deserves to hear those words before you."

He nodded, shifting to take a seat on the bottom step. His elbows rested on his thighs as he wrung his hands together. I continued, "Look, I know I'm not the kind of guy you'd want with your sister–"

"What the fuck are you talking about?" Cole didn't let me finish my thought. "Why the hell would you think that?"

"My history," I answered, feeling like I was exposing all my raw nerves. "I know what the media says about me. But that's not who I am; at least, not who I want to be with Tori. I respect her too much to ever hurt her."

"Jesus, man, I fucking know that," Cole answered. His dark eyes met mine, and I could see the truth in his expression. "You think I don't know what kind of man you are? You fucking dragged me out of the gutter and made sure I got help. You stuck by me even when you had no reason to. I owe you my life."

"Then why are you so pissed?"

Cole shook his head. "I'm not pissed; I'm fucking *worried*, Adam." He let out a tense breath and then stared up at the open sky. "I know I don't get a say in who Tori dates. And, trust me, I have no intention of trying, because that girl is fucking terrifying when she wants to be," He rolled his eyes as if he couldn't believe he was saying his next words. "But if I did, I'd want it to be you."

I couldn't hold back the teasing smile on my face. "Wow, Cole. I think that's the nicest thing you've ever said to me."

"Can it," he chuckled before his face fell again. "But this is going to be a hard road, and I don't want to see my sister get hurt. Or Emilia. Maybe this is really fucking selfish of me, but I've loved having them here. I love that little girl, and I don't want to lose what we have. If something goes wrong between you and Tori..."

"You're afraid it'll screw up your relationship with them too," I finished for him.

"Yeah," Cole reluctantly admitted. "We're just finding our footing again, and I don't want anything to jeopardize that."

"Neither do I," I said as I took a seat next to him. "I promise, no matter what happens between Tori and me, it's not going to come between you guys. I'll make sure of it."

"I believe you," Cole answered. "Just do me a favor?" I nodded. "Be careful with them. Because I'm pretty sure she's falling for you too. And Emilia," Cole chuckled. "That girl is head over heels for you. She talked about you all last night. Probably should have been my first clue that something more was going on."

"I'm sorry I didn't tell you before," I said. "We were just trying to figure things out for ourselves before we told other people. If it makes you feel any better, we were planning on telling you today."

"It oddly does," Cole chuckled. "And as much as I'd like to erase the image of my sister in your clothing, that's not even the worst part."

"It's not?"

"Nope," Cole groaned, rubbing his hand over his face. "Because this means Alex was right, and I am *never* going to hear the end of it."

THIRTY-SIX

Victoria

The next few days, the town seemed to transform into a completely different place. With Fall Fest coming up this weekend, everyone was preparing for the influx of tourists and visitors. Besides the summer season, this was the biggest draw for the town of Saint Stephen's Lake, a final hurrah for many of the seasonal business owners. When the winter months came, many people shut down their shops, not opening their doors again until the snow finally melted away.

While there was a hectic, frantic energy everywhere I went, I loved being a part of it. In fact, most of my days were spent with Cole and Alex, helping them figure out last-minute details of their booth.

After Cole's talk with Adam, he'd said he was happy for the two of us but wanted absolutely no details of what happened behind closed doors—not that I would tell him anyway. Still, Adam couldn't help but tease him, kissing me every chance Emilia wasn't in the room.

Even though we hadn't told her we were dating yet, I knew she was starting to suspect something. While Adam made a big show of leaving at bedtime every night, the moment Emilia was asleep, he'd sneak back in, leaving as soon as the sun came up in the morning. It was the fun type of sneaking around, compared to the stress I felt when we were hiding from Cole.

There was no doubt in my mind that Emilia would be thrilled about my relationship with Adam. He spent almost as much time with her as I did, and she'd started to naturally assume he'd be eating all meals and hanging out with us. In fact, on the one night he had dinner plans with the guys, she'd cried into her pasta, unable to hide her disappointment he wouldn't be there to tuck her in.

He'd remedied it immediately, coming over last night with a bunch of extra cat cookies from the local bakery and reading her three different stories before bed.

The day before Fall Fest, I turned over in bed, reaching out to see if Adam was still at my side. Instead, all I found was a note, something he did whenever he woke up before me. I read the scratchy handwriting, smiling as I looked at his words.

You were sleeping so soundly. I didn't want to wake you. See you soon, trouble.

I stretched my arms over my head as I crawled out of bed, grabbing my robe before I went to Emilia's room. Peeking inside, I could see she was still out. I smiled to myself as I softly shut the door. I'd never tell her this, but some of my best mornings were when she slept in a little. While waking up to her smiling face was one of my favorite sights, it was nice to take a breath before diving into the day.

As I pressed the coffee maker's button, a soft knock came on the door. I rolled my eyes, already knowing what would be waiting on the other side. Opening it up, I saw the same long, white box with a deep purple bow. For the past week, Adam sent me flowers every morning. He claimed it was because he couldn't be there when I woke up, but I think he just liked knowing they brought a smile to my face. He'd been sending different bouquets each day, all in shades of purple because it made Emilia happy. After almost a week, it was starting to look like I'd opened a flower shop of my own. Maybe I'd bring some downstairs for the other guests to enjoy.

But as I lifted the top of the box, I let out a sharp gasp, the smell of decay and rot filling my nostrils. I quickly pulled it back down, almost vomiting at the noxious odor. *Shit, had something happened at the florists?* After a week of near-perfect blooms, it seemed like something must have gone wrong for this arrangement to be so vile.

Without looking again, I ran downstairs and dumped the flowers in the back dumpster. Hopefully, they could give Adam some kind of refund. But as I walked back inside, I was stopped by the sight in front of me.

"Cam?"

My ex turned around at the sound of my voice, greeting me with a bright smile. "Hey, Vic," he said as he stepped forward, wrapping me in a tight hug. "It's so good to see you."

"You too," I said as he put me back down. "But what are you doing here?"

"I have a meeting in Boston on Monday, so I thought I'd come up a little early and surprise my girls. Plus..." He nodded off to the side. "I brought you a little something."

I glanced around his shoulder, squealing when I saw a swatch of bright blonde hair checking out the breakfast bar. "Hadley?"

"Oh my God!" she said, almost dropping her full plate when she ran to hug me. "I have missed you so, so much! I can't believe you didn't tell me about this place sooner. It is adorable. Your brother owns the whole thing?"

"Yup," I said, my chest filling with pride at all of Cole's hard work. "He runs it with his wife."

"I can't get over how much I love it here. I can see why you'd want to come for a visit." She tugged my hand before realizing I was still in my robe. "Shoot, I didn't realize how early it was. Sarge over there made us take the red eye, so my sense of time is all thrown off."

"Some of us have a schedule, Menace," Cam called out from the stairwell. "Is it cool if we head to your place? I'm dying to see Em."

"Of course," I chuckled, leading them up the stairs to my apartment. But as Cam went through the door, Hadley held me back. "I want every single detail about you and Adam Rice. Leave *nothing* out."

"Never going to happen," I chuckled, wrapping her in another hug. As much as I loved it here, my world wasn't right without Hadley at my side. "But you can tell me how you survived an entire plane ride without murdering Cam."

"Trust me," she groaned, "it was the biggest challenge of my life. But it was worth it to see you and Emilia again. I missed you so much."

"Missed you more."

AN HOUR LATER, we all sat at the island in my kitchen, listening to Emilia tell tales of our trip. She spared no details, making sure Hadley and Cam knew precisely what they had missed out on. As she told yet another story featuring Adam, Cam arched his brow at me with a sly smirk. "Seems like you two have been hanging out with Adam a lot, huh, Em?"

"Oh yeah!" she exclaimed. "He's the bestest. He got me all the paints, and we've had *so* many tea parties." She leaned in to whisper, "And he told me we're going to see horses soon."

"Oh, he did?" I mused, hiding my smile behind my coffee mug. Adam had gone all out this weekend, not only making sure that there would be ponies at Fall Fest, but also offering a donation to make sure Emilia's dreams come true. He'd even given them extra to make one look like a unicorn, complete with a purple felt horn.

I looked up, finding Hadley and Cam staring at me with twin smiles. While Hadley knew all too well how much time Adam and I were spending together, Cam could probably tell from the look on my face—definitely a downside to our almost lifelong friendship. The man knew me way too well.

"And what about you, Vic?" Cam smirked as he leaned back on his stool. "Do you think Adam is the *bestest*?"

Before I could answer, a knock came from our front door, and the man of the hour stepped in. Adam's face practically glowed when he spotted me, and he held up his usual breakfast treats. I swore, the man was trying to spoil us, not realizing we didn't need any perks to stick with him. Both my daughter and I were head over heels for Adam.

As Adam turned to greet us, his face fell slightly when he realized we weren't alone. His false smile was back in place as he stepped up to my side, dropping the bag on the counter. He leaned in and kissed me on the cheek. "Sorry, Tor. Didn't realize you had company."

"No worries. We were just talking about you," I chuckled. "Adam, you remember Cam, Emilia's dad." I nodded down the island. "And this is my best friend, Hadley."

"Charmed," she smirked as she held out her hand. "And yes, we've heard all about you from Emilia." She turned that saccharine smile toward me. "Tori's been a vault, however."

My eyes narrowed at her as Adam chuckled. He placed his hand on my lower back, "Glad to hear someone is singing my praises." He smiled down at me. "Maybe if you try some of these new pastries, you'll have nicer things to say about me."

"Oh, she hasn't said *anything*," Hadley teased, pulling the bag over to her to look inside. "Maybe you'll be willing to spill more secrets than your friend here."

Cam rolled his eyes. "Ignore the menace, Adam. She's only happy if she's torturing an innocent soul."

"Aww, Cammy baby, are you feeling left out?" She booped his nose. "I'd ask you questions about your love life, but frankly, I don't think anyone could stomach you long enough to date you."

Just as Cam was about to snap back, Emilia's voice rang out. "What's a love life?"

I glared at Hadley as I turned back toward my daughter. I tucked a strand of hair behind her ear. "It's another word for dating. You know how some of the ranchers have partners back home?" She nodded. "So that's their love life—who they're with, if they're married, something like that."

She furrowed her brow then stared at me. "Like you and Adam?"

My eyes widened as I looked at him over my shoulder. He just shrugged and mouthed *no idea*. Still, he had a smile on his face, probably ecstatic that our secret was finally out in the open.

Cam met my eye and gave me a subtle nod, as if encouraging me as well. As I stared back at him with uncertainty in my eyes, he chuckled, grabbing Hadley's arm. "C'mon, Menace. Let's give them some space to talk."

"Boo," she sighed. "I want to see how this plays out."

Despite everyone else's reassurances, for a moment, I debated lying to my daughter. I hated to do that, only lying when it was entirely necessary. And even though I knew she loved Adam like family, it was hard navigating dating as a single parent. All the books had mixed responses in terms of a timeline, but most stated it was best to wait until you were sure the person would be a long-term partner, not a passing entity in your child's life. And no matter what other questions I might have had about our new relationship, one thing was for sure: Adam fell into the former category.

"Yes, baby," I said, exhaling slowly with each word. "Like Adam. He's my boyfriend." I ran my fingers through her hair. "Are you okay with that?"

She scrunched her nose and turned toward Adam. "Does that mean you're going to come to dinner every night?"

"I hope so," Adam answered. "I might not be able to be there every night, but I'm going to try. And if I can't, I'll be sure to call and talk to the two of you."

She nodded, seemingly pleased with his answer. "Are you going to live in our house?"

"Not right now," Adam said. "But maybe one day. We'd talk to you about that before it happened. And if we did...maybe we could all get a big house and fill it with lots of animals."

That made her eyes light up, but she wasn't entirely done with her questions. "Are we gonna cross the thing off Mommy's list?"

Adam's face blanched, and even when I arched a brow at him, he didn't look in my direction. "Not yet," he said, lowering his voice conspiratorially. "But soon. I'll let you know."

My eyes narrowed at the two of them, trying to read through the lines. When Adam pulled back and wrapped his arm around my hips, I glared in his direction. "Are you ever going to tell me what she wants me to do?"

"Nope," he chuckled as he pressed a kiss on my forehead. "But trust me—I think you're going to like it."

Within the hour, news had gotten out about Cam and Hadley's arrival. Victoria's small apartment was soon crowded with all our friends. In between questions, though, everyone made their way over to us, telling us in different terms that they knew Victoria and I were going to get together eventually. Alex and Calla were particularly smug, claiming that they were the first ones to see a spark between us.

I just stood next to Tori, touching her every chance I got. It was nice not having to hold back anymore. I liked the way her eyes lit up when I grabbed her hand—almost like she felt the same way. The only detractor was Cole, who groaned every time I kissed her or pulled her against my chest.

"You know this is karma," Theo said after Cole made another comment. "You and Alex have been disgustingly touchy since the moment you got together. It's about time you felt our pain."

"It's not the same," Cole grumbled. "Wait until it's your baby sister, and then you can talk."

"I don't have that problem," Theo smirked. "Don't have a sister."

"Then your daughter," Alex quipped back. "That will be really fun for you. And if she's anything like Calla, you're in for it."

"Oh God." Theo's face paled at the thought. "That's it. *If* I have a daughter, she's not allowed to date until I'm dead."

His eyes narrowed at Alex as she smiled innocently at his side, busying herself with another set of magnets she was putting together for Fall Fest. After everyone had gotten to know each other, this had become the unofficial headquarters for the event tomorrow. With our group responsible for three different booths, it was all hands on deck to get everything ready.

Calla and her sister, Devyn, were putting together sample fall-themed bouquets in one corner while Theo and Cole were waiting for Gray. They were going to help him figure out how to set up the equipment for The Lost Tavern's food stand. Meanwhile, the rest of us were putting together swag bags for Fox Creek, complete with brochures, magnets, and other little trinkets to bring in more guests.

Cam and Hadley tried to help as much as possible, but they were eventually relegated to Emilia duty. Even though she wanted to be involved in what everyone was doing, there was only so much a four-year-old could handle safely.

"Shit," I hissed as I sliced my finger on the paper slicer, sticking it in my mouth before I could think better of it. As I pulled it out, I smirked at Alex. "You know, most people get paid for their work..."

"Consider it your payment for all of the free lodging," Alex popped back at me. "And not to mention, my excellent match-making services."

"Umm, no," Calla said. "I'm totally taking credit for it. I have a reputation to uphold."

"Neither of you get credit," I chuckled. "As much as I love

you guys, it was in the works long before you guys said something."

"How long?" Alex asked.

I turned to look at Tori, smiling softly at her curious frown. "From the moment she got here. She almost crashed into me downstairs, and I thought she was the most beautiful woman I'd ever seen. I didn't even realize who she was."

"I knew it," Tori chuckled before turning back to the rest of the group. "He tried to play it off like he knew exactly who I was."

"I was in shock!" I argued. "You looked nothing like I remembered. But as soon as she smiled up at me, I knew I was done for."

"You're such a softie," Victoria teased as she came closer. "For me, it was a little bit later. Obviously, I thought he was attractive. But I started falling for him when he tried to teach me poker." She winked at me. "You still owe me a rematch."

"Name the time and place, trouble."

Story time ended when Gray crashed through the door, his dog, Elsa, leading the way. As he stumbled with the bags of groceries and craft supplies, Elsa had other plans, barging through the room and right into Emilia's waiting arms.

"Elsa!" she cooed, wrapping her arms around the dog's neck. "I missed you! I saved you all the bacon from breakfast." She pulled a couple of strips from her pocket. "I hope you like them."

"That explains why she almost pulled my arm off," Gray grumbled as he dropped the bags on the counter. Calla instantly went over, kissing him on the cheek as she started to empty his supplies.

As most people greeted Gray, Cam grabbed Tori's arm, his eyes widening at the sight of his idol in the same room. "Holy shit, it's Grayson Anders. The living legend." He took Victoria's hand and brought it to his arm. "Please, you gotta pinch me. There's no way I'm awake."

"I volunteer," Hadley grinned at their side, holding up her fingers.

"Don't touch me, menace," Cam sneered, taking a step behind Victoria. "You'd probably rip a layer of skin off just for fun."

I rolled my eyes at Victoria, quickly getting used to the odd dynamic between the three of them. I had to admit, there was a little jealousy that lingered in my chest at their closeness. Not so much on the romantic side with Cam, even though my fists clenched every time he touched Tori, but more about how well they knew each other.

As I pulled Tori next to me, her eyes were glued to the other side of the room, ignoring her friends' bickering for another face-off. Devyn and Gray stared at each other, neither taking a step any closer to the other. Gray shook his head, as if coming out of a daze. "I didn't know you'd be here."

"It's fine," Devyn snapped. "I was just about to leave. I have some work to do at the hotel."

"Don't run out 'cause of me," Gray grunted. "Just dropping some supplies off. Gotta head back into town." As he headed to the door, he glanced at her once more over his shoulder, "Good to see you, Devy."

"Don't call me that, *Grayson.*"

His hazel eyes crinkled with amusement as he turned to look for his dog, who was still wrapped up in Emilia's arms. He shook his head as he snapped his fingers. "Time to go, Elsa."

Devyn's eyes bulged out of her head. "You named your dog Elsa?"

"Yup." Gray smiled wider than I'd ever seen. "Always had a thing for ice queens."

As soon as the words left his mouth, he closed the door,

cutting off Devyn's muttered string of curses. With the rest of the room devolving into chaos, primarily thanks to Calla interrogating her sister about her interaction with Gray, I took the opportunity to get some alone time with my girl. I took her hand and placed my finger to my lips. We snuck out into the hallway and headed down the stairs. Once we were clear of the main dining area, I brought her into the unoccupied maintenance office, letting the door close behind us.

"Thank you." Tori placed her hands on my chest. "As much as I love all of them, my apartment is not nearly big enough to have everyone in one room."

"Tell me about it, trouble," I grumbled, leaning down to kiss her lips. As she stared up at me, I dragged my fingers through her hair. "How are you handling everything?"

"What do you mean?"

"You know, with telling Emilia about us, Cam and Hadley being here, everyone camping out in your living room. How are you handling all of it?"

She sighed and placed her head against my chest. "It's okay. Most of it is a relief. I'm happy Emilia knows and that she's cool with us being together. And honestly, it's good to see Cam and Hadley, even if their bickering is making me want to strangle them." She peered up at me. "I like that we're this loud, ridiculously crazy family. But it also makes me incredibly thankful that they're all going to their own homes tonight."

"What about Cam and Hadley?"

Victoria chewed on her lower lip. "I told them that they could stay with me for the weekend. Hadley can sleep in my bed, and Cam's going to sleep on the couch." Her eyes studied me with apprehension. "Is that okay?"

"It's not up to me," I chuckled. "It's your home. Am I thrilled about your ex sleeping ten feet away from you? Not really. But I trust you."

Victoria's smile turned devious as she looked up at me. "Well, I was actually thinking, since they're going to be there tonight, maybe after Emilia goes to bed, I can stay the night at your cabin."

I didn't give her a moment to say anything else, instead bringing my lips to hers with a newfound vigor. My hands found her ass, pulling her up against me. I groaned as she slid against my length, bringing my cock to life. He was desperate for another taste of her tight pussy, not caring how many people were on the other side of the door.

I gripped her hair and dropped my head to her forehead. "Shit, trouble. I don't know if I can wait that long."

"Me either," she groaned, palming my length through my jeans. I cursed as she tugged open the fly and tucked her fingers around me. "I need you inside me, Adam."

I pushed her against the door, gripping her thighs so they wrapped around my waist. Sliding my pulsing cock against her core, I let out a muffled groan. "Is this what you want, baby?"

"Yes," she moaned, arching her back to bring her closer to me.

My hands dug through my jeans, searching for the condom I thought I'd tucked in there earlier. "Dammit," I said, dropping my head to her shoulder. "I don't have a condom. Left them all over at my cabin."

"I have an IUD," she said, the words rushing out as she ground her pussy against my cock. God, just the touch was enough to remind me how perfect it felt inside her. It almost made me lose all rational thought. My hand shifted to her cheek, shifting her eyes up to mine.

"Is that what you want?" I asked, the words catching in my throat. "We don't have to do this. We can wait until later–"

"I'm sure—I trust you, Adam, and I want to feel you without

anything between us." Her warm eyes never left mine. "If you're not comfortable, I understand."

"You have no idea how badly I want that, Tori," I said as I pushed her back against the door. "You want me to fuck you bare right here? You want me to fuck you so hard, you can feel where my cock leaves its mark all day?" She whimpered a yes. I reached into her long, dark hair, tugging it so her eyes were glued to mine. "Then you better hold on, baby. Because by the time I'm done with you, everyone here will know without a doubt that you're mine."

THIRTY-EIGHT

Victoria

My back slammed against the wooden door as Adam's lips branded me like an oath. Each touch of his skin on mine was a relief. With the room full of people asking questions about our relationship, it was tempting to take him and run, leaving the chaos behind. Just a few minutes alone with Adam had already helped me breathe and allowed my anxious brain to handle the people currently invading my space. While I loved all of them dearly, the entire morning, I was craving a couple of minutes alone with him.

Granted, hooking up in the maintenance office was not what I had in mind; it was infinitely better.

Each brush of his fingers along my hem felt forbidden, like someone could interrupt us at any minute. It made everything feel heightened, my skin electric with the need to feel him closer.

Adam toyed with the bottom of my skirt, pushing it up to rub his hands over the globes of my ass. He let out a sharp curse as he squeezed my skin. "Fuck, baby. You have no idea what this ass does to me. Makes me want to worship you all day, every day."

"Then you better get to it," I teased. "Before people come looking for us."

"Let them come," he answered. "But they better be prepared to hear you screaming my name, because you feel way too fucking good to stop."

I didn't get to respond as his fingers bunched in the fabric of my panties and gave them a sharp tug. The fabric bit my skin as it ripped away, leaving my core open and exposed. He shoved down his jeans and lifted me back up, using his fingers to explore my entrance. He smiled at me as he found me wet and ready. "Is this all for me, trouble?"

"Of course," I groaned back to him. "It's only ever for you."

He circled my clit a few times, and my head fell back against the wooden surface. As his fingers explored me, all I could do was hold on, not so patiently waiting for him to fuck me. There was something so raw, so primal about him taking me without protection. Even with Cam, we'd never done this. Emilia was the result of a broken condom and unfortunate timing.

However, I trusted Adam more than anyone else in my life. I knew he would rather hurt himself than risk harming me. As his thick cock nudged my entrance, our eyes met, and I felt the bond between us growing even stronger. Our gazes never drifted as he pushed inside me, my body almost fighting the intrusion. Even after taking him so many times, the first couple of thrusts were a little uncomfortable. But as soon as he gripped my hips and started to handle me more roughly, the hint of pain turned into the most intoxicating form of pleasure.

"Oh my God, Adam," I moaned, feeling every inch inside my body. He fucked me with abandon, as if he couldn't get enough. I tried to meet him thrust for thrust, rocking my hips against his.

"Shit, baby, keep doing that. Keep squeezing me like you never want me to stop."

Words couldn't form; my brain was too wrapped up in the pleasure he was giving me. It felt like we were the only two people in the world, and the rest of it had faded away. I met his eyes, and I felt wholly consumed by this powerful, beautiful man. How was it that someone with so much strength had the biggest heart out of anyone I'd ever met? I sent silent prayers to karma, the gods, and whoever would listen to thank them for bringing Adam into my life.

As his thumb found my clit, my back bowed with pleasure, giving into the waves crashing over me. But Adam's hands gripped me tightly, ensuring I wouldn't fall. I'd never felt as thoroughly fucked, as ruined, and as treasured at the same time.

"Atta girl," Adam said as he nipped my lobe. "So beautiful when you fall apart. The most beautiful thing I've ever seen."

With a couple more thrusts, Adam roared his own release, clutching me tight against his damp skin. As he emptied inside me, I held onto him, wanting to savor this moment for a little bit longer. When he finally came down, he pulled back, smiling brightly at me. He thumbed away a few stray locks of hair before kissing my forehead. "You never cease to amaze me, trouble."

As I stared into the depths of his eyes, the same three words fought to break free. *I love you.* I was dying to say it to him, to tell him how much he meant to me. But with the rest of our friends upstairs, it felt like we'd already crossed more lines than we should have when we weren't alone.

Instead, I kissed him slowly, hoping to show the depth of my affection with my actions if I couldn't give him my words just yet. "You have no idea how lucky I feel that I found you."

His resulting smile was so bright, so genuine, it almost made my knees buckle. He held me close, placing my hand on top of his heart. "Same here, Tori. All my life, I've been searching for something like this. And I gotta be honest—I was starting to think this kind of relationship wasn't meant for me." He pulled back, his hand going to my cheek. "But really, I just needed you."

AFTER WE RETURNED to the apartment, my brother avoided us entirely, grumbling something under his breath about all of us needing boundaries. But nothing could dull my joy. It was odd; for so long, I thought words were my love language. But with Adam, as much as I wanted to hear him say 'I love you,' it felt almost unnecessary. He showed me, *showed us*, how much he loved us every day. It was in the way he played tea parties with Emilia and helped me with my studies. Every time he tucked Emilia into bed or kissed me goodnight, I could feel the depth of his adoration.

Cam knocked into my side, giving me a knowing smile. "So, you and Rice, huh?"

"Yup," I chuckled.

He turned and stared at me, his usual grin missing. "You know I'm happy for you, right, Vic?"

"That means a lot, Cam." I nodded, giving his hand a quick squeeze. "What about you? Anyone you're interested in?"

A rare blush filled his cheeks, and all my senses went on high alert. There *was* someone. But Cam just shook his head, obviously unwilling to admit it to himself, "Nah, you know me, Vic. Between baseball and Em, I have everything I need."

"That's what I told myself too," I chuckled. "Maybe you're not ready yet. And that's okay, Cam. But just promise me, if you find someone who makes you want to open up again, you're not going to let them go before you give it a chance."

"Maybe once I get this whole contract thing settled," he sighed. "I love my team, but I'm ready for something more. Hopefully, my meeting will go well on Monday." He crossed his arms around his chest. "Plus, Boston is only a couple of hours away from here, so I could come up on my days off and spend time with you and Emilia."

I almost dropped my water cup. "Wh–What do you mean?"

"Come on, Vic." He smiled at me. "I'd have to be blind not to see how much you love it here. You've got your man, your brother—a whole life in this little town. Back home, you've been coasting for years."

"Ouch."

Cam chuckled, pulling me into a hug. "That's not how I meant it. I'm just saying that I'm happy for you. And if you want to stay here, we'll make it work."

I pulled back, searching his eyes. "But that wasn't the plan. We were supposed to–"

"Plans change, Vic," he said, leaning back to squeeze my shoulders. "You've spent the last eight years working around my schedule. You're at every game, even lived with my parents to make my life easier. It's my turn to do the same for you. Besides," he nodded behind me, "then I get to hang out with Adam Rice and Gray Anders regularly. Pretty sure that would make any length of drive worth it." He bopped me on the nose. "And I guess seeing you girls."

"Funny," I deadpanned. But as I turned to look at Adam on the other side of the room, my heart almost burst with happiness. In truth, I'd been dreading going back to Texas, not wanting to give up this little life I was creating here. I'd found a family beyond my brother, people who would be in our corner no matter what. It was a sense of belonging I never realized I was missing, and now that I'd experienced it, I didn't think I'd be able to live without it.

And not to mention, Adam. We'd already talked about how life would look different if he went back to taking acting roles, but his home base would likely be here. He felt the same way I did—despite there being bigger, more luxurious places in the world, Saint Stephen's Lake felt right.

Knowing I might be able to build a real life with him in a town we both loved, with our newfound family surrounding us, made my heart almost burst with hope for the future.

My words got caught in my throat as my eyes filled with happy tears. "Thank you," I choked out to Cam, reaching out to pull him into a hug. "For everything."

"Anything for you, Vic," he mumbled. "After all, you gave me the best thing in my life. I'll never be able to repay you for that." He pulled back, "If anyone deserves to be happy, it's you. And I'm rooting for you. Always and forever."

He held up his pinkie, one of our childish habits that followed us into adulthood. I smiled and wrapped my own around his. "Always and forever."

THIRTY-NINE

"Shit," Alex hissed, running her hand over her face. "Where are all the medium-sized shirts? I swear, I had them in this bin."

"I've got them," Victoria called out from under the table, lifting one up into the air. "You put them in the green bin at the last minute."

Alex let out a relieved sigh then tightly hugged her sister-in-law. "Thank fuck you're here. If it was just me, I would have lost my mind hours ago."

"What about me?" I smirked from the other side of the booth.

She rolled her eyes after handing the customer a Fox Creek shirt. "You, my friend, are eye candy. So smile big, pretty boy."

I shook my head, returning to the back of the Fox Creek booth to restock some of our supplies. We were on hour three of the Fall Fest, and there had been a steady stream of guests ever since we opened. Everywhere you looked, people were enjoying the festivities, families and children running down Main Street without a care in the world. The air smelled of spiced apple cider and fresh fried donuts, filled with laughter that brought a smile to my face without even trying.

I took a moment to look around, letting a sense of rightness wash over me. Ever since I came to this town, I wanted to be a part of its community, and I never felt like more of it than today. When Alex and Cole first asked if I wanted to help out at their booth, I hesitated, unsure if I was ready to show my face to so many strangers. But after months of tucking myself away, I was done letting anyone else decide my fate. With Victoria at my side, I felt invincible, as if I could take on the world if she asked me to. So, when I left my hat and sunglasses at home and walked out into the world, I felt a new sense of hope.

Maybe, if I was lucky, this could be my life. The audition still hung over my head, but instead of nerves, excitement filled my chest. Last night, after Cam put Emilia to bed, Victoria came over and helped me run lines. It was the kind of quiet domesticity I always thought would bore me, but with her, everything else made sense.

As Alex turned toward a new group of visitors, Victoria nuzzled up to my side. I wrapped my arm around her shoulders, dropping a kiss on the top of her head. She sighed against my chest. "You know, when you said this was a big deal, I didn't quite realize how many people would be here. It's kind of insane."

"Seriously," I chuckled. "Glad Alex made me make another hundred buttons, even if my fingers were about to bleed."

Victoria's phone vibrated in her pocket, and she pulled it out and smiled at the photo filling her screen. She tilted it so I could see the image of Cam covered in purple glitter makeup, Emilia placing a headband in his hair. Victoria chuckled. "Glad to see they're having a good time."

"Me too," I answered. As much as I was looking forward to spending the day with Emilia, after weeks apart, she needed this time with her dad. While they were hanging out at the apart-ment, Hadley had decided to make herself the unofficial photographer of the event, running around to try to get as many portraits of our town's residents as possible.

Meanwhile, the rest of us were on booth duty. Victoria and I agreed to help Alex at Fox Creek's booth while Cole assisted Gray at his food stand down the street. In the booth next to us, Calla had enlisted her sister and Theo's assistant, Eloise, to help her with her business. The only people missing were Marta and Curt, but they were taking the year off. After twenty years, they'd passed their duties on to the new generation, enjoying the festivities as guests for the first time.

As much as I loved seeing all my friends in action, a part of me was itching for the next part of the day. Cam was going to bring Emilia by this afternoon so she could see the animals and enjoy the carnival in the Town Square. I couldn't wait to see her face when she saw the pony ride we'd arranged with the local farm.

I looked down at Victoria in my arms as she texted Cam, a slight grin on her face. There would always be a tiny nudge of jealousy at their tight bond, but I had no question that Tori and I belonged together. I wasn't the kind of man who believed in destiny or fate, but if I did, I would think the stars sent this woman right to me. There was no other explanation for how she came into my life at the exact right moment and fit so perfectly against me.

As I held her a little tighter, Eloise came over, staring at my arms wrapped around Victoria. For a moment, something passed over her features that I hadn't seen before, but it passed as quickly as it came, and she gave me her usual shy smile. "Hey, Adam. Theo told me about the audition. I'm glad you found a script that worked for you."

"Thanks," I chuckled. "Hopefully, I'll do okay. I'm feeling a little rusty."

Victoria turned and lightly smacked my shoulder. "Stop

that. You're going to be amazing." She shifted her attention to Eloise. "Hey, I'm Victoria, Cole's sister."

"I'm Eloise. I'm Theo's assistant." She beamed at the woman in my arms. "I've heard a lot about you. And if you've had anything to do with Adam's decision to step back into acting, *thank you*." She grimaced. "Theo's been much easier to deal with lately."

"Eloise was a god-send," I said to Victoria. "She'd drop off scripts every single week and passed along my messages to Theo." I turned to the other woman. "Sorry if I put you in an uncomfortable position."

"It's fine." She waved me off. "Theo is...demanding. But I'm learning a lot from him, so it helps. And Calla's amazing, which makes dealing with her husband worth it." She snapped her fingers. "Speaking of, she asked me to come over here and ask if Alex had any more of those little candies. Her stomach's been in knots all day because of the booth, and they're the only thing she can keep down."

Victoria turned to Alex, seeing her busy talking to a potential guest about hosting a work retreat in the winter months. She smiled. "I'll take a look around. I'm sure she has them in one of the bins." She shuffled through the different containers under the table, scouring them. When she popped back up, there was a bright smile on her face. "Here you go. Tell her I hope they help."

"Thanks!" Eloise called out as she headed back to the booth.

But even as she left, the same secretive smile remained on Victoria's face. I shifted to look down at her. "Something I need to know?"

"Nope," she smirked, lifting onto her tiptoes to kiss me. "But I have a feeling things are going to change around here pretty soon."

"I THINK IT'S OFFICIAL," Cam sighed, leaning into the back seat of my truck. "Batteries power this kid. That's the only possible explanation for how she has that much energy."

I had to agree with him. After hours of working the festival and then following Emilia through the entire carnival *twice*, I was dead on my feet. The trek to my truck was far enough, and I couldn't wait to get back to my cabin. My bed was calling my name, and all I needed was my girl in my arms to make this day complete.

As I hit my blinker to turn off Main Street, Victoria chuckled in the passenger seat. I dropped my hand back into my lap, and she reached over and linked it with hers. "Yeah, that's the reason, Cam. Not the eight sugary treats you let her pick out."

"It was a special event, and it made her happy." He shrugged. "Besides, I had to do something to improve my reputation after this guy blew her mind."

I couldn't help but smile at the memory, remembering how Emilia's little eyes filled with happy tears when she saw the "unicorn" waiting just for her. Even after the horn fell off, she kept beaming at me like I had made all her dreams come true.

Earning Victoria's smile was one of my favorite things in the world, and I was desperate for each and every one. But seeing her daughter look at me with stars in her eyes? That was the kind of feeling I wouldn't forget for the rest of my life.

As we pulled up to the lodge, I checked the back seat, seeing Emilia's head on Hadley's lap. Both slept soundly, exhausted from a long day at the festival. But that wasn't what caught my eye. No, that was the way Cam's brow furrowed as he looked at them together, as if finally connecting something in his mind. I grinned to myself, bowing my head so no one else would catch on.

But apparently, it wasn't quick enough, because Victoria turned toward me, searching my expression with her eyes. "What's that look for?"

"Nothing, trouble," I said as I leaned in to kiss her. "You gonna come over after Emilia gets settled?"

"Yup," she said. "Just going to get changed and make sure she's still out, then I'll be there."

"Make it fast, Tor." I leaned in so only she could hear me. "After all of our hard work, I think we both deserve a little reward."

She sucked in a sharp breath, tucking her lower lip between her teeth. "Can't wait."

Cam's head popped between our seats, making us jump apart. As he placed his elbows on the tops of our seats, he looked at each of us with a grimace. "Listen, I love you guys together, but could you save the dirty talk for when I'm out of earshot? These child locks are making it impossible to escape."

Victoria playfully rolled her eyes as she stepped out of the car. I opened the door for Cam, reaching in to grab Emilia as he said good night to Victoria and tried to wake up Hadley. She growled at him as she slowly opened her eyes. "Waking up and the first thing I see is you? I must be having a nightmare."

"You wish, menace. Get your ass inside."

I kissed the top of Emilia's head as I passed her over to her father then reached out and pulled Victoria into my arms. She nuzzled my chest, letting out a content sigh. While Cam, Hadley, and Emilia walked up the front steps, she lifted her chin. "Thank you for today. It was definitely chaotic, but getting to spend the whole day with you was worth it."

"Same here, trouble." I grinned as I tucked her hair behind her ear.

"And thank you for the surprise for Emilia. I'm pretty sure her little heart gave out when she saw that unicorn standing there."

I chuckled, kissing the top of her hair. "No problem at all. Love making my girls smile."

She leaned back and grinned at me. "Oh, we're your girls now?"

"Have been for a while, Tori. Cam might have had you first, but I'm claiming you two as well. He's going to have to get used to sharing."

She placed her hand on my chest. "You aren't jealous of Cam, right? You know that stuff with him is long over. We're just friends."

"I know that baby," I chuckled, leaning down to capture her lips. "I'm not worried that he has your past."

"You're not?"

"No," I said, gripping the back of her neck so she'd look at me. "He can have it. Because I get your future, and that's all that matters to me."

Victoria sucked in a sharp breath. "You're making it really hard to walk away from you right now."

"Tell me about it," I groaned. "But the faster you get in there, the faster I can have you screaming my name."

"Deal," she said as she kissed my lips one last time. "You really know how to motivate a girl."

Victoria waved at me as she stepped inside the main lodge, and I waited until the door shut behind her to head to my cabin. Even though the sun had set hours ago, there was still life around me, bugs humming in the air and squirrels scurrying across the yard. I waved as I walked by the fire pits, a couple of families up late making s'mores and telling tales by the fires.

What would it be like here when the winter started? Would this all be a sea of white, the snow transforming the mountains yet again? I stared at my little cabin tucked at the edge of the woods and wondered how it would feel to leave it behind. I'd toyed with the idea of creating permanent roots here for weeks, but now, the idea was starting to grow teeth. Even though I told Emilia I wouldn't be moving in anytime soon, eventually, I wanted us all under one roof. It would be hard enough splitting time with Cam. When she was home, I wanted us to be all together.

Maybe it was time to look into some real estate, something we could all grow into. As I glanced over my shoulder at Victoria's apartment, I wondered what she would think about that. Hopefully, she'd be on board, but she had yet to tell me her plans for the future. While it'd be great if she stuck in town, I knew better than to give that dream a voice just yet. She needed to decide what would be best for both her and Emilia, not to mention, Cam.

And as much as I wanted our home to be here, in the end, it didn't really matter. Home was the two girls upstairs, the ones who held my whole heart. I'd go anywhere they wanted to go.

Shaking my head, knowing a long talk with Victoria was coming, I stepped closer to my cabin, but as I reached the bottom of the steps, the hair on the back of my neck started to rise. The door was mostly closed, just a sliver of the wooden strip showing it wasn't wholly latched. I gave one more glance over my shoulder, making sure Victoria wasn't anywhere near before I climbed up the steps and pushed it open.

There was no sound, only darkness that washed over the room. The only light was the glow through the patio doors, the moonlight reflecting off the lake. There was no sign of anyone else, but I could sense it—someone had been in here.

It was the same feeling that haunted my nightmares, the knowing feeling that someone unwanted had invaded my private space. As I walked through the kitchen, nothing looked amiss, but there was a lingering odor in the air, like the smell of sulfur or smoke.

As I stepped into my bedroom, I could feel the air shift, my entire body telling me to turn around and walk back out the door. But I couldn't. I had to see what was waiting with my own two eyes.

I flicked on the light, stifling a sharp curse as my bed came into view.

My sheets and my pillows had all been doused in some kind of chemical, leaving nasty stains and burns on the fabric. I had to cover my mouth with my hand, the smell causing my stomach to flip. The sensation only grew as I spotted a lump in the middle of the bed. My heart sank at the sight, terrified of what was waiting for me under the thick blanket.

Run. Leave, my intuition called out, desperate to get out of this room and return to earlier in the day, when everything seemed to be going well. But I couldn't. I needed to know what happened, what this stalker had done to invade my home.

With shaky, uneasy steps, I returned to the kitchen and grabbed a metal spatula. The room ebbed in and out of focus as I walked over to the bed, and pulled back the comforter. Before I could even get a proper look, a powerful odor crashed into me, causing me to turn and empty the contents of my stomach all over the carpet.

When it was thoroughly empty, I forced my back to straighten, trying to ignore the smell of rotting flesh filling my nostrils. Turning toward the bed, I was met with the dead eyes of a large fish carcass lying in the middle. From the look of its skin and innards, it had been doused in the same strange chemical as the rest of my belongings, or it had been the source. Either way, my bed was ruined, and that wasn't the worst part. Sticking out of the fish's flesh was a large carving knife, similar to the one that stuck out of my walls in New York.

My vision started to darken as I stared at it, taken right back to that night so many months ago. It was as if no time had passed, and I was stuck in the same cycle of terror, waiting for someone to jump out of the shadows and take me out for good.

As I turned to walk toward the balcony for some much-needed air, I finally faced the opposite wall, and my blood ran cold. The wall that had once housed my television was covered with *hundreds* of pictures of Tori and me. From our first interaction to our more intimate moments, our entire relationship was spelled out in an angry rhythm. My stomach lurched again as I read the words carved into the paint just above the photos.

I warned you—you are MINE.

FORTY

Victoria

"Did you see anyone suspicious while you were attending the Festival?"

The police officer sat on the opposite side of the kitchen table, studying me as he asked dozens of questions. But as much as I tried to pay attention, I could barely hear what he said. My mind was too chaotic, too busy trying to figure out when things had gone so wrong.

If you had asked me an hour ago if I would be sitting in the remnants of Adam's ruined cabin answering questions from the police, I would have thought you had lost your mind.

Yet, here I was, still trying to reconcile the image in front of me with the events of the day. I could barely even look behind me, too traumatized by the sight of Adam's bed covered in some harsh substance. Even with the windows and doors all open, the smell remained, making my stomach twist and turn. How had the place where I had experienced so much pleasure and joy been warped into a scene straight out of my nightmares?

"I already told you!" Adam's voice rang out from the balcony. "I don't fucking know! Do your damn job and figure it out!"

I flinched at his tone, hating the desperation covering every word. Even from two rooms away, I could feel his anger, feel how vulnerable and violated he felt. When I first arrived, I knew something was wrong, finding Adam almost despondent on the front porch with his cell phone still in hand. I tried to go inside and see for myself, but he held me back, not letting me take a step inside the cabin until the cops arrived.

But even after seeing him so distraught, nothing could have prepared me for the sight inside. The words carved into the wall cut a hole deep in my chest, making it hard even to breathe.

Even though the police were hesitant to say the word stalker, I knew Adam and I were thinking the same thing—it was the same person who had been tormenting him in the city. Our conversation about his stalker from weeks ago came rushing back to me, and I could remember the fear in his eyes. He'd fought like hell to get away from them, and was just starting to regain his confidence in the world. For so long, his stalker hadn't made any moves against him, so we assumed they were gone for good. But now, it appeared they were just biding their time. The pictures proved they'd been following him, *us*, all this time, lying in wait for the moment to attack.

"Miss?" the officer asked from the seat across from me.

I shook my head to clear my mind. "Sorry, I'm having trouble focusing."

"I understand," he answered solemnly. "About the festival—was there anyone who stuck out to you? Who seemed out of place?"

"No," I sighed. "We met a lot of people today. I didn't get a weird feeling or anything from anyone, but I also wasn't really looking that closely."

The officer noted something in his notebook as the front door burst open, my brother appearing on the other side. He scanned the area, and his relief was evident when he met my eyes. Without a word, he crossed the room and pulled me into his arms. He leaned back, scanning my face. "Are you okay? What happened?"

I shook my head. "I'm fine, just a little rattled. Emilia?"

"She's good," he breathed. "Cam brought her and Hadley over to my house. When I left, she was sleeping soundly in the guest room."

"Good," I sighed, pressing my hand to my chest. It was a slight relief to know she was in good hands and away from all this chaos. As Cole watched me, I took a step back, wrapping my arms around my middle. "You should go check on Adam. He's barely hanging on. I'm afraid he's going to snap pretty soon."

Cole nodded, watching his friend through the pane of glass. "Did you know this was happening?"

"I knew that something happened in the past, but he was hopeful it was over." I smiled softly up at him. "Sorry, I can't say anything more than that. It's not my story to tell."

Cole stared at me, worry and fear etching his brow. "Look, I know you two are together, but maybe you should think about getting out of town until all this clears up. I don't want you or Emilia in any danger."

"No," I insisted, steeling my shoulders to face him. "I'm not leaving Adam, not when someone is threatening him because of me."

"That's precisely why you *should* go," Cole insisted, rubbing his brow. "Clearly, this fucking psycho is pissed you're dating Adam. This time, they came after him, but what are you going to do if they start to target you? What if something happens to Emilia?"

"I...I–" My voice stuttered, unsure how to even answer his questions. It felt like my heart was being torn in two. My primary duty was to my daughter, to make sure she was safe no matter what. And even though I knew leaving was the best option, my entire heart rebelled at the thought of leaving Adam. There was no way I could walk away, not when he needed me most. "Cole, I can't–"

"He's right."

My head whipped to Adam, finding him now standing in the doorway. His eyes were rimmed red, and raw anger radiated off his body. I stepped closer to him, needing to soothe some of his pain, but he held his hand out, stopping me from coming any closer. "You need to go home, Tori. You shouldn't be here."

I swallowed, bowing my head. "That's fine. I can head up to my apartment. Call me when you need to crash, and you can stay with me."

As I turned, Adam's voice called out, "No." I turned, meeting his stern expression. He continued, "I meant you should take Emilia and go back to Texas."

"What?" I snapped. "How can you even say that?"

Adam stared at me, his gaze set and determined, without saying a word. The rest of the room faded away as we faced off, our anxieties and fears blending into desperation. Before either of us could speak, one of the police officers came to Cole's side. "Sir, are you the owner of this establishment?"

"Not now," Cole snapped.

"We just have to ask a couple of questions about your security system." The cop swallowed, his nerves evident by the wobble in his throat. "Could you please come with us?"

"Fine," my brother grunted out. He pointed at Adam. "Make sure she's safe."

Adam nodded, but his eyes never left mine. This was the first time I hated being able to read him so well. I could see it all: his fear, his nausea, how much he wanted to protect me. But none of it was enough to send me away, not when my heart broke staring at this defeated version of the man I loved.

Between the weight of Adam's stare and the hundreds of images of us watching our every move, I couldn't stay inside the cabin for a moment longer. I pushed past Adam, heading to the balcony. I gripped the railing in my hands as I slowly inhaled, staring out at the lake like I often did, begging it for one more moment of peaceful tranquility. But it didn't come. Not when my world felt like it was spiraling out around me.

I could feel Adam join me before I even turned around. As I shifted to face him, all my words died on my tongue. The look on his face silenced me. His nose flared, and his lips were flat, as if his whole body was tense beyond measure. I'd never seen this side of him, and if it was anyone else, I would have been terrified. But I knew Adam, knew the depth of his heart. He wasn't trying to scare me—he was afraid *for* me.

"I know what you're going to say," Adam said, his voice gruff and unnerved. "But you need to go home, Tori."

"I'm not leaving you right now," I insisted. "Not when all of this is happening."

"It's my fault," Adam dryly chuckled. "It's my fucking fault that this is happening, Tori. I should have known. I thought that maybe, just maybe, I could get my life back, but I should have known that was too much to ask. My therapist tried to warn me, but I refused to listen. And now look what happened." He threw his arm out toward his bedroom. "So you need to leave. Get as much space from me as humanly possible."

"No," I said, refusing to let him see me waver.

"Don't you get it?" Adam snapped. "You should want to go. You should fucking hate me, Tori. I put you and Emilia at risk because I was too fucking reckless to walk away."

"No," I repeated, stepping into his space. He shuddered as I placed my hands on his chest, my thumbs running over the wrinkled fabric. "You did nothing wrong, Adam. The police are going to find this person and then—"

"No, they're not." His pain-filled eyes met mine. "I've been down this road before, Tori, with a much bigger police force with more tools at their disposal. If *they* couldn't find the person responsible, how will this one?" I rolled my lips together, looking over the group gathered in his home. They did seem lost, unsure where to even start with a case of this magnitude. "This is never going to stop."

"Yes, it will," I insisted. "If the police can't figure it out, we will. We'll look through everything and find who's watching you."

"You're not getting involved," Adam said, but I continued.

"If they've been watching you, then there has to be some evidence. Maybe one of Cole's cameras picked them up, coming in or leaving the property—"

"Goddamnit, Tori, I said *no*."

My lips quivered as I met Adam's furious stare, not used to having him upset at me. And even though I knew he was angry at the situation, not me, my temper rose in response. "Then what do you want to do, Adam? Run away and bury your head in the sand? What good is that going to do? Clearly, this person is willing to follow you. You can't let them steal your life away."

"You don't get it," he said, shaking his head.

"Then explain it to me!" I exclaimed. "Because all I can see right now is a man who is giving up. And that's not you, Adam. Remember? You fight for everything in your life? Then fight, dammit! Push through this fear and fight for us, for this life we're creating together."

"I can't."

"You won't," I bit back. We stared each other down, neither one of us giving an inch. As my anger started to recede, all that was left was my breaking heart crumbling to ash in front of him. My lip trembled as I stared up at him. "Why won't you try?"

"Because I can't risk something happening to you," he

quietly admitted. He reached out and brushed his thumb along my cheek. "Don't you get it, trouble? I'd give up everything rather than risk your safety, for even a minute. If this was just about me, yeah, I'd fight like hell. But it's your picture up there right next to mine. I put a target on your back, and for that, I'll never forgive myself. So please, do this for me."

"You stubborn idiot," I hissed through my teeth. My hand reached up, gripping the back of his hair. "Do you think I feel any differently about you? Your safety matters to me, Adam Rice, and I'm not letting some lurker in the darkness take you from me. Not today, not ever. Do you understand?"

He shook his head. "You have Emilia, Cole, a whole family to worry about–"

"And you," I insisted, bringing my forehead to his. "You are my family, Adam. I walked away from my family once, and it's taken me almost a decade to get it back. I'm not risking that with you, Adam. I want a lifetime of loving you, and I'm not letting anyone steal a minute of our time together."

His dark blue eyes studied me, looking for doubts, but he would never find one. I'd risk everything for him: my heart, my body, and so much more. Because there was no doubt in my mind that this man was my forever, and I'd never let him face his demons alone again.

Adam sighed as his hands found my waist, pulling me closer. "A lifetime, huh?"

"You said you wanted my future," I said. "I'm more than happy to give it to you." My fingers tightened in his shirt, holding him close. "Because I love you, Adam."

"Yeah?" I could feel a tentative smile form on his face. "Even with all of this?"

"Yes," I answered, peering up at him through my lashes. "No matter what comes next, I'm with you. Every step of the way." I flicked his shoulder. "So stop trying to send me away when you need me the most."

He exhaled, crushing me against his chest. I could feel the relief radiating off him, knowing I wasn't about to abandon him during his darkest moment. "I love you too, Victoria Campbell, with every broken and frayed part of me. And no matter what happens next, I'm with you too."

"Good," I said, lifting my head to softly kiss him. "Then let's figure out who is responsible for this mess and put an end to it, once and for all."

FORTY-ONE

"Holy shit," Theo hissed from behind his computer screen as he flipped through hundreds of my emails from my stalker. "This is...extreme, to say the least."

An hour after the police declared my cabin an active crime scene, my entire group of friends gathered in Alex and Cole's living room, ready to discuss what had happened. I wasn't sure if I was prepared to talk openly about what had gone down, but after a long phone call with Dr. Kedir, it was clear it was time. I'd grabbed the envelope filled with emails and letters before leaving my cabin, at least the ones I had kept just in case. There were still a few more sitting in an evidence box in the police precinct in the city, but after months with no word, I was sure they wouldn't give us any more insight.

Victoria stood at my shoulder the entire time I spoke, her hand never straying too far from my back. If I hadn't already known I was in love with this girl, tonight would have cemented that fact. I was prepared for her to run away, closing off my heart so she couldn't destroy it as she left. The last thing I expected was for her to demand to stay at my side and help me track down the person responsible for so much pain.

Maybe it was selfish of me to hold on so tight, but in truth, I couldn't get through this without her. She was my port in the middle of the storm, my light guiding me to safe passage. Without her, I would have let the darkness absorb me, falling back into the crater I created months ago.

When I finished, Cole sat back on the couch, running his hand over his face. I knew he wasn't happy she was still here, petrified his sister would get in my stalker's crosshairs. But once she insisted it was her choice, there was nothing he could say to change her mind.

The only concession Victoria made was that Emilia leave town with Cameron. With his meeting in Boston in two days, they decided to head down to the city early, telling Emilia it was so they could explore the sights together. Hadley had even agreed to go along with them to watch Emilia while Cam was meeting with the team. Victoria would have nothing to worry about.

Watching her drive away was painful for me, but it was downright torture for Victoria. I held her as the tail lights went up the path, whispering in her ear, "You could still go with them. No one would blame you for wanting to sit this one out."

"No," she insisted. "My place is here, with you." She turned and linked our hands. "We're fighting for a life together. All three of us. So let's figure this out so Emilia can come home."

I nodded as we walked inside, half-heartedly smiling at the people who came to support us. By the time everyone showed up, there was barely any room to breathe, but no one wanted to leave, hoping to help in some way. Even Devyn and Gray had cast their differences aside, working together without an issue.

Seeing this group, this community, band together to fight my demons made hope rise in my chest. Maybe we'd actually be able to find this person and put an end to all this misery.

As the shock from my admission wore off, everyone started

assigning themselves tasks. Alex and Cole pulled up the recordings from all the security cameras around Fox Creek, trying to align the angles with the pictures my stalker had taken. The only good news was that there were none from inside Victoria's apartment. Whether it was because the front entrance was covered or because of the constant people around, we couldn't be sure. But there were only a couple of pictures with Emilia in them, and it was clear she wasn't the focus of my stalker's rage.

No, that had been saved for Victoria.

As we started pulling down the photos, it was clear she was the target of their rage. Her face was scribbled out of almost every single image, either with a marker or a sharp object. Victoria tried to stay calm when she saw them, but I could tell she was rattled—we all were.

"Nothing," Alex hissed, slamming down her laptop lid. "Whoever this fucker is, they know where our cameras are located. They managed to avoid them for months."

"Do you think it could be someone on the staff?" Javi asked.

Alex looked at me in question. I ran my hand over my face. "No one stands out. Most of them know me, but they've kept their distance. The only one who might have shown an interest was that one waitress...What's her name?"

"Delia," Cole answered. "Can't be her. She's out of town for her grandmother's wake."

"Unless she's not really," Calla said. She glanced around the room. "What? This person clearly has some issues. Can we really assume they wouldn't stoop so low as to claim a fake grandparent's death?"

"I'll stop by her place first thing in the morning," Cole said. "If she's not involved, I don't want to scare the shit out of her by showing up in the middle of the night."

"Good call," I said, looking around at the tired faces

surrounding me. "In fact, all of you should go home. It's late, and you all deserve some sleep."

"Not going to happen," Alex said, standing up with her hands on her hips. "Whoever wants to leave is more than welcome to, but I'm not going to bed knowing this person is out there, possibly plotting their next move against you." She shifted, moving toward the kitchen. "I'll put on another pot of coffee."

"Alex is right," Cole added, turning to me. "But you should crash, and it's been a long night already. The guest room's all yours."

I shook my head. "I can't impose on you any more than I already am."

"I'm sorry. Do you think I meant that as a question?" Cole's eyes narrowed in reprimand. "You're staying with us until this thing blows over." He gave the same look to his sister. "The same goes for you, trouble. Neither of you are leaving this house alone until this person is behind bars, got it?"

"Got it." My voice caught in my throat, so I didn't risk saying anything more. It was hard for me to put into words how much I appreciated everyone in this room. Even after I suggested they all leave for the night, no one moved toward the door. All my life, I'd tried to be the guy people could count on, the one with the ever-present smile on my face. I hated asking for help, hated to let anyone see any of my weaknesses. But looking around, I realized how foolish I had been. I would have laid my life on the line for any of these people, and how could I have been so blind as to not see they would do the same for me?

My eyes started to water from both the gratitude and exhaustion of the day. Victoria pressed a kiss to the top of my head. "Go lay down."

"I can't," I said. "Not while everyone else is working to help me."

"Yes, you can," she insisted, pulling me up to stand. "You've lived with this alone for long enough. Let us carry this weight for a little bit."

I shook my head, starting to argue, but I stopped when I saw that determined look on Victoria's face. My body slumped from the exhaustion, finally feeling like I could unload the weight for a little while. I squeezed her hand, "I love you."

"Love you, too, Adam. Now, get some rest while we try to work all of this out."

I started toward the stairs, but my feet paused when I saw Theo lurking in the darkness of the kitchen, alone, his computer screen illuminating his face. I glanced over my shoulder at Victoria, who was occupied with Alex and Javi, before heading in his direction. When I approached, Theo's face lifted, regret filling his features like a mask.

"I'm sorry, Adam," he muttered as I took a seat next to him on the kitchen island. "I should have seen something like this was going on."

"You have nothing to apologize about," I answered. "I didn't tell you for a reason. I...I was embarrassed. I thought I could handle it on my own, and when I realized it was more serious than I thought, I didn't want to burden anyone else with my problems."

"Never do that again," Theo said, his dark eyes boring a hole into mine. "You have a problem, we work through it together. Even if I can't help you as your agent, you sure as fuck know I'll be there as your friend."

I nodded, trying to keep the catch out of my throat, but it was useless. "Thanks, Theo."

"Thank me after we catch this asshole," he grumbled, returning to his computer screen.

I peered over his side. "What are you looking at?"

"These emails from last year. I can't put my finger on it, but there's something familiar about the language your stalker uses. I think an old client of mine might have had a run-in with someone similar."

"Can you talk to them?" I asked. "Find out what happened?"

"I can try," Theo groaned. "The problem is, I don't represent them anymore. They stuck with Jack and the agency when he took over my old office."

We both sighed, guessing this would probably be a dead end. Jack was Theo's former co-worker, one he once considered a close friend. But when Theo needed him the most, Jack betrayed him and forced Theo out of the office he helped build. There was still a lot of bad blood between the two, so it was unlikely he'd be willing to help us out.

"Actually, there might be one way to get that information out of him." Theo smirked as he leaned over, calling out into the other room, "Devyn, can you come here for a moment?"

She strolled into the kitchen, her usual frown firmly in place. I didn't know Devyn as well as her sister, but everyone could tell they were polar opposites in most ways. Calla was always smiling, a human version of eternal sunshine, while you could never quite know what Devyn was thinking. She watched everyone like a snake poised to attack, and it made it hard to relax around her.

But I'd also seen the lengths she'd go for her sister and anyone else she cared for. Hell, she even rushed over here in the middle of the night, having no qualms about losing sleep over two people she barely knew.

"Need something?" Devyn asked as she leaned across the counter from us.

"You're in contact with Jack, right?"

Her resulting smirk was utterly devious. "Yes, everything is in place. I'm just waiting for you to give the word."

"It's going to have to hold off a little longer," Theo sighed. "We might need his help."

"Who's help?" Calla asked as she walked into the kitchen and poured herself a glass of water.

Theo's gaze flickered to Devyn's, and a rare moment of uncertainty crossed both of their features. It was Devyn who relented first. "We might need to call Jack."

"What?" Calla gasped. "Why on Earth would you need to talk to that cretin? Do you think he's involved?"

"No, I don't think he'd dirty his hands with something like this, but he might have crossed paths with Adam's stalker through one of his clients," Theo answered. "I hate involving him as much as you do, but it's worth the risk. He might give us something to go on. Because otherwise, we could be running in circles for a while."

Calla hummed in understanding before turning to her sister. "And why are you the one contacting him? Didn't you block him months ago after everything came to light?"

"I unblocked him." She shrugged. "I needed him for a...*special* project, so I reached out and convinced him he might have another chance with me."

"But he doesn't, right?" Calla's whole face paled. "I swear, if you get back together with that asshole..."

"Relax. He doesn't have a chance in the world." She waved off Calla's concern. "I'm just letting him think he has one."

"And what is he really doing?"

Devyn's smile turned from devious to downright lethal. "Digging his own grave."

FORTY-TWO

Victoria

As the morning light started to climb over the hills, I reluctantly went to bed. Everyone else was still in the living room, mostly passed out in the chair or couch, where they'd been scouring through the evidence Adam had collected over the past year.

With each note I read, my heart broke a little more for him, hating that he'd gone through so much alone. But one thing was evident from the people camping out downstairs—that wouldn't happen this time.

As I pushed open the guest room door, I smiled at Adam's sleeping form. We'd forced him to call it a night first, knowing how much this had been weighing on him. Even in sleep, it looked like he'd gotten no relief, his brow furrowed and his body twisted, like he'd been fighting his demons in his dreams.

I laid down at his side, brushing back some of the dark blond tresses that stuck to his sweat-soaked skin. When I pressed a kiss to his brow, his eyes fluttered open, taking a moment to recognize me. But when he did, his bright smile made my heart melt, knowing this man was my person and that we would see this through. There was no other option, not in my mind. I wouldn't let him continue to live on edge, wondering when someone would strike out and take away his happiness.

Not after he'd done everything to bring mine back to me.

"Hey, trouble," he said as he pulled me to his side. "What time is it?"

"Early," I answered, dropping my head to his firm chest. "Get some more rest."

"Trying," he said, rubbing his hand over his face. "Tell me something good to help me fall asleep."

I chuckled as I ran my nails up and down his arm. "What do you want to know?"

"One more thing from your list. The most extravagant one." He leaned over to kiss my forehead. "So we can do it when this whole thing is over."

"Honestly?" I said, furrowing my brow. "I've always wanted to travel. Go off to one of those island resorts I see on social media all of the time." I shook my head, "But it's always been a pipe dream. There's no way I can afford it, even when I'm done with school."

"Well, then it's a good thing you're with a guy who has some money tucked away," Adam chuckled. "Because that's what we're doing. A week away, just you and me. At one of those beach resorts with the glass floors so you can see all the fish swimming underneath."

"That's not somewhere you just go." I grinned against his skin. "That has to be like a special occasion, like a honeymoon or anniversary or something."

"You proposing to me, trouble?"

"Not yet, Rice," I giggled. "I think maybe we should wait a bit for that, don't you? After I'm done with school, and we're more settled. Besides, I think I'd like to get a house maybe first. Somewhere near Fox Creek so we can see the lake in the morning and stay close to everyone."

Adam's eyes popped fully open, and he shifted so he was on top of me. "Does that mean you're staying?"

"Yes," I said, unable to hold back my grin. "We're staying here. I talked to Cam about it a couple of days ago, but I was waiting to tell you until we were alone. He's going to make it work so we can live here full-time, and he'll visit. With any luck, he'll be in Boston, so that's only a couple of hours away. I still have to figure out how to ship all of our stuff—"

My words were cut off when Adam's lips met mine in a passionate, soul-consuming kind of kiss. It was the type that became a core memory, one I'd look back on years from now and forget all the darkness surrounding us. All I needed was my family—my daughter and the loving man in my arms. We'd find a way through everything else. Together.

"Shit, Tor," he smiled against my skin. "I didn't think it was possible for anything to make me happy today, but you just made me feel like the luckiest man in the whole damn world." He kissed me again, softly, slowly. "I can't wait to find a home together, baby."

"Yeah?" I chuckled. "Are you sure you're ready for Emilia and me full-time?"

"More ready than I've been for anything in my entire life. You just wait, Tor. I'm going to find you the house of your dreams, and we'll make it a home. Fill it with animals and more babies, if that's what you want."

"Slow down," I chuckled, pressing against his chest. "Maybe for now, we should start with more sleep, and then we can figure out everything else later."

"Fine," Adam groaned, flopping back onto his side of the bed. "But just so you know, the moment we're alone again, I'm showing you exactly how much you staying means to me."

"Now that's the best motivation I've ever heard."

A COUPLE OF HOURS LATER, I reluctantly rolled out of bed, feeling like I hadn't gotten a single moment of rest. The entire time, I dreamed of unseen people stalking Adam and me, interrupting all our happy moments with their vile and wicked ways. I reached out to the other side of the bed, finding it cold and empty. With a frown, I sat up, sure everyone else was probably downstairs still working.

I pulled on the clothes Cole had set aside for me and made my way down the stairs, stopping at the landing at the sight in front of me. Overnight, it was like Alex and Cole's living room had turned into the set of one of those crime scene shows, complete with a whiteboard and photos lining its edges.

I shook my head as I walked downstairs, stopping in front of it to see what they'd come up with while I was sleeping. There were dozens of names on the side, some scratched out, others circled.

"Good morning," Calla said as she handed me a giant cup of coffee. "How'd you sleep?"

"Terribly," I sighed. "Where did all of this come from?"

"Theo," she chuckled. "He called in every single favor and cleared out his office. He had Eloise bring this thing over at 5 am." She glanced over my shoulder, frowning at her husband, still working hard in the kitchen. "I'm starting to get worried about him. He hasn't closed his eyes, not for a moment. He's going to crash pretty soon if he keeps going like this."

"Guessing he'll refuse to go home even if we ask?"

"Oh yeah," Calla sighed. "He feels responsible for this whole thing, as if he should have been able to see the signs of what was going on with Adam."

"No one could have known," I said, my hand on her arm.

"I'm just glad we do now." Calla smiled, placing her hand

on top of mine. "I've been meaning to thank you. I've known Adam for a while, and this is, by far, the happiest I've ever seen him. Even with all of this..." She motioned around the room. "You brought a light back into his eyes, and I can't thank you enough for that."

"He did the same for me," I said, finding Adam watching me across the room. "The least I can do is make sure he has someone at his side while we figure out what's going on."

Calla smiled at me as Adam walked over, dropping a light kiss on my lips. I ran my hand through his hair, taming his erratic waves. "Any luck?"

Adam's face fell. "Not yet. Devyn's been on the phone with Jack most of the morning. He's agreed to help us out, but he wants a favor from Theo that he can call in at any point."

"What kind of favor?"

"No idea, but Theo already agreed, so Jack's going over all his files. He agrees with Theo; all of this seems really similar to what happened to his client. He can't tell us who for confidentiality reasons, but he'll let us know if there are any connections we can explore."

"And how are you?" I asked, running my fingers along the creases in his brow. "You look terrible."

He smirked down at me. "Ouch, that's harsh, trouble. I'll have you know, I was named one of the Sexiest Men Alive three years in a row."

"Just calling it like I see it, Rice." I sighed as I rested my head against his chest. "So, what's next? What do you need me to do?"

Just as Adam started to answer me, Cole walked through the door, a haunted expression in his eyes. He scowled as he surveyed the room, his eyes dropping when they met mine. My heart sank in my chest. Even though I'd already heard from

Cam and knew Emilia was settled and safe far from here, my mind immediately went to her.

He grabbed Alex and dropped a kiss to her head before coming over to us, looking between Adam and me. His gaze landed on Adam before he said, "Can we talk? Alone?"

I grabbed Adam's hand. "What happened?"

Cole shook his head and turned to his best friend. Adam just nodded in agreement. "Whatever it is, I'm going to tell her. You might as well get it out of the way."

Cole ran his hand over his face. "It's the apartment. Apparently, someone broke in during the night and destroyed the cameras leading up to your place. We'd already cleared out the lodge, just in case, so there was no one there to hear or see anything." He walked to me, placing his hand on my shoulder. "I'm so sorry, Tori. It's all destroyed. Looks like they doused the whole thing in some sort of chemical."

My heart broke for a moment, but not for me. I knew how much that space meant to Cole, how much time he and Alex had put into making it memorable for Emilia and me. I shook my head, pulling him into a hug, "It's just stuff. As long as everyone is okay, that's all I care about. I'm more upset they destroyed all your hard work."

"Don't care about that," Cole mumbled against my hair. "Would have never forgiven myself if something happened to you." He pulled back and ran his hand over his face. "But this shit ends now." He glanced over at Theo. "Any more clues from the emails?"

"No," Theo called out, exhaustion plaguing each of his words. "But there's something here. I can feel it."

"Could it be someone you know?" Calla asked, her hand going to her stomach.

"I'm not sure. It's like all of the pieces are laid out in front of me, but I'm missing the one that bring everything together." He ran his hand over his face. "I"m going to grab some files from my office. See if there's anything else that can help connect the dots."

His wife came to his side, placing her hand on his arm. "Not alone. I'm going to come with you."

"Absolutely not," Theo barked. "I'm not a target. I'll be fine, beautiful." Theo's eyes narrowed on Cole and Adam. "She does not leave your sight. Am I understood?"

Calla started to argue, but Theo silenced her with one look. She grumbled but hugged him anyway. He whispered in her ear before pulling away, giving us a wave as he headed out the door.

Tension ripped through the room as the door slammed shut behind him. We silently prayed this would be it, that Theo would be able to make the pieces fit. Calla exhaled first, turning around to face everyone else. "Alright, what's next?"

FORTY-THREE

Adam

For hours, we worked in shifts, piecing together a timeline of all the messages and comparing them to events I had attended and other dates on my calendar. It was an odd feeling, looking at your life through an objective lens, watching back each choice you made, wondering if that was the moment you made yourself a target.

Because as much as everyone could say it wasn't my fault, it wasn't easy to convince myself. Not when the people I cared about were putting themselves in danger's path all because they wanted to help me. Each smile I gave, each interview I sat through, only reminded me of the man I used to be, the one so consumed by his career that his life was all smoke and mirrors.

My worldview had been so narrowed, so focused, that it took something of this magnitude to pull me away from it. If it hadn't, who knows where I would be right now? And as much as I hated feeling like a victim, at least something good had come out of it. I found the love of my life during my darkest period, and as much as I wished she wasn't in danger right now, I couldn't say I regretted being with Victoria.

I glanced down at her, softly slumbering in my lap. When I

insisted she sit on the couch and take a break, Victoria tried to fight me. But after only a couple of minutes of my fingers running through her hair, her breathing softened, and her eyes reluctantly closed. Looking down at my girl, I tried to keep up the fight, to match the fierce determination she held when she told me we would end this together. But with each passing hour, my faith started to wane. After all, if trained professionals had no idea who they were looking for, what chance did we have?

Across the coffee table, Alex let out a little gasp, her eyes darting up to meet mine. She motioned to the kitchen, probably trying to keep Victoria or the others from waking up. Sliding out slowly, I took a pillow and placed it under Victoria's head, kissing her brow before following Alex.

She held her laptop open, placing it on the kitchen island. I frowned when I looked at the screen. "What did you find?"

"I'm not really sure," she mumbled. "I've been playing around with our calendar from the lodge, trying to think if anyone else might have seen something while we're all looking in another direction." She pointed her finger at one date. "This weekend last month, right after Victoria came into town, a group of hikers wanted to check out the local wildlife. They'd asked if I would mind if they placed some cameras up behind their cabins to capture anything coming into our property."

"Which cabin?" I asked.

"The one right next to yours," she answered as she pulled up another browser window on her computer screen, showing the details of her property with some x's marked behind the back row of the cabins. "This is where they wanted to place the cameras. I know none of them are directly pointed at your cabin..."

"But they might have caught an image of someone sneaking around," I said, excitement filling my veins. It was a lead. Not necessarily one that showed us my stalker's face, but it was the closest thing we'd come to one all day. I reached out, hugging Alex tightly against me. "You're a genius."

"Don't say that yet," Alex sighed. "I sent them an email about their footage, and they just forwarded it over to me, so that's the good news. However..." She chewed on her lower lip. "There's data from six different cameras, and they were recording for over twenty-four hours. It's going to take a while to comb through everything."

"I can help," I said. "Send one set over to me, and I'll look through it while you take on the others."

"We can help, too," Calla said as she joined us, resting her head on Alex's shoulder. Devyn reluctantly joined us, pouring the biggest cup of coffee I'd ever seen. I couldn't help but smirk as I looked at her, only now noticing the large glasses that covered almost half her face.

"Not one word," she said, pointing her finger at me. "One comment, and I'm out of here. I could use about three days' worth of sleep right now, and my fuse is even shorter than normal."

Calla rolled her eyes. "Ignore her. She doesn't mean a word of it." She tilted her head, "Well, except for the lack of sleep part. She can be mean when she's tired."

"What's her excuse the rest of the time?" Alex teased.

"Ha, ha," Devyn groaned. "Send it over to me as well. I'm pretty good at spotting discrepancies. Calla can use Theo's to look at the other." She looked over at her sister, who was staring at her phone with a concerned frown. "Calla?"

"Yeah, sorry," she said, popping her phone back into her pocket. "Have any of you heard from Theo? I texted him almost an hour ago, and he hasn't responded."

Alex and I shared a look, one that spoke of our concern and worry about her statement. But stressing out Calla wasn't an option, so I lied. "You know Theo. When he gets involved in something, it's hard for him to break his focus." I placed my hand on her shoulder. "Plus, given how tired he was, he probably just fell asleep at his desk."

"You're right," Calla said. But anxiety continued to roll off her shoulders, the feeling almost palpable in the air.

"How about this?" I asked. "You three start combing through the footage, and I'll take a drive over to his office and give him hell for worrying you."

Alex chewed her lower lip. "You really shouldn't be alone right now. Maybe one of us should go with you."

"That's not gonna happen, Alex," I chuckled. With Gray and Cole out, trying to track down the waitress who'd taken an interest in me, it was only the girls left at the house. Although I didn't doubt their strength, I knew the guys would kill me if I put any of their women in jeopardy. Peeking over at Victoria sleeping on the couch, I could understand the feeling. I would do the same if any of them put her in harm's way. "I'll be fine, trust me. Just..." I nodded over to Victoria. "Don't wake her up until I get back. She'd wring my neck if she knew I was going out by myself."

"She's not the only one." Alex glared at me, but she softened as she looked at her best friend, who was still staring at her phone like it held all the answers. "Fine. But make it quick, and don't take any unnecessary risks."

"I'll be back before you know it," I said as I grabbed my keys and headed out the door.

IT ONLY TOOK a few minutes to get to Theo's office on the other side of town. With Fall Fest over and most of the tourists returning home, the roads were empty. While in the past, this might have made me thankful and happy to have our sleepy little village back to normal, tonight, it set me on edge.

As I turned each darkened corner, I waited for someone to jump out, some unknown force looking for this moment to take me out. I had to hope my stalker didn't want to do me any physical harm, but from stories of other celebrity stalkers, I knew these situations could escalate very quickly.

I pushed that thought out of my mind, focusing on the task at hand. All I needed was to get Theo and bring him back to his wife. Calla was under enough stress; she didn't need this fear leaching into her as well. All I could hope was that Theo was furiously working at his desk, trying to find a connection in the evidence I gathered. I'd kick his ass for making his wife worry, but it was the best possible outcome.

As I pulled into the parking lot of the office park, relief flowed through me at the sight of his SUV parked in its usual spot. "This fucker," I hissed under my breath. "You better be in there."

I took a look around before pushing my door open. There was no one in sight, but I knew better than most what could be hiding in the shadows. I quickly moved to the front door of Theo's office, a nondescript, rented room in a former textile factory. It had been bought out by a developer a couple of months ago, and they were slowly dividing it into offices to accommodate our growing town. But as far as I knew, Theo was the only current tenant because the rest of the spaces weren't ready yet.

Walking up to his door, I jiggled the handle, unsure how I felt when it refused to turn in my grip. Luckily, Theo had given me a key in case of emergencies, and I had no qualms about using it now.

After shoving open the metal door, I looked around,

squinting to see in the darkness. As I flicked the light switches on and off, nothing happened. Shit.

"Theo?" I called out. "Are you in here?"

No answer.

My blood chilled more with each step inside, that same feeling of wrongness coating me. It was the same as when I walked into my cabin last night, and before, when I entered my penthouse apartment and found my home vandalized. The same icy tendrils of fear ran down my back, making me stand even straighter.

Refusing to give in to my nerves, I pulled out my phone and pushed the button for my flashlight app. I scanned the door, finding no sign of a break-in. In fact, the entire reception area was pristine, looking as if they had just stepped away for the weekend. But as I continued to walk toward the office in the back, something on the floor grabbed my attention, my pulse instantly thundering in my ears.

Three drops.

Three dark red drops marred the floor.

Blood.

"Theo!" I bellowed, moving closer to his office. The first thing I saw was his dark hair, the rest of his body obscured by his high-back chair. My whole body tensed as I moved closer, twisting his chair so he would face me. Theo groaned as he slumped forward, his hand clutching the handle of a knife buried deep in his side. His color was pale, almost ghostly, his breathing labored with each rise of his chest.

"Shit," I hissed, searching for a pulse. "Theo, can you hear me?"

He grimaced, but no words left his lips.

As a faint thump of his heartbeat hit my fingertips, I exhaled slowly, sending up a silent prayer for it to hold on. I pulled his jacket back to take a better look at his wound. The weapon was small, closer to a kitchen knife than a carving one, but it seemed deep.

"Get the fuck up, Theo," I hissed as I ripped off my sweater and pressed it around the weapon, trying not to jostle it. Relief rippled through me when he grunted at the impact. Even if he was in rough shape, at least he was breathing. As I continued to apply pressure, I lifted my phone. My fingers shook as I dialed emergency services, refusing to let my eyes leave Theo for even a second.

"911, what's your emergency?"

"My friend..." The word rushed out of me. "I think he's been stabbed."

"Where's your location?"

"We're at—"

But I never got to finish the words before my world went black.

FORTY-FOUR

"It's fine, it's going to be fine," a voice echoed around me, saying the exact words over and over again. It took a minute for the sound to solidify into a feminine voice, one I knew but couldn't readily place. "It was a break-in, that's all. No one needs to know anything else. They can't know anything else."

My head fucking pounded, making it hard even to open my eyes. But there was some baser part of me, some instinct, that knew I was in danger, even if my mind was scrambling to right itself.

I twisted to my side when I realized my hands and feet were bound. With my hands behind my back, it was impossible to tell how they were held together, but dark green climbing rope was wrapped around my ankles. The bindings made it almost impossible to move more than a few inches. With a solid grunt, I shifted onto my side, squinting to see what was lurking in the dark. It took a few moments for the room to come into focus, the sleek office furniture a familiar sight.

Theo's office.

At least they hadn't taken me to a second location. From what I knew from true crime podcasts, I hoped it was a good sign. My ears still rang from the pounding in my skull, but I tried to ignore it, hoping to find some way out of this mess.

But as I twisted my wrists together, checking the ropes for any weakness, a groan came from the other side of the desk.

Theo.

Panic made my stomach twist as I tried to find him, seeing his office chair empty. I shuffled over, inching my knees and elbows into some sort of crawl. As I got to the edge of the desk, a dry, wheezy chuckle came from the other side.

"About time you woke up," Theo groaned, his voice raspier than I'd ever heard it.

"Shit," I said, seeing he was weakly holding my sweater to his wound. "How bad is it?"

"Not sure," Theo answered. "Hurts like hell, but it doesn't seem like it's too deep. She got me with this kitchen knife when I caught her going through my computer."

My eyes jumped up to his, trying to understand. For a moment, my brain refused to believe it, refused to connect the dots. But then, the name jumped into my mind, making all the other noises around me fade out in a dull buzz.

Eloise.

Anger radiated through me, remembering all the times she stood in my home, smiling to my face while plotting my destruction behind the scenes. We'd laughed together, shared coffee more than once. I always tried to look out for her, making sure she was settling into town okay and that Theo was treating her well. I'd never once considered her a threat, not in the months I had known her. Little did I know, she was a snake in the grass, waiting for the perfect moment to strike me down. And now, she was trying to take Theo with me.

"I'm going to kill her," I grunted, narrowing my eyes at her shadowed figure through the window.

"Not if I get there first," Theo groaned, shifting to sit up a little more. I tried to reach out to stop him, but my bound hands made it impossible. Even that little movement caused more blood to spill onto the carpet around him. My throat dried up at the sight, unsure how much more Theo could lose before the damage was irreparable.

As he saw me staring at his wound, Theo shook his head. "I'm fine."

"Yeah, I'm calling bullshit on that," I hissed. "We need to get out of here and get you to the hospital."

"I've been trying to figure that out," Theo replied, staring at the window. He sighed as he dropped his head back down to the carpet. "How did you know I was here?"

"Your wife sent you a text, and you never responded, so she was worried."

"Tell me you didn't bring her with you." Theo's eyes widened, and I could see pure terror reflected at me, not for himself, but for Calla. "Adam, tell me she's safe."

"She's still at Cole's," I said, and he visibly deflated with relief. "I'm here alone."

"Well, I'd like to say that was stupid of you, but given our situation, I'm fucking relieved Calla's not with you." He shifted up a little taller, his eyes tracking Eloise as she paced in front of the window, chewing on her nail bed. "There's something you need to know in case I don't get out of here. Calla... She's pregnant."

"Yeah, I know." As Theo stared at me, I sighed. "It wasn't hard to figure out. First, it was all the nausea she tried to claim as nerves, and then she stopped drinking wine and coffee. The wine wasn't a big tip-off, but the coffee..." I shook my head. "That girl never goes more than a couple of hours without an iced latte in her hand. But I wasn't going to say anything until you told everyone."

"It's still early," Theo said, his voice now low and pensive.

"We had to have some genetic testing done, and thank God, everything is good. But we found out it's a girl. I'm going to have a daughter." His dark eyes met mine, determination aimed at me. "If I don't make it out of here, make sure they know how much I loved them. That I would do all of it again just to get this time with Calla. Promise me you'll make sure my little girl knows I went down fighting because I wanted to see her face."

"Don't talk like that, Theo." I shook my head. "We're getting the fuck out of here."

"Just trying to be rational."

"Well, knock it the fuck off. I need you to focus and help me figure out how to get the hell out of this mess." I tried to look around the room. "Is there a backdoor in this place?"

"Next to the storage closet, in the back of the main room." Theo motioned to the side door. "It leads to the fire exit."

I cursed under my breath. "So Eloise knows about it?"

"I'm sure she does." Theo shook his head. "I hadn't gotten around to showing her everything here, but she probably figured it out. It's marked on all the plans."

"Okay, then that's probably not an option if we want to get out of here without alerting her."

"There is no option for that," Theo groaned. "If we try to go out the window, she'll see us, and everything else requires going past her. Even if we can find a way to get out of these ties, there's still the gun to deal with."

I rubbed my wrists together, digging at the knot with my nails. It gave a little bit, enough that I could slip my finger through. I turned to Theo. "Pretty sure I can get out of this rope. I just need to buy some time."

"How?"

"Haven't figured that out yet. I just need to deal with this knot, and then—" My mouth snapped shut as Eloise walked inside, seeing us both awake. She cocked her head to the side and stared at us, her wide, green eyes alight with some odd emotion. It was like looking at a different person, a far cry from the shy, put-together assistant I'd gotten to know over the past year. Her strawberry-blonde hair was falling out of its usual bun, all the strands standing up, as if she'd been pulling them for hours.

But what struck me the most were her eyes. Gone was any hint of warmth or kindness, only a cold indifference peering back at me. It was enough to put all my nerves on alert, every part of my mind screaming to get away from the danger.

"Well, well, well," she cackled. "Look who's awake and ready to play."

Eloise took a step closer, leaning down to get a better look at us. As her head swiveled between the two of us, a chill cut into my bones. I was prey caught in her web, only seconds away from being consumed.

But instead of harming us further, she just sighed, pressing her elbow into her knee and resting her face in her hand. In her fingers, she held a cell phone, one that looked suspiciously like mine. However, the other hand was what held most of my attention.

I'd done enough time on set to have handled modified weapons before, gaining a healthy respect for how much damage a gun could wield. True terror coursed through my veins as she tapped it against her thigh, knowing how easily one bullet could take our lives.

"This wasn't supposed to happen," she finally muttered, pushing up to her feet. As we watched silently, she paced the length of the room, continuing to tap the gun against her leg. She suddenly turned, pointing it in my direction. "You weren't supposed to be here. Not yet." Eloise groaned, looking up at the ceiling. "Why did you have to come here, Adam? *Why?*"

"Eloise," I said slowly, trying to keep emotion out of my tone. "We should talk about this. You don't want to hurt us."

"You're right," she laughed. "I don't. But this is *your* fault." She bent down, her eyes meeting mine with a furious flame. It took everything in me not to sneer in her direction, to keep my mouth sealed while she stared at me like she wanted to paint the walls with my blood. As she watched me, my fingers worked nimbly, tugging and twisting the knot until it eventually loosened.

Eloise continued, "I waited for you for years, Adam. *Years!* From the moment we met. You remember, don't you?" She smiled at me, but there was zero warmth in her expression. "It was on the set of your first action movie. I was an extra, and you smiled at me. Told me I was beautiful and brought me back to your trailer." She placed her phone on the ground and toyed with the ends of her hair. "I *knew* we were meant to be together. That I had to save you from all the other *whores* who wanted your attention. To prove to you I was *worthy* of your love."

"Eloise," I repeated, softening my voice as much as possible. "You don't have anything to prove to me–"

"Then, I was finally ready," she sang, pushing up to her feet. "Spent *years* making myself into the woman of your dreams. I found my way to New York and got a job at this..." She pointed her gun at Theo. "This *asshole*'s office just to surprise you. To give us one of those movie moments. You would look at me across the room, and you'd remember everything about our time together, realize I was the one who got away. But you know what happened instead?" Eloise sneered at me. "You. Didn't. Remember. Me."

"I'm so sorry," I said, meaning the words despite her actions. She was right—I didn't recognize her, couldn't have picked her out of a crowd, even after I slept with her. I might not have been the whole reason this woman broke, but I was one of the factors, and self-loathing coursed through my veins. How could I have been so selfish? Through my actions, I'd broken something inside Eloise that had turned into such a twisted, ugly obsession. "I never meant to hurt you."

"Oh, I know, baby," she cooed, reaching out to stroke my cheeks with the muzzle of her gun. It took everything in me not to recoil from her touch. "I know you would never hurt me. You know why?" Eloise leaned forward, whispering in my ear, "We're soulmates. Made to be together. And now, it's even better." She shifted back, smiling softly at me as she ran her fingers through my hair. "Now, we can leave this world together and spend eternity in each other's arms."

"Please," I said, not caring that I was getting dangerously close to begging territory. I had too much to live for, too many people waiting for me to come home. As I closed my eyes, I pictured Victoria's face, imagining her soft smile one more time. This was not how our story ended. With one desperate tug, the rope around my wrists slackened, and I was able to pull one of my hands out of it. But I kept them locked together, taking a page from Eloise's book, and waited for the ideal moment.

"Baby, we don't have to die to make that dream come true." I put on my most charming smile. "I screwed up before. I should have recognized you, known how much you meant to me. But I see you now, Eloise. How many mornings did we spend together in my cabin, talking about our lives? You were there for me through all of it."

"I was?" Her eyes sparkled as they met mine, hope filling their formerly dead expression. "How come you never said anything?"

"I was struggling," I admitted, "and didn't think you'd be interested in me while I was trying to get my life back on track. Why do you think I was trying to take on new roles?" I said, injecting as much innocence as possible into my words. "It was to be a better man for you."

"Aww, Adam," she cried as she wrapped her arms around me. As her more petite frame crushed mine, I lifted my head, rearing it back as far as I could in this position. But it was enough that when I brought my forehead down on her nose, a loud crack echoed through the air, and blood gushed into my face and lips.

Eloise screamed as she recoiled from me, anger and hatred blaring deep in her eyes. But she stumbled, and it was just enough for me to finish undoing the rope around my wrist. As she scrambled to find her gun, I shoved off the wall and tried to grab it before she could aim. But I wasn't quick enough; my fingers were only centimeters away when Eloise snatched it, and the last of my remaining hope died away.

She tutted her tongue. "Adam, you really shouldn't have done that." She leveled her gun at my chest. "You know, I was really trying to be nice. I was willing to let your little bitch live. I do hate to think of her daughter growing up without her mother. But now you've gone and messed everything up." She pulled up my phone, showing my text chain with Tori. "So maybe I'll just have to bring her here and show you what happens when you upset me."

FORTY-FIVE

Victoria

A chime came from my phone, forcing me to open my weary eyes. I had no idea what time it was, feeling exhausted even after resting. I was still on Alex's couch, curled up against the backrest. My eyes fluttered closed again, begging for a little more sleep. But my phone jingled again, and I groaned, reaching out to grab it on the coffee table next to me. As I opened the screen, I looked around the room, finding Javi and Gray asleep on the armchairs across from me. Adam was nowhere to be found, a pillow underneath my head where his lap used to be.

At first, I assumed he'd gone back to work, but that hope died in my chest when I saw his name on my phone's screen.

ADAM:

> Hey Victoria, need you to meet me at Theo's office. No time to explain, but we found something you're going to want to see.

"Victoria?" I whispered as I reread it, alarm bells blaring in my mind. There was only one other instance I could think of when Adam called me by my full name, and that was because he was trying to respect my boundaries. Other than that, I was *always* Tori or trouble to him. I continued to stare at the text, searching for hidden clues until my eyes felt dry. Despite his plea, something stopped me from reaching back out to him. I tried to call his number, but there was no answer. The line rang a couple of times, and then it went to voicemail.

I clicked off the call and followed the sound of voices into the kitchen, where I could tell Cole was having a quiet but tense conversation with Alex. His arms were wrapped around his chest, and he glared at her, disappointment written all over his features. When I crossed the threshold, everyone's eyes darted to me, all in various shades of guilt and shame.

"What happened?" I asked.

Cole glared at Alex until she sighed and shifted closer to me. "Adam went to check on Theo at his office. We were concerned because he hadn't responded to any of Calla's texts, and you know that's not like him. He's been gone almost thirty minutes, and now, neither of them are answering their phones."

"I just heard from Adam," I said, holding up my phone. "He texted and asked me to meet him at Theo's office, but something doesn't feel right."

Cole shook his head as he placed his palms on the counter. "How so?"

"It's more of a feeling than any hard facts," I said, pulling the text chain to show them the message. "He called me Victoria, which Adam never does."

"He always calls you Tori," Cole finished my thought, staring daggers at the screen. "Feels too convenient, like it might be a trap."

"I agree, but it doesn't matter," I said, tucking my phone in my back pocket. "If he's there, then I'm going. Adam could be hurt, could be–" I couldn't finish the thought, unwilling to even bring those words to life. Adam had to be okay; we had too much to look forward to, too much life left to spend together. I refused even to entertain any other option. "I have to go."

Everyone tried to stop me, but no matter what they said, nothing mattered to me. At least, not until Calla stepped in my way. She placed her hands on my shoulders, "I get it, Tori. It's taking everything in me not to go rushing over there when I know Theo might be hurt." She lowered her gaze to meet my eyes. "But we have to be smart about this. Even if they are in danger, the last thing they'd ever want would be for us to take that risk."

I placed my hands on top of hers, holding her tight. "I can't just stay here and wait to see if he's okay. I need him, Calla. I need to see him, to tell him–" My throat closed as my eyes filled with tears, unable to stop my body from trembling. She pulled me in for a hug, holding me close.

"I know," she whispered. "It's killing me too. But we have something, and we're getting close. I can feel it."

As I cried in her arms, someone cleared their throat behind us. "I might be able to help with that."

We shifted to face Devyn, who was holding a laptop in her arms. "I heard back from Jack about his client. He couldn't give us any details, but he did send over some of the messages with the pertinent information blacked out." She showed the screen, "And with that, I also found a restraining order filed in Chicago five years ago. They're public record."

"What are you saying?" Calla asked.

"I have a name." Devyn smirked. "If it's the same person, we can find them. Right now."

"THERE'S no one named Jennifer Portland in any of these

directories," Alex sighed as she pulled up another website. "Are you sure the restraining order was filed in Chicago?"

"Yup," Devyn said, her fingers moving furiously over the keys of her laptop. "Most of the information is redacted, but I can see her full name and address. I'm finding no trace of her anywhere the past five years."

"So she must have changed her name," I groaned, pressing my palms into my eyes. We all sat at the dining room table, studying different computers in hopes of finding more clues about this stalker. As we read the messages from Jack, it was easy to see how Theo made the connection between his former client's experience and Adam's. The words in the notes weren't just similar; they were identical—the same threats and pleas. Everything had almost been copied and pasted. But now, Jack's client was home safe, while Adam was out there in the world, still not answering his phone. I shook my head, trying to resume my focus. "What about social media? Does she have an online profile?"

"Nothing," Calla said, her voice tense with worry. Her head dropped to the table. "We're never going to find her. This woman is a ghost."

Alex reached out, placing her hand on top of Calla's. "Keep going, Cal. Did you see anything in the footage I sent over?"

She shook her head. "I can see someone skulking outside Adam's cabin, but it's completely obscured. It looks like they came prepared, wearing all black, and their face is hidden the whole time."

I glanced over to the living room, watching Cole pace as he tried to work out a plan with Gray. We were all hopeful the name would lead us to more clues about who we were dealing with, but if it didn't, I refused to waste another moment. Cole was furious I was putting a clock on our search, but time was of the essence.

"God, that gives me high school flashbacks," Alex teased, trying to lighten the heavy mood. "I had a disastrous experience with trying to dye my hair neon blue and wore a hoodie over my head for almost a month until it washed out."

"Wait," Devyn said, her head popping up. She pulled over Alex's laptop, searching through the messages. "In this one, she says she first met Jack's client in high school." She started furiously typing, her smile growing with each click of the mouse.

"Something you want to share with the rest of us?" Alex called out.

"A lot of high schools are digitizing their old records and yearbooks to make them more accessible to alumni. Between that and Facebook pages for high school reunions, all I need is to know where they went to school. And considering this town is a smaller suburb of Chicago, with an eagle as a mascot, we shouldn't have to search far to find any records... Got it. And if we look through the pages and tagged alumni..." She grinned. "I've got her. Jennifer Portland, class of 2014. And if I click here, I should find...Oh, *fuck*."

"What?" I snapped as I ripped the laptop out of her hands. When the image came into view, my stomach bottomed out, and I had to hold my hand over my mouth to keep the limited contents inside of me.

"Oh my God," Calla whispered, "Is that..."

"That's Eloise," Alex answered for her. "Different hair, maybe a tweak to her nose, but that's definitely her."

"I'm going to be sick," Calla said as she burst out of the room, slamming the bathroom door behind her. I wasn't faring any better, all my fears and anxieties crashing over me like a riptide. Adam called her a godsend, singing her praises when we met the other day. Even Emilia had met her—Eloise hugged her after she gave my daughter a couple of pieces of candy. She'd integrated herself into all our lives while all along, she was plotting to hurt the man I loved.

Devyn leaned back in her chair, crossing her arms over her chest. "She's been around forever. I met her when Calla was still living in the city."

"I thought she had a boyfriend," Alex said, staring off into space. "She said she followed him to New York, but..." Her voice trailed off as she lifted her gaze to meet Cole's. "Then she said he wanted to leave the city. That's why she was willing to follow Theo up here." She held her hand to her face. "Do you think she was talking about Adam?"

"Right now," Cole said, "none of that matters. We've got to assume she subdued Adam and Theo somehow, and now, she's using them to draw Tori out of hiding."

"Then that's what we do," I said, standing up from the table. "We know who we're facing, so we already have the element of surprise on our side."

"Absolutely not," Cole insisted. "We need to call the cops and let them handle it."

"If we do that, both of them are probably dead." Everyone turned to face Calla, who returned from the bathroom with renewed anger on her expression. "This bitch has been in my home. I hired her, let her into our lives. I *refuse* to let her take Theo and Adam from us. I'll kill her first."

"This is what we can't do," Cole said, running his hand over his face. "Look, I still think we should call the cops. But if no one else agrees, then we need a solid plan. Neither of you are running in there and risking yourselves. Theo and Adam would never forgive us." He looked at Calla with a resigned expression. "You need to stay here."

"Not a fucking chance," she spat.

"Please," Cole insisted. "There's more to think about than just you and Theo. You need to stay safe, or Theo will skin me alive when he gets back." He stepped closer to her, taking her hand in his. "I promise we'll bring him back to you."

She stared at him for a long moment, her chin quivering as she looked into his eyes. "Fine," she eventually sighed. "I'm holding you to that, Cole."

"I'd expect nothing less," he said. "You helped Theo design the office, right?" She nodded. "Then we're going to know everything. Leave no details out."

FORTY-SIX

"You know what's sad?" Theo said, his voice barely above a whisper. "Of all the ways I thought I'd die, I always thought it would be stress-related. Heart attack at my desk. Maybe a stroke." He chuckled as he turned to face me. "Being stabbed by the world's worst assistant never even crossed my mind."

I chuckled as I tested my hand restraints for the fiftieth time. After I escaped the last time, Eloise knocked me out with the butt of her gun and tied them in an even more intricate pattern. There was no escaping, not this time. "I'm not that surprised. Remember how many assistants you went through before Calla? Wasn't there one who only lasted an hour before you fired him?"

"Oh yeah..." Theo sighed. "Tried to swap out my coffee for some green juice, vegan concoction. Always thought he'd be the worst of all time. But stabbing me? Definitely gives Eloise that honor."

He coughed, and the sound rattled in his chest. I glanced over at him, hating the gray pallor his skin had taken. Theo was running out of time, and if we didn't get out of here soon, no one would be able to save him. Even though my energy was draining and my head pounded from the subsequent blows, I refused to give up. I wouldn't sit back and let my friend die all because some deranged woman decided she could claim me.

I lifted myself to check Eloise's location. She'd been spiraling since she stole my phone, muttering to herself about why Tori hadn't shown up yet. No matter the reason, I was relieved Victoria hadn't come, hoping she realized that there was something wrong when Eloise texted her on my phone. That hope was a tiny ember in my chest, but I held onto it, nurturing it until the last possible moment. I had to keep it going, not just for me, but for Theo as well.

But it almost died out when a sound came from the front of the office, the shuffling sound of the door being slowly pushed open. All my limbs suddenly went numb as footsteps walk toward us. "No, no, no," I whispered, arching my back to try to see more clearly. My heart pounded in my chest, praying Victoria hadn't turned herself over to try to save me.

But my thoughts died out when Eloise shrieked in disappointment, "You're not supposed to be here! Where is she?" She waved her gun toward the person, "Where is she?"

"At home," a deep voice called out, and a weight dropped in the center of my chest. *Cole.* He stepped forward, and I could make out the outline of his shadow through the window. I strained closer, trying to pick up on their conversation. Cole's voice was muffled, but I could make out most of his words. "I know what you want, Eloise, but I can't let you take her, not when I just got her back. So I'm here instead, willing to take her place."

"This is all wrong," she cried out. "None of you were supposed to be here. Do you think I want to kill you too?" She hit the gun against her head, pulling out strands of hair with her free fingers. "All I needed was Adam. That's all I wanted. I wanted to be left alone, to die with *Adam*." She lunged toward him, shoving the gun in his face. "But now, you've all fucked everything up!"

As Cole said something else to Eloise, my attention shifted to the window on the other side of our room. The bottom creaked, wiggling slightly before it popped up with a spring. I exhaled a sharp breath as I saw a crowbar continue to pry it open, ruining the seal on the antique windows. But any relief I felt died in my chest as Victoria squeezed through the small opening to lift herself into the room with us. She landed quietly and shifted to her knees, her gaze immediately meeting mine.

I didn't know what to do, paralyzed by the fear coursing through my veins. While I was more relieved than I could put into words to see her face, deep terror froze all my muscles. When she dropped to my side, tucking behind my shoulder, I shifted to try to stare at her, emotions making it hard to speak. "You shouldn't be here, baby."

"Neither should you," she whispered back. As the knot came undone behind me, I brought my hands back to my front, rubbing the raw skin. Before Victoria could move, I pulled her in, kissing her deeply. "How did you know something was wrong?"

"In your message, you called me Victoria. You've never done that before, so I knew something was off."

"God, I love you," I said. "Please tell me you have the cops outside?"

"They're down the block," she admitted, chewing on her lower lip. "We might have lied and said we'd wait for them before we tried to get inside."

"Jesus Christ, Tori, are you trying to kill me?"

"The words you're looking for are *thank you*."

"No, no, please keep going," Theo's voice called out, now barely above a whisper. "I'm just bleeding out over here. Don't let it ruin your moment."

"Oh my God," Victoria hissed as she dropped to his side. Her hands shook as she looked at his wound, as if unsure how even to move him without shifting the knife. Her wide eyes met mine, trying to decipher what we should do.

I shook my head, looking over at her. "You go back out the window. Get an ambulance here as quickly as possible."

"What about you?"

I pressed a kiss to her lips, trying to pour in as much devotion as I could with one single touch. "I'm going to deal with Eloise."

ONCE I WAS sure Victoria was a reasonable distance away and Theo could hold on a little longer, I stood, trying to ignore the trembling in my legs. Armed with only the crowbar, I walked toward the main part of the office, saving one last look for my friend in the corner.

All night, I'd been drenched in terror, trying to keep my emotions in check so I wouldn't risk angering Eloise. But now that I knew help was closing in, I let that rage wash over me, let it reinforce my determination to bring this whole mess to rest. My hands tightened on the cold metal as I twisted the door's handle, slowly pushing it open a crack. Through the sliver, I surveyed the scene, ignoring the tremble in my hands. As I pushed it open a little more, I found Cole standing by the front door, his hands in the air as he stared down Eloise.

But when I looked toward Cole, his face wasn't what I saw.

I only saw the gun pointed at his chest.

"You shouldn't be here. You're not supposed to be here." Eloise glared at Cole, raising her voice. She stood only a couple feet away, her arm waving as she became more and more incensed. While Cole was the picture of calm composure,

Eloise was unraveling, a ticking time bomb in front of our eyes. "She should be here!"

As I pushed the door a little more, I snuck around the other side, hiding behind a bookcase so Eloise couldn't spot me. She never even turned as I walked into the room, too focused on Cole. When I got into position, Cole met my eye, giving me a subtle nod. After decades of friendship, we'd gotten pretty good at reading each other's cues, so I hoped like hell he could read mine now. All we needed was a distraction, something to get Eloise to lower her weapon long enough to subdue her.

Cole's eyes shifted to Eloise, almost as if he was telling me to get ready. Seeing him so composed made me wonder what he had seen in the military and if this was the first time he had faced someone so dangerous. He was a fortress, and his words and body language were completely at ease despite the tension filling the room.

I, on the other hand, could feel my nerves coming out to play, my fingers trembling as I tightened my hand around the bar. As I moved a little closer, the floor creaked underneath my weight, and Eloise started to turn in my direction.

"I'm begging you," Cole called out, pulling her attention back to him. "Take me instead. Let everyone else go, and I'll stay with you. Just..." He exhaled slowly. "Leave my sister alone."

She cocked her head, studying him like the predator she was. "You love your sister?"

"Very much," Cole nodded. "From the moment Tori was born, all I ever wanted to do was protect her, to make sure she was safe. I might have failed her before, but I'm not letting that happen again." His eyes narrowed at Eloise. "I won't let you hurt her."

"Well, you made my decision easier, then," she sighed, toying with the gun in her hand. She laughed to herself, the sound hollow and frightful to my ears. "I was going to kill her, but there might be something even more poetic about this." Eloise twisted the gun, moving closer to Cole. "Fine. You can sacrifice yourself for her. Maybe once she loses you, she'll know how it feels when someone steals the person you love most."

My arm swung out as her finger started to squeeze the trigger, using all my force to bring the crowbar to the side of her head. She let out a little yelp as she collapsed to the floor. Her body crumpled into a heap, and the gun broke out of her grip, landing on the carpet near Cole's feet. As soon as she was down, Cole leaped on top of her, pulling her arms around her back. With one hand holding her wrists, the other dug in his pocket, pulling out a pair of handcuffs.

As I looked at him, he just shook his head. "Don't ask."

"Theo needs medical attention," I huffed out. "Tori went to call an ambulance."

"Should be out front," Cole grunted, shoving Eloise off to the side. Her chest rose and fell with shallow breaths, enough to show she was still alive but unconscious. Hopefully, she'd be out for a while. Rage simmered in my veins, staring down at the woman who'd made my life hell for the past year. All the nights I spent worrying, all the time I missed out on, all because she thought she was entitled to a part of me.

As much as I hated that my actions had led Eloise to this place, I knew most of the blame lay on her shoulders. I might have made a mistake, but she was the one who escalated it, unable to accept I would never be hers. Honestly, if it wasn't me, she would have found another target and made their lives hell instead.

Cole placed his hand on my shoulder, breaking me out of my spiral. "Go get Tori. I'll stay with Theo until the ambulance gets here." He walked over to the gun, emptied the chamber, and tucked it in the back of his jeans. "Hurry, Adam."

I nodded and rushed to open the door. My chest almost

seized when I looked around, finding four cop cars with their lights trained on me. My legs started to give out with the weight of relief. It was over. It felt like it had been years of my life, but in reality, it had only been hours. And now, it was over. I was free.

My legs started to buckle as the adrenaline drained from my body, but I stayed standing by sheer force of will. The officer who'd interviewed me at my cabin stepped forward first, holding his gun out at his hip. "Is she subdued?"

I nodded, unable to form words. Even though I'd tried to keep hope, there was a small part of me that thought I would die in that tiny room, that Theo and I would never get to hold our loved ones again. But standing here, in the middle of a parking lot, I inhaled slowly, closing my eyes as the officers and paramedics rushed behind me. It wasn't until I heard my name called that I opened my eyes.

The floodlights blinded me, but I knew she was there. Victoria rushed out from behind a couple of officers who were trying, but failing, to keep her away from the building.

As she ran across the pavement, I walked as quickly as I could, catching her in my arms as she jumped toward me. I held her tighter than I ever had before, savoring the sweet smell of her shampoo and the way she fit against my chest.

This moment—this was what I fought for.

Why I refused to give up, even in our darkest hour.

Because I would go through all of it again just to have my girl back in my arms.

Tears filled her face as she pulled back, searching my face. "Tell me you're safe. Please tell me she didn't hurt you."

"I'm okay, trouble." I glanced behind my shoulder, seeing the paramedics pushing out the stretcher with Theo on top. Calla broke out of the crowd, moving over to his side. She let out the most anguished sob as she held her husband's hand, cradling it close to her chest.

One of the paramedics tried to block her path. "Ma'am, you need to move. We need to get him to a hospital as soon as possible."

"Then do it," Calla snapped. "But there's no way in hell I'm leaving him, so you better figure out how to work around me."

As the paramedics moved them both to the back of the ambulance, we stood there, watching as they attended to Theo and drove away. No one said a word, mesmerized by the cycling lights as they faded into the distance, sending up silent prayers. If anyone would make it out of this through will and sheer determination, it would be Theo.

When the siren finally died out, our attention was drawn to the front of the office, Cole walking outside with the rest of the cops trailing behind him. Eloise was at the back of the pack, her arms held by two officers at her sides. While the officers pushed her into the back of their patrol car, Cole came to us, offering an apprehensive smile. Victoria rushed forward, pulling her brother into a tight hug. But when she let him go, she slugged him in the shoulder. "Don't you *ever* put yourself in danger to save me ever again."

He wrapped his arm around her shoulders and kissed the top of her head. "No promises, trouble."

FORTY-SEVEN

Victoria

Hours ticked by as we sat in the hospital waiting area, desperate for any news about Theo. With each passing minute, our anxiety only grew, unsure of what was going on behind the scenes.

When we met up with Calla, all she knew was that he'd lost a lot of blood and had been rushed into surgery. The doctors were trying to repair the damage inflicted by the knife, but they wouldn't know how bad it was until they opened him up. They promised Calla they would update her on his state, but the last one had been hours ago. Now, she sat off to the side of the surgical waiting area, staring at the blank space on the wall.

Devyn was right at her side, holding her hand, even though Calla never said a word. On the other end of the room, Gray stood watch, his eyes never traveling far from the two sisters. Opposite them, Cole sat in one of the chairs with his head against the wall, Alex curled into his lap like a kitten. Her eyes were closed, but they opened every time someone shifted, on high alert for any news.

In our own set of light blue linoleum chairs further down, Adam and I were side by side, staring off in the direction of the surgical hallway. There was barely any sound, just the quiet voices of the nurses fluttering through the halls. Given the late hour, no one else was in the waiting room, so our group took up most of the chairs. Vending machines and a coffee bar sat against the far wall, but none of us even glanced in its direction, too worried to think about food.

Adam's hand curled around mine, holding it tightly in his lap. He hadn't let go since we'd left the office park, holding onto me like he was afraid this all was an illusion. I couldn't blame him. After only minutes with Theo, my stomach was in knots, terrified about what would happen to him, the guilt of being unable to help sooner weighing on my chest.

I couldn't imagine how Adam felt.

But he was locked up just as tightly as Calla, barely saying anything to any of us. The police tried to speak to him, but given the extent of his ordeal, they agreed that he should get checked out by medical personnel before giving a statement. As one squad car drove away with Eloise locked in the back for processing, Adam and I went in another, letting them drive us to the hospital. Behind us, everyone else piled into Cole's truck, sticking with us every step of the way.

The thirty-minute drive to the hospital was horrible, every minute making my anxiety grow in my chest. Even though Adam was safe at my side, the impact of the day's events was far from over.

Once we arrived, Adam reluctantly let the staff check him over, declaring he had a concussion but no other significant injuries. While I almost crumbled at the relief, Adam's face only tightened, as if he felt guilty that he wasn't the one who was grievously injured.

"This wasn't your fault," I whispered, dropping my head on his shoulder.

Adam sighed, his eyes turning red as he glanced down at

me. "That's what I keep telling myself, but everyone is in this mess because of me. Theo's hurt because of me. Calla..." His voice cut off. "I just need to know he's going to be okay."

I nodded, hating that I didn't know how to help him. None of us knew what would happen when Theo got out of surgery, and even though I refused to think of the worst possible outcome, it was lurking in the back of my mind, making my stomach swirl with fear.

All I could do was hold his hand and pray we all made it through.

"Calla..." Cole called out, shifting Alex out of his lap. He nodded to the doors to the surgical wing, where two doctors were heading in our direction. Calla exhaled slowly, Devyn's grip tightening on her hand.

When they crossed through the doors, Adam closed his eyes, but I held fast, trying to give him the strength to get through whatever came next.

As the first doctor approached Calla, a slow smile formed on his face, "Your husband is going to be fine." He continued speaking, but none of us heard anything else. We were too busy breathing loud sighs of relief. Calla collapsed into her sister's arms, sobbing at the news. Devyn held her tight, whispering quiet reassurances in her ear.

The doctor waited, pulling off his skull cap and running his hand through his hair. "Mr. Ayad's still sedated, but he should be waking up any minute. If you'd like to see him..." We all stood at once, but he just shook his head. "I'm sorry, only family right now. The rest of you can visit in the morning."

"They are our family," Calla said, shaking her head. "Please..." Her voice cracked as she looked up at him. "Can they please stay?"

The doctor sighed and looked at their partner. The other doctor just shrugged, so they nodded. "I don't see why not. The rest of you can wait out here. Only two people in the room at a time. He's going to be groggy and medicated, so try not to get him too excited."

Calla looked at Devyn, and she nodded, both of them following the doctor through the automated doors. The silence that followed their exit could have been cut with a knife. Exhaustion ached deep in our bones, and we were the ones watching from the outside. I had no idea how Adam was still functioning.

I turned to him, softly wiping away the tears that gathered in the crease of his eyes. "Theo's going to be okay."

"Yeah..." he cried, rubbing his eyes on his thumb. "Thank god." He chuckled, and it brought some lightness into my chest. When Adam shut down, I was terrified that he would never recover, that Eloise would have taken my beautiful, kind man and traumatized him into a shell of himself. But with that one light laugh, my fear started to dwindle. "I'm going to give that guy the biggest fucking raise."

A COUPLE OF HOURS LATER, Calla finally emerged, a large smile covering her face. She'd washed up somewhere, all the blood and carnage from the night now erased from her skin. She came up to us, lightly shaking Adam awake from where he slept on my shoulder. "Hey," she whispered, trying not to wake everyone else around us. "He's asking for you."

Adam nodded, wiping his hand down his face as he stood. He glanced back at me, then over to Calla. "Can Tori come with me?"

"Of course." She grinned. "Just...be warned. He's on some very heavy pain meds, and they're making him a little more...*vocal* than normal."

Adam's brow furrowed as he took my hand, following us down the hall. When we reached the room in the ICU, Calla motioned for us to head on in. "If he asks, I'm going to get one very, very small cup of coffee. No more than eight ounces, I swear."

We nodded as we stepped inside. While the room had the same pastel tones as the waiting room, the air in here felt much more sterile. Machines beeped from Theo's side, various tubes and wires attached to his body. In the middle of the bed, Theo smiled up at us, his face tired but very much still with us. I let out a sigh of relief, so happy to see some color back on his face. As much as I tried to stay strong for everyone else, seeing him so pale would probably haunt me for the rest of my days. If I hadn't spoken to him, I would have thought he was already dead, looking more ghostly than alive when I left him behind.

He smiled brightly at Adam. "God, I am happy to see your pretty face."

"Right back 'atcha," Adam sighed, stepping up to take Theo's hand in an awkward handshake-fist bump. He pulled up a chair, his eyes looking down at his friend's bandaged side. "How are you feeling?"

"Not feeling much of anything," Theo chuckled, but the sound felt forced. "Luckily, she had terrible aim, so she missed anything vital. Should be good as new after a couple of weeks."

Adam cleared his throat, nodding along with his friend's words. "Theo... I'm so sorry you got involved in this. It should have been—"

"If you finish that sentence, I'm going to make Calla hit you." He motioned to his middle. "I don't have the best range of motion right now. Otherwise, I'd do it myself."

"It's my fault."

"No," Theo said. "It was that psychotic bitch's fault." He grimaced as he tried to sit up, and I reached over to help him. "I don't hold you accountable, not even for a moment. If anything, I blame myself."

He cleared his throat, his face contorting with pain as he tried to reach out and grab his water cup. I jumped up, holding it out for him as he sipped through the straw. His eyes met mine, filled with kindness and gratitude. "Thank you, Tori. For coming to rescue us. I don't know if I'd be here right now without you." He turned toward Adam. "Without both of you."

Adam shook his head. "I didn't do anything."

"Bullshit," Theo hissed. "You fought like hell, Adam. Stop beating yourself up over what happened. You couldn't have known what she was doing. We're both here; we're both alive. That's what matters."

Adam just stared at him, taking in his words. Because as much as anyone else could try to say them, Theo was the only one who was there during the whole ordeal. I reached out and squeezed Theo's hand. "Thank you, too. If it wasn't for your hunch, we never would have put the pieces together."

He smiled so wide, he looked like a different person. Calla was right; the meds were definitely kicking in. There was no sign of the usual grump who wore his frown like a badge of honor—or maybe surviving the night had given Theo a new outlook on life. It didn't matter. I was just relieved to see him and to know he had many years left with his wife at his side.

His eyes started to drift closed just as Calla knocked on the door, softly looking down at Theo. He pulled open one eye just enough to scowl at the cup. "That better be decaf."

"Sure," she smirked. "Whatever you want to tell yourself, sunshine."

Theo grumbled something under his breath as he drifted off to sleep. Adam squeezed my hand as he stood, making room for Calla at his side. But before she sat, she walked up to Adam and wrapped her arms around him. "Thank you for bringing him back to me." She reached out and placed her hand on my cheek. "Both of you."

Adam shook his head. "He would have done the same thing for us."

She smiled as she let go, settling into the chair next to Theo's bedside. As her fingers trailed through his hair, Adam took my hand and led me out into the hall. When we exited the ICU, he pulled me into his chest, letting out a long exhale. "I can't believe he's going to be okay."

"Believe it," I sighed into his chest. When I pulled back, I brushed my thumb over his cheek, hating the defeat still in his eyes. "We all are."

Adam leaned down and pressed his forehead against mine. "It's going to be a long road, trying to get back to normal after everything, trying to remember that I don't have to look over my shoulder anymore." He smiled softly at me. "That's not what you signed up for, Tori. If this changes things...."

I lifted to seal my lips with his. As I pulled back, I whispered, "This changes nothing. I'll always be yours, Adam. The hard times don't scare me as long as I know we're in them together."

He smiled, the first one I'd seen all day. "Gotta admit, I really like the sound of that."

"Good, Rice. Because you're stuck with me for a long, long time." I reached down and intertwined our fingers. "C'mon. Let's go home."

EPILOGUE

SIX WEEKS LATER

"You know, if this is some kind of weird role-play thing, I think it's a bit too soon."

Victoria tried to lift the blindfold, but my hands covered hers, trying to keep her from ruining the surprise. Emilia giggled at my side, unable to hold back her excitement a moment longer. When I told her that today was finally the day, she almost screamed, only holding back because I promised her it would all be worth it.

Over the last week, fall had faded away to winter, and there was no question that snow would be on its way soon. As much as I hated to see the bare trees after months of warm colors, I had to admit, I wasn't sad to let this season of my life go.

The past six weeks had been some of the most challenging of my life, and I was still having trouble sleeping through the night without nightmares. But slowly, I could feel their hold lessening on me, in no small part due to the almost daily therapy sessions I had with Dr. Kedir. She was helping me process all my emotions, from the guilt that continued to plague me to the bouts of anger I had at how Eloise had harmed the people I cared about. But with the help of our sessions and an antianxiety medication regimen, I was starting to feel like myself again.

It also helped that Eloise, or whatever the fuck her real name was, decided to take a plea deal instead of taking things to trial. With all the evidence against her, there was no way she would have been exonerated but I liked knowing she'd be locked in an institution for the rest of her life. As much as I hated her, I also pitied the woman and was grateful she'd be able to get help and wouldn't be able to hurt anyone else.

Theo had returned home from the hospital a couple of days after his surgery with strict orders not to work or exert himself, which he almost immediately ignored. Still, Calla made it her mission to get him to relax.

Victoria held her arms out in front of me, trying to feel out where we were. "If you make us late for Calla's party, Adam..."

"Relax, trouble," I chuckled at her side. "Just a couple more feet, and then we'll be there. Although, I gotta admit, isn't it kind of weird to have a "we're pregnant" announcement dinner when everyone already knows?"

"Maybe," Victoria chuckled. "But after everything we've been through, I think we need to celebrate the good stuff."

"The good stuff, huh?" I said, leaning close to her ear. "And when are we going to have some good stuff to announce, trouble?"

She shivered as my breath coasted along the shell of her ear. "I thought we agreed, Rice. House first, maybe some traveling, and then we'll talk about the whole baby thing."

"I'm just teasing you," I said, pulling her against my chest. I smirked as I looked out at the view, silently hoping this would go the way I wanted it to. Still, apprehension started to fill my veins as I looked at my love in my arms, unsure if I'd done the right thing. "Okay..." I eventually sighed. "You can take off the blindfold."

She pulled off the black fabric, her face furrowing at the sight in front of us. As she took a step closer to the old farmhouse, she turned to face me. "Adam...this is a house."

I held up the keys. "Yeah, baby. It's our house."

Victoria's eye widened, her head snapping back to me. When I nodded, she turned back toward the house, taking in the aging structure. In truth, it looked worse for wear. The paint was peeling, half of the shutters were missing, and a lot of the porch needed to be replaced. But Cole and his team assured me that it was all cosmetic fixes, things that we'd probably want to change anyway a long the way.

"I'm sorry," Victoria said, turning to face me. "You bought us a house?"

I shifted closer to Victoria. "I know you wanted something close to town, and this is only a ten-minute walk if you don't feel like driving." I stepped around the porch, motioning for both of them to follow me, pointing at some of the rotten planks. As Victoria spotted the view from the backyard, she brought her hand over her mouth. I continued, stumbling over my words, "I know it's not quite the same, but you can still see the lake, especially from the kitchen and the dining room." I pointed to the far corner. "Em and I talked about getting a swing set over there so she could play outside. Maybe add a fence if we want to get a dog or two. It's going to be a lot of work, but I figured that was what you wanted, that way we can really make it our own..."

But as I kept talking, all Victoria did was stare at me, her dark eyes wide with an emotion I couldn't quite place. I moved in front of her, cupping her cheek. "Baby, please say something. If you hate it—"

"Hate it? This is..." She shook her head and then launched herself into my arms. "This is everything I could have ever wanted and more. I can't believe you did this for us."

"You wanted a home, Tori," I said as I held her. "And this is one we can make together. And I know it's soon, and maybe it's too fast, but if life has taught me anything, when you find something this good, you hold onto it." I took the keys and placed them in her hands. "So, say you'll live here with me, baby. Because this house isn't a home unless Emilia and you are in it."

"Of course," she said, nuzzling into my embrace. She reached out and pulled Emilia into our hug, her tiny arms circling our knees. When we finally separated, she tugged the hem of my shirt.

"Can we finally cross the thing off the list?"

"This again?" Victoria asked.

I looked down at Em and pulled my wallet from my pocket. Fishing out the scrap of paper, I passed it to her. She grinned at me as she looked it over, recognizing the wish we'd written months ago. I kneeled and whispered to her, "I don't know, kiddo. I think you need to ask your mom if it's okay to cross it off."

Emilia smiled as she shifted to her mother, handing it over. Victoria's brow furrowed, and she looked over at me. I stood, chuckling as I pulled her hand into mine. "I know we never got around to writing out that list of yours, but this was one Emilia and I felt very strongly about."

"Find a prince and fall in love," Victoria read. She smiled down at Emilia and ran her thumb over her cheek. "That was very sweet of you, baby."

"Adam helped me," she giggled, looping her arms around Victoria's legs. "He also said we could paint all the walls and have the biggest garden. Ever."

Victoria held Emilia close, then looked up to meet my eyes. She mouthed *thank you*, then turned her attention back to Emilia.

"Are you gonna cross it off, Mommy?" She beamed up at us. "Are we staying here with Adam?"

Victoria nodded, chuckling as I passed her a pen. "Yeah, baby, we're home."

LATER THAT NIGHT, our entire group gathered at the Lost Tavern, celebrating the good stuff, as Victoria called it. She beamed the whole time, showing everyone pictures of the inside of the house. It needed a lot of work, having been empty for the past couple of years, but we were both excited to tackle it together. Cole had already mocked up a new floor plan on one of the napkins, showing Victoria all the options to reshape the dilapidated kitchen.

As the night wore on, Emilia's eyes reluctantly closed, and I picked her up and held her in my arms. My whole heart almost burst as she snuggled against me and whispered, "Love you, Adam."

"Love you too, kiddo," I said back to her. Although Emilia wasn't mine by blood, I swore an oath to myself that I'd never let her feel it, loving her every day as if she were my own. From the moment she placed her sparkly tiara on my head, I was doomed to fall for her and her beautiful mother.

Glancing across the room, I met Victoria's eyes, loving that she was in the middle of the conversation. I didn't know if she realized it, but she'd been the missing piece—not only in my life but in all of ours. Alex and Calla loved her like a sister, and she and Devyn had become fast friends. Hell, even Gray came out of his shell more when she was around, which was often because his dog was obsessed with our little girl.

Cole nodded over to me. "I think it's time we call it a night. Someone's ready for bed."

"He does look a bit tired," Victoria teased as she joined us. She looked over at Devyn, tugging her arm as we all exited the bar. Gray hung back to lock up as we headed toward our separate cars. "When do you head back to New York?"

"Not for a couple of–"

But her words were cut off as a car raced toward us, pulling sideways into the parking lot to face us. The driver's side door flew open, and a man stormed out, his blond locks erratic and anger rippling off him in waves. He stopped when he spotted Devyn. "You bitch."

Theo stepped in front of Calla and her sister. "Jack, what the hell are you doing here?"

"Ask her," he spat, motioning to Devyn. "Although you probably know, don't you? This reeks of your bullshit, Theo," Jack cursed, shaking his head. "I bet you think you're really clever, milking me for information and then luring my clients to other firms?"

Devyn just looked at the beds of her nails with a bored disinterest. "Yes, I did think that was pretty clever of me." She nodded to Theo. "See, I don't have a pesky non-compete like he does, so there was no reason I couldn't talk to a few people about your unscrupulous behavior and persuade them to look for alternative representation."

"A few people?" Jack screamed. "You poached *all* of my clients."

"Whoops." Devyn shrugged her shoulder.

Jack rushed over to her, grabbing her arm and dragging her close. "Listen here, you little bitch–"

Theo took a step forward to defend Devyn, but he was too late. Jack was already falling backward, courtesy of Gray. None of us even noticed Gray approaching, not until his hands were shoving Jack to the ground. As Jack scrambled on the concrete, trying to stand, Gray's imposing stature loomed over him, the promise of violence flickering in his eyes.

When Jack stepped back toward Devyn, Gray stopped him, growling in his face. "Don't you *ever* fucking touch her."

Jack snarled, not backing down despite the rage radiating off Gray. He shoved against the bigger man's chest, and Gray pushed him back, Jack's knees buckling at the force of it. He glared as he rubbed his chest "This is none of your business, Anders."

"It is my fucking business if you put your hands on my wife."

Everyone's eyes darted to Devyn, daring her to contradict his words. But she just stood there, staring at Gray as all the color drained from her face. Jack took a step toward his car, pointing his finger in Devyn's direction. "This isn't the end, you stupid bitch."

"Yes, it is," Gray answered calmly, moving closer to block his view of Devyn. "Because if I *ever* see you in my town or near my wife again, I will end you. That's a promise."

Probably sensing his imminent demise, Jack quickly walked back into his Mercedes, speeding off down the road before anyone else could say anything. As his tail lights faded into the darkness, Gray turned to Devyn, reaching out to brush her arm where Jack had grabbed her. "You good, Ace?"

She nodded, not looking up to meet his gaze. The rest of us just stared, unwelcome witnesses to their brief exchange. But while we were content to watch silently and not interrupt the moment, Calla had no such qualms.

"I'm sorry, but did he just call you his *wife?*"

ACKNOWLEDGMENTS

Someone pinch me because I cannot believe I am here, finished with book THREE. Even though I am still at the beginning of my journey as an author, my gratitude only grows more and more with each of these I write. This story was one I wasn't sure about, from the characters to trying romantic suspense for the first time, but from the moment Adam and Victoria appeared on my screen, I was addicted to them. They are the couple I never knew I needed, but they are so incredibly special to me.

I would never have gotten to this point without the love and support of my family. So much of Victoria's motherhood journey was pulled from my own experiences, especially about how you can lose yourself in the experience. But even in my darkest days, all of you had my back, offering unconditional love and support. You are my reason for everything, and nothing in my life would matter if you three weren't by my side.

To my fantastic team of readers. Lauren- you were such a godsend! I am so grateful that our paths crossed because your feedback was invaluable throughout this process. When I doubted Adam, you were the best cheerleader, and I am so grateful to you.

Emily, my write-or-die, thank you so much for all of your support, vent sessions, and tough love. You've always been the one I can turn to when I'm questioning everything, and I am so grateful for your years of friendship.

To my beta readers—Heather, Meghan, Brandi, Katie, Katherine, Maeghen, and Nikki—you guys are the very best!

Thank you so much for reading through the unedited version of this story and giving me the best reactions. You helped shape this story into the best possible version, and it means more than you'll ever know.

Lemmy at Luna Literary Management—thank you so much for all of your help managing ARCs and the beautiful graphics you created. You take so much off of my plate, and you have no idea how much that helps. Thank you for being such a bright light in this community.

To Alexa, my editor, thank you for all of your time and support. You are such a rockstar! Sorry for my overuse of the word that lol.

To Ainna, you knocked another one out of the park. I always love watching you take my HORRIBLE stick figures and turn them into masterpieces. I am in awe of your talent and so grateful that you took a chance to help me create the illustrated covers of my dreams.

To Books & Moods- thank you so much for the BEAU-TIFUL covers you've created. Each time, I never know how you're going to take my scrambled ideas, but you never fail to blow me away.

Last but never least, thank you to my readers. Anytime you drop into my DMs to squeal about my characters, my heart almost bursts with joy. Your excitement gives me life and makes me keep going when the doubts start to sink in. Thank you so much for loving my stories and my characters as much as I do. It is the greatest gift.

Now, it's time to fix what Devyn and Gray broke....

ABOUT THE AUTHOR

K.C. Brooks is an avid romance reader who has always dreamed about turning her ideas into a book of her own. She lives for sunny days, iced cold coffees, and stories that make your heart ache for more. When not living in the fantasy worlds of her books, she resides in upstate New York with her husband, two children, and two fur babies.

www.ingramcontent.com/pod-product-compliance
Lightning Source LLC
Chambersburg PA
CBHW030753310726
48969CB00005B/1395